CORRUPTED

CATHRYN FOX

FAST DEAL

FAYE AVALON

MILLS & BOON

First Published in Great Britain 2020
by Mills & Boon, an imprint of HarperCollins*Publishers*
1 London Bridge Street, London, SE1 9GF

Corrupted © 2020 Cathryn Fox

Fast Deal © 2020 Faye Avalon

ISBN: 978-0-263-27765-4

MIX
Paper from
responsible sources
FSC
www.fsc.org   FSC™ C007454

This book is produced from independently certified FSC™ paper
to ensure responsible forest management.
For more information visit www.harpercollins.co.uk/green.

Printed and bound in Spain
by CPI, Barcelona

CORRUPTED

CATHRYN FOX

MILLS & BOON

This one is for my lovely and supportive cousin,
Nicole Johnson.

Thanks for always cheering me on!

CHAPTER ONE

Cason

LONG SPLASHES OF purple and pink bruise the night sky as the sun sets low over the Vieux Port. The gorgeous harbor front is busy tonight, compliments of an unusually warm December in the French Riviera. Numerous tourists stand shoulder to shoulder, admiring the luxurious yachts bobbing gently in the warm Mediterranean Sea, while others line up to ride la grande roue, or as we call it back in New York, the Ferris wheel.

The view is picturesque and worthy of a photo, but after spending a week at the International Festival of Creativity, I just want to drive back to my villa, eat something home-cooked and climb out of this suit. Except late-night drinks with one of my long-time designers await me, which is why I'm currently headed for Movida's, an exclusive gentleman's club in the heart of downtown Cannes.

I pull up in front of the impressive architectural building and hand the keys over to the valet. Long strides carry me up the aged stone stairs two at a time. As my name is checked off the exclusive invitation list, I catalog the smoky room in search of Luis. His arm lifts in his fashionably cut Luis Laurent original, as he waves me over. I smooth the lapels of my jacket, and admire the extravagance of the drawing room as I make my way across the marbled floor. I circle large white pillars and nod to men of all ages and ethnicities, while they nurse topshelf liquor around rich mahogany tables.

A chuckle catches in my throat as I consider the exorbitant amount of wealth in the room. I'm a long way from the streets of Philadelphia, where my sister and I were tossed around in foster care, oftentimes getting separated. When we were kids, I swore to Peyton that when I got older, I'd make something of myself and would never let anyone or anything tear us apart again. Thanks to Penn Pals, the dating app I created at Penn State University—while I was an undergraduate computer science student—as well as my online clothing business, Hard Wear, I now have the means to create a better life for my sister and me as well as other kids who are unwanted and unloved.

Luis stands as I approach, the lines around his eyes crinkling as he pulls me in for a hug. I bend to accommodate his short stature and pat him on the back. His silver hair has thinned a bit since my last visit, but his smile is just as bright and welcoming.

"Nice to see you, my friend," he says in a thick

French accent that is as rich and smooth as the man himself.

"How have you been, Luis?" I ask, as he waves a hand to the seat beside him. I lower myself, and give a curt nod to the others seated around us. They return to their conversations, and it's clear Luis and I are the only two conducting business in the club this Friday night.

"Never better," he says and leans toward me. "Shall we get our business out of the way before drinks and entertainment?"

I laugh. "I do love how you always get straight to the point."

As he reaches into a leather satchel and pulls out a tablet, I steal a glance at the elevated stage. I've never been to a gentleman's club before. They have them in New York, but it's not really my thing. What is my thing? Hell, I can't remember the last time I did something just for fun. But I do wonder what kind of entertainment they have in store for the crowd of men tonight. Not that I plan to stay. After days of hard-ass negotiations with other suppliers, I'm dead tired on my feet. Luis powers up the tablet and turns it my way, dragging my focus back to the reason I'm here.

"Here is what I've worked up for you," he says, and I look over the designs created exclusively for Hard Wear. Money was tight at Penn State and I held down three jobs to save for my sister's tuition, often wearing secondhand clothes to keep my monthly budget in line. Hard Wear was born out of my personal need for quality, yet affordable clothing. Young professionals who must look their best, but either hate to shop or are struggling financially, now have somewhere to turn. That was my end goal.

Luis takes a big drag from his cigar, and I run my finger over the tablet, sliding it to turn the pages. Impressed at what I'm seeing, I study the specs for the new young casual line I want to introduce to my loyal customers.

"These are perfect, Luis." I lift my head to find him smiling at me. "You've worked up the numbers?"

"A little higher than you'd like," he explains with a frown. "Shipment costs are increasing."

Trust doesn't come easily to me; it's one of the first things to go when you're in foster care. People tell you one thing, only to turn around and do another. I might have learned distrust in the system, but my cynicism was fortified back in college when I fell for Londyn Harding, a spoiled little rich girl from the right side of the tracks. I shared my clothing app idea with her, talked animatedly about it for days on end, only for her to turn around and share it with her entrepreneurial daddy, giving them the jump on the market share. But the man I'm sitting across from, well, we've been working together for many years, and I have faith in his designs and his numbers.

He presses a few buttons on his tablet, and presents me with a spreadsheet. I study the figures carefully, and mentally do a cost breakdown. The numbers are higher than I would have liked, he was right about that, but I can work with them. My new line is going to be a hit. After seeing the mock-ups, I'm sure of it.

"We could use a different fabric," he explains. "But it won't give your customers the quality they've become accustomed to."

"We're a company that stands behind what we promise," I recite. "Customer trust is important." Hell, any kind of trust is important to me. Luis nods in agreement. "Okay," I say. "Send these to me, and we'll get the contract signed." I hold my hand out and he shakes it. I wish all negotiations were as easy as this one, but when push comes to shove, I don't back down, which is how I managed to build a multimillion-dollar business before the age of thirty.

"Always a pleasure doing business with you, my friend," Luis says and snaps his fingers. A moment later we're presented with two snifters of brandy. I lift mine in salute and we both take a swig. The amber liquid burns down my throat and I welcome it. I set the glass down, and I'm about to conclude the night when Luis puts his hand on my arm.

"You must stay for the auction."

"Auction?" I look around but find no items being presented. I'm about to ask what kind of merchandise is up for bids, when music filters in through overhead speakers, and an impeccably dressed middle-aged man walks onto the stage, a microphone in his hand. A new kind of excitement buzzes through the establishment and slides over my skin. The hairs on my neck stand as I soak in the vibe. Thanks to survival instincts, I've always been good at picking up on other people's emotions—even though I keep mine close to my chest—and while I'm not sure what's about to happen, the men in the room are now wide-eyed with enthusiasm.

My body feeds off the excitement, and while I have no desire to purchase anything—I have everything I need—I have to admit, I am intrigued. My brandy glass is refilled and I shift my chair until I'm facing the stage. Whatever items are about to be sold have recharged the atmosphere in the club and every man is sitting up a little straighter, their laser-sharp focus latched on the stage.

"Welcome," the announcer says and briefly goes over the rules for bidding. "All bids start at five hundred thousand dollars," he says, and the high price tag piques my interest. No one else in the room shows any sign of surprise, however. They've all clearly done this before and whatever they're selling these men are buying, no matter the expense.

The lights dim around us and brighten on the stage as an attractive girl, in her late twenties or early thirties, walks onto the platform. She's dressed in some kind of lingerie, and her smile is soft, demure almost, as she parades herself in front of us all. Despite her bashful composure, I sense her excitement. Perhaps she's feeding off the enthusiasm in the room, much like I am. Although I still can't quite figure out what she's doing up there. Will she be showcasing the items? I lean forward for a better look, as something niggles in the back of my brain. Why the hell is she so familiar?

"Who would like to open the bid?" the announcer asks. "For two weeks or more Chanel can be your companion," he adds, and I nearly swallow my tongue.

They're auctioning off women?

You've got to be kidding me!

I press back into my chair and turn to Luis, sure I'm mistaken, but he simply offers me a smile.

"She's a beautiful woman," he states, and there is no denying that. "Perhaps you'd like to keep her for a couple weeks, or better yet, the entire month of December."

Voices call out around me as the bidding starts, and in seconds the price is well over a million dollars.

"Is this legal?" I ask as I try to wrap my brain around all this.

He arches a thick white brow. "You think this is any different than your Penn Pals app, Cason?"

I blink and do a fast comparison. My app was designed to provide a number of services to the women on Penn State campus. We provide male companionship, a bodyguard to protect those walking home after night classes, or simply a date to an event. There was never anything sexual going on. No money was exchanged for bedroom services—contrary to what little miss rich girl's father, Randolph Harding, presumed and was happy to accuse me of, repeatedly.

"This isn't about sex?" I ask.

"Not at all. These women provide companionship. What happens behind closed doors with two consenting adults, however, that is not for me to judge. As long as *she* initiates it. You may not touch her first, if you do, you void your end of the contract and she is free to leave, payment in full," he says as he gestures to the stage. I follow his gaze. "Some of these women are from European royalty, others are models, CEOs, CFOs, but all of them are confident powerhouses," he tells me, and that's when I realize why this girl looks so familiar. I've seen her face in lipstick and other cosmetic ads. Luis takes a pull from his cigar, and waves his hand, like he always does when he's trying to get a point across. "They do it for the excitement, the thrill, but downtime in the hands of a companion who will pamper them, that is nice, too, no?" His chuckle curls around me, followed by a thick ribbon of smoke.

"I… I guess I heard about auction houses before, I've just never been to one."

"Then you must leave with a companion tonight," he says.

I turn back to the stage as the bidding winds down, the woman going to some young billionaire for three million dollars. Truthfully, I'm not looking for any type of companionship. I've been screwed over enough in my life, thank you very much. A soft body under the covers might be nice every once in a while, but my bedroom has a revolving door. Sex is for sex and I don't go out with the same woman twice. Having one underfoot for two weeks or more, well, I wouldn't know what to do with her. My work is my life, and with the launch of the new casual line later next year, I don't need the distraction. If I want a woman, I'll get my own, and make sure the ground rules are clear.

"There are rules," he says, and I chuckle. That man is too good at reading my mind.

"I'm good," I say. "I have some work to do tonight."

He tsks teasingly. "All work and no play."

"That's me." I finish my drink, and push to my feet as the next girl is brought onto the stage. I'm about to leave but stop dead in my tracks. The tall pillars before me sway, and I'm certain I must be hallucinating. I blink once, then twice but the image doesn't change.

No fucking way.

My heart jumps into my throat and I sit down seconds before my legs give. I take a breath, but can't fill my lungs as the announcer introduces the gorgeous girl as Desiree. Except that's not her real name. No, that's Londyn Harding, Penn State's spoiled rich girl who did me wrong in so many ways. I have no idea why she's selling herself. I only know one thing.

It's on.

CHAPTER TWO

Londyn

BRIGHT LIGHTS SHINE on me, making it impossible to see who's out there bidding. With my luck it will be some ninety-year-old man with one foot in the grave. Not that that matters. I'm not doing this for fun or the thrill of it, like these other women. To each their own, and no judgment on my part. But for me, well, I'm doing it to save my father's business before he marries me off in some ridiculous merger. I'm a woman for God's sake, not a commodity he can barter with to better his position for his companies in this turbulent market, and this is the twenty-first century, not the nineteen hundreds. I'm a capable, confident twenty-nine-year-old woman, and I'd be an asset to any of my father's businesses, if he'd only give me a chance. But no, in his old-world way of thinking, women should be home, doing charitable work while catering to their families. That's fine if that's what the woman wants. I just don't happen to be that woman.

Leave the business to a man, Londyn.

Oh, and why is that, so he can make one bad investment after another and put the entire future of his conglomerate at risk? As his familiar words grate on my nerves, I question my sanity. I should be raising this money to start my own business, instead of trying to save my father's. Then I'd show the damn fashion industry I was more than Londyn Harding, spoiled, rich brat and pampered daughter of Randolph Harding. I *am* more than that, yet every time I apply for a job I get turned down, or worse, laughed at. No one takes me seriously. I have a fashion degree from Penn State University to put to use, if only someone would give me a chance and believe in me.

The bidding starts as I walk along the stage, the bright lights overhead warming my barely clad body. While this isn't my finest moment, no one is holding a gun to my head. I'm here on my own accord, fixing a problem the best way I know how, thanks to Jennie Sanders' little nudge. She's a friend, a model, a rich socialite who loves it up here on stage, even though she has access to her trust fund, as well as her own earnings, and can pay for her own adventures. Me, well, I'm on a ridiculous allowance. I'm heavily involved in my father's charity work, but would rather earn my pay by being a contributing member to one of his businesses. If I was, I bet I could get them back in the black in ways that don't involve near nudity.

Someone in the crowd bids a million dollars, and a small thrill trickles down my spine. Who the heck would pay a million dollars for my companionship? When it comes right down to it, I'm a nobody. Another man raises it to two, and I push my hair back and smile, urging them on. It works, because soon enough many voices are chiming in. I prance around the stage and give an extra little shake to my hips. Excitement needles through me, and I catch a rush of breath as the energy in the room vibrates along my skin. Only problem is, I'm beginning to wonder what's really going on with me. Is this all about raising money, or am I prancing for other reasons?

I hate to admit it, but Jennie was right. She told me the second I walked onto the stage I'd enjoy it. Normally I'm not one to flutter under a man's gaze, and I don't seek out validation for my personal appearances, but it's oddly titillating to be the object of so much attention. I almost snort. The last time I was the sole focus of any guy's anything, I stabbed him in the back. I hate myself for it. I really do. But when I heard all the horrible things he said about me—*Londyn is nothing but a silly joke*—I stopped fighting my father and let him pursue stolen ideas that nearly destroyed the guy I was in love with. I should have been the better person, and while I never stopped caring for Cason Harrison, I learned a valuable lesson in trust—mainly, who to let in and who not to.

Someone in the back of the room, with a deep husky voice that slides down my back and awakens some dormant part of me without warning, ups the ante, and I peer out. Who just bid three million dollars on me, and what is it about his muffled voice that intrigues me? Dammit, I wish they'd dim the lights up here so I could see who's outbidding everyone else. A man near the front, his voice deep, scratchy and gruff, a side effect from years of smoking, increases it to three and a half million, and I nearly falter in my too-high heels. The money will go a long way in helping my father regain control over his businesses. More important, it will stop him from trying to marry me off.

At least this is all aboveboard, and really, providing companionship to a lonely man isn't the worst thing in the world. Still, my father might not be proud of the way I'm getting paid, but it will show him I'm a girl who will do what it takes to succeed—within reason of course. It's not like I'm going to sleep with the guy who wins me. This is about friendship, and sort of reminds me of the app Cason created back at Penn State.

But I don't want to think about him. Every time I do it creates a huge knot in my stomach. I push him to the recesses of my mind as the gentleman at the back of the club bids fiercely. Slow whispers go around the room and chairs scrape the floor as everyone turns to see exactly who is refusing to be outbid. I hate that I can't see.

With the audience distracted, the announcer steps up to me and lowers his microphone, his words for me only. "You'll have to come back, Desiree. You're causing quite a disturbance out there."

"Probably because I'm new," I say.

"Maybe, maybe not, but Mr. Laurent's guest sure is hell-bent on winning you."

"Mr. Laurent as in the famous designer Luis Laurent?" I ask, blinking rapidly. Good God, am I really in the presence of one of my idols?

His smile is big and toothy. "The one and only."

I narrow my eyes and strain to see into the crowd. "Who is his guest?"

"A new member. First time here, actually. Perhaps you know him. His name is Mr.—" he begins, but stops when a loud voice gains our attention.

"Five million," the man at the back of the room says flatly.

A hush falls over the crowd, signaling the end of the bidding. I have no idea who just bought me, all I know is his voice is low and sexy, filling me with deliciously dirty images of him taking me up against the wall while doing depraved, corrupt things to my body.

Whoa, what the heck is the matter with me?

I turn to the announcer, and work not to sound breathless. "This is all safe, right?"

"You're in charge, Desiree," he assures me with a pat on the arm. "The power is in your hands. If anyone so much as lays an unwelcome finger on you, or even looks at you the wrong way when you leave here, they'll be banned from the club. Don't worry, everyone knows the rules and I'm quite certain you're about to have a couple luxurious weeks in the hands of your host."

I relax. Two weeks of luxury. Wouldn't that be nice. Heck, I haven't had a luxurious anything in far too long. I've been too busy trying to prove myself capable, and applying for fashion jobs. If only Mr. Luis Laurent had bid on me. To be in his brilliance would be a dream come true. I could pick his brain about the industry and learn so much.

Then again, who's to say his guest isn't also in the fashion industry. A fresh wave of hope pushes back those last remnants of worry, and I suddenly can't wait to meet my new companion.

I leave the stage and find Jennie, or rather Chanel, there waiting for me.

"Ohmigod, Londyn. You went for five million dollars. That's incredible!" She pulls the curtain back slightly and scans the crowd. "Who was that? Do you know? I usually know everyone out there."

"No idea." I stand there, still trying to wrap my head around the five million, half of which I receive now, half when the contract is fulfilled in two weeks.

"Well, come on," Jennie urges. "Let's get changed and go meet our hosts."

"Jennie?" I ask as I follow her down the hall to the change room.

"Yeah?" she says as she enters. She takes off her lingerie and slides into a little black cocktail dress.

"Have you ever…"

She plants her hands on her hips and meets my gaze in her makeup mirror. "Slept with my host?" she asks.

I chuckle. God, I am such an easy read. "Yeah."

"Once," she says, turning to face me. "He was midthirties, looking for a companion to a fundraising gala. I liked him, and he liked me. It happened on his yacht one night. But you should know, I was the one who made it happen. These guys know better." Her eyes go wide. "Wait, are you thinking of sleeping with your host?"

"No, I don't even have any idea who he is," I say and give a casual roll of my shoulders to shrug off all the dirty thoughts that raced through my mind when I first heard his voice. "I was just wondering."

"Well, sweetie." She pulls a tube of lipstick from her purse and swipes a layer of bright red cream across her lips. "If he's young and hot, I say go for it. You work too hard and play too little."

I don't disagree, and the thoughts of a man's big warm hands my body does sound nice, but I'm not the type of girl to jump into bed with a stranger. Heck, I've only ever slept with a few guys who were lackluster at best. My first was Jackson Freeman, a guy my father insisted I date after I'd been spending too much time with Cason Harrison in college. I'd given Jackson my virginity out of spite, I think. I wanted my first time to be with someone I loved, but Cason had said some horrible things about me behind my back. I guess in the end I'm glad I didn't give him my body. Unfortunately, he's been holding on to my heart for quite some time now. Damned if I don't want that back.

"Here, try this," Jennie says and hands me a fresh tube of lipstick. "If your guy is young and hot, he'll go crazy for this color red. Oddly enough, it's like an aphrodisiac for men," she says with a chuckle. "It hasn't failed me yet."

"Thanks." I slide the lipstick into my purse and change into a jumpsuit, stylish yet comfortable and, more important, designed by me.

A big man in a short-sleeve T-shirt that shows off muscles covered in tattoos sticks his head into the room. "Ms. Desiree, your car is here."

I suck in a fast breath but it does little to settle my sudden bout of nervousness. Am I really doing this? Going home with a stranger who just bought me? Hell yeah, I'm doing this, and you know what, I have two weeks away from home, away from all the stresses and parental pressures to marry me off to a man with a pedigree. For the next couple weeks, I get to spend my time with a man who is going to dote on me, and I damn well plan to take advantage of it.

Jennie blows me a kiss. "Go have fun, *Desiree*," she says. "I mean it."

"Yeah, I will, *Chanel*." I tease but mean it, as well. "You, too."

I gather up my small suitcase and my purse, then slide into much more comfortable heels before following the bodyguard down the long hall. We make our way through the massive building, and I take in a rejuvenating breath when I find myself back outside, standing on the top step in Cannes's downtown core. It's quite breathtaking, actually, and for a brief second I wonder if we'll be staying in the French Rivera. Apparently, the hosts come from all over, and I pray mine isn't from New York. This place is straight out of a fairy tale, and I am not ready to go home just yet.

"You have a good night, ma'am," the guard says as he hands me off to the concierge, who takes my luggage and leads me down the stone steps toward a rare sports car. I shouldn't be surprised by my host's wealth, considering the amount he paid for my companionship. We circle the vehicle and he opens the door behind the driver's seat and I'm a bit disappointed. I was hoping I'd be in the front, or on the other side of the backseat, to get a glimpse of the man who fought for me. It's almost like he purposely positioned me behind him. Does he not want me to know who he is? I mean, sooner or later I'll find out, right?

"Good night," I say to the concierge as he closes the door behind me and puts my belongings into the trunk. I shift, buckle my seat belt and angle my head, trying to see into the rearview mirror. The driver taps restless fingers on the dashboard as I situate myself.

"Are you comfortable?" he finally asks, his hushed voice deep and rusty, thick with something

I can't quite identify. There is something so familiar about it, though. Do I know him?

"Yes, thank you."

He starts the car, and I look out into the night, admire the bright lights and the Christmas decorations on the lampposts. It's such a pretty sight. But if he wants the full two weeks with me, I won't even be home for the holidays, not that my absence will be noticed. Mom will likely be off to some fancy ski resort with her friends, and my father will be buried in business as usual. Jennie won't even be home this year. She'll be enjoying Cannes with her new host. Her folks always celebrate the season in a big way. They always invite me over and when I was younger, I'd go. A part of me longs for big family dinners, opening gifts around the tree at the crack of dawn, and passing the day away with laughter and board games. I sigh inwardly as I recall those joyous days with Jennie's family. But she's been working and traveling, and we're not kids anymore. Last year I didn't even bother to put up a tree. But as much as I want a loyal man in my life, and a big happy family, I refuse to succumb to parental pressure and marry for any other reason than love.

Good God, I wish I wasn't such a romantic at heart.

I shake off my loneliness—my stupid wish that happily-ever-after really did exist—and when the driver puts on his signal and takes a left, I peer into the vehicle's side mirror and try to get a look at him.

The dim light of the dashboard highlights the hard, yet sexy angles of his face as well as the light dusting of whiskers on his chin. That dark shadow, combined with a full head of thick chestnut hair warns me that he's young.

Warn?

Maybe that's the word that jumped to mind because of my current mood. But maybe it's a warning for him, and not me. It's been so long since my body has been touched that there is a part of me that might not only accept all to come, but let go and really give myself over to this man—in ways that might even shock him. A little shiver goes up my spine, and once again I ask myself the question, am I really doing this?

Yes, I'm doing this.

He drives a few more blocks and pulls into a private villa overlooking the gorgeous Mediterranean Sea. It's absolutely breathtaking. I almost can't wait to get inside and make myself at home.

"We're here, Ms. Harding," he says, his muffled voice an octave lower.

He exits the driver's seat and goes to the trunk to retrieve my luggage. As I watch the way he moves, something niggles in the back of my brain, although I can't quite figure out what's suddenly bothering me. But then alarm bells ring loud and clear, and fight-or-flight instincts kick in as understanding hits like a punch to the gut.

He just called me by my real name.

My thoughts race, and I take a minute to recall his voice, his age and those hard yet sexy angles of his chin. The second the tumblers fall into place my jaw drops open.

Oh. My. God.

No.

It can't be.

Can it?

CHAPTER THREE

Cason

I THOUGHT SHE would have recognized me long before now. Then again, I was purposely keeping my features hidden and my voice muffled. Hell, if she knew it was me, she would have bolted. But two seconds ago, when she finally figured out my identity, her resounding shock buzzed through my body like a million angry hornets.

I close the trunk, and the sound reverberates in the quiet night and ripples along the rocky shoreline below my villa. I lift my head, and find her glaring at me through the back window, her mouth slightly open, her eyes bulging out of her head. Keeping my calm, despite the raging storm sweeping through my gut, I step up to her door and open it.

"Are you coming?" I ask in an even tone, but she doesn't move. Instead, her mouth opens and closes, and I can almost hear the wheels spinning in that brilliant brain of hers. "I asked a question, Londyn. I'd appreciate a response."

"I...what the hell is going on?" She glances around and scans the quiet neighborhood. What is she looking for? An escape route? She's safe with me, despite our history and anger toward one another. Or rather, my anger toward her. What does she have to be angry about? She's the one who stabbed me in the back and her daddy made a fortune from it. I open my mouth but she blurts, "What the hell am I doing here? What is this all about, Cason? What the..." Her words fall off and she lowers her head in thought.

I give her a moment, and when she remains silent, I say, "It seems pretty obvious to me. You were at the auction house, and I bid on you. Now you're here, mine for the next couple of weeks." I narrow my eyes, take in the flush of color on her heated cheeks. Honestly, if she thought I was going to let her go home with any other man, then she doesn't know me at all. I almost scoff at that because *I'm* the one who really doesn't know her. Yet, the second I saw her up there and felt a hint of her trepidation I would have emptied my entire bank account to bring her home. I understand there is nothing sexual in this arrangement, but I didn't like the vibes I felt off a few of the men around me.

Or maybe that's just a damn excuse.

"What exactly is it you don't understand?" I ask.

"Never mind."

Her eyes flare hot, the blue turning a cold shade of ice, and I hold my ground. If she thinks this is some revenge plot on my part, she'd be wrong. I think. Truthfully, I have no idea what I'm doing. All I know is that there was no way in hell she was going home with any other man than me. Everything about her on that stage tonight, from the nervous way she studied the crowd to the excitement at that first bid, warned that this was a new experience for her. Unlike those other women who do it for the thrill, my gut tells me she has other reasons, and I damn well plan to get to the bottom of the matter.

Don't think of her bottom, Cason.

"Are you coming?" I ask.

She lifts her chin an inch and I fight back a grin when her glare turns venomous. "I'm coming," she says, each word punctured with a sureness that doesn't reach her eyes. "You don't have to be such an ogre. A lady needs time to get from the backseat of a car like this."

"An ogre?"

She stands, and shakes out her long blond hair. The curls fall down her back and as much as I don't want to remember, my mind instantly goes back to the nights I held her while she fell asleep in my arms. So much was lacking in her life, and she was so incredibly lonely. I'd lie beside her, smooth her hair from her face, run those long strands between my fingers and fight the urge to kiss her as she drifted off.

She wronged you, Cason.

I can't forget that. Ever. My sister and I have been through so many battles and I made a childhood promise to her. Simply put, I'm completely overpro-

tective of Peyton, and if anyone tries to stand in the
way of my career goals, which prevents me from ful-
filling my pledge to my sister, they become the enemy.

Londyn Harding is the enemy.

"Yes, an ogre," she says and reaches for her bags
but her hands are shaking. She's as rattled by this
unexpected turn of events as I am and working hard
to hide it.

I move the bags from her reach and she nearly
stumbles into me, nearly pressing that soft warm
body of hers into mine. Jesus, after all these years I
still can't get her sweet citrusy scent out of my brain.
When I walked her home, or held her in bed, it would
wrap around me, tease all my senses. Since I'm still
a man, and she's still a beautiful woman, the want
hasn't vanished, but succumbing to it would be di-
sastrous in so many ways. She's the last woman on
the face of the earth I plan to sleep with.

"I'm sure there's no need for name-calling," I state
flatly, portraying a calmness I don't feel, and it gives
me a measure of satisfaction when it rattles her even
more. That probably makes me a complete asshole.

She regains her balance and stands before me.
While she might be many inches shorter, she lifts
her head like she's a mile taller, but the confidence is
feigned. "What is there a need for, *Cason*?" she says.

Oh, for me to fuck you and get you out of my system once and for all. But that is not going to happen. Ever.

"We'll figure that out over time, *Londyn*," I snap

back, adding emphasis to her name, the same way she did with mine.

"There are rules you know."

"Fully aware of them," I say, and pat the pocket of my suit. I was briefed on the rules while she was brought to my car. They were simple enough, and the only one who can break them is Londyn. I might have bought her, but she's holding all the cards.

"You can't touch me."

"Good, because I don't want to." As I push that lie through my teeth, she glares up at me, and for a second I'm pretty sure I spot disappointment in those big blue eyes of hers. Good, I'd hate to be the one hogging all the disappointment in this relationship... or whatever this thing is between us.

"I'd like to go to my room."

She turns from me, and my gaze drops to her perfect heart-shaped ass, all nestled snug in that stylish yet sexy jumpsuit, no doubt, designed by her. The sight grabs me by the balls and squeezes.

"If you could stop drooling over my ass, maybe you could show me."

I meet her gaze, and my smile is slow, maybe even obnoxious. "Is that what you think I was doing?" I ask, even though it's exactly what I was doing, but I can't let her know that. And for some twisted reason, I like watching her fall off her high horse, and lose control of her game.

She opens her mouth, and closes it again. Shaky hands swipe her hair back, and under the bright floodlights embarrassment rushes over her face, turning her cheeks that pretty shade of pink I like so much. "I didn't mean to suggest—"

"I'm pretty sure you were suggesting that I want you. Rest assured, Londyn. You've been hired as my companion, and that does not include bedroom duties."

"Good, because I'm not a prostitute."

"No, not a prostitute, but you have sold out before," I state. She flinches at the dig. I instantly feel like a grade-A prick.

Her shaky hand grips the handrail leading to the front door. "Cason…" she begins, her voice quieter, but I'm done dredging up memories. We both know what happened in the past, and we have two weeks to get through, so for the time being it's best we leave the past in the past.

"Your room," I say and sweep my hand toward the door.

"Right." She turns and her steps are swift as she climbs the stairs. "Your villa is beautiful," she says, and I open the front door.

"Thank you."

"How long have you lived here?"

We step inside, and I get it, she's making small talk, wants to start fresh. Considering our history, I'm not sure it's possible, but I'm exhausted, and the fight is slowly draining out of me.

"I bought it a few years back."

I set her bags on the floor as she begins an exploration, taking in the living room, the dining room that never gets used, the kitchen with every high-end appliance a person could want and lastly my den.

She turns back to me, and her throat sounds as she swallows. "You did really well for yourself, Cason…"

I wait a second, wait for her to add the words, *despite me*, but they never come. Her smile is genuine, and holds all kinds of warmth as her eyes meet mine, and I soften a little more. What the hell is it about this woman that brings me to my knees so easily?

Keep it together, Cason.

"Thanks," I finally say.

"How's Peyton?"

I smile as I think of my sister. "She's doing well. She's applied for a teaching job in Malta."

"Wow, that's amazing. Good for her."

"Only problem is it's a small community with certain values, meaning they don't hire single female teachers. She'd have to be married. It's not the law, the marriage bar was lifted years ago, but behind the scenes it's still practiced."

"Wow, I never heard of that before."

"Not in North America, but it's different in other countries."

"Sometimes in North America people want you married, too." I narrow my eyes at her and she continues with, "What's she going to do?"

"She swears she's not interested in marriage, so I guess she's going to pretend for a while. Once they see she's good at what she does, perhaps her marital status won't matter. That's what she's hoping for, anyway. It's her dream job and she's so good with kids even though she doesn't want any herself." Londyn nods, and I say, "Do you remember Rylee Jenkins?"

"I do. She was dating your friend Sebastian Marshall, right?"

"Yep, they're married now."

"Oh, wow." Her eyes go to my left hand.

"No, not married," I say. "I wouldn't be here with you if I were. I'm loyal like that," I add with a cock of my head.

"Yes, of course." She holds her own bare finger up and wiggles it. "Single, too."

I arch a brow. "Daddy hasn't managed to marry you off to one of his business associates yet?"

She glares at me, but hey, it's a legit question. After her father accused me of running a prostitution ring, she started going out with that douchebag Jackson Freeman, a man with the right pedigree and someone her daddy handpicked, of course.

"That's why I'm here," she says so quietly I have to strain to hear it.

What is she talking about? "You're saying you're here to get married?" I ask. I mean the room was full of wealthy men, all of whom her daddy would approve I'm sure. Well, with the exception of me. I might be a self-made millionaire with two extremely successful online businesses, despite the Harding family sabotage, but no matter what, in his eyes I'll always be that boy from the wrong side of the tracks.

"When I marry it will be for love," she states, her voice steady, but the turbulence in her eyes is a sure sign she's fighting some internal war.

"Of course it will." Leaving the matter for the time being, I tug off my tie and toss it aside. Her gaze drops as I shrug out of my jacket and toss it over my shoulder. "I've been wanting out of that all night."

"Is it one of yours?" she asks, and waves her finger up and down the length of my dress shirt and pants.

"This style sells at Hard Wear, if that's what you're asking."

"It is and I bet it sells well. It's perfect…you're perfect." Her gaze jerks to mine. "I mean you look good. In the suit." She blinks a few times, her gaze panning the length of me a second time. Okay, obviously our attraction to one another hasn't diminished over the years. If anything I think our absence has strengthened the pull, and seeing her tonight has lit a spark inside me that I can't quite seem to extinguish. She lets loose a flustered sigh. "What I mean is the suit looks good. It's a nice cut."

"What's going on with you, Londyn?"

Her gaze jerks back to mine and she stands a bit straighter. "Nothing, um, I didn't mean to stare. I wasn't looking at your body or anything like that. I have no desire to sleep with you. I was just admiring… wait, maybe *admiring* isn't the right word. None of this is coming out right." She takes a breath, lets it out slowly and tries again. "I was noticing the excellent fit and I like the way your pants hug your…" A garbled sound crawls out of her throat, a half laugh, half snort. "I don't mean hug—"

"Londyn," I say, effectively cutting off her ramble. "When I asked what was going on, I meant are you working in fashion." She's not, and as much as I hate to admit it, I have kept tabs on her. "It's always been your dream and you were good at it."

"I…um… I'm sort of in between jobs. I've been doing charitable work with my mother. So, Peyton, she's doing well?"

Clearly, I've hit a sore spot.

Giving her a reprieve, I say, "Come on, I'll show you to your room." I pick up her suitcase and she follows me up the stairs. "This one has a nice view of the ocean. Peyton loves this room," I say, and she steps in, runs her fingers over the soft bedding.

"It's very pretty."

"I'm glad you like it." I set her luggage on the stool, as she sits and bounces on the bed. My throat tightens, and I try not to look at her breasts. "Comfortable enough for you?"

"Yeah, not that I'll sleep."

I soften. "Still have a hard time?"

She points to her head. "I can never shut this down."

"How about a glass of wine and something to eat. That might help."

Her grateful smile screws me over. "That sounds perfect. I forgot to eat earlier." She squeezes her hands together, an anxious gesture of hers I'm familiar with. "I was so ner…"

Her words trail off, but I push. "You were what?" I ask as she follows me back out into the hall. We head downstairs, and I guide her into the kitchen and pull out a stool at the island.

She sits. "I was so busy getting ready for the auction, I forgot," she says, but she's forgetting something else. This is a girl who shared all her hopes and dreams with me—only to steal mine—but I know what makes her tick, at least I thought I did. But what she's not saying is that she was *nervous* about tonight because this isn't something she usually does. Why was Londyn really up on that stage?

"You do this often, then?" I ask, deciding to call her out on it as I open the fridge. I pull out a bottle of white wine and hold it up to her. She nods and I uncork it.

"Oh, yes," she says, her voice light and breezy as she waves her hand. "It's quite the thrill."

"I bet it is. I've never seen you onstage before," I say, testing her.

"Wasn't this your first time at the club?" she counters, and I fight a grin.

"Maybe that's why I've never seen you onstage before," I say and it brings a wide grin to her face, one that reminds me of our happier days and messes with me a bit. I turn from her, and pull myself together as I fill two wineglasses.

"I guess I just happened to be at the right place at the right time," I say, turning back to slide a glass across the island.

"Or the wrong place at the wrong time," she responds and clinks glasses with mine.

I look at her over the rim of my stemware before I take a healthy sip. While she's probably right about that, I still ask, "Are you sorry I bid on you, Londyn?"

She goes quiet, too quiet, and her lids fall slowly. When they lift again, she says, "I guess that depends on why you bid on me so fiercely."

"You have a degree in fashion design," I begin and she eyes me. "I have numerous upcoming meetings, and I really need someone who knows a thing or two about fabric."

Her eyes light up. "Really?"

"Yes, I have shirts and pants to be laundered and ironed," I tell her.

Her cheeks redden and I brace myself, waiting for her to hurl that glass at my head. I'd deserve it. She takes a deep breath, like she's considering it, then calms herself.

"I hardly think you need me for that."

"What other reason would I need you?" Jesus Christ, could I be any more of a prick? Probably not, and I sort of hate myself right now. I've been needing to vent for far too long, obviously, because the truth is, I'm protective—maybe even overprotective—of those I care about, so why I'm purposely saying things to hurt her is beyond me.

Wait, what? I care about her?

Of course, I genuinely care about her. I never

stopped, but I can't forget how deeply her betrayal cut. How that goddamn wound has never healed and how the sight of her on the stage tonight ripped it raw all over again.

"Maybe this is a mistake," she says and glances over her shoulder as she sets the drink down.

"No one is forcing you to stay."

As I give her time to reconsider and figure out her next move, I go back to the fridge and take out the seafood I've been thawing. I've always been a good cook. A necessity when you have no mother or father to take care of you. It wasn't always like that, though. I was seven when they died in the car accident, Peyton was only two. Our grandmother took us in until she said she was too old and frail to care for us anymore. But that wasn't the real reason. She blew through our childcare money like a house on fire—and not on us. Child services stepped in and we ended up in the system.

I turn back and find Londyn watching me. "I'd never keep you here against your will," I say and gesture toward the door. "You're free to go. I can drive you myself, or call you a car if you prefer."

She hesitates, and looks past my shoulder, but her thoughts seem a million miles away. What is going on with her?

After a moment, her focus returns. "What are you making?" she asks.

"Seafood pasta."

"With those small scallops, and white fish?"

"Yes," I say and take out the milk, garlic and onions.

"Oh, my God, I've been dreaming about that pasta for a year." She makes a sound, one that reminds me of the sweet noises she used to make before she fell asleep in my arms, and my goddamn dick twitches. "You always were such a great cook, Cason. I tried to replicate that recipe once, but it didn't turn out like yours. What's your secret?" she asks.

"I don't have any secrets," I say flatly. Her question was innocuous, and I get that she's not looking for any insider information, but even if I did have any secrets, she's the last person I'd tell. Fool me once, right?

"Right." Her shoulders tighten at the remark, and unease radiates off her as she takes a big drink of wine and tries again. "I meant, what do you put in it that makes it so special?" She forces a smile, working to ease the tension between us, and holds up her finger, like she just had an epiphany. "Wait, let me guess, you make it with love," she adds.

I hold up the big stick of butter. "Wrong," I say, and she laughs. It lessens the strain in my body and I relax.

"You always did have a great sense of humor," she says, her smile big and heart-stopping. "Some things never change."

"And some things do," I say. "So, what will it be, Londyn. Will you be staying, or leaving?"

CHAPTER FOUR

Londyn

WELL ISN'T THAT just the question of the hour, the day…the century. He turns from me, and reaches into his cupboard. Even though I can't see his face, I can still feel those dark brown eyes drilling into me like a fine-tuned laser. Disappointment radiates from his every pore, and I can't say I blame him. But he's not as innocent in all this as he might think. Back in the day, he said some pretty hateful things about me. I thought there was more between us. I thought he used to believe in me. He didn't. Regardless, I should have been the bigger person and never should have let my father run with Cason's original clothing app idea—although I'm not sure I ever could have stopped him. Anger and hurt made me act out and do something rash and reprehensible, something we can never come back from. I'm older now, wiser, but there is no undoing the damage that has been done. From here we can only go forward, and that direction does not include a future for us.

My stomach coils and I take a huge sip of wine. Cason spins back around, his fingers wrapped around the neck of the wine bottle, and I try hard not to think about the way those strong hands used to care for me. Back in college, he always walked me home, accompanied me to fundraising events, and would stay the night in my dorm room, holding me until I fell asleep. I'm still a terrible sleeper—especially in strange places. I used to think Cason was my knight in shining armor and thought some-day we'd ride off into the sunset together. But that stupid romantic image isn't helping this situation, so I bury it as he grips the wine bottle and arches a questioning brow.

I give a resigned nod. "Yes, thank you."

"You're staying, then," he says, a statement, not a question.

Of course I'm staying. If I left now, I'd lose all that money.

Is staying really about the money, Londyn?

If only it were. An unguarded groan catches in my throat.

"Is there a problem?" he asks as he refills our glasses and I hate him right now. How the hell can he be so damn unfazed by this situation when my insides are bouncing off my abdomen like a wres-tler bounces off the ropes in a prizewinning match.

Honest to God, I never in a million years thought I'd end up in his villa tonight. Yet here I sit, every goddamn emotion I had for him back in the day rising to the occasion and begging to be noticed. Back at the club, it's no wonder his voice—muffled or not—elicited tingles in my body.

"No, no problem at all," I lie and fiddle with my wineglass. I look past his shoulders, check out the ingredients on the counter. "Is there anything I can do?"

"You could get started on pressing my pants," he says, and I'm about to toss my glass at him until I catch the twitch in his lips. Okay, so maybe he's not as calm and collected as he's pretending to be, and maybe he's using humor to hide the insanity of all this.

"If you don't need them ironed this very moment, perhaps I can do them later." I hold up my glass. "Wine and ironing don't mix."

"Toss in your dislike of me, and I don't want to be anywhere near that fiasco waiting to happen."

A humorless laugh catches in my throat. "You probably don't," I say, even though I don't dislike him. Quite the opposite, really.

He laughs at that, and the sound skitters down my spine, and settles deep between my legs. My God, no man, and I mean no man ever stirred my body from a simple laugh.

Imagine what his touch would do.

Another sound crawls out of my throat and Cason arches a brow. Okay, I seriously need to get myself together, and contrary to what Jennie and I talked about at the club, no way am I going to sleep with my host, no matter how young and hot he is. Despite our fun and easy banter, I'm sure the only thing Cason wants from me is vengeance.

"I thought I could help cut the onions," I say, wanting his focus off my face before I reveal what I'm feeling. He does not need to know what his mere presence is doing to my body.

"You cook now, do you?" he asks and drops pasta into a boiling pot.

I shrug and push off the counter. "Not as good as you, but I try."

He pulls a big knife out of the drawer. "Have at it, then."

My hand touches his as I take the knife into my palm and a needy little gasp catches in my throat as his warmth penetrates my skin.

"Everything okay?" he asks.

"Yeah." I weigh the knife, "This is just big in my hand."

As soon as the words leave my mouth, my gaze drops to his zipper, seeking out something else that might be big in my hand. His chuckle curls around me, and I throw up a silent prayer. *Dear ground, please open up and swallow me whole.* I didn't mean for those words to come out sounding so sexual, and why the hell did I look at his crotch? Tonight is just getting better and better.

"I just mean—"

"Here," he says, handing me a smaller knife and

wood cutting board. "This might work better in your small hand."

"Thanks," I say, grateful that he's letting it go. I cut into the onion, and Cason moves around the kitchen, searing the scallops in the hot pan. My entire body is in hyperdrive, fully aware of his presence, his movements, his every damn breath. Once again, unbidden memories from our college days infiltrate my thoughts and skip down my tingling spine. How I'll make it through the next two weeks is beyond me. The alternative is to go home empty-handed, which I'm not about to do. But hey, after two weeks cooped up with a man who doesn't really want me here, well, that might work out to my advantage. Maybe when we're done, I'll be able to go home with my heart back in my chest, instead of in his palm. It's not like he wants it, or even knows he has a tight grip on it, right? So yeah, maybe something good will come out of all this. My lips twist at that thought.

"Something funny?" Cason asks, and I lift my head. He takes the board full of chopped onions and tosses them into a sauté pan.

"What?"

"You're smiling."

"I am?"

"Yeah, what were you thinking about?" he asks and leans against the counter, his body so close to mine, it generates instant heat and my stomach takes flight. I resist the urge to squeeze my thighs together to help quell the building ache and the last thing I should be thinking about is my G-spot and how I'd bet top dollar he'd be the first man who could find it.

"Nothing important," I say.

"You sure?"

"Positive."

He reaches out and drags the rough pad of his thumb down my cheek, his capable fingers creating a bone-deep warmth inside of me.

"Tears," he explains.

I sniff and pray my voice doesn't come out as shaky as I feel. "Onions. Cutting them always does that to me."

His smile is soft, so damn full of love when he says, "When Peyton was young, she used to put on swimming goggles when she helped me cut onions." He goes quiet, like he's remembering old times, and he chuckles softly. "She was a funny kid."

His eyes lift, meet mine, and the admiration I see shining there steals my next breath. I remember when he used to look at me like that, but now that adoration is reserved for his sister. But it does remind me how much I loved and respected that about him. Those he cares about always come first—he'd run through fire for those people. Those who crossed him however...look out.

I crossed him.

"So Peyton has no desire to get serious with anyone?"

He frowns. "No, and she had the nerve to ask me

to set her up with someone on Penn Pals to help with the teaching job in Malta."

"The nerve?"

"She's my kid sister. I don't want to set her up with anyone."

I chuckle at that. Peyton is going to have one hell of a time with her brother when she eventually falls in love.

"She was always beautiful, Cason. Why does she need an app to find a guy?"

"She's not looking for anything serious." He laughs, like he understands fully, and I take it he's in no hurry to change his bachelorhood—or ever. "But she needs it for work and I want her to get her dream job."

"I can understand that," I say. I know exactly what she's going through. I come up against someone wanting me married every day.

"If I don't help her out, she'll just find someone else to pretend to be her fiancé. Some guy I know nothing about."

"You're going to do it, then?"

"As much as I don't want to, I'll set her up with someone who knows the ground rules and understands the consequences if he breaks them." He cracks his knuckles, and reaches above my head to pull out a bowl. His warm scent wraps around me, and as I lose my sense of balance, I wobble, bang into his body. He falters, and nearly loses the dish in his hand as I wrap my arms around him.

"Whoa," I say. "You okay?"

His throat makes a strangled gurgling sound, and he coughs as he breaks from my arms. "It's just been a long work week. Exhausted on my feet."

"Maybe we should get you to bed?" I shake my head. "Wait, I don't mean we. I mean you. You should get to bed."

"I'm fine, Londyn."

"If you're tired, you could sit down, and I can finish this for us. It won't be as good as yours, but…"

Our eyes meet, and heat arcs between us. He steps back, distancing himself even more, but I catch the want in his eyes. Okay, so he clearly feels this pull between us every bit as much as I do, but isn't about to act on it. No worries, Cason. I'm not either.

Wait, why the hell not?

We're not college kids anymore. We're both consenting adults. Maybe having sex with him will get him out of my system once and for all, and put my heart back where it belongs.

The rules are clear. He's not allowed to seduce me. But that doesn't mean I can't seduce him. Yeah, he hates me, and thinks I hate him, too. But unlike him, I don't hold hate in my heart. Regret, however, that's a different story. I'll always regret what I did to him, the hurt he continues to hold close, and the future we no longer have. But tonight, I believe it's time to start anew. We have two long weeks together and let's face it, he only has so many clothes in need of ironing.

I run my tongue over my bottom lip. "If you'll excuse me for a minute." I find my purse, pull out the tube of lipstick and swipe it over my lips. I recap the tube, and slowly lift my lids. But I didn't need to look up to know Cason is watching me, his sole focus on my mouth. His entire body is stiff, his chest rising and falling a little faster as his nostrils flare.

"My lips were a little dry," I explain. "I needed to moisten them."

His low growl punctures the night and rumbles around me, and smoke rises from the pan behind him. I point at the stove, as a little thrill goes through me. Jennie was right. This color is like an aphrodisiac.

"The onions," I say. "I think they're burning."

He blinks once, then twice, and I'm about to repeat myself when he snaps out of whatever trance he was in. "Right," he says.

He turns, and my gaze drops to take in his perfect backside hugged so nicely in those dress pants. Back in college he was more of a jeans and T-shirt kind of guy, and I have to admit he's grown up and filled out rather nicely. I take a moment to admire the man he's become, his body thicker now, his muscles fuller and taut. While he was always a great-looking guy, the put-together man before me is just that—a man. One who has awakened every inch of my body, and I can't help but think we should finish what we never had the chance to start.

I step beside him, and reach for the wine. I splash a little more into our stemware, and take a sip. I'm a lightweight, but the buzz is a welcome reprieve from the stress of the night, and gives me a burst of courage. I step a bit closer, and his muscles ripple. Looking around him, I inhale, but it's the warm scent of his skin, so arousing and familiar, that I take into my lungs.

"Smells great," I say as he tosses the fish into the white sauce.

"Almost done," he grumbles, his voice an octave deeper. I let it wrap around me, let it slide over my body and stroke all my needy places.

"Oh, and here I thought we were just getting started."

His eyes jerk to mine and I blink innocently. "What do you mean?"

"Getting started, you know, on me being your companion, doing what you need me to do for the next two weeks," I say, and he doesn't move. I'm not even sure he's breathing and I can't help but wonder what's going through his head. Is he picturing me on my knees before him, taking him into my hands and mouth? Holy, that hot image sends heat straight to the quivering spot between my legs, and a little moan catches in my throat.

"Can you...uh," he begins, his eyes dilating, his arousal evident in the swelling of his pants.

"Can I what?"

He clears his throat, the muscles along his jaw rippling. My God, if he keeps clenching like that something is going to snap out of place.

"Grab the plates," he bites out.

Disappointment settles in my core, but the night is still young. "Sure."

I set the plates out, and stand back and sip my wine as he finishes making our dinner. He divvies up the pasta and seafood, and steam rises from the plates as he makes his way to the table.

"Maybe we could eat outside. It's such a beautiful night. We should totally take advantage of this unusual heat, don't you think?"

His eyes meet mine, and hold for a long time. He's a smart guy, one of the smartest I know, and yeah, he's well aware of the heat I'm referring to. He's fighting it, but I'm not a girl to go down easily—so to speak. Does he remember my inner determination? If so, is he regretting this situation, bemoaning the sizable amount of money he dropped on a girl who might take him down before he gets his payback?

"Yeah, outside is a good idea," he says. He hands me my plate and gathers our utensils. I follow him out back and gasp when I see the view from his deck. In the distance, Christmas lights in the downtown core illuminate the dark sky, and warmth moves through me.

"My God this place is gorgeous." I set my plate on the table and walk to the railing. Gorgeous. Romantic. The perfect place for a seduction. "Look at all the colorful lights."

"Yeah, gorgeous." I turn to find him staring at me. He tears his gaze away and sits.

"Are you going to stay here for the holidays?" I ask, and press my back against the rail.

"That's my plan."

I spin in a circle, to take it all in again. "It's so strange being in a warm place for the holidays. I think I'm going to miss the snow."

"Not me."

I study the frown on his face. "Are you going to decorate?" I ask, even though it's a question I already know the answer to. But maybe things have changed for him. Maybe he learned to love the holidays instead of running away from them.

"No."

"What about a tree?"

"What about it?"

I roll my eyes at him. "Are you going to put one up?"

"No."

"Why not?" He flattens both hands on the small table, and lifts his gaze to me. His eyes are dark, frighteningly intense as they meet mine. "I didn't think Christmas was your thing either, Londyn," he says, his voice a low controlled whisper that skitters through me.

"You're right, it's not." I'm surprised that he remembers so much about me. What else does he have stored in that brilliant brain of his? I steal another glance out at the town in the distance. "Something about this place makes me feel a little festive inside."

"Sorry about that."

I laugh. "I'm not saying it like it's a bad thing. We're far away from home and things just feel… different."

"Things are different."

"Maybe we could pretend this isn't the real world for a while."

"I don't pretend, Londyn."

"I've traveled to numerous places, but here, I don't know, it's so removed from the real world, it feels like…like…"

"What does it feel like?"

"A fairy tale."

He laughs, and I get it. Life was anything but a fairy tale for him and his sister. Ironic really, considering in college he developed the Penn Pals app, and all the guys he hired became known as the Princes of Penn to the girls using the service.

"That's why you called me an ogre?" he says. "You still believe in fairy tales?"

"I called you an ogre because you were acting like one." He doesn't say anything so I add, "And I guess I don't really believe in fairy tales anymore." His brow knits together, and I can't tell whether he's happy or sad by that admission. "Are you keeping me here through the holidays?"

"Do you want to stay that long?"

"I don't really have any reason to rush back home. You know my mother, she always goes away, and my father buries himself in work. I actually told him I

CATHRYN FOX   55

was in Florida visiting a friend. Not that he'd worry about me, but I just needed a break from…" I shift a little uneasily. I probably shouldn't have brought up my father, judging by the way he's suddenly glaring at me. "What about Peyton? What is she doing for the holidays?"

"Working."

"Don't you two—"

"We do what we can just to get through the holidays. Working helps us move on."

Without thinking, I step closer and put my hand over his. I give it a squeeze and honest to God, I swear I can hear his heart crashing against his chest. I understand Christmas is a bad time for him. It's when he lost his folks in a car accident. I'm just sad that he and Peyton haven't found a way to make new memories for the holiday. Happier ones.

"We should eat," he says and turns from me, but not before I catch that lost look in his eyes, the same one that haunted him in college. Cason Harrison might be a grown man, but deep inside he's still sweet and vulnerable, a guy who cares about others, but had no one there for him. I cared about him—still do. But I wronged him, and lost the privilege of giving affection, as well as receiving it.

"Right," I say, pushing those troubled thoughts to the back of my brain as I settle in next to him at the bistro table. Silence falls over us as we dig into our meal.

I moan as I slide my fork into my mouth, the

flavor dancing on my tongue. "This is better than I remember."

"I've perfected it over the years."

"I've bet you perfected a lot of things," I say.

"You could say that." He twirls the pasta and takes a generous bite. "We learn and grow from our mistakes."

I set my fork down. "I know why you bid so fiercely on me, Cason."

He frowns. "Do you now?"

"Yeah, this is about revenge."

He takes another bite, chews slowly, and gives a slow nod of his head. "Is that what you think?"

"It's what I know, and I was thinking…" I lean forward, and his warm familiar scent wraps around me. Need races through me, floods my body. My breasts swell with heated blood, and ache for him to take them into his big hands. "Most people feel revenge is a dish best served cold, but if you ask me, I think it's best served hot."

He sets his utensils down, and sits up a bit straighter, the frown on his forehead deepening. "What are you suggesting, Londyn?" he asks, a slight edge to his voice.

"You said I'm here to do your laundry. I get it, you're *sticking it to me*." I pause to do quotes around those words. "But maybe there are other ways we can go about that?"

"You're suggesting there are other ways I can stick it to you?"

"Yes."

He leans toward me, his body so close to mine, all I have to do is inch forward if I wanted to kiss him. His thumb slides over my hand, and the touch vibrates through me, stroking the hot spot between my legs. As I bite back a heated moan, my nipples harden, poke through my lace bra, and his eyes drop to blatantly stare. I'm not normally one to put myself out there and boldly lay my needs on the line, which is probably why equal amounts of excitement and nervousness are racing through my veins, both fighting for control.

"There are rules," he says.

I shrug. "Rules are meant to be broken."

His gaze rakes over my face, and without warning, he cups my chin, his touch firm, reassuringly strong. "You think I'm the kind of guy to break trust?"

My heart slams against my chest at the reminder, and he inches back, leaving cold where there was once heat. "Cason—"

With an unnerving look, he says, "Perhaps it's time we call it a night."

CHAPTER FIVE

Cason

I TEAR OFF my shirt and toss it onto the bed as her words continue to race through my brain, teasing my aching cock to the point of pain. The woman is a contradiction. One second she's hell-bent on neutering me, and the next she wants me in her bed. I want that, too, long before she ever coated her lush, bee-stung lips in that fuck-me red lipstick. Then when she turned seductive, suggesting I *stick it to her*, I was seconds from carrying her to this very room when self-preservation kicked in. She broke my heart, tore it from my chest and stomped on it. I can't do this again with her. I can't get involved.

Then why the hell did you bid on her, dude?

Okay, fine, I hated the way the other men in the club looked at her, but there is no point in downplaying what's really going on here. I *couldn't* leave that club without her. Couldn't turn my back. Couldn't walk away. There isn't a single bone in my body that would let me leave without her. But now that I have her here—and no way are we sleeping together—what the hell am I supposed to do with her for the next two weeks? Maybe I should put her in the car and drive her to a hotel and end this sweet torment right now. I clearly have no idea what I'm doing and tonight was nothing but a total disaster. My dick agrees, even though he's hating on me right now. But there was a reason she was on that stage, and I can't let her go until I get to the bottom of the matter.

Across the hall I hear the shower running, and I try not to picture the hot water streaming down her gorgeous naked body and beading on her tight nipples. Is she touching herself, running her hands over her curves and wishing it was me caressing her, the way I dreamed about back in college? Jesus, when her nipples swelled tonight my mouth watered for a taste, and my dick damn near ripped through my zipper.

Why am I putting myself through this kind of torture? Didn't she hurt me enough already? Agitated, I kick off my pants and boxers and take my dick into my hand as I stomp into the en suite bathroom. It's been a long time since I've abused myself but I believe that dry streak is about to come to an end tonight. Either that, or I hit the local pub and find myself a willing woman, one who understands I only do one-night stands. Not that some random stranger would suffice now, not after spending time with Londyn.

Stick it to me.

I turn on the shower, lather my cock under the hard spray and in minutes I'm spurting into the stream. Jesus, when was the last time I came so fast? I scoff. Londyn screwed me over in a lot of ways, and now she's turned me into a damn hormonal teenager again.

You should have walked away tonight, dude.

But no, I couldn't leave well enough alone, now could I? I turn the water off and knot a towel around my hips. You'd think I'd be feeling a measure of relief but my dick is still standing at full attention. I tug on a fresh pair of boxers and climb between the sheets. Outside the near full moon shines in through my open curtains, and I wonder if she's in her bed, staring at the same moon, thinking of me the way I'm thinking of her.

I spend the next two hours tossing and turning. The creaking of Londyn's bedsprings is a sure sign she's as restless as I am. But as I think about her alone in that big bed, in a strange place, my heart squeezes, softens around the edges. She's a bad sleeper even when she's in familiar surroundings. There is probably no chance in hell she'll relax enough tonight to drift off. Come morning she'll be exhausted.

So, what are you going to do about that, Cason?

The bottom line is this: I brought her here, which means I'm responsible for her. I might be an asshole but contrary to what she thinks, I'm not a fucking ogre. Yeah, I'm ruthless in business, but I do not feed on the souls of innocent children.

I kick off the covers, and follow the path of the moon to my bedroom door. I twist the knob and listen for sounds as I quietly pull my door open. Silence meets my ears, and I wait a moment longer. Maybe this is a bad idea. Fingers wrapped tightly around the doorknob, I'm about to close my door again and head back to bed when the sound of her springs squeaking reaches my ears. I pad quietly across the floor, and find her door slightly ajar. I peek in and chuckle silently. In typical Londyn fashion, her sheets are kicked off and tangled around her feet. She's a hot mess and never looked more inviting.

I inch the door open. "Londyn," I say quietly as I walk across the floor, the boards groaning beneath my weight.

"Cason?" she says, rolling over. Flat on her back, I can make out the shape of her body, and I take a moment to admire her generous breasts hugged by a tight T-shirt. Her cotton nightclothes are far from sexy, but I somehow want her more.

"Roll over," I command in a soft voice, and she hesitates, her brow furrowed as her eyes lock on mine. My heart tumbles and I pinch my eyes shut for a brief second to slow it down.

"What's going on?" she asks, her voice husky and deep, her lids fluttering rapidly.

"You need sleep and I'm going to help."

"Are you…" She hesitates, but she doesn't need to finish for me to know what she's asking.

"Yes. I'm sure."

I step toward her and a surprised little yelp catches in her throat as she rolls, and aims her sweet ass my way. Damned if I don't want to slide those shorts down her legs and help her relax with my mouth… my fingers. I lift the blankets, and gently fix the sheets around her shoulder before crawling in behind. Her soft body relaxes against mine, and I nuzzle my face into her hair, breathing in the fresh scent of her shampoo.

After a long moment, she breaks the quiet, "Cason…"

"Shh, everything is okay. Go to sleep," I say. Tonight isn't about sex. I refuse to give in to the demands of my body. It's against host rules but, more important, I'm afraid if I do, I'll fall for her a second time. I care about her, yes. I can't deny that. But I can't, under any circumstance, love her again. She gutted me, and no matter how many millions my businesses are worth, I'm still the unwanted, unlovable boy from the wrong side of the tracks. Her father would see me dead before he'd see my ring on her finger. Not that I care what he thinks, but Londyn does. For as long as I've known her, she's been starved for his approval, but she should stop trying to please him. He's never going to give his approval until she marries a man of his choice and becomes a dutiful wife, and to be honest that's just fucking sad.

She takes a deep breath, lets it out slowly and softens against me. I pull her in tighter, and put my arm around her to hold her close, much the same way I used to do back in college. Her breathing changes, slows, and just when I think she's asleep, she speaks.

"Thank you," she says in a groggy voice, seconds before her body completely settles against mine.

"You're welcome," I whisper. As my words fall on deaf ears, my traitorous heart misses a beat. I swallow against a tight throat, and gently blow a strand of long blond hair from my face. My lids fall shut and the next thing I know, light from the rising sun slants into her room, pulling me awake. Jesus, when was the last time I slept so soundly? With my arm still around her—hard to believe neither of us moved through the night—I slowly lift my head to check the clock on the nightstand. I didn't bother bringing my phone in with me, didn't bother setting any kind of alarm. My routine is set in stone, and my internal clock is pretty good at waking me. But there was nothing normal or repetitive about yesterday, which is why it's an hour past my regular wake-up time.

I slowly inch away, not wanting to wake her, and she makes a sexy little noise of disappointment. I tuck her back in, and stand over her for a second. My heart beats double time against my chest as I take in her beauty. This morning her face is free of makeup, and dammit that natural, girl-next-door look works on her. She used to always wash her face clean before I tucked her in and stayed with her until she drifted off. I always loved this side of her, and I'm pretty sure I'm the only guy she ever let see her that way.

Walking on my tiptoes, I head to my room, and

my heart is somewhere in my throat as my brain dredges up old memories. I tug on my jeans and check my phone for messages. A few business calls that can wait until later, and one from Peyton. What would she think if she knew Londyn was here with me—that I bought her at a damn auction? She'd probably lose her mind. She's the only one who really knows me, the only one I let see the pain under the easygoing facade I present to the world.

I shoot her a text back, letting her know I'll see what I can do about setting her up with a good guy from Penn Pals in the New Year, and take the stairs quietly. In the kitchen I put on a pot of coffee and look out the window. The water is calm today, a good day to take the catamaran out. The dock is decorated for the season, each post sporting a festive wreath. Last night Londyn picked at an old wound when she brought up Christmas. It's not right for me to keep her here over the holiday, but she doesn't seem in any hurry to leave. She can say she hates Christmas as much as I do, but I call bullshit. There is a part of that girl that has "white picket fence and a big house full of kids" written all over her.

I dig eggs and bacon from the fridge, and when the coffeepot beeps, I pour a big mug and take a generous sip.

"Save some for me."

I spin at the sound of Londyn's voice. The second I set eyes on her, my heart stops beating, all the need from last night bubbling to the surface. Her hair is a mess, her eyes wide but still sleepy and those lush, bee-stung lips are slightly parted, like they're desperate to be kissed. I instantly harden, and I fight for a measure of control, but it's fraying along a finely stitched seam like a sail caught in a windstorm. How can I possibly hide what she does to me?

What if I don't want to anymore?

Her pink tongue snakes out, and she swipes it over her bottom lip. I curl my fingers before I grab a fistful of her hair and tug, until her mouth is poised open for mine. Sensations pulse through my body, effectively cutting each threadbare edge of my control.

She makes a small move, but I'm right there, right there on her until we're standing toe to toe, our bodies aligned, our knuckles brushing.

"Last night—" she begins, and I cut her off.

"Did you sleep well?"

She runs her fingers through her mess of hair, and a laugh catches in her throat. "I can't remember the last time I slept that well, actually."

"No?" I ask, self-preservation a thing of the past, as my other head, the one farther south, starts calling the shots. My gaze drops to her mouth. I want to taste her in the worst way.

"Well, maybe I can," she says.

"Yeah?" I lean into her, breathing deeply.

"The last time you stayed with me. You walked me back to my apartment, crawled in bed with me." She sighs. "That was such a long time ago."

"Too long." I lift my hand, and scrape the rough

pad of my thumb along her bottom lip. Her eyes widen, like she's startled by my touch. "A bit of toothpaste," I explain.

"Oh." Heated blue eyes move over my face, then flick away. She looks down, a cascade of blond hair covering her disappointment. "I thought…"

"What did you think?"

"Nothing," she says, her shoulders swaying slightly as she shakes her head. As her gaze shifts away, I drop my hand, let it graze her bare arm. She sucks in a fast breath, not at all unfazed by my touch. I shouldn't like that. I shouldn't want that. But I do, and I can't do a damn thing about it. Tomorrow there might be regret, but today is different. Today holds all kinds of promise. Besides, I'm not going into this blind—like I did last time with her. I'm older, wiser and have learned from my mistakes.

"The rules, remember," I say.

She looks at me through her lowered lashes. "You can't touch me," she responds, her voice soft, breathless, like she's been running a marathon.

I step closer. With our bodies only a hairbreadth away from intimate contact, I struggle to keep up my no-touching end of the contract. Heat and sexual need vibrate between us, and my dick reaches out to her, aches for her touch. Damned if the big guy doesn't know what he wants. But I need her to make the first move. Yes, this is crazy and reckless, and could very well chip at the carefully constructed wall around my heart. But I can't seem to stop myself.

"That's right," I say and hold my arms up, palms out. "You're hands-off, Londyn."

She angles her head, and her hair falls off her shoulder, exposing the long column of her neck. That's where I want my mouth first, right there in that soft nook. After I press warm openmouthed kisses to her flesh, and fill my lungs with her scent, I'll work my way down to her full breasts, her stomach, the spot between her legs that is undoubtedly flushed with heat and beckoning my tongue. Fiery warmth radiates off her in waves, cocooning me in a blanket of need. It's a battle I can't fight…can't win.

"What about if I touch you first?"

My throat closes over as she plays this game with me. Yesterday I might have been sending mixed signals, wanting her in my bed but fighting every second of it. Today I'm pretty sure my actions and words are crystal clear. I want to corrupt this sexy woman, do all kinds of depraved things with the little rich girl. None of which stem from revenge.

"I believe that's allowed," I say.

"That's what I've been told, too."

"Londyn…"

"Yeah."

Walk away, Cason. Run.

"Touch me."

Fuck.

She takes a measured step closer, like she, too, is starved for my touch, and her hard nipples press against my bare chest. *Yes!* Grinning, like she holds

all the cards—and she damn well knows she does—
she moves slightly, rotating her curvy hips and scraping her gorgeous buds over my flesh. The resulting
growl that climbs out of my throat elicits a soft, yet
urgent little moan from her. Slowly, deliberately she
moves against me. Well shit, I never knew she was
a sexual tease. We never got that far in our relationship before.

"How about this?" she murmurs, her voice soft
and needy, but in the far depths I catch a hint of playfulness. I forgot how much I liked the lighthearted
side of her. She so rarely showed it. But if she wants
to play with me today, I'm game.

"I'm not sure that would be considered touching," I explain. "Not to the club's definition, anyway. They're a stickler for details, or so I've heard."

"Oh, okay." She looks up and to the left, like she's
in deep concentration. "Will this work?" As mischief
tugs at her mouth, she goes up on her toes, moves
her hips closer, until our sexes are aligned. I nearly
come in my jeans.

Sweet mother of God, the heat radiating off her
core nearly does me in, but I bite the inside of my
jaw to maintain control.

"Oh, it works," I say through clenched teeth. "But
I'm afraid it still doesn't quite fit the definition of
touching."

The soft pads of her fingers circle my nipple.
"Would you consider this touching?"

I try not to flinch under the warmth of her soft

fingers, and resist the urge to grab her hips and pull her body to mine. I clear my throat. "Close but still questionable."

She takes a step back and frowns. "This is rather hard."

I cup her elbow, tug her back to me, and our bodies collide. I groan as my dick presses against her stomach "Yeah, very hard," I say, and her soft chuckle curls around me, massages my aching balls.

Her cheeks turn pink, her body flushed with the power she has over me. "I don't know what it's going to take to convince the club," she says and nibbles on her bottom lip in a way that makes my dick throb. I want to be the one biting her…everywhere.

"I never thought you were the type of girl to give up so easily."

"I'm not," she murmurs. "I'm just considering my options." She leans forward and places a soft kiss on my shoulder. I vibrate beneath her warm, wet mouth. She inhales deeply, breathing in the soapy scent of my skin, and her moan of approval rocks my world. If she doesn't soon touch me, I'm going to lose my damn mind. Her tongue snakes out, and she runs it along my flesh. I quiver, and it's all I can do to keep my hands fisted at my sides.

She continues to press warm kisses to my flesh, like she's lost in tasting me, and I suck in a fast breath. Big blue eyes lift, blink up at me.

"Do you think the club would consider this touching?"

"It's possible, but there could be room for argument," I manage to get out.

She stands to her full height, confidently reaches out, and places her hand over my aching cock, giving it a firm massage in my jeans.

"How about this, Cason? I believe there is no mistaking this for anything but me touching you."

"I believe that just might be the magic touch," I say, and slide my hand around the back of her neck. I hold her tightly and dip my head.

CHAPTER SIX

Londyn

HE HAULS ME against him, hovering over me, his strength and stature making me feel small against his big athletic frame. I crane my neck to see his face, welcoming him to my mouth—to my body—but he's no longer looking for permission. No, he's taking over, calling the shots and while this is probably a mistake, my lust-rattled brain currently doesn't give a shit. His lips find mine, but not in a gentle exploratory kiss meant to introduce our bodies to one another. No, his kisses are hungry, ravenous, devouring me with a need I've never before experienced, and have only ever fantasized about.

I kiss him back and his hot mouth tastes like mint, coffee and…filthy sex—the kind I'm suddenly desperate for, but want with this man only. My sex tightens, and clenches for something to grip on to as I moan, boldly push my hips forward, wanting more, all of him. His breathing changes, becomes labored as he shifts positions, pulls me against him harder, and as his greedy tongue roughly tangles with mine, I ask myself one question.

Is this really happening?

Last night, after he abruptly shut down my seduction, leaving my ego bruised and my body needy, I figured come morning he'd send me home. Yes, there is an insane chemistry between us, enough to light up every Christmas tree along the harbor front for a month straight, but he walked away, making it painstakingly clear he wasn't going to act on our sexual pull. I'm not sure what changed his mind, and right now, with the way he's kissing and touching me, it's not the time to examine this unexpected turn of events. No, now is the time to just simply enjoy.

The soft bristles on his chin burn my face, eliciting a hot, rippling rush over my flesh. Restless, and so damn needy, a sound rumbles in my throat and I don't try to hide it. He shoves a knee between my thighs, presses it firmly against my sex. I rotate my hips, and slide my arms around him, reveling in the feel of his hard muscles, thicker now that he's grown from a boy into a man.

"That's it. Ride my leg," he growls into my mouth. I rub my clit against solid muscle, riding him boldly. Honestly, I've never been this shameless with my needs before. But the sinful way Cason touches, encourages me, brings out a side I never knew existed, and no way am I going to try to leash it now. Not when this is so much fun, and so deliciously dirty.

I run my fingers over his chiseled body, and deep between my legs I grow wet. My nipples swell, ache for his touch, his mouth, his greedy tongue. Good God, I've never needed anyone the way I need him right now. It's terrifying, and exhilarating all at once.

"Cason," I murmur into his mouth, a new kind of desperation gripping me as his fevered kisses steal the breath from my lungs. But I don't care. I don't want to breathe. All I want to do is feel this man's mouth on mine, his hands on my body. Frantic, I claw at him and his big palms slide down my arms, grip my hips and effortlessly move me around like I weigh nothing. He shifts me, until I'm pressed against the kitchen wall. Holy Hell, this is the kind of sex a girl can only dream about. Well, the kind I've dreamed about, anyway.

He breaks the kiss, and I gulp for breath as his teeth skim my lower lip. A second later he buries his face in my neck. He nips at me, scrapes the coarse edges of his teeth over my skin and I'm pretty damn sure I've died and gone to heaven. Sex has only ever been vanilla, a mundane task that left me unfulfilled, and there is no denying I want this dirty, delicious, up-against-the-wall, no-holds-barred sex with this man—and none other.

Wild and demanding, deft fingers grip the hem of my cotton T-shirt and peel it over my head. His nostrils flare as he stares at my breasts, and my nipples swell under his heated examination. His gaze slides over my body like a hot caress, and as he lavishes me with his undivided attention, I squirm against the wall.

"You are so beautiful, Londyn."

My heart skips one beat, then another as his pupils dilate, pleasure evident in his expression. "Please," I say, even though I'm not sure what I'm begging for.

"These," he says, and runs his palm along the swell of my breast. "I dreamed about having these in my mouth all night."

A surge of pleasure shoots through me, and taking ownership of my desires, I cup my breasts and rub my thumbs over my nipples. As he watches, transfixed, I squeeze the undersides, offering my aching buds up to him. He steps back for a second, studies me too closely, too intently. My pulse jumps. This man is going to eat me alive. I'm about to let my hands drop when he gives a slow shake of his head, and a little thrill goes through me. I glance down, take in his thickening cock. He wants this as much as I do, and I'm finally going to have what should have happened years ago.

I briefly shut my eyes, and turn my head from side to side. My long mess of hair tickles my bare flesh and I quiver. My eyes fly open as his deep, appreciative growl cuts the silence in the room.

"Last night when I crawled in with you, I wanted my cock right here." He cups my hot sex through my shorts and gives a little squeeze.

"I wanted that, too," I say. I wanted that from the first time I met him.

"I wanted to fuck you until sunup, a week from tomorrow," he says, and I quake. Violently.

"Cason…"

"I can't give you more than that, Londyn." His eyes go dark, lock on mine, and I gasp at the frighteningly intense way he's staring at me. "I won't." I gulp and he goes quiet, waiting for a response.

He's protecting his heart. I get it. I should be protecting mine, too. "I don't want more," I say, as his cold, foreboding words echo in my brain. "I can only give you my body. Nothing else." I grip a fistful of his hair, urging his mouth back to mine, and as he tears his gaze away, I'm not entirely sure that we're on the same page or that I'm being honest with him or myself. But I appreciate him laying out the ground rules for this affair, and plan to follow them.

He kisses my neck, licks my skin, his heavy-lidded eyes skimming my face before his mouth once again claims mine. He grips the band of my pajama shorts and I expect him to slide them down my legs. Instead, he dips a finger inside, and slowly inches me open.

"Shit," he curses under his breath as he releases my mouth and runs the rough pad of his finger along me. He finds my clit, circles it cruelly, coming close but never touching, and I gyrate forward, trying to force him to center his touch. His dark chuckle curls around me and I take a shaky breath.

"Cason," I murmur.

He puts his mouth next to my ear and the heat of

his mouth takes me even higher. "You need something, Londyn?"

"Yes," I say and sag against the wall.

"Might this be it?" he asks, and finally applies pressure to my aching nub. A moan rumbles in my throat as his wet fingers deftly swirl, creating heat and friction that rocks me to my core.

"Oh, God, yes. It's exactly what I need." He groans and pushes himself against me, and I gyrate my body to massage his erection. His hips flex, power forward, and I love the needy growl that follows my teasing movements.

"I need something, too," he murmurs into my ear, his breathing harsh and labored.

"I can tell," I respond playfully and rub him a little more.

"Do you have any idea what I want to do to you right now?" he asks and looks me over, like he's gauging my reaction. I get the strangest sense that he could be a little afraid of what he needs. That he might lose control. I've never had a man lose it with me before, and the idea of it happening with Cason, a man I've never stopped thinking about, fills me with a kind of excitement I wish I didn't feel.

"What…what do you need?" I ask, wanting everything with him, even if it means emotional suicide.

He slides a finger into my heat. "I need you bent over the island, until you're wide open for me."

I gulp, as his dirty words and invading finger bring on a shudder. He changes the pace, running his thumb over my clit a bit faster, sweeping side to side until I'm damn near delirious.

"That feels so good," I whimper.

"Yeah, you feel good. So wet and ready for me." His hands shift and I almost cry at the loss of his touch but it turns to a moan as he dips a second thick finger inside, penetrating deeply as he uses the heel of his hand to massage my clit. Blood pumps through my veins double time, and sensations center on my core as an orgasm takes shape. I can't believe he's taking me to the edge so fast. Then again, it's been so long since I've been touched, and no man has ever quite touched me the way Cason is right now.

"Not yet," he says and pulls his hands from my shorts, leaving me hot and achy. God, is this some kind of cruel revenge? Take me to the edge and leave me hanging. Punishment for the way I wronged him.

"Cason," I cry out, about to touch myself and finish this before I'm nothing more than a quivering mass of need on his kitchen floor. His lips twist knowingly, as I imagine the worst.

"The first time you come with me, I want it to be with my tongue so I can taste you," he says, and I nearly sink to the floor, elated. He pushes against my shoulders, anchors me to the wall. His firm touch stabilizes me and my knees stop quivering.

"You good, Londyn?" he asks, his voice changing, becoming deadly serious with worry, and my heart leaps, loving the way he's checking in on me.

"I will be," I say, trying to get my shorts off to

give him better access. He laughs and shoves my hands away.

"You don't get to touch. Only I do," he says and flattens my palms against the wall. "Keep them there. Your orgasms are mine." His chin lowers and our eyes meet as he grips my shorts and peels them down my legs. Far too slowly for my liking. His breath is hot on my flesh, and goose bumps break out on my skin. I try to buck forward, try to hurry him. "Such a needy girl," he whispers.

"Cason."

I lift one leg and then the other. He tosses my shorts away, and goes back on his heels just to stare at me.

"You have the prettiest pussy," he says and pets me gently. I nearly freaking come. I catch the heat in his gaze, the way his eyes are worshipping me. While no man has ever looked at me with such need, I can't take another second of this torture. I've waited, wanted him for too long.

"Please touch me," I cry out.

He parts me with strong fingers, and taunts my sex. I roll my hips, a low moan rumbling from the depths of my throat. God, yes.

"Don't move," he says, and I go perfectly still, not wanting to do or say anything that will prolong this seduction. I suck in a breath and let it out ever so slowly when he leans into me, sweeping his tongue over my swollen clit, with slow leisurely strokes that heat me to the boiling point. Holy God. I grip the wall, to hold on.

His tongue lazily laps at me, and I want to move, want to shove myself onto his face, grind against him, hard, force his mouth to ravage me, but I don't do any of that. Instead I stay still, giving him the control, and I have to say, remaining motionless comes with its own twisted pleasure.

He finally, *finally* buries his face between my legs, eats at me like a man starved, and his finger thrusts inside, faster and faster as he changes the tempo and pressure, his tongue plundering, taking everything it wants, until I sink into a haze of sensations. My breathing grows rough, and I gulp for air as he drives into me with filthy, blunt strokes that shut down my mind. Tension builds inside me, and I cry out his name, needing release before I shatter into a million broken pieces. My skin grows taught, and I whimper as a powerful orgasm tears through me.

Dizzy and gasping, I feel my hot release drip down my thighs, and he slows the pace, removing his mouth from my clit as I ride out the waves. He takes my hands from the wall and puts them on his shoulders. I squeeze, and work to ground myself as I slowly come back down from that high.

My God, is this what I've been missing out on?

He stays between my legs, pressing soft, open-mouthed kisses to my pussy, and I struggle really hard to keep myself together, in more ways than one. He slides up my body, his cock pressing against me, and my mouth waters for a taste but he seems to have other ideas. He steps back and I ache at the loss of his heat. But it's short-lived. Two seconds later, he has me bent over the kitchen island, and the hiss of his zipper as he releases his pants sends shivers of anticipation down my spine. My entire body quakes.

I try to look over my shoulder but he puts his hand on my back, and presses my swollen breasts against the cold marble. It does little to push back the heat building inside me. He jerks forward, shoves his hard length against my ass, and I wiggle. That movement gets me a small slap on my backside. I yelp, but it's from pleasure not pain.

"Such a tease," he says, leaning over me to whisper in my ear. His heat trickles through my blood, and my breathing grows shallow. I catch his scent, breathe it in and lose myself in it as it swirls around me.

Strong fingers grip both ass cheeks, and squeeze. I'm sure I'll have little finger bruises come tonight, but I love that he's a little bit rough and wild, and those marks will be a reminder of this moment. My belly draws in tight as he pulls on my cheeks until my sex is wide-open and wet for him.

"Shit," he curses, and his hands clamp tight as he nudges my feet a little farther apart, spreading me more. His erection is now between my thighs, pushing, and probing, big and needy, but then he's gone. I wait a second, but it feels more like an hour. When he doesn't rush back, I'm about to turn, to get down on my knees and beg him to finish, when I hear the foil crinkling. I nearly cry out with relief.

Once sheathed, he reaches around my body, and pinches my clit with slick fingers as he positions himself at my opening. He pulls in a deep breath, and then another, like he's a sprinter about to run the race of a lifetime, one he's been training for since childhood.

I know the feeling.

He pushes into me, offering me one sweet inch after another and I claw at the counter as he stretches me open. "More," I cry out, and his hips power forward. He grunts, and holds my hips for leverage as he seats himself high inside me, filling me completely.

My heart pounds against my ribs as he buries himself so deeply, I'm sure he's going to ruin me for any other man. But I don't care. Right now, all that matters in this moment is that Cason is inside me, and how incredible that feels.

"You good, Londyn?" he asks, his rough voice rumbling through me as he strokes a finger down my spine. A quiver rushes through my entire body and he groans as the movement squeezes his cock.

"Yes," I lie, fearing I'll never be good again. "You?"

"You feel so fucking good," he growls and pulls almost all the way out. I whimper as the heated friction hijacks my ability to think with clarity. He drives back in again, and I lift my ass, my sex growing wetter and wetter as my peaked nipples nearly score the marble countertop.

His lust-saturated groan curls through me, and he

moves with steady thrusts. He cups my ass, kneads my flesh and pounds into me. His length teases me as his girth stretches me in the most delicious ways, and the second he reaches around my body and races a finger over my clit, another climax takes hold. I've never climaxed twice. Never. Not even with Mr. Right, the battery-operated toy that hangs out in my nightstand. Why the hell is sex so good with him?

"Oh, my God, yes," I cry out.

He presses hot kisses to my back, the moisture on our bodies sealing us together as he drives harder, his movements frenzied as he chases his own pleasure. I rock against him, meet each speeding thrust as he sinks into me, and my hot wet sex muscles clench around him until his control is a thing of the past.

"Londyn," he growls, and hearing my name on his tongue as he lets go does the stupidest things to my heart. He groans as he depletes himself and I grip the counter harder, doing my best to hang on— to my sanity.

My God, that was the most erotic experience of my life.

Sated and spent, he falls over me, his lips warm on my back as he silently peppers me with lazy kisses. His soft touch creates a new kind of need in me. One I'm not about to explore. A long time later, he lifts me from the counter, and wraps his arms around my waist. With his chest against my back, he just holds me, his forehead pressed to my shoulder and we breathe together. My mind trips back to last night, to when he crawled in bed with me, holding me just like this until I fell asleep. He may be a hard son of a bitch on the outside—but there is a warmth and kindness in him he can't hide from me, no matter how hard he's trying. But I'm here to get my heart back from him, not let him get a tighter hold on it, right?

I touch his hand, pull one away from my body and peel his fingers open to expose his palm.

"Looking for something?" he asks.

CHAPTER SEVEN

Cason

I PACE AROUND my office, and try to concentrate on work, but I can't take my mind off Londyn. I've had sex before, plenty of times, but holy shit, it's never been that good…that right. I can still taste her sweetness on my tongue, still feel the clench of her sex around me as she tumbled into orgasm. My only regret is that she was face down. Next time, I want to see her eyes, want to watch the ecstasy spread across her face, and know I'm the guy who put it there.

Next time?

Shit, there shouldn't even have been a first time but when it comes to her, I'm so goddamn weak I have zero restraint. But hey, at least we both made it clear this was sex and sex only. No misunderstandings. No expectation. No future.

No mistakes.

I sit back at my desk and answer a few emails, but don't have to look up to know Londyn is standing in my doorway. I can feel her eyes on me, smell her sweet citrusy scent as it fills the room and teases me until I'm thickening in my damn pants.

She knocks gently on the doorframe and I glance up. My God, she is beautiful. My pulse beats a little faster as my gaze moves over her face, taking note of her cheeks, which are still a bit red and abraded from the bristles on my face. I scrub my chin, and make a mental note to shave as my mind revisits that incredible round of sex in my kitchen. After I had my way with her on the island, I cooked us breakfast and we both showered, in separate rooms. While things weren't awkward between us—being inside her created a new kind of intimacy I'd rather avoid—we went our separate ways. But there is no avoiding her now, and I have to figure out a game plan for the next two weeks. I mean, we can't just have sex all the time.

Why the hell not?

"Sorry to interrupt," she says.

I wave my hand for her to come in, and my gaze moves over her tight curve-hugging jeans and white blouse I'd like to remove from her body—with my teeth. Lust saturates my brain, flooding my veins with need. But is that all this is? Lust? Lust I can live with. Love, however. There is no place for that here.

"What's up?" I ask.

"Well," she begins as she settles herself in the chair across from me, and primly folds her hands. I almost laugh at the reserved position. While she might come across as proper, this pampered little rich girl has a very sensuous side of her. One I like very much.

Another thing I really like is her fierce determination. Back in college she was a hard worker. Yeah, sure I might call her a spoiled rich girl now, but those words come from a place of anger and betrayal. What I can't take away from her is her drive and dedication. She's a woman who isn't at all afraid of backbreaking work, and I admired the hell out of her for it.

She glances past my shoulders to the sea below. "I didn't want to go into your bedroom without permission, but you did mention you had some pants you needed me to press."

I laugh, and shake my head. "You don't have to do that."

"I want to," she says quickly. "I'm here for you, Cason." She draws her bottom lip into her mouth and once again all I can think about is nibbling on her. "Being here is way better than being in New York, and you bought me, so whatever you need."

"I don't need anything," I say.

She takes a deep, fortifying breath. "Then what do you want with me?"

Since I don't really know the answer to that, I stare at her long and hard, and try to piece the puzzle together. "Why were you really on that stage?" I ask.

She sits up a little straighter. "I told you, for the thrill of it."

Her cheeks turn a deeper shade of pink, and her lashes blink rapidly. I read her body language and say, "I'm not sure I believe that."

"I'm not sure you need to," she responds, her chin

inching up, and I tap my pen on my desk, study the way she's suddenly avoiding my gaze.

"Fine, then. Don't tell me." My cell phone pings and we both glance at it. I ignore it for the time being. I flip it over, and close my laptop.

"What are you working on?" she asks.

"Going over a contract and looking at designs."

Her eyes light up. "If there is anything you need help with—"

"There isn't."

Her smile slips as she deflates, and her shoulders sink, and damn if I don't feel like a prick. But I'm not about to share business secrets with her. For all I know she was on that stage to hook up with me again and steal more secrets. But that's too coincidental, and too ludicrous for even me to believe.

"Okay. I guess if you don't need me for anything…" She puts her hands on the arms of the chair, about to lift herself, but stops. "Can I ask why you were at the club?"

"I had a business meeting," I say honestly and try not to blatantly stare at her lips, which are still bruised and swollen from my kisses. I went at her like a goddamn horny teenager with no finesse. That's how much I wanted her, but next time, next time I'll go slower, savor her longer.

Next time?

Yes, of course there's going to be a next time. I've given up trying to fool myself. I have zero control around her. As I consider that, I instantly decide that for the next two weeks, I'm going to live in this fairy-tale world with her, pretend we're in a magical place where hurt and backstabbing don't exist. After our two weeks, it's life as usual, and that life does not include Londyn Harding.

"Your business was with Luis Laurent?"

I push back in my chair and study the longing and admiration in her eyes. "How did you know that?"

"I just heard." She smiles, and looks down, her thoughts a million miles away. "He's only my idol."

"I'd imagine he is. Wait, is that why you were at the club? Were you hoping to get bought—"

She grips the arms of the chair again, effectively cutting me off when she says, "No, no, nothing like that. I didn't even know he'd be there. Well I should let you get back to work." She stands, and flips her hair from her shoulder but my stomach tightens as another thought hits. What if she's in some kind of trouble. "Cason?" she says, her frown deepening.

"Yeah."

"I don't normally have so much free time on my hands. I'm not sure what to do with myself. If there is any way I can help you…"

"Why don't you head out, explore the city." I push from my chair and go to my window. "Come here," I say, looking for an excuse to touch her, as weak as that makes me.

Her heels tap on the floor as she comes my way. I take her shoulders and move her in front of the window. Standing behind her, I press my mouth to her ear, and breathe in her scent as I point. "See that café right there?"

"I'm not sure I do," she says, her voice a bit breathless as she scans the city below. She bends forward, presses her forehead to the glass. Her sweet ass bumps my groin, and my pulse beats a little harder in the base of my neck as she fiddles with the top button on her blouse, like she needs to occupy her hands.

"Right there," I say and step closer, until our bodies are touching. "The one with the bright orange sign." She nods and I add, "They make the best croissants."

"You want me to get you a croissant?"

"Get us some," I say.

"You paid an awful lot of money to hire an errand girl."

"I know," I say and run my hands down her arm. "How well did you pack?"

"Just a few outfits, pajamas…"

I groan as my cock thickens, remembering how I removed those pajamas only a couple hours ago.

"I'd like to go out on the boat later," I tell her.

She turns to face me, our bodies merely inches apart. "You have a boat?"

"Yes, and I'd like to take advantage of the nice weather. Did you pack appropriate clothes for boating?"

"Not really."

"Why don't you go shopping, get what you need. Charge everything back to me."

Her shoulders sag, the glow on her face dimming at my suggestion. "Okay, it's better than sitting around here twiddling my thumbs, I guess." Her gaze moves to my laptop, a longing in her eyes. "Are you sure you don't need my help with anything else?"

"Positive," I say.

She gives a curt nod, pushes past me and walks out of my office. I stand there for a few minutes, and my insides turn. Yes, I get it. She's a brilliant woman, capable of doing more than running errands for me, but I can't—won't—task her with anything that involves my business. That would make me the stupidest man on the planet. I sit down, and the sound of the front door clicking shut pulls me from my reverie.

I grab my phone and text my sister back. She knows I always spend the holiday in Cannes, secluded from the real world, so I have no idea why she's asking about my plans when they've been established for years. I wait for an answer but when none comes, I dial her number. She answers on the fourth ring.

"Hey, big bro, what's up?"

"I should be the one asking you that question."

Papers rustle in the background, and I tap a restless finger on my laptop. "What are you talking about? Wait, have you forgotten your meds this morning?" She cracks a joke. Like me she sometimes uses humor to hide what she's really feeling.

"And here I was wondering if you overdosed on your morning concoction of *smart-ass*."

She chuckles and I relax. It's good to hear her voice. We've both been working so hard, it's actually been months since we sat down and talked face-to-face. But with the holiday upon us, hanging out in person is not going to happen anytime soon. Not because we're busy but because we both hole up and just try to get through the festive season the best way we know how.

"I'm calling because you asked if I would be home for Christmas."

"Yeah, sorry," she says, a hitch to her voice. "I don't know what I was thinking. Maybe *I'm* off my meds."

My heart constricts at the uncharacteristic longing I hear in her voice. "Are you okay?" I ask, struggling to loosen that imaginary band squeezing my chest.

"Never better," she says, injecting a fake ounce of lightness into her voice. "What about you? How did your meeting go with Luis?"

"Great, actually. I think the new line is going to be a huge success."

More paper rustling, and a stapler clicks. "What are you not telling me?"

I chuckle inwardly. My little sister is too smart for her own good. "You wouldn't believe it if I told you."

"Try me, bro. I need a good story. Something to cheer me up."

I stiffen, and my heart stills. "Why do you need cheering up?"

A beat of silence and then she replied, "Ah, nothing really. You know, the holiday."

"Yeah, I know." I spin in my chair, and glance out the window, debating on how much I should divulge.

"Spill," she says, "Or I'll hunt you down. You know I'm a teacher. I have ways of making you talk," she teases.

I laugh at her antics, and a bit of the tension leaves my chest. "You're not going to believe who's here with me."

"Ooh, do tell."

"Londyn Harding."

Peyton goes so quiet I think she might have hung up on me. I wait a second for the dial tone, and when it doesn't come, I say, "Are you still there?"

"Bro, seriously, what the hell is going on?"

"I actually bought her at an auction house."

"You…bought her?"

I wave my hand even though she can't see me. "It's not quite like it sounds. It's all aboveboard. So don't worry."

"You…bought her," she says again, and I don't need to be face-to-face to know hers is scrunched. A familiar gesture when she's trying to puzzle something out. "Like, you own her?"

"It's not quite like that. It's just—" I pinch the bridge of my nose. What the hell possessed me to open my damn mouth, anyway?

Oh, maybe because you need someone to talk to about Londyn.

Nope, I don't. I really don't.

Liar.

"It's hard to explain," I say.

"Wow, fate is a funny thing, isn't it?"

Fate? Fate isn't what brought us together. Five million dollars is what brought us together. No way am I about to admit that though. I actually still can't quite believe I doled out that insane amount of money.

"Why would Londyn be selling herself? Does she need the money or something? Did her father cut her off?"

"I'm not sure," I say. The one thing I do know, however, is that she was lying when she said she was on that stage for the thrill.

"How long do you own her?"

"I don't own…" I stop, my protest dying in my throat. Once Peyton gets something in her head, there is no changing her mind. Clearly, I taught her well. "She's here until after Christmas."

Another pause and then in a soft voice she says, "That is so nice, Cason." The sigh that follows those words surprises the hell out of me, but the longing in her voice is what nearly knocks me off my damn chair. What is going on with her?

"There's nothing nice about that, Peyton," I say, exasperation in my voice as I shoot that answer back quickly, maybe too quickly.

"Yeah, Cason. There is." She chuckles into the phone like she knows something I don't. Whatever she thinks she knows, she's dead wrong.

"I don't even like her," I say, my denial so fast and furious I wonder exactly who I'm trying to convince.

I am so screwed.

"I know," she says, her voice lacking conviction.

I slump a little in my chair. "Then why would you say it's nice?"

"I think you'll see soon enough," she says, a hint of something in her voice, something that sounds like melancholy, but my sister isn't a dreamer. Like me, she's grounded in reality. Then again, I am suspending reality for the next two weeks to live in some fairy tale with Londyn.

I snort and say, "Okay, you really are off your meds. You're worrying me, kiddo."

"No need to be worried, and you can stop being overprotective. I'm a big girl and can take care of myself and while I'd like to talk longer, I have to run to a meeting."

"Yeah, okay," I say, reluctant to let her go as concern niggles at me. Maybe I am just being overprotective.

"I love you, big brother."

"I love you, too, crazy little sister." I shake my head and wonder what's really going on with her as I slide my finger across the screen to end the call. As soon as I get back to the city, I plan to pay her a visit.

I go back to my computer, and work to focus on business. I make a few calls, check in with human resources regarding a staffing problem and somehow manage to lose myself in work for the remainder of the day. By the time I lift my head, and blink my eyes into focus, I realize that it's nearing dinnertime. Nighttime will soon be upon us. So much for taking the boat out today.

I push from my chair and as the quiet of the house beats against my ears, worry weaves its way through my veins. I stand and step up to my window to glance out. Where the hell is Londyn? She should have been back hours ago.

I leave my office to search the villa. Maybe she came back and I didn't hear her. I check the main level but she's nowhere to be found. Worry hits like a punch. Is she lost? Hurt? She would have called if she needed me, right? Shit, we didn't exchange numbers. Another thought slams into me. Maybe she left. While I had my head down, buried in work, maybe she cabbed it to the airport and hopped on the next flight back to New York? She said she didn't want to go back, but maybe she changed her mind after I sent her on a menial task. But no way can I talk to her about business, or let her help.

I work to quell my panic and wonder why the hell I'm panicking in the first place. Jesus. Her hopping on a plane would probably be for the best for both of us. The fact that I can't find comfort in that thought nearly paralyzes me. Shit.

Forcing my legs to work, I dash up the stairs, and three long strides take me to her room. Her suitcase is still sitting where I left it and I don't even want to examine how happy that makes me.

If she didn't leave, where the hell is she?

CHAPTER EIGHT

Londyn

I SWING MY PURSE, looking far more carefree to the tourists flocking about than I actually feel deep inside. Honest to God, I can do more than run errands for Cason. I have thoughts, ideas and skills that can be put to better use. But why on earth would he ever let me near his work again? If I were him, I sure as hell wouldn't.

He bought you for revenge, Londyn, not to help him with his business.

With that thought bouncing around inside my brain, I walk along the streets, and work to ignore the empty ache inside me. I find the stupid café and step inside. The delicious smells instantly lighten my mood, and as I walk up to the counter, I shake off the rest of my angst. I'm here in Cannes for two weeks, with the hottest guy on the planet. Sure, he hates me, but the hate sex was pretty damn phenomenal, and definitely something I want to experience again.

My body quakes in remembrance. I always wanted

Cason, wanted him to be my first in fact. Somehow, I knew sex with him would be wild, wicked, devastatingly delicious and so deeply satisfying. Never in my life has a man pushed me against the wall, or bent me over a counter. I'll never be able to go back to vanilla sex after that. The man is corrupting me. Maybe that's his plan. Ruin me for any other guy, and then leave me cold. But I'm not currently cold. No, my body is warm, flushing as I think about how skilled he is with his hands, his mouth. Heck, while I'm here I'm just going to go for it. Live out every fantasy that's ever crossed my mind. Give myself to him in a way I've never given myself to another. I'm so lost in my thoughts that I almost don't hear the woman behind the counter asking for my order.

"Oh, sorry. Everything looks so good," I say, pretending I was debating on what to choose. "I can't make up my mind."

She smiles at me, and I check the display, finally deciding on a six-pack of croissants and a cappuccino to go. A few minutes later, I'm back strolling the streets. I sip my delicious coffee and take a bite of the croissant. Holy God delicious. Cason wasn't kidding. I put the remainder of them into my big purse and walk aimlessly, wasting time as I glance into clothing shops, looking for something suitable for the boat, but not really in the mood to shop. I browse, and because I'm not looking where I'm going, I come to an abrupt halt when I bump into a man with a camera, nearly knocking it from his hands.

"I'm sorry," I say and check the camera to make sure it's okay.

Before he can answer, a girl in her early twenties, dressed in jeans, an oversize thrift store sweater and a stylish black beret, takes hold of my arm. Her nostrils flare as she glares at me. Heck, if looks could kill.

"You're not supposed to be behind him," she says, impatience lacing her voice. She points to a crowd gathered around a gazebo. "Over there." After a good hard eye roll that would leave me with a headache, she throws her hands up and says, "Extras. They'll be the death of me yet."

Extras? What the heck is going on?

I walk to the gazebo, and slide in next to some elderly gentleman. He has kind blue eyes and a nice smile. "Hi," I say, and he puts his fingers to his lips to hush me.

I wince, and try to see over the heads of the people in front of me. I shift, and spot a man dressed as Santa, children on his lap. Cameras are zeroed in on him as he laughs joyously with the little wiggling boy. Ohmigod, they're filming a movie here. The girl with the beret circles the gazebo, and when Santa stands, his suit gets caught on the chair and rips.

"Cut," Beret Girl says, and the crowd around me relaxes and starts talking. "Where is Bethany?" she calls out. "Bethany, where the heck are you?" We all glance around for Bethany, not that I have any clue what she looks like.

"She's not well. She had to leave," one of the cameramen shouts.

Beret girl throws her hands up. "Great. How are we going to fix this costume?"

I push through the crowd, and tentatively walk up to her. "I can help."

Beret Girl eyes me for a moment. "What do you know about costume design?"

"A lot actually."

She studies me for a moment, and gives me that big eye roll again. "There's no budget. We're a small production. I can't pay you."

I don't even care about the pay. I'm excited to do something beneficial, and put myself to better use while I'm here. "It's fine. I'd be happy to help." I turn to Santa, and examine the clothing on the other actors and actresses. "Come on, Santa. Let's get you fixed up."

Santa pulls his beard down, and I see the young man beneath the costume as he exchanges words I can't hear with Beret Girl. A moment later he's leading me to a small space in the back of a fruit-and-vegetable market, the doors open to the rear of the building. I glance around and examine the antiquated equipment.

"Can you work with this?" Santa asks with a big frown. "It's sort of all we had the budget for."

I laugh, a new lightness inside of me. "I don't think I have a choice," I say, and he grins and holds his hand out.

"I'm Raphael by the way," he says. "The director is Marci. She's a bit of a tyrant." He scrunches up his face, like he's just eaten something distasteful, but it's clear how much he admires and respects Marci. "Being a perfectionist and all."

"I understand." I run my hand over a sewing machine and check the thread. "I'm a bit of a perfectionist myself."

"We really appreciate you doing this." His gaze strays, and I spot a pile of clothes, all in need of fixing, in one way or another. These kids really are on a tight budget.

I jump to help. "I can work on all these."

His shoulders relax. "Really? It's not too much to ask?"

"Not at all."

"Bethany has been a bit of a flake and we need this done right if we want to enter it into the film festival next year. We're all film students from UCLA, if you haven't figured that out by now. This project is for our six-week program here in Cannes."

My heart leaps. I'm elated to be a part of something important like this. "That's fantastic."

He exhales and scratches at his face, little white fluff from the beard is stuck to his skin. "It will be, if we can get it done."

"I'll work as fast as I can."

"We're shooting some other scenes tomorrow, so we won't need these ones until the next day."

From the corner of my eye, I spot the script. Christmas isn't my thing, but maybe I'll glance through it later. "I'm going to do my best to make that happen, then."

His eyes narrow in on me. "Really? Who are you?"

"I'm...nobody."

"Why would you help?"

My phone rings, and I glance into my purse to see that it's my father calling. I told him I was visiting a friend in Florida for the holiday. He's probably calling to check in on me. Ignoring it, I turn my focus to my new friend. "The better question is, why wouldn't I?" I say, and don't bother telling him I'm doing this for me as much as for them. But I love the arts, can sew and I need to do something with these idle hands. "Get undressed, Santa."

"Jeez, you didn't even offer to buy me dinner first."

I laugh as he grins at me and slips out of his jacket. "I can do this really fast, so you can get back out there."

"No worries, she's on to another scene."

"Okay." I spread the jacket out on the table to examine the work that needs to be done.

"Let me at least get you another coffee."

I reach for my purse. "I'd really appreciate that."

He holds his hands up to stop me. "It's the least I can do."

I smile as he disappears out the back way, and I take a deep breath, a sense of purpose building inside me. This is going to be fun. I sit myself down, and get to work, stopping only when Raphael returns with my coffee, and before I know it, the day has gotten away from me. I reach for my coffee, which is stone-cold, when someone clears their throat at the door behind me.

"You've been working so hard, everyone thought you could use another cup."

Startled, I spin, and my hand goes to my chest. "Cason," I say. "You scared me."

His smile dissolves and he pushes off the door-frame. "I'm sorry."

"No," I say quickly as his long legs close the steps between us. My gaze rakes over him as he approaches. He's now dressed in jeans and a dark wool coat. One of his designs, no doubt. My brain buzzes, the sexy look setting off fashion ideas inside my head. Ideas he'd probably never want to hear. "It's okay. I was just so lost in my thoughts." He stops in front of me, his big frame eating up the small room and overwhelming me. My breath flutters and I ask, "I… How long were you standing there?"

"A long time, actually," he says, a softness to him that I haven't seen in years. It slides over my skin, and my cheeks warm, despite the chilly room. "Your coffee is still warm though."

"Why didn't you say something?"

"I don't know." He hands me the coffee, a smile on his face as he looks at the old sewing machine, and I get a sense his thoughts are elsewhere. "I guess it was just your concentration. I remember when you used to get like this in college." He taps the sewing machine. "I've never seen such focus, Londyn. You by far, were the most determined woman I'd ever known. I always admired that about you. Did you know that?"

"No." I gulp, pretty sure he has no idea how much that compliment actually means to me. "Thank you," I say quietly, then another thought hits. If he thought that about me, why did he say I was a joke, a silly little rich girl. I want to ask, but I'm not sure if I want to hear his answer, and I'm not ready to leave this place if we get into an argument. It's crazy and not a great idea, but I want my full two weeks with him. Things have been easy with us, and I want to savor that for as long as I can. "Wait, how did you find me?"

"I was worried when you didn't show up back at home."

Cason was worried about me? That thought curls around me like a warm blanket, and hugs so tight it squeezes the air from my lungs.

Breathe, Londyn, breathe.

"I wandered the streets and asked people." He steals a glance around the small space. "Heard you volunteered to help with the costumes."

"Yeah, their designer is out sick." I shrug and pat the pile of clothes beside me, but I brace myself inside. Is he going to think I'm ridiculous? "They're students. I thought I could help."

"I'm just glad you're okay. I thought you might have been abducted by aliens."

I chuckle. "Wow, aliens, huh? I never knew you had such a wild imagination."

He wags his brows at me. "I guess we'll have to see about rectifying that," he says, his voice full of promise and dirty innuendos.

"When you put it that way," I say, trying to keep the mood light.

His teasing smile dims and his Adam's apple bobs when he swallows, his amusement dissolving like honey in hot tea. "What you're doing here. That's really nice."

I study him, warmth traveling all the way to my curled toes. "You don't think it's silly? That I'm silly?" I ask, his words from all those years ago still cutting deep.

He frowns, the worry lines in his forehead intensifying, and I can practically hear the gears churning. What, were those harsh words not important enough to remember?

"Of course not," he says. "Why would you even say that?"

"No reason," I answer, not wanting to dredge up old memories, and reopen old hurts. The truth is we both messed up.

"Next time just leave me a note or text me, okay?" he says.

"I didn't mean to make you worry." I glance at my watch and my eyes bug out of my head. "Ohmigod, the time." Panicked, I glance back up at him. "I'm sorry. I didn't realize. I should have been back by now." The man bought me in an auction for God's sake. I'm supposed to be his companion, not run off and disappear for hours. I'm probably violating the contract and giving him grounds to ship me back home.

"Hey," he says, his gentle voice cutting into my thoughts. He pulls up a stool and sits, and my gaze rakes over the concern in his face. When he looks at me like that, like I'm the most important person in the world to him, it creates a deeper intimacy that goes well beyond what we shared this morning, when he was inside me.

Keep it together, Londyn.

He paid for you and simply wants his money's worth. As that harsh thought leaves a bitter taste on my tongue, a breeze blows in through the open door and a chill moves through me. The temperature was well above the normal for Cannes in December when I left the villa this afternoon, but has since dropped. A cold front must have moved through, and I'm definitely not dressed appropriately. "It's okay. I found you. You're safe. That's what matters."

I take a gulp of my coffee, giving my heart a second to settle. "I totally lost track of time," I say.

"Actually, I'm kind of glad this happened." He shakes his head and grins. "You have no idea what it's like to see you work." He reaches out, tucks a wayward strand of my hair behind my ear, and his closeness teases my senses. "I just… I forgot how much I liked this about you."

A little bubble wells up inside me, the way it always does when I'm doing what I love. "This is what I was meant to do," I say, the excited fire in my belly flaring as I glance at the pile of clothes in need of my attention. I root through them. "I love fashion, fabric and creating."

The smile he aims my way pierces my heart. This is the Cason I remember from our youth—vulnerable, a little off his game and a whole lot of sweet. How could I have hurt the one guy who was always so nice to me? I don't deserve these two weeks with him. I don't deserve any of his kindness.

"I know you do, and I'm the one who should be apologizing," he says.

"What do you mean?"

"I can't expect you to sit idle for two weeks. It's not who you are, and I should probably send—"

I take hold of his coat, grip the lapels, as lightning bolts of worry burst through me. "I don't want to go back," I blurt out. If I leave, I won't get the rest of the money, and I'll be damned if my father is going to marry me off in a merger. But I can't tell Cason that. He hates my father, rightfully so, and if he knew his money was actually going to help his businesses, he'd kick me to the curb faster than my father stole his app idea. But there are other reasons I don't want to leave, more important reasons that hit close to my heart.

His warm expression changes, worry pushing back the smile. He waves his hand in front of my face. "Hey, where did you go?" he asks, the genuine concern in his eyes, and the tenderness in his voice, nearly bringing me to tears. I can't remember the last time someone asked me that, the last time someone cared about me or my well-being. Actually, maybe I can. Maybe it was back in college with this sweet man. Which makes the things he said about me all the more hurtful, and a bit confusing actually. I guess he was just playing with the rich brat. Having a good time talking about her with his friends behind her back.

"I'm here," I say, not wanting to talk about my father. "And here is where I want to stay. I want to help out with this film, if you don't need me for anything in the day, maybe I could spend a few hours here."

I hold my breath, a part of me desperate to hear him say he does need me.

The words don't come. Instead he gives a small chuckle and says, "I wasn't going to send you back. Actually, if you have the time, I'd like to show you some of the designs Luis sent me. You have a great eye for fashion."

"Really?" I shake my head, positive I'm hearing things.

"Sure."

My heart wobbles, and stupid tears prick my eyes. I swallow against a painful throat, and work my words past the lump forming. "I would love that."

"It's settled, then."

He's about to stand, but I tug on his coat. "Cason."

"Yeah?"

I inhale a sharp breath, and as I let it out, I work to keep my voice steady when I say, "I'm… I'm so sorry." His head jerks back and his dark brown eyes move over my face as I say the words that should have been spoken many years ago. "So sorry…for everything."

He looks at me for a long, still moment, his expression blank, unreadable. As the quiet fills the room, takes up space between us, the muscles along his jaw clench. I stare at him, trapped in the emotions passing over his eyes. Pain, sorrow, regret… loss. My body convulses, and I briefly close my eyes as my head spins, lost in a vortex of sadness and guilt. After a long moment, he scrubs his hand over his face, nods and stands.

He taps the pile of costumes, and I look at those big hands that touched me with such heated skill this morning. "How about you gather this stuff up and finish at home."

"I can't do that." I swallow and push my next words past the lump in my throat. "I don't have a sewing machine or any supplies."

"You will," he says matter-of-factly. "By the end of the night, you'll have everything you need. I promise."

This time my throat completely closes over and it takes all my strength to lift my trembling body from the stool. He's wrong about that. I'll never have everything I need. There is one big thing missing from my life that I'll never have, and his gaze is currently roaming over my face.

Turning from him before he can see my shaky smile—the man has always been great at reading other people's emotions—I gather up the clothes. He helps me and puts them in a plastic bag and I scribble a note to let the crew know that I'll bring them back as soon as I fix them. Before we leave, I snatch a script from the pile on the table for a little bedtime reading.

"If there is something specific you need, just let me know. I'm not an expert on sewing machines or anything like that."

"Cason, you…don't have to do that," I finally manage to say after finding my voice. "I can come back here tomorrow, and use this machine." Okay, yeah, sure it snagged up on me more times than I can count, but he does not have to buy me one.

"Yes, I do. And I won't take no for an answer."

"Still bossy, I see."

"Is that what you think?"

"It's what I know." I blink up at him, my heart pounding at his generosity. "I don't know how to thank you."

He wags his brows playfully and a streak of need sizzles in my blood. "I can think of a few ways." I grin at his teasing words, and appreciate how he's working to lighten the mood between us. "Besides, maybe I'm doing it more for me than you."

"What do you mean?"

He grins, and gives me a nudge. "You're kind of hot when you're focused." He laughs and releases a measure of tension in my shoulders.

"Always watching me when I don't know. That's kind of perverted."

"I know, right?" he says, his voice full of playful tenderness.

He shrugs out of his wool jacket and drapes it over my shoulders. I sink into the warmth as he puts his arms around me, his big body dwarfing mine. Secure in his arms, with the strength of his body flooding my system, he leads me out of the building and onto the street. He puts his hand on the small of my back, his touch achingly familiar, warm and comforting. I never found my place in this world, never felt I belonged, but Cason has always represented safety and security, something I never had with anyone but him.

"Christmas, huh?" he says, breaking the quiet between us as he gazes at the script sticking out of my bag. "The one holiday we'd both rather avoid and here you are in the thick of a damn Hallmark movie."

I laugh, and give him a sidelong glance. My heart quivers a bit. "Next thing you know, I'll be wanting to put up a tree," I say and brace myself for his reaction. When I was a kid, my mother always put up a huge evergreen. It was lush and gorgeous, with frosted tips and blue and silver bulbs. I wasn't allowed anywhere near it when I was a child. Sadly, she'd never hung the decorations we made in middle school. Apparently they clashed with the professionally decorated tree that was on display like a Picasso at the Guggenheim, but still…unlike Cason, I had a tree and even though there weren't people around it, there were tons of presents beneath it. I would have preferred it the other way around.

Cason's brow furrows and his lips curl in distaste. My heart goes out to him, wishing I could smooth away the years of loss and loneliness. If I could, I'd go back in time and change what happened to him. Losing your parents so young, and at Christmastime no less, is a double dose of pain no child should ever have to endure. Then to be tossed around from home to home. But maybe when I'm here I can somehow help him create new traditions. Happy ones. Then again, he might not want any traditions with me, but what about his sister? I'd love to do something, anything, to make this time of year a bit easier for them. With Peyton in New York and him here though, it's an impossible task.

"Would a tree be so bad?" I ask.

"Yes," he says flatly, his eyes trained on the sidewalk.

Teasing, but half-serious, I say, "You'd probably hate me if I snuck one into your living room." I snort at that. "What am I saying, you already hate me."

His head lifts and his eyes slowly move to mine. "Is that what you think, Londyn?"

CHAPTER NINE

Cason

LONDYN'S LUSH LIPS curl in a know-it-all smirk as she nods her head and declares with authority, "Uh, it's what I know."

I shake my head at that. Since I first brought her home, she's been making some pretty big assumptions, telling me what I think, adamant that she knows the reasons behind my actions, when really, she has no idea. How could she, when I don't. Christ, I'm supposed to be the one in charge, the one who knows what they're doing, and I'm walking around with my head in the clouds not knowing which way is up or down.

The thing is though, I want to hate her. I really do. She gutted me back in college and started dating some asshole from the right side of the tracks, someone Daddy approved of. Why she cares what her old man thinks is beyond me. He never gave her the praise and encouragement she needed, or deserved. I guess that's how it is with parents though, and I wish I knew that firsthand. No matter what, a kid will fight for their respect and approval, whether the parent warrants it or not.

Maybe someday her father will wake up. Hell, maybe someday Londyn will. I truthfully wish he could see what I saw today. The concentration, the small smile on her face as she donated her time to help some college students. There aren't too many people I know who'd bother. That was beauty in its purest form. So yeah, while I want to hate her, I can't. In fact, the second I saw her sitting there, happily working with some antiquated sewing machine—totally in her element, even in a cramped room that could pass as a closet—something warm and needy flared inside me, something I refuse to put a name to.

You can't go there.

"Are you hungry?" I ask, redirecting the conversation. No way am I about to let myself get wrapped up in her again. I won't. The rational side of me understands that, the rest of me…well, the rest of me doesn't give two shits if I fall flat on my face a second time.

Her stomach takes that moment to grumble, loudly.

Chuckling, I nudge her with my shoulder. "I'll take that as a yes."

Her eyes go saucer wide as she puts her hands over her belly to hide the sound. "That wasn't embarrassing at all."

"No need to be embarrassed. Not with me." I take

the bag of clothes from her. "Do you want to drop these things off and go out and grab a bite to eat?"

"Sounds like a good idea. I haven't eaten since the croissant earlier. Oh, speaking of…" She reaches into her purse and pulls out a white paper bag. She opens it and frowns. "They're kind of squished."

"No worries. We can get more. Did you like it?" I ask, hoping for a yes. Christ, I'm not sure why pleasing her, and wanting her to like what I like, has become so damn important to me.

Oh, Cason, don't screw yourself over here.

"It was delicious," she says and makes a little moaning sound that teases my cock. A gust of wind rushes down the street, blowing a paper cup. I stop to pick it up, drop it into a garbage can, and when I find her shivering, I lift the collar to cover her ears. Jesus, she's adorable, and I take a moment to envision her in one of my button-down shirts, and nothing else. I bite back a groan as I imagine her long legs sleek and bare…wrapped around my shoulders. My dick grows, but the streets of Cannes, filled with tourists, is no place to be sporting a boner.

"Such a gentleman," she says and gives me a smile as I secure a button that came undone. The appreciation in her eyes warms me more than a layer of wool ever could, and reminds me I was far from a gentleman as I ravished her this morning. Dammit, I'm not a teen, I shouldn't have acted like a hormonal pubescent, an amateur with zero finesse eager to get into his girl's pants. But this woman…and what she does to me is absurd.

"Ogre, pervert and now a gentleman," I gruff to hide the way my heart is skipping around my chest like a child hyped up on sugar. "You're going to have to make up your mind, Londyn. All these mixed messages are confusing me."

She laughs, and the easy, carefree sound, one I haven't heard since our college days, surrounds me, batters the wall around my fractured heart. Even though she apologized, and it came straight from a good and honest place, I tighten my guard, reconstruct those cracked walls before I bleed out again. I can't go there with her.

"Give me time, I'll come up with the perfect description before the two weeks are over," she says.

I scoff. "Yeah, that's what I'm worried about." I step closer, wanting the contact with her for reasons I don't want to identify.

She kicks at a pebble, her smile falling as her eyes lift to mine. "What were you going to say earlier, when I thought you were going to send me home?"

"I was going to say, I will send out for some supplies, fabrics, whatever you wish. You can create, design, do whatever you like while you're here. I have lots of spare rooms. This is supposed to be an epic week for you, too, right, with lots of pampering. Since I'm not whisking you off to Paris, or wherever else you'd like to go—"

"There's nowhere else, Cason," she says, her words

rushing out on a fast breath. "Right here is where I want to be. With you."

"Okay," I say. Tortured eyes lock on mine, and my gut clenches. What is she really doing here in Cannes, selling herself at an auction house, and why is she determined to stay here with me, a man she screwed over years ago? There was no denying her panic when she thought I was sending her home, and I want to know why that idea rattles her. Does it have something to do with her father? Perhaps what I should really be seeking answers to is, why am I so hell-bent on keeping her? A car speeds by, its revving engine pulling my thoughts back. We dodge a few tourists and continue down the sidewalk. "We'll create a studio for you," I say.

She stops walking, and it takes two long steps before I realize she's no longer beside me. I turn to find her staring at me, her jaw open. "Was it something I said?" I ask and slide my hands into my pockets. I rock on my feet, studying her beautiful face as I meet her unwavering stare and wait for an answer.

"I…" She shakes her head and her honeyed hair falls over her shoulders. "That's all too much. I'm supposed to be a companion for you."

"It's like this." I reach out, take one of her hands and brush my thumb over her soft skin. Her fingers twist in mine as she visibly quivers under my touch and I wish I didn't like her reaction so much. "I've never bought a woman's companionship before, and you've never put yourself on the bidding block at an auction house before," I say and wait for a counter argument. When none comes, I continue with, "So how about we write our own rules, and just live in this fantasy world you have going on in that head of yours."

Her soft laugh curls around me. "You mean fairy tale?"

"Yes, same thing."

She gives me a big smile and, catching me off guard, goes up on her toes and throws her arms around my shoulders. "This morning was sort of like a fairy tale to me."

I tug her to me, her body warm, soft and pliable against mine. I breathe her in. Jesus, she smells like cake and candy and everything I want to put in my mouth. "If you play your cards right, tonight…" Before I finish, I lean forward and press my lips to hers, giving her a small sampling of things to come. I'm not normally one for public displays of affection, but I'm not about to let that stop me, not when I am pretty damn sure I'll go up in a burst of fire and die a painful death if I don't get my mouth on her. The tourists who are staring from across the street, well they can either fuck right off, or stay and enjoy the show.

Her lips are shaky and cold at first contact, but I deepen the kiss to warm her up, inside and out. We stand there and I hold her to me, sinking into a wet, sensuous kiss full of want and need. Only problem is, I fear my mouth on hers is less about kissing and more about claiming. With my brain barely working, a part of me registers that her hands have moved to my ears as the wind swirls around us. She covers them to keep them warm. As that thoughtful gesture pokes holes in my armor, my traitorous heart skips a few too many beats. I break the kiss and work to get my shit together.

"What is this about playing my cards right?" she asks, her voice heady and breathless, full of playfulness.

I scrape my thumb over her kiss-swollen bottom lip and work to ground myself in reality as a sexy, urgent little sound rises in her throat. An unbearable tightness grips my heart and I quickly remind myself we're having sex, playing a game. Nothing more.

"Play them right and tonight maybe I'll play the part of Prince Charming in this fairy-tale world of yours."

"Hmm." Her eyes narrow in thought as she bites her bottom lip.

"What, you have to think about it?" I ask with a laugh. I give her a playful shove, and she grins as she falters backward. "Hey if you don't want Prince—"

"Actually, I always favored the Big Bad Wolf."

Dammit.

I groan and tug her back to me. Her body collides with mine and need zaps my balls. Heat rockets through me, sizzling up my spine, and nearly fries my last working brain cell. "There's a whole side of you I don't know, isn't there?"

"Who, me?" she asks innocently as she pokes her finger into my chest. "And what I'm thinking is instead of going out to eat, why don't we stay in. We can order takeout, or we can cook, and when I say we, I mean you."

"Come on," I say and put my hand on the small of her back and usher her along the sidewalk.

She doubles her steps to keep up with me. "What's the hurry?"

"I just realized how hungry I am."

She reaches for her purse. "Why don't you have a croissant to hold you over? I mean, I know they're squished, but…"

I grin at her sweet naivety. "Oh, sweetheart, did you think it's food I want to put into my mouth?"

"Oh," she says, her eyes widening with anticipation, lust and want.

"Yeah, *oh*," I say.

A sexy little moan slides past her lips, like she has no trouble with that revelation. Good, I want her hot and willing when we get home. "My mistake."

That's when I remember her grumbling stomach. "Dammit, we need to feed you though."

"Come to think of it, there is only one thing I'm interested in putting in my mouth. This morning I didn't get the chance."

Need boils my blood, and I almost trip on an imaginary crack in the sidewalk. "Jesus, you didn't just say that to me, did you?"

"I believe I did."

A second later we're practically running back to my villa. We're both laughing and breathless by the time we reach the front door, and I'm so goddamn anxious to get my hands on her, I can barely get the key into the lock.

"Want me to do it?" she asks with a chuckle as she reaches for it.

I brush her hands away. "You don't have to do everything you know. There are things I'm quite capable of handling myself."

"Oh, I know, and I must say I do love this alpha side of you."

"Alpha? You think this is alpha?" I tease.

I get the door open and haul her in with me. I pull her against me, hard. "You were this morning," she says.

Shit. She's right. I went at her like a goddamn caveman, breaking my own etiquette rules, and while she didn't seem to have a problem, fast and furious is not my normal style. I wanted to slow it down with her and savor each sweet minute, but I couldn't calm myself down and summon any sort of control. She's the one girl I couldn't get my hands on quick enough, and she deserves better than that.

I brush the back of my fingers along her jaw, a soft caress. "Yeah, about that. I—"

She goes up on her tiptoes, and presses her lips to mine. "I should probably tell you. A gentleman is nice, but totally overrated."

Her breasts press into my chest, and she moves

her hips, massaging my growing cock. "Are you say-ing you like it rough, Londyn?"

"I'm saying I never had it rough before."

"Yeah? That was your first experience?" A pink hue crawls up her neck, flushes her cheek. "What?" I ask.

"I haven't been with very many men," she be-gins, dark lashes fluttering over big blue eyes. Her innocence and her insecurities twist me up inside. "I'm not that experienced, Cason. What sexual en-counters I've had, have left me unsatisfied. But it's partly my fault. It's not easy for me to open up, and growing up under scrutiny all the time, makes me feel like I'm always being judged. I shut down when that happens."

Okay, I hadn't expected her to say that, and while on one hand I'm happy that she's not been with many men, on the other I want to punch them in the face for not making it good for her.

"There's nothing wrong with you. You have to know that."

Her warm palm goes to my face, and she says, "I don't want to talk about those other guys. I want to talk about you, and how this morning you gave me the best sex I've ever had. I've never experi-enced anything like it." A wobbly laugh churns in her throat, and she turns her head, breaking eye con-tact, like she's a bit embarrassed.

"Hey," I say and tuck a strand of hair behind her ear, bringing her gaze back to me. "Don't shut down on me. I'm not here to judge you, Londyn, and for what it's worth, this morning you rocked my world, too."

A wide smile splits her lips, and her eyes glisten. "I'm not sure what it is about you." She crinkles her nose. "Then again. Maybe I am. Maybe I can be myself with you and open up in a way I never could with anyone else. We used to be so close."

"Yeah, we were. I told you things about myself that I've never told anyone else."

"Same, and for the next two weeks I want that."

She blinks rapidly, rays of hope moving into my eyes, and as my heart pounds a little harder I find myself saying, "Okay." Jesus, if I know what's good for me, I'll get out now, stop pretending nothing happened between us.

"You're the only man who's ever made me feel safe, and when I'm safe, I have an easier time expressing myself. I'm not so afraid to put myself out there."

I do that for her? I stand there blinking, her admission filling me with pride and seriously flooring me.

"I want you to be who you are. You're safe with me, Londyn." It's not a lie. I'd never let anything bad happen to her.

"I know."

"I want you to express yourself, no embarrassment, no judgment."

"Okay," she says, a hint of mischief curling up her lips. "I loved the way you seemed to lose control. No man has ever looked at me with worship in his eyes before."

"You're a woman who should be worshipped, and those guys were assholes for not figuring out what you needed."

Her palm lands on my chest, covering my rapid heartbeat. "I had no idea how much I liked being ravaged, until you ravaged me. I want that again, Cason." Empowered, she lifts her chin and asks, "So what are you going to do about that?"

I grip the lapels of my coat and back her up until she's pressed against the door. Her breathing changes and heat floods her cheeks. My mouth finds hers in a deep bruising kiss and her resulting moan wraps around my dick and tugs.

I tear at the coat, practically rip it from her body as I devour her mouth, unable to taste deep enough. Jesus, this woman is everything…and I swear she's going to be the death of me.

"I'm going to fuck you, babe. So goddamn hard, you're going to still feel me inside you when you leave here."

Her entire body quakes as she tugs at my shirt. "I want that, too. I want to feel you when I'm gone."

Gone.

Shit, I can't think about that right now. Not when her heat is beckoning my fingers and mouth. I slide a hand between her legs, lightly brush her sex. I can ravage her, give her what she wants, but first and foremost her comfort is of the utmost importance.

"You're not too sore?"

Her smile is warm. "Not for you." She puts her hand on my cheek. "Never for you."

"I might ruin this hot, tight pussy," I say. Honestly my mind is a little blown. I shouldn't be surprised by her lack of innocence. She wasn't a coed who slept around, but liking it rough and dirty, yet afraid to give in to her desire? I didn't see that coming. My cock thickens a little more. Jesus, I'm having a hell of a good time discovering all the sides to her and I have to admit, I'm feeling a measure of pride that I'm the first guy to give her what she needs. "I might actually ruin this sweet mouth of yours, too," I say and slide my thumb in.

She sucks on it, and need grips me hard. Her fingers slide over my shoulders, dip under my shirt and score my skin. "What are you waiting for, Cason?"

I groan, pull my finger from her mouth and work the tight button on her hip-hugging jeans. I need her naked. Now.

I grip the belt straps, tug until her jeans hover around her round hips, but she pushes me off her body. For a moment I go still. Has she changed her mind? I'm about to ask, but my words stick, then morph into a moan when she turns, and puts her hands on the door, high up, near the rack where my scarves are hung. She grips the fabric, runs it around her fingers, letting me know in no uncertain terms what she wants. My glance rakes over her quivering body, and every dirty scenario that has ever played out in my mind when it came to her crashes over me, like a hot Caribbean wave.

"I'm going to make you mine."

I reach above her head and tie the scarves around her hands, securing them to the rack. The binds are tight enough to hold her in place, but loose enough that she can get out of them if she has a change of heart. Although, judging by the way her breath is coming in jagged little bursts, like she'd just sprinted through a marathon, I don't see that happening any-time soon. Oh, yeah, sweet Londyn Harding likes this hot little setup, and she wants me to play.

Play I will.

I reach around her, and run my fingers over the ridiculously small buttons on her blouse. I breathe against her ear, and her entire body quakes in re-sponse. I grin, loving the reaction my closeness pulls from her. I present calm, but I'm not as together as I'm letting on. No, I'm two seconds from losing myself in her, and never finding my way out again.

"These buttons, they're kind of pissing me off," I growl.

"What did my buttons ever do to you?"

"They're too small for my fingers. If I were de-signing women's clothes, I'd buy up every small but-ton and burn them."

She chuckles. "I never would have worn this shirt if I'd known it was going to prevent you from touch-ing me."

"Your hands are tied, so you leave me no choice."

I grip the edges of her blouse, and with one quick yank tear it wide-open. The silly little buttons clatter to the floor and her resulting yelp wraps around my balls and gives a delicious squeeze. Fuck yeah. "Much better," I say and continue to rip the shirt until it's gone from her body. "I'll replace that," I say and run my fingers over her delicate shoulders.

"No need. I have plenty." Her breathing grows harsh, and fingers coil around my scarves, like she's doing her best to keep herself upright.

"You good, Londyn?"

"Never better."

I press my mouth to her shoulder, and slowly tug down her bra straps. "This is much easier to remove." I unhook the latch and free her breasts.

"Yes," she whimpers, her hair falling down her back as she lifts her head, and arches her spine, putting her lush tits right into my palms. I knead her, pinch her nipples until they're swollen and hard. Her hips move, her sweet little pussy desperate for something to squeeze. I'd be more than happy to help with that. But first I need to play with the sexy woman who's tied up and at my mercy.

With one hand on her breast, I slide the other down her body, and jerk my hips forward, massaging my dick against her sweet ass. I slide my palm down her stomach, dip into her jeans and cup her wet sex. She rocks and moans, and rubs up against the door. She is so damn open and sexy, the sight of her writhing like this is pure heaven. This woman makes me weak in the knees and that's a whole lot scary.

"I've been suffering all day," I whisper into her ear.

"Suffering?"

"Yeah, for a taste of you." She moans, and I slide a thick finger into her hot wet core. "Shit, you are so wet for me."

"You're not the only one who's been suffering," she tells me and bucks backward, a greedy little thrust as she rides my finger. It's the hottest thing I've ever seen.

I keep my hand there, let her use me, take what her body needs.

"I should just tug these jeans down and put my cock inside you, fuck you hard for making me worry about you." Her body convulses. "You'd probably like that though."

"I don't think so," she says, and I chuckle. She cries out as I remove my finger from her tight pussy. I grip the band of her jeans and slide them down, just enough to expose her hot ass. I take her cheeks into my palms and spread them. "Maybe I'll bend you over right here and push myself into this tight hole," I say, lightly running my finger along her puckered crevice.

She gasps.

"Ah, look at you. Not so sure you like that idea, huh?"

"Cason," she moans as I insert a pinky finger into her. She quivers around me, and I cup her sex again, rub my palm over her clit as I slowly introduce her ass to a new kind of pleasure. "I've never…"

"I know, baby. I know." I tease her back passage a little more, stretching her out, wanting to fill every inch of her. My mouth goes to her neck and I slide my tongue over her. "I want my tongue on your pussy," I say and slowly turn her.

Her hands twist in the scarves, and the sight of her, her cheeks pink, her eyes so lust-imbued and needy, it nearly brings me to my knees. I have never seen a woman want me the way this one does right now. It screws me over in the worst way.

I stare, take my time to burn this image into my memory. As my gaze rakes over her, my body aroused at the rising and falling of her lush tits with each breath, I take a measured step back. I tear my own shirt from my body and shove it away. Her eyes widen at my impatience, and the hunger raging inside me fills the room, curls around us like a wild animal ready to claim its prey.

"You're mine," I growl.

"Cason…please."

"Say it," I demand, not wanting to think too hard on why I need those words to spill from her lips.

"I'm yours."

Her fingers wiggle, like she's desperate to get them on me, and while I want that, too, I like having her tied up like this. I bend forward, take one breast into my palm as my mouth goes to the other. Need blazes through me, lighting a fiery path to my balls.

They tighten, beg for release, and I groan against her breasts as I scrape my teeth over her delicate nipple. It swells painfully in my mouth and with little finesse and much greed, I shove my hand between her legs. I run the back of my palm over her sex, pressing into her, and sliding it back and forth to part her lips.

"You want my finger in you?" I ask.

"Cason... I can't..." she murmurs, her voice a hushed whisper. "Touch me. Please. Now."

I suck her nipple so hard, my cheeks form hollows, and she whimpers. "What makes you think you get to tell me what to do?" I tease, mercilessly spreading her but avoiding direct contact with her swollen clit. She struggles against the bindings, but doesn't pull her hands free. She's so damn delirious with need she's tossing her head from side to side, her eyes glazed, her cheeks rosy red. I love this wild look on her and if I had it my way, I'd ruthlessly toy with her every goddamn day.

Who says I can't have it my way?

"Does this little pussy need me?" I brush her clit, and she yelps and writhes like a restrained animal. "Maybe I'll just keep you tied up like this all night, and touch you when I feel like it." I lightly stroke her sex, opening her up for my girth. Her small tremors vibrate through me and I nearly lose my damn mind.

She bends forward, curls her body as her orgasm pulls at her. A moment later, restless and edgy, her head flails back and I reach behind, fist her hair and tug until her eyes open.

"Look at me." Her eyes fly open. "I want to see you when you come."

"Yes. I'm so close." She wets her bottom lip and I close in for the kill. My lips find hers and I devour her mouth, my dick so hard, it's a wonder I have any blood left in my brain. I eat at her delicious mouth, tangle our tongues until she's moaning. I tear my lips away, and her eyes are so dazed I'm not sure she's still with me.

"Londyn?" I ask, my voice rough and shallow, as I try to keep a measure of control.

"I love the way you kiss me," she says.

"You like my mouth here," I begin and roughly run my thumb over her bruised bottom lip. "Or perhaps you'd prefer it here." I probe her opening, offering her a finger up to my first knuckle, and she whimpers and moves. Her muscles try to clench around me, but I'm not done torturing her.

"Please put your finger back in me."

"The second I do, you're going to come, aren't you?" I dip my head, and lick her nipple again. As I brutally prolong her pleasure, I twirl her marbled nub between my teeth and she sags against the door, a quivering mess of need. I suck harder, and beneath my finger, her clit pulses. "Does my baby need to come?"

"Yes."

Deciding to end the sweet torment, I slide one thick finger into her and she lets go, her muscles clenching hard as her body releases in a rush of hot liquid. It bathes my fingers and hand, and drips down her legs, preparing her sweet pussy for my throbbing cock. She comes and comes and comes some more and when she finally stops, I pull my finger from her sweet pussy and put it in my mouth.

"Fuck you taste good."

She pants for breath, and watches me with aroused eyes. "Cason…"

"Yeah." Giving her no time to recover, I untie her hands, take hold of her chin and lift it until her mouth is poised open. "Is there something specific you wanted to put in here," I ask, and run my finger over her bottom lip. She shakes my hand away from her jaw, and before I realize what she's doing, she bends forward and draws my index finger into her mouth. She sucks, rolls her hot wet tongue around it and moans.

"Shit," I curse as the pressure builds, the greedy little bastard between my legs screaming at me to put her on her knees and fill her mouth with something a whole lot bigger than a finger.

Dammed if I don't like that idea. A lot.

I put my hands on her shoulders and push. She grins, and I get it. She likes the power she has over me. Likes that I'm amped up like an addict on crack and so lost in her I can't wait one goddamn second to feel her lush lips around my dick. Yeah, she's an addiction I don't want to quit and the image of my dick sliding between her full lips has been taunting me since she first told me there was only one thing she was interested in putting in her mouth.

"Still hungry?" I ask.

"Starving."

"What do you want?"

"I want you to feed me your cock, Cason. I want all of you, every inch in my throat, and I don't care if you choke me."

A hard quake rocks my body and I shove my jeans to my knees and cup the back of her head. I almost laugh at my roughness, at my lack of grace, but it's what she wants, and I have no restraint left in me. Hell, no one can accuse me of being a gentleman tonight.

She parts her pretty lips, and I grip my cock and feed it to her, giving her one inch at a time, until I'm groaning and hitting the back of her throat. She chokes a little and I try to pull out but she cups my ass cheeks and holds me to her.

"You keep that up and I'll come down your throat," I say, and that simply seems to encourage her. Down on her knees, her head bobs as she takes me in, and every time she pulls back, sucking only my crown, it's the most erotic thing I've ever seen.

"You give the best head," I say, and her eyes lift in pure pleasure. Jesus, she flourishes under my appreciation and encouragement.

Her hands go to my balls, and my dick slips from her mouth. "I never used to like it," she murmurs.

"You like my dick, Londyn?" I desperately need her to say yes.

"With you, I like everything, and yes that includes your dick in my mouth."

"Show me," I say and cup the back of her head, guiding that sexy mouth back to my crown. She fucks me with her mouth, and I clench my teeth to hold on.

"Your mouth…so good." I fist my fingers in her hair. "More. Deeper." I've never needed any woman to swallow me whole, or take as much of me as they could but with her it's different. I need every inch of myself inside her, an impossible task, but it's not preventing her from trying and I love that about her.

Love?

No, this is sex, I remind myself, but that thought evaporates as she moans around my cock, the vibrations pulling an orgasm from my deepest depths. My cock thickens, my veins bulge and I try to pull her off me but no, she's not having any of that.

"Londyn," I say, and as she moans around my cock, I let go in her mouth. Keeping me to the back of her throat, she swallows me, and I grip her hair tighter, my heart pounding out of my damn chest.

She releases my dick, and smiles up at me. She wipes the back of her mouth with her hand and I haul her to her feet.

"You good?" I ask and assess her face.

"I've never done that before," she admits honestly.

"Since we're sharing secrets, I've never done that before either."

Her face lights up. "That was the first time you…"

she lowers her voice "…came down a woman's throat."

I laugh. "Why are you whispering?"

She starts chuckling, and I hold her to me. "I don't know. I guess I'm glad I was your first."

"Yeah."

"Since we're being honest. I always wanted you to be my first, Cason."

"There were a lot of things I wanted from you, too," I say, and to keep this light, I reach around and slap her backside. "This week I plan to take…"

She nibbles her lip, a teasing warmth in her eyes. "And I plan to give."

My heart stops beating, as a bone-deep need grips me tight.

Yeah, you're not in any trouble here at all, dude.

CHAPTER TEN

Londyn

A COOL BREEZE slides over my skin as I shift, and my lids slowly flutter open. For one split second I have no idea where I am, but as memories from last night infiltrate my sleepy brain, I sink into the mattress, a satisfied moan catching in my throat.

I turn, and a hollow feeling seeps into my bones and takes up residency in my chest, right around the vicinity of my heart, when I find the other side of Cason's bed empty. After that incredible round of sex against the door, we ordered a pizza and ate it in front of the fire. It was romantic and intimate, the wind whipping outside as he shared his upcoming new spring collection with me. We talked for hours on end about his new line, and afterward he carried me to his bed where he buried himself in me again. As I revel in the memories, I give a lazy catlike stretch and enjoy the ache in my muscles, some of which I didn't even know existed. Last night was perfect, which makes me wonder why he didn't want to be here when I woke up.

My gaze goes to the crack in the window, and I jerk upright when I find the sun high in the sky. What the heck? I check the nightstand clock. Holy hell, it's late morning. No wonder Cason is up and gone. He probably has a ton of work to do. Work I'd love to help more with. My stomach rumbles and I can't believe I'm hungry again, but given the time of day…

"Good morning."

I turn, and the sight of a freshly showered Cason leaning against the doorjamb, two cups of coffee in his hands, pushes back the cold skating over my skin. Could he be any more adorable and how is it he's getting better looking by the minute? The cool air chills my skin, and I reach for a blanket and cover up.

"A very good morning," I correct. He gives a slow shake of his head and makes a tsking sound that has me sitting up a little straighter. My stomach tightens, "What?"

With a nod he gestures to the blankets covering me. "I was enjoying the view."

Flutters erupt in my stomach and I relax as he teases me. "You're kind of a creeper, Cason." He arches a playful brow. "How often do you watch me without me knowing, anyway?"

"As often as I can," he says and pushes off the door. He comes my way and I roll toward him as he perches on the edge of the mattress.

"Is that for me?" I ask, and he hands me the cup. I take a big sip and moan.

Cason groans and sets his cup on the nightstand. "I like that sound. Although I like it better when I'm the reason behind it." He's in a different mood today. Lighter. Playful. I like it a lot. He usually has the weight of the world on his shoulders, and it's nice to see the edge is gone, and his shoulders are no longer around his ears.

"I'm sure you can figure out a way to rouse that sound in me," I tease.

He reaches out, lightly runs his finger over my mouth, and it travels lower until he's cupping my sex. My body responds but the warmth in his eyes when he looks at me, holy hell…my heart is wide-awake now, doing the damn macarena. I set my cup down before I spill hot coffee on myself.

"I'm going to hold you to that, but we have to go out," he says quietly as he lightly touches my sex.

I move against his hand. "What's on the agenda today, Prince Charming? We never did get out on your boat yesterday. Is that what you're thinking?"

"Prince Charming, huh?" He rubs the pad of his thumb over my flesh. "Is that what you want?"

I crinkle my nose. "I might be a romantic at heart, but honestly I'm not sure I believe in happily-ever-after."

His hand leave my body and I want to cry out at the loss. I pull myself together as he reaches for his coffee and takes a sip. "You said you were a girl who wanted to marry for love," he says matter-of-factly.

"Yeah, I know…"

His brow rises. "But you don't believe in happily-ever-after?" he asks, his head angled, his look dubious.

Dammit, I hate that he can see right through me.

"That's right."

He nods slowly. "Then I guess we have that in common." Once again he sets his coffee on the night-stand next to mine, and shifts closer. "I talked to Luis this morning."

My spine stiffens. "Luis as in Luis Laurent?"

He rakes his fingers through his damp hair. "The one and only."

"What…what did you talk to him about?"

"I needed his advice."

"Oh, about your new spring lineup?" I ask, ignoring the flare of disappointment sweeping through me. He asked me for my thoughts last night, and I had some good ideas on the accessories to best show-case the clothing on the app, but I guess he wanted to hear from a true professional.

"No. We talked about the kind of machine you'd need to help with the costumes."

My breath stalls in my lungs. "Are you serious?"

"Do I look like the kind of guy who'd joke about that?"

"No." Cason did this, for me? Truthfully, I really do not deserve it at all. I shake my head and my hair falls over my shoulder. "Cason, I—"

"You're not going to argue with me, are you?" I'm about to continue my protest, but he laughs. "It's not going to get you anywhere, Londyn. I'm supposed to be pampering you, and I plan to do it. I guess you're right. I am bossy, so zip it." He runs his thumb and index finger over his lips.

"Zip it?" I blurt out.

He laughs. "Yeah, zip it or I'll zip it for you."

I lift my chin, all indignant-like, even though his sweetness wrecks me a little more with each passing moment, and releases a need inside me that I'm too frightened to acknowledge. But what we're doing here, this isn't the real deal. He's playing the part of Prince Charming by day, Big Bad Wolf by night, and the combination isn't something a girl can walk away from unscathed.

"I'd like to see you try," I say, my objection sounding weak, even to my own ears.

"You asked for this." He leans into me, and any further protest dies a fast death as his lips capture mine and terminate my flow of words. The last time a man kissed me speechless was…never. But oh, this is so much better than arguing. As I clamor for more, one hand goes to my bare thigh, making it impossible for me to think as his fingers draw lazy circles on my trembling flesh. His lips devour mine, and I moan, my tongue tangling wickedly with his.

He inches back and his warm chuckle, rich and sexy, curls around me, and my entire body shudders. "Ready to zip it?" he mutters into my mouth, my lips still parted, poised and waiting for more.

"You don't play fair," I say with a sigh.

"No, I don't."

"You're going to pay for that."

"Or maybe instead, later tonight, when I get you back here alone, we can pick up where we left off."

"Okay," I say dreamily.

What the hell, Londyn? When did you get so easy?

He laughs, and kisses my nose. "Come on."

"Wait, where are we going again?"

"Don't you have some costumes to deliver?"

"Yeah, but we sort of got sidetracked last night, and I still don't have a sewing machine."

"Yeah, about that little interruption up against my front door. Sorry, not sorry," he jokes and takes my hand to pull me up. I stand before him completely naked and his nostrils flare. Without a word, he goes to his closet, grabs a button-down shirt and drapes it over my shoulders. I grin, loving the way he looks at me with such hunger. I do this to him. I can't even begin to describe how that makes me feel.

"Come with me." He takes my hand, and leads me down the hall and into another room. I come to an abrupt halt when I see a Janome HD-3000 heavy-duty sewing machine.

"I promised this last night, and I'm a man of my word, so I apologize for not having it here then, but under the circumstances..."

"Cason."

"What, you don't like it?"

I step farther into the room, my gaze going back and forth between the top-of-the-line machine and the man who is seriously slaying my heart, scoring it so many times I'm not sure I'll be able to put it back together when I leave here.

He dumps the bag of costumes onto the table. "Luis said this one would be the best for thick fabrics."

I open my arms, my palms up. "How…when… I don't understand?"

He grins. "You needed a machine, so I got you one."

"How did you get it here so fast?"

"Let's just say I have friends."

I nod. "Good friends."

"Good friends," he agrees.

I turn to him, and put my hands on his cheeks. I'm so glad he has good people in his life, people he can count on. He deserves that. "Thank you. I'll be able to get the costumes fixed faster now, and I can deliver them later today. They don't need them until tomorrow, but I'd like to get them done right away just in case."

"We have another machine coming, one more suited for delicate material, in case you want to work on some of your own designs. Later this afternoon we can go pick out some fabric. Luis suggested a great manufacturer just outside of Nice. It's where he goes, and he called ahead to give us access. I think it will be a nice drive today."

Incredulous I stand still and stare at him. What did I ever do to deserve all this from him? His knuckles brush with mine, and from downstairs my cell blares. I tense, instantly recognizing the caller from the personalized ring. I ignore it, and Cason frowns.

"Aren't you going to get that?"

"No," I say quickly, too quickly. Cason's eyes move over my face, but I don't want to tell him I'm avoiding my father and all the ridiculous demands he's placing on me. I'm not going to risk Cason kicking me to the curb if he found out what I was really up to.

"How about something to eat," he says, and I'm grateful when he doesn't push. "Then you can get to work on the costumes." He gives me a tap on the ass. "Go ahead and shower. I'll make us something to eat."

I nod and force my legs to carry me to the master en suite. He's being so incredibly sweet and giving, I can't help but want to do something special for him, something important. I turn on the spray and as I wait for it to warm, an idea forms, takes shape in my brain. I'm not sure if I'll ever be able to pull it off, especially without him finding out, but dammit, I'm going to try. Yeah, a Christmas morning to change his outlook and give him happier memories is just what Cason needs. What we all need.

With a renewed determination about me, I shower quickly, and within twenty minutes I step into the kitchen and find Cason on the phone. He has that familiar smile on his face and his words are soft. He hangs up and turns my way.

"Was that Peyton?" I ask.

"How did you know?" He hands me another cup of coffee and divvies up the eggs and bacon. The toast pops and he slides a piece onto each plate.

"I remember that smile."

He laughs. "When did it get so hard raising a kid sister?"

"Ah, that's your problem," I say as I slide a mouthful of eggs into my mouth. Cason's gaze drops, settles on my lips and my insides buzz to life.

"Meaning?" he asks.

"She's not a kid anymore, Cason."

"She'll always be a kid to me," he snarls grouchily.

"I'm sure she loves that attitude." He snatches his fork from the table, his scowl still in place. "What did you guys like to do as kids? What games did you play?" I ask.

"That's a strange question."

"I used to love snakes and ladders."

He smiles. "That was one of Peyton's favorites, and one Christmas we were together, with foster parents, and she got this Tamagotchi that she was crazy about, but it went missing. I actually think it was stolen."

"Really? By who?"

He toys with his eggs. "The fifteen-year-old who didn't want us in his house. Things got physical between us." He shakes his head. "Shit, if I hadn't decked that asshole, maybe we wouldn't have gotten tossed out. I wasn't the easiest kid."

My heart goes out to him. Something tells me he got himself kicked out before they could kick him out. Maybe it was easier leaving first, and skipping all that rejection. My heart tumbles. I sort of did the same thing to him. I rejected him and dated a boy my father approved of. I can't even imagine the scars imprinted on this man's heart.

"You were just protecting your sister," I say. "You know I always loved that about you." As soon as that *L*-word leaves my mouth, his head lifts. "I just mean, you're protective of those you care about." I toss a piece of bacon into my mouth and chew. "What were your favorite toys or games?" I ask, hating the sadness in his eyes.

He gives a noncommittal shrug. "I never really had a favorite anything."

"Okay," I say and let it go. He clearly doesn't want to talk about it, and I don't want to open old wounds. I take a few more bites. "I'll help you clean up and then get sewing," I say, excited to have something productive to do.

"I got this." He stands, takes my plate from me and drops a tender kiss onto my head. Whoa, where the hell did that come from? "You go. Those kids are probably waiting on you."

I nod, and as he gathers my dishes I dart upstairs, my mind on the lost little boy with a good heart, who grew into a man with an even bigger one. I get to work and the next thing I know, I hear movement at the door. I turn to find Cason standing there. I shake my head.

"Honest to God, I'm going to put a bell around your neck."

He laughs and perches himself on the corner of the desk. "How are you making out?"

"Good, I'm just finishing up."

He checks his watch. "Perfect, we still have time to deliver these and get to the manufacturer before it closes." He huffs, but there is a hint of teasing in his eyes when he adds, "I don't mean to rush you but if you hadn't wasted your morning sleeping—"

"Hey," I say and grab his shirt and pull him toward me. I press my lips to his and say, "You're the one to blame. If you hadn't carried me to your bed and put your cock in me again, I might have woken earlier."

His eyes turn a darker shade of brown, my dirty words obviously surprising and delighting him. His fast arousal curls through me, teases my nipples as well as the swelling cleft between my legs. "But we'll discuss that later," I say. "Right now we need to go."

He grips the back of my head, bringing my mouth back to his. "Now look who's not playing fair."

"You don't like when I play dirty?"

"I like it."

"But payback's a bitch, right?" As soon as the words leave my mouth, acid eats at my stomach. We'd both wronged each other in the past which means we can never have a future, and that makes my heart ache.

Thirty minutes later, I'm back in the small room at the back of the fruit-and-vegetable market. Marci is in a pink beret today, and she's going over instructions with one of the crew. Cason is wandering around outside and talking to a few of the cast members.

Marci finishes and turns to me as I pull the costumes from the bag. "All fixed," I say. "If you have anything else I'd be happy to help you."

"I appreciate that," she says, warming up to me.

"I'm glad to help."

"Although now with the new budget, we'll be able to buy better costumes and props, anyway."

"New budget?" I ask.

"Yeah, some anonymous donor invested in my film last night. I got a call from the school. Crazy, right?"

Warmth streaks through me. "I guess there really is a Santa Clause."

Cason steps into the room and I look at him. Goddammit, I'm so far down the rabbit hole, I'm not ever going to find my way out.

"All set?" he asks.

I look back at Marci, "I'm looking forward to seeing the end product."

"Come back for some of the filming. We'd love to have you as an extra. It will really put you in the holiday spirit."

"I'll try," I say and head outside with Cason. I slide my arm around his. "Did you hear?" I ask as we walk to his car.

"Hear what?"

"Some anonymous donor made a huge donation to their film."

"Nice," he says with a slow nod of his head. "But you were enjoying the costumes. I hope you're not too disappointed about that."

"I helped a bit, and I'm happy about that."

"I guess it's a good thing we're getting you fabric for your own designs today. Good timing."

"Yeah, it is, and I wonder who the donor was."

"If they wanted anyone to know, they wouldn't have done it anonymously."

I hug him tighter as we walk. "I'm thinking it was Santa."

He laughs. "No such thing as Santa, Londyn."

"I beg to differ," I tell him. "Santa brings joy and that's what he did here." I grin up at him. "Hey, maybe if I'm good, I'll make the Nice List and Santa will bring me something, too."

He smirks at me. "I think after last night, you're on the Naughty List. No worries though. I might not be Santa, but later tonight, I'm going to bring you all kinds of joy."

CHAPTER ELEVEN

Cason

I STAND OUTSIDE the door as Londyn works on her sketches, going back and forth from her drawing to her fabric. She studies the designs, examines the fabric and lays it out this way and that, as her brilliant mind races through ideas. Honestly the fashion industry needs her as much as she needs it.

I love seeing her like this, lost in her work. For the last week, after our trip to the manufacturing store, she's been sneaking in here every spare moment and working all hours. But I'm not complaining; after every piece she makes, she models it for me, and after I give my opinion, I then help her out of the outfit and straight into my bed. It's been one hell of an amazing week, and I have to say I'm finding myself in a place I swore I wouldn't go.

A small grin curls up the corners of her mouth. "Can I help you?" she asks.

"Yes, we're going out to dinner." I push off the door. "You've been cooped up in here too long."

She smiles up at me. "That actually sounds like a great idea." She drops her pencil and I step farther into the room. I flip through her sketch pad.

"These are fantastic."

She nibbles her bottom lip, her gaze darting between me and the sketches. "You don't think they're silly, or that I'm silly trying to pursue a career in fashion?"

I frown, and pull her into my arms. "Why do you keep asking me that?"

She rests her head on my chest. "You know why." she says, her voice muffled in my shirt.

"Actually, I don't." I'm about to press, when her cell phone rings. Her head lifts, and her eyes go wide. This isn't the first time she's ignored whoever is calling. "Come on, let's get changed and out of here," I say, desperate to protect her from whatever, or whoever, is filling her with anxiety.

She nods in agreement, and follows me to the master suite. She moved her meager wardrobe in here a few days ago, and she's yet to take me up on my offer to go shopping, buy whatever she wants. She slips into a sexy little black cocktail dress, followed by a pair of heels. I pull on a suit and tie, and we head to the front door where we put on our coats.

"What are you in the mood for?" she asks.

I laugh at that. "Do you really have to ask?" I say. This woman has turned me into a hormonal teen without even trying, so what I'm always in the mood for is sex. No matter how many times I've claimed her, I can't seem to get enough.

She rolls her eyes at me. "Never mind. Forget I asked."

I tug her to me, and my lips graze over hers. "What, don't you want that, too?"

"Oh, I do. As a matter of fact, I have a new outfit to put on for you tonight."

"It's nice how our interests work so well together." She gives me a strange look. "You know, you like putting clothes on, and I like taking them off you."

She laughs at that and gives me a small shove. "Come on, let's go or we'll never get out of here." I lock up and we head toward my car. "How about we walk?" she suggests.

I look her over. "You're in heels."

"I can't get anything by you, can I?"

"Smart-ass." She chuckles as I scan her face. Her smile is genuinely happy, and she's far more relaxed than she was when I first brought her here. "Will you be warm enough?"

She gives me a grateful smile and my heart squeezes. She's a strong, independent woman who likes it when I care for her. "I am," she says and slides her arm around mine. We head toward the downtown core and she takes a big breath and exhales slowly.

"I love it here, Cason."

"Me, too," I say.

"How long do you spend in Cannes each year?"

"I'm usually here the winter months."

"I'd live here all year round if I could."

"You don't think you'd miss your family?"

Her chin drops, and her gaze goes to the ground. "It's not like my father would miss me at work, and my mother is busy with other things. My closest friend is Jennie and she's here a lot." She laughs. "Jennie is from the auction."

"Yeah, I actually recognized her."

Since she brought it up, I decide to walk through that door. I tug her a little closer to offer my warmth and support. "What were you really doing on that stage, Londyn?"

Her mouth opens, and it's obvious she's going to recite the same lies about it being a thrill. She stops when her eyes meet mine. Her breath comes out heavy. "It's a bit of a long story."

As we approach town, I snort and glance around. "We're in Cannes, with all the time in the world," I tell her.

"You're right." She bites her lip, the struggle in her eyes tugging at my heart. Whatever is going on with her is causing her a tremendous amount of stress. "I don't want you to hate me."

"Londyn—"

"What am I saying, you already hate me."

"Is that what you think?"

"It's what I know, but I don't want to go back, Cason. I want to stay the rest of the week. Promise me I can?"

"Yes," I say quickly. Shit, I don't want her to go back either. Although now I'm not sure I do want to know the reason behind the auction. She opens her mouth but is suddenly cut off by Marci.

"Londyn," the student director belts out. "You're back. Just in time for the filming of the final scene."

Londyn shakes her head. "Oh, I wasn't…we weren't." She glances up at me, the emotions in her eyes a mixed bag of excitement and concern. It's a Christmas film and she knows how I feel about the holiday, but right now, in this moment, it's not about me. It's about Londyn. She wants to watch and I want to do this for her.

"I'm not starved to death," I say. "We can stay and watch the final scene if you like."

The wide smile that splits her lips hugs my heart. "Really?"

"Yeah, really."

She goes up on her toes and rewards me with a kiss. I hug her to me, and a second later her mouth is gone. She claps her hands as she turns to Marci.

"Can we be extras?"

"After a kiss like that, you two are perfect." She waves her hand. "Come on. The hero and heroine's Christmas wishes came true, and they're about to share their first kiss. The extras hug and kiss, too, as they watch them accept love into their hearts."

"Sounds corny," I say, and Londyn whacks me.

"Do you not have any romance in you?"

"Not really."

"Well maybe the scene will melt some of that ice." She takes my hand and tugs. We go silent as we stand around the gazebo, and the couple inside exchange loving words. Christmas music plays in the background, and Raphael, who I met last week, comes on to the scene dressed as Santa. He speaks to the couple, but we're too far to hear. I caught Londyn skimming through the script over the last week, and her big smile is a clear indication she knows what's being said.

"He's telling them wishes made at Christmas do come true."

I nod and avoid looking at her. I don't believe in anything Christmas, but I'd be a real prick if I didn't let her live in this fantasy world a little while longer. We continue standing, and when the couple kiss and the cameras span the crowd, everyone is hugging and kissing, and I pull her to me. Her face is awash in happiness as I kiss her. My God, she's so into this, gobbling up the festive season like it's a big turkey dinner and she hasn't eaten in weeks. Am I a total prick for not putting up a tree, decorating it together? For not going back to spending the holidays with my sister when I caught the melancholy in her voice?

Dammit.

Marci yells out, "Cut," and I dip my head.

"Do you want to hang around a bit longer, or head to the restaurant?"

She smiles up at me, all dreamy-like. "I'm ready to go."

The walls around my heart crumble a little more

and I shake my head. "Let's go." I put my arm around her and lead her through the crowds.

"Did you notice the costumes?" she asks.

"Yeah, they went with the ones you fixed. You did such a good job they didn't need to order more. I'm sure they put the donations to better use."

"It kind of makes me happy that they went with the original costumes. It sort of fits with the rags to riches story they're going for."

"Couldn't have happened without your sewing talents."

She smiles, a new lightness in her step as I lead her into the well-known seafood restaurant. I open the door and put my hand on her back to guide her in.

"This place is gorgeous," she says quietly. "I'm sure we'll need a reservation."

"I called ahead."

She gives my arm a squeeze and it travels to my damn heart. "Here I've been ignoring you and you've been planning this."

I bend and whisper in her ear. "Is that what you think, that you've been ignoring me?"

"It's what I know."

The hostess takes our coats, and puts us at a quiet table for two, a nice private spot in the corner like I asked. I unbutton my suit jacket and sit. As she admires the aesthetics of the place, I open the wine menu and scan it.

"Chardonnay?" I ask.

"Still my favorite."

"Since we're walking…" I close the menu and order a bottle when the server comes.

"Are you trying to get me drunk?" she asks, as bread, oil and vinegar are served to us.

I wait until we're alone. "When I get you in my bed, I don't want you drunk, babe. I want you wide-awake and aware of everything I'm doing to you."

She visibly quakes, and I grin. The bottle of wine is brought over and served, and when it's just the two of us again, I tap glasses with hers and we both take a sip. I don't want to spoil tonight, or pierce her balloon of happiness, but I lean forward, wanting to talk about the auction, and her eyes meet mine. Her body stiffens. Clearly she knows what's on my mind.

"So, the auction house," she begins, takes a big sip of her wine and sets it on the table. She toys with the stem, her gaze flitting to mine. "As you know my father can be controlling at times."

I smooth my hand over my coat, and push back in my chair. "I know."

"Unfortunately for me," she says, twisting her cloth napkin in her hand. "He's made some very bad investments." Her lashes lift slowly. "From what he said, his conglomerate is in real trouble." She laughs but it's humorless. "I have ideas, of course. But he won't listen to a word I have to say."

"That's a mistake on his part."

"Thank you for saying that." She takes another sip of wine, and the server comes to take our orders. We both have a quick look at the menu but after what

I just heard, and what I fear she's going to say, my stomach has soured.

After she orders, I close my menu. "I'll have the handmade ravioli," I say. At least that will give me something to move around my plate.

"He doesn't believe women belong in 'business.'" She does air quotes around that word. "I've mostly been doing charitable work with my mother." She cringes like she's embarrassed at what she's about to say next. "I'm basically on an allowance for that."

I nod, and she continues. "It's not that I'm not trying to get work. I-it's just no one takes me seriously."

"I take you seriously."

Her eyes widen, and she almost looks like she's going to offer a counterargument, when I say, "Why is this unfortunate for you, Londyn?"

"You're going to find this hard to believe. Heck, I still can't wrap my brain around it. It's the twenty-first century for God's sake." She shakes her head, and goes quiet. Her thoughts a million miles away.

"What will I find hard to believe?"

"He wants me to marry to better position his businesses," she blurts out, and a wave of disbelief and anger screech through me.

Bastard.

"So you go onstage to raise a sizable amount of cash to flood the company."

She glances down, and her face is a bit paler. "In a nutshell, yes. Crazy, right?"

"What's crazy is what your father is doing. Forc-

ing you into marriage, to someone of his choosing."
I clamp down on my jaw. I want to say more, I do,
but I'd rather her find out from someone else, or for
herself, that her father is likely full of shit. Everything in my gut is telling me this is a stunt to marry
her off to a guy with the right pedigree, and less to
do with him needing a business partner.

"I'm not even sure if my father likes me."

My heart cracks, right down the center. Her whole
fucking life she's been seeking his approval. I don't
want to hurt her feelings, but can't stop myself from
saying, "Maybe you should spend all that energy on
someone who does, Londyn. I know he's your father,
and I would probably do the same if mine were still
alive, but it rips me into pieces to see how hard you
work, and how little respect he gives you, as a designer and as a woman. You have more talent in your
little finger than most, and you're a good person." I
take a breath. "I know what you did to me…it was
all for your father. Your way of getting approval." I
swallow the lump in my throat. "Why did you think
I was going to send you back once I found out?"

"You bought me, Cason. That money is going to
save my father's business. I can't even imagine how
that would make you feel after…"

"The money is going to keep you from a marriage
you don't want. I'd spend it all to stop that from happening, Londyn."

CHAPTER TWELVE

Londyn

I'M STILL A LITTLE stunned to be honest. I thought Cason would be livid once he learned where the money he spent on me would be going, but instead he showed more concern about my well-being, more concern about protecting me from a forced marriage. Over the course of the meal, while he seemed infuriated that my father would put me in such a position, not once did he direct any of that anger at me. In fact, he was incredibly sweet and charming, engaging me in conversation and encouraging me to talk about my work, which I could go on and on about for hours, and pretty much did. Dammit, I really did hog all the conversation, although he seemed to enjoy sitting there listening to me. I love that about him.

I love a lot about him.

"You all set?" he asks as we finish our last sips of coffee and Kahlúa.

"I'm glad they finished up the film," I say, and he gives me a strange look. I rub my tummy. "They might mistake me for Santa with a bowl full of jelly when we walk by."

He laughs, and the easy sound wraps around me. After he pays the bill, we head outside and the night is a bit cooler. I hug myself, and he moves closer. His mere presence, his proximity, leaves me light-headed. How I'm ever going to go back to "normal" after this week is beyond me. Actually, maybe it's not. Maybe there is just no coming back from this fairy tale.

"Do you think it will snow for Christmas?" I ask as my shoes tap on the dry sidewalk.

"Doubtful." He glances at the dark night, the stars shining against a black velvet backdrop. "They don't get much snow here. I think something like only three days a year, but I've yet to see it."

I scrunch up my nose, disappointment swirling through me. While I don't like the cold, snow at Christmas would be the perfect ending to this fantasy I'm living. "Bummer."

"You want snow?"

"I think it would be nice." I smile and nudge him. "Maybe if I wish really hard for it, Santa will bring it."

"Yeah, maybe, and maybe I'll get that Transformer I always wanted?" he says, and then curses silently under his breath. "I mean, it's probably not going to happen," he redirects, like he said more than he wanted to and is desperate to get his words back. Too late.

I stop walking. "What?"

"Nothing," he says, slowing his steps but not stopping. With his back still to me, he adds, "I guess I was just making a point that Christmas wishes don't always come true. It's best not to get your hopes up."

"I know," I say and start walking again, hurrying my steps to catch up. This man has faced far too much disappointment, and I hate that I added to it. I look up at him and he briefly pinches his eyes shut. "What?" I ask. "Are you okay?" Jeez, he looks like he's in total agony.

"I can't believe I'm about to do this."

"Do what?" I glance around but can't figure out what he's talking about.

"Come with me," he says, putting his arm around my back to lead me down toward the port. "I hope you don't have any work that can't wait."

"My work can always wait for you, Cason," I say with an honesty that makes his brow furrow. I glance down as we walk, my mind on Cason. Now what did I say to give him grief? "What do you have in mind?" I ask, assuming it's something to do with us both getting naked. The man sort of has a one-track mind, and I'm not complaining, not one little bit.

"This," he says, and I lift my head to see all the Christmas trees being sold in the lit-up lot.

My entire body shakes, and my knees turn rubbery, as I take in the festive display before me. It's gorgeous with all the colored bulbs flashing, and a hot chocolate stand set up. If I didn't know better, I'd think it was part of the Christmas movie.

"Why are we here?"

"You want a tree, don't you?"

I stand there, sure I've heard him wrong. Perhaps the hustle of the people around me has distorted his words and has me hearing things.

"I… I don't understand."

He laughs.

"Would you like to put up a tree, Londyn?"

"I…yes," I say. "Only if you do."

"I do," he says.

I narrow my eyes. "Who are you and what have you done with my friend?"

"More like what are *you* doing to *me*?" he mumbles under his breath, and my heart does a little happy dance against my rib cage. I love seeing him get into the holiday spirit, love that he's feeding off my happiness. Although I don't want to get too excited. I'm still not sure I haven't taken a wrong turn, and stepped into the twilight zone.

"Are you just going to stand there, or are you going to pick out a tree?"

I snap out of it and give him a playful glare. "You don't have to be an ogre."

He laughs harder, and takes my hand. "Oh, we're back to that are we?" We weave in and out of all the gorgeous trees, until I find the most perfect one.

"This one," I say.

"Seriously?" He gives me a look that suggests

I'm crazy, and I'm not sure he's wrong. I am crazy. Crazy to get mixed up with him again, to fall into his bed, to make something of this holiday season, and to try to bring a new kind of joy into his life. But in the end, while I'm going to leave here heartbroken, if it brings a modicum of happiness to this amazing man, then the pain will be worth it. He deserves more than this life has given him. "You had to pick the biggest one on the lot?" he asks, dragging my thoughts back.

"Hey, you told me to pick one out, and you never said there were restrictions, so if we're going to do it, we're going to do it right."

"Have you never heard of moderation?"

"If you're going to do it, then overdo it."

"Right, moderation is for the weak," he says. "I remember that was your motto back in college."

I laugh at that and he puts his arms around me. His lips find mine for a warm kiss. "You're kind of crazy, you know that?"

Crazy about him? Yeah, I know that.

"Funny, just a minute ago I was thinking the same thing."

"I'm not too far off either, so again something we have in common."

I arch a playful brow. "Does that mean we can get this one?"

"Of course," he says, and as he reaches for his wallet, happiness wells up inside me. This tree goes hand in hand for what I want to plan, and speaking of, with Christmas just around the corner, I need to hit the ground running.

"Now we need to find a store with all the bulbs."

He groans, but there is a new kind of happiness about it. "What have I gotten myself in to?"

"Save that thought for later…" I tease.

He grabs my arm. "Come on, I'm getting a boner."

"Oh, that reminds me. We need to get some *logs* for the fire."

He groans. "Really, Londyn?" I burst out laughing and he shakes his head at me. "Let's go find these bulbs and logs."

A little over an hour later, we're back at his villa with a fire raging in the hearth. We've both slipped out of our formal wear and into our casual clothes. Cason looks edible in his jeans and a T-shirt that showcases his broad shoulders and trim waist. I'm currently in my yoga pants and one of his button-downs, which he seems to enjoy, judging by the way his gaze keeps going to my cleavage as we move furniture so we can put the tree in front of the big window.

"We won't be able to see the sea," Cason says.

"I want to look at the tree, not the water."

There's a knock at the door, and Cason goes to answer it as I finish rearranging his place. As he brings in the tree, I dash to the kitchen to put the kettle on. There will be no decorating without the prerequisite hot chocolate. A bubble of happiness wells up inside me, and I almost burst, until my ringing phone brings me back down to earth. I grab my purse, stare at the number and debate on answering it.

If I don't, he's soon going to start worrying, and for all I know he'll send out a search party. Since Cason is busy, I run my finger over the phone and answer the call.

"Hello, Father," I say.

A beat of silence and then, "Londyn."

"Ah, how are things? How's Mother?"

"Your mother is preparing for her holiday in the Alps. Will you be home for Christmas?"

I lower my voice, not wanting Cason to overhear. "No, I told you I'd be spending my holidays in Florida with a friend."

"Is that right?" he asks, his voice hard, doubtful.

I straighten my spine. Honest to God, I'm a grown woman, and I no longer have to answer to him. Let him cut off my monthly stipend, or as he calls it *my allowance*. That's ridiculous, considering I work for every last dime, and if you ask me, he's not paying me nearly what I'm worth, or utilizing me the best way he could. I wish I didn't have to depend on him. Wish I could make it on my own. The second that thought hits, so does another one. I gasp, and cover my mouth as a brilliant complementary idea to Cason's Hard Wear app pings around in my brain.

"Londyn, are you still there?"

"I'm here," I say, struggling to tamp down my excitement. Cason curses under his breath in the next room and I chuckle silently as he struggles to get the tree in the stand. I should be in there helping him not trying to placate my father.

"I can't really talk," I say. "I'm a bit busy."

"Is that why you haven't been answering my calls?"

"Yes," I say.

"Are you sure that's the only reason, Londyn?"

A chill goes down my spine, taking me back to my teenage years, when my father reprimanded me for one thing or another. Was there ever a time I could do anything right in his eyes? Ever a time where he was impressed or told me he was proud of me? Over the last week, Cason has been filling me with confidence, giving me the courage to run with my ideas. My creativity has come back under his care, which is likely why that brilliant idea hit moments ago. I can't wait to tell Cason about it. I'm sure he's going to want to run with it.

"I'm positive," I say.

"You are visiting the parks."

"The what?" I ask, trying to focus on his words as Cason grunts and groans in the next room.

"You said you were visiting a friend in Florida. I assume you're visiting the parks."

"Right, the parks. For sure," I say, hating to lie but having no choice in the matter. I can't let him know who I'm with. He considers Cason, a boy who was tossed around in the system, from the wrong side of the tracks. If you ask me, that's why he has so much character and integrity, and is so unlike the judgmental, unyielding stuffed shirts my father wants to see me with.

Cason said horrible things about you, Londyn.

Why am I suddenly second-guessing that?

Oh, because it just doesn't fit with his character.

"Is everything under control, Londyn?" he asks.

Wow, not "How are you, really?" Or "I'd really like to see you for Christmas," but instead, "Is everything under control?"

"Yes, of course everything is under control," I say, and when I hear movement at the door I lift my head and find Cason watching me carefully. One hand goes to my chest in surprise, the other clutches my phone tighter when it nearly falls to the floor. "I have to go," I say quickly. I end the call and slide my phone into my shirt pocket.

"You okay?" Cason asks, his gaze moving over my face.

"I'm good," I say and push my father from my mind. "I'm just about to make hot chocolate. The tree is up?"

"Yeah, but not before it gave me a hard time."

"Logs and hard times. I don't know what I'm going to do with you."

He laughs, and reaches for the mugs. His body brushes mine and a soft sigh catches in my throat. I scoop chocolate into the mugs, pour in the hot water, and we make our way back to the living room.

"Ready to start decorating?" he asks, putting one

hand on his hip, like he has no idea where to start. Why would he?

"Can we sit for a minute?"

He turns to me. "Are you sure you're okay?"

"Actually I'm great and I want to talk to you about something." I shift on the sofa barely able to contain my excitement.

He lowers himself across from me and I say, "You know all the designs I've been working on all week."

"Yeah, personally," he teases with a wag of his brow. "I've been the lucky guy to take them off you."

I laugh and playfully whack him. "I had an idea and I'd love to run it by you."

"Run away."

"Your business is Hard Wear. You cater to busy men on the go, men who hate to shop, or simply don't have a lot of money to spend on quality, fashionable clothes."

"That's it in a nutshell."

"What about women? There are lots of women in that same category, too. Lots of women who hate to shop—" His brow raises like I've truly gone crazy.

"If that's what you think."

I laugh. "It's what I know."

"You do seem to know a lot about a lot," he says, and for a second I'm not sure what he's referring to. "Anyway, go on."

I take a breath and let it out. "What if we did a complementary app to Hard Wear, and call it Soft Wear for women? Get it? Men are hard and women are soft, and like Hard Wear is a play on *hardware*, because of your computer science background, Soft Wear is a play on *software*, for the same reason."

"Oh, I get it."

He sits there staring at me, his expression unreadable and I hold my breath. Oh, God, please don't let him think it's a stupid idea.

"You just thought of this?" he asks.

"Yeah, like just a few minutes ago." I wave my hand. "I have all these designs, and no place to sell them."

"Londyn," he says, giving a slow shake of his head. "I can't believe you just thought of this." He snorts and scrubs his face. "Actually, I can."

I blink up at him, my heart crashing in my ears, eager to hear what he has to say next. "You can?"

"Of course, I can. It's brilliant. You're brilliant."

CHAPTER THIRTEEN

Cason

I PEEL MY eyes open, and darkness surrounds me. I'm not sure what's pulled me awake, I only know I'm having a hard time staying asleep. After Londyn shared her Soft Wear idea with me, we stayed up all hours, making notes and sharing ideas, and I sent emails off to my programming team as well as my lawyers. She hasn't asked, or even brought it up, but if I go with her concept and designs, we have to have legal documentation drawn up to give her ownership in the idea and new business plan. Honestly, I can't believe why I hadn't thought of it myself. The idea is downright brilliant.

Whispers from the other room have me sitting up in bed. I swipe at my eyes and glance at the clock. It's three in the morning. Who could Londyn possibly be talking to? I supposed if it's someone from back in New York, that would make sense. It's only nine at night there. I kick the blankets off, pull on my boxer shorts and pad quietly down the stairs to the living room. The tree is fully lit. How long has she been out of bed, and why is she up at all?

I step closer, but can't hear her whispered words. Beside her on the table, I spot my cell phone, lit up like the tree in the window. I don't normally lock it in the privacy of my own home and it's possible she grabbed mine thinking it was hers. What other explanation could there be? It had to have been a mistake. Why then is an uneasy feeling infiltrating my stomach?

Maybe it's because she seemed a bit spooked when I found her in the kitchen deep in conversation. I'm not sure who she was talking to, and she wasn't interested in telling me, but she seemed upset until she spotted me standing in the doorway. Her demeanor instantly changed. I honestly had no idea she was on the phone when I went looking for her. In fact, I was surprised to find her on a call, which she quickly ended when she noticed me standing there.

"Really?" she says, her voice rising a little from excitement. "That would be amazing. Okay, just text me the details. I'll be waiting."

She spins abruptly, and her eyes widen when she finds me standing there. "Okay, I have to go." She ends the call, blinks several times, and toys with the top button on the shirt she's wearing—my shirt. Goddammit, it's hard to think straight when she's standing before me, half-naked and sexy as hell. But it's more than just physical arousal with her, more than just wanting to strip bare, and slide her underneath

me. What I feel goes so much deeper and it terri-
fies the hell out of me. But the truth of the matter is,
where I want her most is in bed beside me, every single morning when I wake up—for the rest of my life.

"Did I wake you?" she asks.

I scrub my face, briefly glance past her shoulder
to take in the romantic ambience of the room as the
fire burns down and the tree lights twinkle. Last
night, as much as I wanted to be inside her, we had
so much to discuss that we talked until we were exhausted and fell asleep. I was content to hold her as
she drifted off, like I had all those years ago. Now,
however, with us both wide-awake...

"I'm not sure. Something woke me." She sets her
phone on the table, screen down. I glance at it.

"Oh," she says and gives a flippant wave of her
hand. "I had to call New York. The time difference is
a killer." She steps closer, and puts her arms around
me. "Sorry for waking you."

"It's okay." Worry slides around inside my stomach, but Londyn doesn't appear to be upset. Quite
the opposite, actually. "You seem happy."

She turns in my arms, presses her back to my
chest and wraps my arms around her. As I hug her
tightly, her heart pounds a little harder against my
hand. She rests her head against my shoulder, and
her soft hair tickles my face. My body relaxes against
her as she exhales a contented little sigh.

"Cason," she says quietly.

"Yeah," I say and brush my mouth over her ear.

A quiver goes through her and I revel in the movement of her body, the way it wraps around me and squeezes my heart.

"I am…happy. This gorgeous tree. This beautiful fire. The French Riviera."

"Your new Soft Wear idea."

She chuckles slightly. "That's the icing on the cake." She goes quiet, and we watch the tree for a bit. She finally breaks the silence and says, "It just feels like things are coming together for me." Her head dips. "Why do I find that so frightening?"

I spin her in my arms, and catch the turbulence in her eyes. "Because you don't believe in yourself, Londyn. You're afraid of failure. I think that's what's been holding you back. You're so goddamn afraid of disappointing your family, your confidence isn't what it should be."

"I try," she says meekly, and my heart reaches out to the girl seeking approval from a man who will never give it. Sometimes I think I'm the lucky one. No father at all is better than one who is manipulative and controlling. Londyn deserves so much better than that.

"I know you do. But you need to believe in yourself. Anything worth having is worth fighting for."

"I think I read that somewhere."

"Yeah, on a poster in my dorm." I chuckle. "Don't you let anything hold you back. Failing is better than not trying and you can't succeed if you don't give it your all."

She opens her mouth, closes it again and steps away from me. I follow her to the tree as she lightly touches the bulbs.

"Londyn?"

"Sometimes when things are too good to be true, they usually are."

"I know," I say. I pull her to me, and drop my gaze.

"Have I been living in a fairy tale, and none of this is real?"

Her frightened look breaks me and haunts my soul. "It's real, Londyn," I say, wanting to make her whole again, even though she once tore my heart from my chest and trampled it.

"You don't think I'm just fooling myself? That I'm not a foolish girl with no talent?"

I shake my head, frustration gripping my throat. I have no idea why she keeps asking me that, or what it's going to take for her to see that I believe in her— for her to see her worth.

"No, and when it comes to things being real, this is as real as they get," I say and press my mouth to hers. She melts against me, and all thoughts evaporate, all but one. I need to be inside her.

I draw in an unsteady breath as my chest tightens. "I want you."

"I want you, too."

I grin at her. "Look at that," I tease. "We have so much in common." My shaky fingers go to the buttons on her shirt. I begin to release them, one at a time, slowly, drawing this night out. Tonight there will be no hurried sex, no frantic fucking, no matter how much we both like that. No, tonight, when I put my cock in her—when I make love to her—I plan to savor ever second of it, plan to make it so goddamn good for her, she'll never forget this night. Honest to God, when it comes to her, I'm fighting a losing battle.

She moves restlessly, and places her warm hands on mine. Our eyes meet, our gazes lock and I smile at her. I widen the shirt, run my fingers over her slowly, gently, and cup her lush breasts in my palms. As I fill my hands, her head falls back and I brush the rough pads of my thumbs over her nipples. Jesus, I can't wait to bury myself in her.

"That feels so good, Cason."

Her hands go to my face, and she brings my lips to hers. Her breath quickens and her fingers drop, explore my body, her soft touch like a healing balm to my heart. I moan to let her know what she does to me, even though the raging erection between my legs is a pretty good indication.

I break the kiss, bury my mouth in the crook of her neck and she quivers. My cock stretches more, pushes against the band on my boxer shorts. I groan against her soft flesh, and begin a leisurely journey downward. I press wet kisses to her skin, take her nipple into my mouth. I kiss it gently, and treasure it like it's a prized possession before continuing my exploration.

Her nails rake my hair, and I dig my fingers into the soft flesh of her hips. Her eyes close and her body quakes with want. I slide the shirt from her body and it falls to the floor. Backing up an inch, I let my gaze race over hers. She's so goddamn perfect. We're perfect together.

I back her up until we're in front of the fire, and I lay her out on the soft rug. She reaches for me and I quickly rid myself of my boxers, and take my cock into my hand.

"You want this?" I ask, and her head nods. "Show me."

She widens her legs, and I can see every inch of her in the firelight. She writhes on the floor, her finger racing over her flesh, until she finds the needy spot between her legs.

My spot.

I growl, and her mouth parts, her fingers sliding over her sex. I drop to my knees, wedge myself between her legs, and she sits up and wraps those gorgeous lips around my cock. She takes me deep, like she's been waiting, starved for a taste of me, and the sight of my dick sliding to the back of her throat shakes me to my core. I move my hips, plunge a bit deeper, and she moans around the length of me.

"You like sucking my cock?" I ask. She nods, and cups my balls. "You like it when I fill your mouth with my cum?" She whimpers, and I push her hair back to see more of her mouth. She works her mouth over me like it's her goddamn job, dragging her lips along my length. I want to stop, need to stop, but how can I possibly when she's so good at this.

She licks her lips, and glances up at me, a teasing warmth in her eyes. "You like me sucking you?" she asks.

I glance at my rock-hard dick, as it sits on her bottom lip. "Fuck yeah."

She smiles and I get it, she loves the power she has over me. I growl and she takes me back into her mouth, treating me to a hard suck until tightness coils inside me. Moments before I reach the point of no return, I grip her hair and gently drag her off my dick.

"Lie back. Open for me," I command in a soft voice. "I want my mouth between your legs."

A needy sound slips from her throat and her hands go to her breasts as she falls back, her hair wild and sexy around her. I stroke her with a light caress, parting her. Finding her hot and wet like this screws me over a little more. I drink in the sight of her, and her body moves restlessly, but I take my time to enjoy the view.

"Please, Cason…put your mouth on me."

Shit, I love the way she gets for me. I bend forward, and swirl my tongue over her clit, teasing the hunger in her body. I lick slowly, taking my time. As I draw out this seduction, her hands go to my shoulders, and her nails drag on my skin. Fuck yeah. I groan as she leaves her mark on me, and slide my tongue lower, plunging inside of her as I place my thumb on her clit.

Her ragged breath washes over me as she inches

up, taking hold of my head and grinding against me. Attagirl. Take what you need. Knowing exactly how she likes it, exactly what her body needs, I slide a thick finger inside her, and just hold it there.

"Cason," she cries out and tries to shift, but I press down on her to hinder her movements. I almost laugh. She likes it when I lose myself in the moment, and although I'm acting like I'm the one in control here, the truth is, she's got me by the balls and has complete power over me. Londyn has always had the upper hand when it comes to me.

Her muscles ripple around my probing finger and I pull it out. Her hands grip my forearm, and she holds as I sink back into her, a leisurely pace that has her eyes rolling back in her head. Slow and steady, that's how she's getting it tonight. I continue to finger her, eager to see how high I can take her before she tumbles over.

"Cason…" Her back arches, and an urgent little sound catches in her throat. I slow the pace, ease off on the friction, and her eyes glaze over as I keep her hovering on the edge. "What…what are you doing to me?"

"Don't like it?" I ask with a chuckle.

"Yes…yes…but…"

"You need to come?"

"Please."

"You want to come in my mouth?"

"Cason…"

"Rub yourself all over my face, sweetheart. I want

you to get my mouth nice and slick. Can you do that for me?"

Her answering moan prompts me into action. I take her clit back into my mouth and her skin grows tight against my tongue. I tilt my head, needing to see her face when she tumbles over. Her lids flutter, her eyes fall shut. As she loses herself in pleasure, the gorgeous sight squeezes my aching cock. I move my fingers a little faster, answering the hunger reverberating through her quaking body. Heat shoots through me as her muscles tremble and squeeze my fingers, and I keep my face buried between her legs until she finally lets go.

Everything in the way she comes undone is sensuous and beautiful, something I'll never tire of seeing. My skin grows hot, and I'm dangerously close to losing it, simply from watching her.

"So good," she murmurs as each light stroke over her sex provokes a quiver in her body. I touch her softly, bring her back down gently, and her look is one of euphoria as her glazed eyes refocus on me.

"Welcome back," I say.

She smiles and reaches for me. I crawl up her body, my cock nestled between her damp thighs. I kiss the hollow of her damp throat, and her moan reverberates against my lips. I inhale her sweet scent into my lungs, and cover her lips with mine. Her mouth moves, a lazy slide of our tongues, our movements less rushed, but no less profound. My dick probes her opening and she lifts, inviting me inside.

"You ready to disappear again?" I murmur.

"God, yes," she whimpers. "Disappear with me." Her hands wrap around my neck, and I flatten myself on her body. I'm about to sink into her warm depths when a working brain cell stops me.

"Shit. Condom," I say. Jesus I can't believe I nearly forgot. I'm about to move, run to the bedroom at lightning speed, until her hands on my arm stop me.

"It's okay," she says.

I shake my head, confused. "What are you saying, Londyn?"

"I'm on the pill, and I'm clean."

My heart misses one beat, and then another. I'm a dead man, and I know it. Yeah, I'm a complete and utter goner if I put my dick in her with zero barriers between us. Heck, I might as well be slipping the noose around my neck.

"I'm clean, too. I always use a condom."

"I know. I trust you."

My throat tightens. "Are you sure?" I ask, my voice thick and rusty, as the last barriers around my heart come tumbling down. "It's what you want?"

"It's what I want."

Maybe I could be stronger if I wasn't in love with her, wasn't the guy who'd run through fire to give those I care about what they need.

I fall over her, slide myself between her folds. Our eyes meet, and the need I see reflecting in her gaze matches my own. I hold for one second, one long second that feels like a millennium, as I struggle to figure out how I'll ever come back from this.

Maybe I don't want to.

I slide my hands under her ass, and lift her hips. As she lies there, her body poised and open to me, I inch into her, stopping when I can't go any farther, but wanting more, all of her. I seat myself high, and pant against her throat. Her soft hands race over me eagerly, as we hold one another, like our very lives depend on it—like we both know there is more going on here. I set the boundaries from the start of this thing, drew a line in the sand, and we both agreed. But we've crossed the limits so many times, all that's left is scuff marks in the dirt, and a wide open heart. We hold tighter, stay like that for a long time, and I revel in the feel of being buried in her hot flesh.

I move slowly, and her whimper curls around me. She lifts her hips to meet me, and again I can't help but think how perfect we are together. I shift to look between our bodies.

"I love the way you take me," I say as my cock re-emerges, only to disappear into her hot depths again. "Shit, you feel good."

"I love the way you fill me," she says and draws my mouth back to hers. We kiss, deeply, and I pick up the pace, move a little faster and rub my pelvis against her clit. She moans into my mouth, her sweet pussy gripping me tightly as I plunge hard, blunt strokes that bring on her second orgasm. She shatters around me, her sex muscles squeezing tight, gripping my cock, like it's a lifeline in the storm, as her cries of ecstasy vibrate through me.

"Yes," I groan and close my eyes, exploding inside her and filling her with my cum as I disappear with her, overwhelmed with my need for closeness, her touch. I come and come and come some more, filling her completely. I find her mouth, kiss her deeply, possessively, leaving my mark of ownership. She kisses me back, and my heart pounds faster as I collapse on top of her, a pressure swelling in my chest, as she hugs me tight.

She might have hurt me in the past, wronged me in a way that gutted me, but there is no denying I love this woman. I love her with every goddamn fiber of my being. I always have.

So what the hell am I going to do about that?

I go back on my knees, and pull her until she's sitting. I brush her hair from her face, and her soft demure smile, the smile of a well-fucked woman, shuts down the last of my thoughts.

"Come on. We're not finished," I say.

"We're not?" she asks.

"Not by a long shot."

CHAPTER FOURTEEN

Londyn

I'M PRACTICALLY HOPPING around the villa as the clock strikes seven. I dart to the front door to look out, then back to the living room to admire the tree. Judging from my anxious state, you'd think I'd just downed a dozen espressos, but I haven't had any caffeine since this morning. I'm just insanely excited about what's going to happen, any minute now.

I truly can't believe I pulled it off. Cason caught me sneaking around a few times, whispering on the phone and dashing out when he was busy working. He has no idea what I'm up to and I'm secretly thrilled. I just pray, *pray*, this turns out the way I want, and he doesn't get angry with me for overstepping.

Good Lord, that first night I called Peyton, getting her number from the contacts on Cason's phone while I thought he was still sleeping, was nearly a bust. I had no idea I'd woken him and when I turned to find him behind me, I was sure my mission to cre-

ate new Christmas memories had been foiled. But
he didn't ask questions, and I didn't supply answers.

I wasn't sure how Peyton would react to my idea,
and I'm sure she hates me, although she didn't seem
at all surprised to hear I was in Cannes with Cason.
Nevertheless, she jumped at the idea, and I can't
help but wonder if she was a bit lonely all by herself
back in New York. Even if she does hate me, what
I'm doing isn't about me. It's about a boy and his sister and helping them find a new, happier way to get
through the holidays.

"What is the matter with you?" Cason asks, as
he comes from his office and plants a warm kiss on
my lips, like it's the most natural thing in the world,
like we're an old-time couple with an easy comfort
and intimacy between us. I almost laugh. We do go
way back, and the truth is, I've never felt this way
with anyone. In his arms, I feel safe, cherished and
appreciated. He brings out the best in me, and his
belief in me has bolstered my confidence and makes
me want to get out there and leave my mark on the
world. The hell with those who never believed in my
abilities. I don't need them. I'll do this on my own.
Well, with a little help from my friend. The man I'm
in love with.

God, I love him.

Really and truly love him. I'm done denying it,
and if I'm being truly honest with myself, I'd never
stopped, not even after he said terrible things about
me. He's always held my heart.

He represents a safety that allows me to put myself out there. He was right though, when he said I didn't fight hard enough. I *have* been letting fear of failure hold me back.

"Londyn, are you okay?"

His voice pulls me back. "I'm fine," I say quickly, and he arches a brow.

"Then why are you so agitated?"

"I'm not agitated. I'm excited. It's Christmas Eve!"

He turns and looks at the tree. There's a sadness about him he's trying to hide—for my sake. My heart swells with all I feel for him. Over the last week we've had so much fun talking about Soft Wear, planning ideas, and talking about having the launch next fall. He even surprised me with a fashion show in Nice, and that night I finally met my idol, Luis Laurent. We actually talked about my idea. I pretty much needed cement shoes to keep me grounded. Afterward, Cason had a private meeting with him, and I don't know who they were discussing—I think Luis's newest intern, a position I'd die for—but words like *lacking in skill* and *pedestrian* were tossed around. I feel sorry for the designer, and is it awful of me to think that I could apply for the position if she's let go? Yeah probably. Nevertheless, these last two weeks have been a true fairy tale, one I never want to wake from.

A knock comes on the door and I nearly jump from my skin. "Who could that be?" I ask.

Cason frowns. "I have no idea. I don't usually have visitors on Christmas Eve, or…ever."

I grip the sofa to stop myself from leaping. "Why don't you get it?"

He dips his head, and examines my face. I'm sure I must look like the village idiot with the way I'm smiling.

"Are you sure you're okay?"

"Yes, go," I say and shoo him away.

"I'll get rid of whomever it is, and then you can try to convince Santa you've been nice instead of naughty," he says, his voice full of warmth and playfulness. My heart twirls in my chest.

I follow behind him as he heads to the door. He swings it open, and when he finds Peyton standing there, suitcases and shopping bags in her hands, his head rears back.

"Peyton, my God…" He reaches for her, pulls her inside for a hug. A second later he has her by the shoulders, and is holding her at arm's length. "Wait. Is everything okay? Are you okay?"

She laughs and whacks him with her bags, and I hug myself as I watch the beautiful exchange. "Of course I'm okay, big brother. Stop worrying about me all the time."

He looks past her shoulder for a second. "What… what are you doing here?"

"If you let me in, I'll tell you."

"Right." He pulls her in and kicks the door shut behind her. "What's going on?"

"You weren't coming back to New York, so I thought I'd come spend Christmas with you instead."

The muscles in his back ripple as his shoulders tense. "You want to spend Christmas together?" he asks, and I don't miss the hitch in his voice. Happiness wells up inside me. This is what he never knew he needed and I'm thrilled that I could do it for him, and that he's not angry about it.

She drops all her bags to the floor. "Of course I do, you big oaf."

"Oaf?" he asks and relaxes.

I chuckle and Cason turns. He takes one look at me and his expression changes, softens, as realization dawns. "You—you did this, didn't you?"

My eyes fill with tears at the warmth in his gaze, the love I see shining there. "I thought it would be really nice for you two to create new memories. There are some presents I put under the tree for you both."

"This? This is what you've been up to? All the sneaking around and secret phone calls?"

My eyes widen. "You knew?"

"Yeah, I notice when you're not here, Londyn."

I grin. "Oh." A frown turns down his lips. "Wait, what did you think I was doing?"

He scrubs his face and my heart sinks as he averts his gaze. He still doesn't trust me? After these last two weeks, I thought we'd moved past so much. Then again, he did share ideas with me, and vice versa. If he thought I was doing something disloyal behind his back, he would have called me out on it, right? Yeah, he would have, and maybe I'm wrong. Maybe he does trust me, and old insecurities are just seeping back in.

"I didn't know," he says. "I guess I just never thought…this." He points to Peyton.

I smile. "Merry Christmas, Cason." I reach for my coat, about to put it on.

"Where do you think you're going?" he asks.

"I want to give you two private time together."

"What if I don't want you to leave?"

Peyton walks around him and I expect her to wave me out, but she sides with Cason. "I don't want you to leave either, Londyn."

"Are you—"

"We want you to be a part of our new memories, too," Peyton says, her dark eyes full of honesty and sincerity. How does this woman not hate me?

My gaze slides to Cason, and he's nodding in agreement. Their kindness, openness and inclusiveness hugs me like a blanket. I want to be a part of this small family more than life itself.

"I'd like to stay," I say.

Peyton skips toward me. "Good. Now, where's the eggnog?"

"I'll get you eggnog," Cason says. "First there's this 'oaf' thing we need to discuss, and why is everyone calling me names?"

"Probably because you deserve it, Cason," Peyton says and drags me down the hall. She wraps her arm through mine. "Put my bags in my room will you. Leave the pink one, it has the presents."

As Cason stands there scratching his head, Peyton and I head to the kitchen for drinks. I go to the fridge and pull out the eggnog. I toss ice into two glasses and pour a generous amount of the delicious alcoholic creamy mixture into both. Her crystal glass clicks on the marble island as I set it down. She quickly picks it up, taps it with mine and smirks at me.

"What?" I ask.

"You and Cason."

"Oh, it's not like that," I say and take a big drink to cover the heat infiltrating my cheeks.

"But you want it to be. I always knew you two belonged together," she says matter-of-factly. I open my mouth to speak and she continues with, "He's been a miserable prick, Londyn."

I laugh at her language, but sober quickly. "Because of me."

"Exactly."

"He hates me."

She snorts. "Is that what you think?"

I shake my head. "You sound just like him."

"All I know, girlfriend, is I've never seen him look at any woman the way he looks at you. He's been a prick because you haven't been in his life. Fate brought you two back together, and this time you guys had better not screw it up."

My heart tightens. "I never meant to hurt him."

"I know, and now you two have a second chance."

A bubble of hope wells up inside me, but I'm afraid to let myself get too excited. "Do you really think so?"

"Uh, yeah."

"We have a history, you know that."

"I know." She takes a big drink of eggnog and holds her glass out for me to refill it. "Don't judge me," she says. "It's been a bad year."

"I'm sorry. Is everything okay?"

Instead of answering, her eyes narrow, and she shakes her head. "Everyone deserves a second chance, Londyn. Well, not everyone," she says with a snarl.

I run my finger over the rim of my glass. "What do you mean?"

She glances over her shoulder, all conspiratorial like. "Do you remember Roman Abbot, Cason's good friend since college?"

"Yeah, why?" I ask. What the hell did Roman do to make her snarl like that?

"Well, he—"

"Bags are in your room, and the pink one is under the tree," Cason says, coming into the room. He stops when he spots us leaning toward one another. "Am I interrupting something?"

"Girl talk," Peyton says, and rattles the ice in her glass.

"Is it about me?"

She rolls her eyes. "Oh, please. The world does

not revolve around you, brother. Such an ego." Cason grabs her in a headlock and runs his knuckles over her head.

"Smart-ass," he says.

I can't help but laugh. I'm not sure what Peyton was about to tell me but the mood has shifted, so I let it go. I pour Cason an eggnog, and wave him and his sister over.

"Come on," I say. "I can't wait until morning."

I lead them to the tree, and as we all stare at it, I look beyond it and gasp.

"What?" Cason asks, his eyes wide as he assesses my face.

"Look." I point to the window, and both Cason and Peyton step up to it.

"It's snowing," Cason says and shakes his head. "I can't believe it, although nothing should surprise me now."

"Santa came through," I say.

Peyton glances back and forth between the two of us. "Okay, you two, I'd tell you to get a room, but there are presents under this tree, and I want to open them."

"You don't want to wait until morning?"

She rolls her eyes at Cason. "It's like you don't even know me."

I laugh, loving the ease between brother and sister. Peyton is smart, funny and her adoration of her brother is as bright as the Christmas star. We would have been good friends.

Maybe we still can be. Maybe she's right and Cason and I do have a second chance.

Peyton picks up a gift and shakes it. "Maybe don't do that?" Cason says. "You don't know if it's break-able."

"Calm down," Peyton says and glances at me. "Can you lend my brother a tampon?"

I burst out laughing and Cason scowls, but the love for his smart-ass sister is all over his face.

"See what I mean?" he says to me and throws his hands up. "Kid sisters." I grin. This man is going to make an incredible father.

"Okay, you two behave before I have to separate you." I drop to the floor, and cross my legs. I tap the floor. "Come sit."

They both drop down beside me, and Cason scrubs his face, agitation rolling off him in waves. "I didn't know we were exchanging gifts."

Here I told this man I couldn't give him anything other than my body, but that was a lie because he was already holding my heart. Heck, he might as well hold the rest of me, too.

"I don't give to receive," I say. "Besides, Cason, being here in Cannes, at Christmas, with you, is the best gift I've ever been given." I squeeze his hand, and his face warms. "Okay, Peyton," I say, needing a distraction before I launch myself into his lap and kiss the living hell out of him. I hand her gift over.

"Ooh, it's small."

"Good things come in small packages," Cason says.

"Really?" Peyton responds. "That's *not* what she said."

Cason groans, and I hand him his present. "Yours is bigger." Peyton coughs to hide a chuckle, and I roll my eyes at her playfulness.

Peyton rips into hers and goes perfectly still, her eyes latch on the gift. I spot tears and my heart sinks. Oh, no, I made a huge mistake.

Her head slowly lifts. "You…you got me this?" she asks as she removes the Tamagotchi from the packaging.

"Cason told me a story and I—" Before I can finish she throws her arms around me.

"I always knew you were special, Londyn. Thank you. You can't even believe how much this means to me." My heart overflows with happiness, and my breath stalls when I turn to see the intense way Cason is staring at me.

"Open yours," I manage to get out.

His throat makes a gurgling sound as he swallows. "Londyn," he begins, his grip on his present tight.

"Open it already," Peyton says and tears at the paper to expose the Transformer inside. I never was certain which one he wanted, Peyton wasn't either when I posed the question, but after a bit of research I discovered Optimus Prime was a sure bet.

He breathes heavily, his brow furrowed as his mouth turns down in a frown. My heart races, and once again, I hope I didn't make a mistake.

"Thank you," he says quietly.

"Who is this one for?" Peyton asks.

"Um, all of us, actually. Go ahead and open it."

She tears into the package, and laughs when she discovers snakes and ladders. Cason's head finally lifts, and I can't stop staring at him, even though he's looking everywhere and anywhere but at me.

"I'll, uh, I'll be right back," he says and takes the eggnog glasses into the kitchen. I debate on going after him to make sure he's okay.

Peyton nudges me. "I think you broke my brother, in a good way."

I point to the kitchen. "Should I—"

"No, give him a minute. This is a lot to take in." She leans into me and wraps her arm around my shoulder. She presses her lips to my cheek, and I feel her tears slide over my skin. "Thank you, Londyn. This is exactly what we needed, and the fact that you knew that…" She breathes deeply and lets it out. "My brother is the luckiest guy on the planet. We both are."

Cason comes back. We both turn, and I'm stunned, silent when I see how dilated his eyes are. Peyton, however, she stretches her arms out and feigns a yawn.

"You know what, I'm exhausted from all the travel. I think I'm going to call it a night." She covers her mouth and yawns again. "How about we pick up here tomorrow, and after breakfast, which Cason is cooking of course, we can spend the day playing snakes and ladders?"

"Are you sure, you just—"

"I think that sounds like a reasonable plan," Cason says, his voice thick and deep. My blood pulses as his gaze zeroes in on me. Being the sole focus of the man's attention—his hunger—is like a powerful aphrodisiac. I blink, and when my eyes open again, Peyton is gone.

"Oh, okay, then," I say and climb to my feet.

Cason holds his hand out to me. "We should probably get to bed, too."

"Are you tired?"

"No."

CHAPTER FIFTEEN

Cason

I STAND OUTSIDE the security check-in and drag my sister in for another hug. I can't believe her time with us is already over and while she says she has paper-work, over the holidays, I don't really think that's entirely true. She just wants to give Londyn and me time alone. I still can't believe Londyn arranged all this, or how full my heart is at this very moment.

I finally let her break from the circle of my arms, and say, "Call me when you get back to your place safely."

She gives me that familiar eye roll. "I'm a big girl, Cason. I can take care of myself." She pokes me. "Londyn is a big girl, too, but I think she likes it when you take care of her."

"You like her, Peyton?" I ask, glancing over her face.

She looks at me like I'm dense, and she's probably right. "What's not to like?"

"We have a past," I say.

"Londyn said the same thing to me, and I'll give you the same answer I gave her. Everyone deserves a second chance." She pokes me again, harder this time. "You two need to talk."

"You're right, we do," I say, my heart wide-open and defenseless, as love swirls around inside me.

"I'm in love with her Soft Wear idea," she says. "It's brilliant."

I put my finger over my lips. "Shh, it's a secret until the big launch."

"Well, I'll be your first customer, you know that."

"You'd better get going," I say as the line thins.

She goes up on her toes and throws her arms around me. "Love you, bro."

"Love you, too, kiddo."

She arches a brow. "See that wasn't so hard, was it?"

"What wasn't?"

"Telling me you loved me."

I frown at her. "I always tell you I love you."

"Yeah, now you need to tell someone else."

"Did I ever tell you that my life is not your business, and you're too nosy for your own good?"

Her head rears back and she plants one hand on her hip. "Now, if that's not calling the kettle black."

"You're my kid sister, and protecting you is what big brothers do, and do not roll your eyes at me."

She laughs. "Okay, fine. But I still need you to set me up with someone from Penn Pals." She scrunches her face. "I can't believe I have to be married for this job. Just make sure he knows the deal. I'm not looking for anything more than pretend. You and Londyn work, but marriage isn't in the cards for me."

My mouth tightens, not sure whether that makes me happy or sad. While I hate the idea of a guy near her, or hurting her—yes, I get it I'm far too overprotective—I want her to find happiness. I'm just not sure any guy will be good enough for her though.

"I'll set it up and make sure the rules are clear."

"Thanks." She glances over her shoulder, and picks up her carry-on bag. "Okay, I have to run. Talk soon."

I stand outside of security until she clears and she gives me a wave before she disappears up the escalator. With a new lightness in my step, I head outside, jump in my car and drive back home.

Home.

I never really considered my villa in Cannes home. With Londyn there, leaving her mark on the place, and in my bed, it feels more like home and hearth than any other place I've ever lived. I can work anywhere, heck I can fly back to New York anytime I need to, and with my businesses being online, I can log in from anywhere in the world. Londyn said she'd love to live here…

Whoa.

Okay, I'm getting far too ahead of myself. Here I am making plans and we've yet to even have a conversation about our future. Sure, we've been having fun sexually and not once have I told her I wanted more. In fact, right from the start I told her I couldn't give her more. I *wouldn't* give her more. She agreed. Which means, I might be jumping to conclusions. Yeah, I realize her father would likely disown her if she goes against his wishes. I'm just hoping over the last couple weeks, her eyes were opened, and she can see that she doesn't need him or his approval to succeed.

I drive through the downtown core, quiet now as everyone is home enjoying the holidays with their family. I meander through the port area, and do a double glance when I think I spot Londyn. I wanted her to come to the airport with us, but she insisted we go alone to spend our last few minutes together, and that she needed to go for a walk to work off all the food we've been eating. I drive a little closer, and see that she's talking to some elderly gentleman. That's just like her, always so open and friendly to everyone. I'm driving past them and I'm about to head home when I turn back. Maybe Londyn would like me to join her on the walk or perhaps offer a ride home, as it's rather cold outside.

I cruise back to the port, and I'm about to pull into a parking spot, until I see who she's with. My heart jumps into my throat, and my vision goes a bit fuzzy around the edges. Okay, I must be hallucinating, because no way would Randolph Harding be here in Cannes, on the street talking to Londyn. She told him she was in Florida. Why would he be here unless…

Randolph's head lifts, and he makes eye contact with me. Londyn turns and when she sees me, her eyes go wide. She grabs her hood and pulls it up. Does she really think she can hide from me? I'd know her anywhere. But what I really should be asking myself is, why is she with her father, and why the hell is she trying to hide that fact from me?

Her father says something to her, and she turns back to him. He takes her arm, and a minute later, they've moved behind a building, out of my line of vision. With my heart in my throat and my stomach somersaulting, I pull back onto the road and drive straight to the villa. The first thing I do is check to see if her suitcase is there. Once I see that it is, I dash to my office and boot up my computer. With an uneasy feeling rolling through me, and a sense of déjà vu coursing through my veins, I do a few on-line searches, and within seconds, my world turns upside down.

"Holy shit."

CHAPTER SIXTEEN

Londyn

"ARE YOU READY to come back now?" my father asks, as Cason drives away. I stare after his vehicle, my mind spinning a million miles an hour.

"Why are you doing this?" I ask, swiping at the stupid tears welling up in my eyes.

"It's for your own good."

I shake my head, and try to wrap my brain around all this.

"Come on, Londyn. Do you think he bought you for any other reason?"

No, actually, I understood from the beginning that Cason was out for revenge. I told him so myself, and he never disputed it. But over the last two weeks, not only did I think we recaptured our feelings from our youth, but we built upon them. Apparently, I thought wrong, and the proof is in my father's hand—or so he says. Were Cason and Luis really talking about me after the fashion show?

"Wait," I say as I shake my rattled brain to clear it. "How did you know I was here, anyway?"

My father waves a dismissive hand. "None of that matters."

"It kind of does. I told you I was in Florida, how on earth did you find me here, and figure out what I was up to?"

He turns from me. What is it he doesn't want me to see?

"All that matters is you need to come home and take your rightful position in the family."

"Rightful position? Meaning, you want me to marry your colleague's son to better your position in the markets." I wave my hand. "Haven't I done enough?"

"Yes, you have. Raising money in such a manner is a disgrace, Londyn, to you and the family."

I glare at him. "I was trying to help, and short of marriage, you left me no choice."

"Selling yourself to some lowlife was the answer?" He makes a tsking sound. "You'll be lucky if Theodore's son Sheppard will have you after this."

I can't stand Theodore's arrogant, spoiled son, and the thought of any sort of relationship with him sickens me. As my father continues to look at me, disdain all over his face, fire burns through my veins, and my cheeks flare hot.

"Excuse me? Who I'm with is my choice, not yours, and Cason is anything but a lowlife. He's a good man, a kind man, and he believes in me."

My father presses a button on his phone, and Cason's voice comes through. I listen for a second, and my insides twist. I swallow the bile punching into my throat as I hear the conversation between Cason and Luis, except this time I hear Cason use my name. *I'm* the one he's calling pedestrian! My blood drains to my toes, and the world around me grows fuzzy. It can't be true. It just can't be.

"Where did you get that?"

"I have people everywhere, Londyn."

I lift my chin, glare up at him. His blue eyes are narrowed in on me. "So that's how you knew I was here? You have someone watching me?"

"Well…" he begins and stops.

"Well what?" I demand as wind blows down the street and chills my bones. But I won't get into his car with him.

"Can we go to the airport already?"

"No, I want answers. Right here. Right now."

"Fine." He grabs my purse. "You have a device in your bag."

I rip open my bag. "A device, what kind of device?" I root through it but find nothing. "There's no device in here."

"It's in the lining."

My jaw drops. This purse was a birthday gift, a one of a kind purse, made by one of my father's trusted designers.

"Oh, my God. I can't believe you did this." I rip into the lining, and tear at it like a crazy person. "You've been listening to all my conversations? What is the matter with you?"

"You're my daughter." He scoffs and looks around. "You obviously need looking after."

"I do not need anything from you." Not anymore, anyway. I used to think I needed his approval but this is too much. He's gone too far. My stomach coils, and I try to get my breathing under control. "Are your businesses even in trouble?"

He shoves his hands into his pockets and gives me a reprimanding look, treating me like I'm a child who's dared to question their parent's authority. "Business is fine isn't it?" I give a humorless laugh. "I did all this for nothing, and you only told me that to finally get me married to the right man of your choice."

"Londyn," he begins, and I shake my head.

"No, you don't get to say anything to me."

He waves his phone at me. "What are you going to do now? Run back to lover boy who thinks you're nothing but a joke."

"No," I say. "You're wrong. He didn't say those things back in college." I point to the recorder. "And he's not saying those things now. You're manipulating this somehow." He opens his mouth and I shake my head. "Don't even try to deny it." I refuse to believe anything he says to me. Not after what Cason and I have been through. Yes, many years ago, I was quick to believe my father, when he had a lot more influence on me, but he's not a good man. A good man would never treat his daughter the way mine treats me. He'd care about what I wanted, not what made the family look better, or the fiscal bottom line.

He frowns. "Everything I've done has been for your own good."

"So you admit it then?" I glare at him "You edited the recording?"

"I'm not admitting anything…"

I breathe in and out, and as my breath turns to fog, my father continues to talk, but I'm not listening. No, I'm remembering all the times I asked Cason if he thought I was silly. It confused him. Not because he forgot, but because he never said those cruel words in the first place. My father will stop at nothing to get what he wants, even breaking Cason and me up all those years ago so he could get a jump on the app idea.

Oh, no!

Had he overheard our conversation about Soft Wear? He doesn't have access to my designs, but it's possible he heard me talking about the styles and details that would appeal to Soft Wear clientele.

My throat tightens, a gurgling sound caught in the depths. "I have to go."

"Don't you dare—"

I turn and walk away, my footsteps fast on the pavement. I can't let my father come between us again. I won't.

I pinch my eyes shut and pray it's not too late.

CHAPTER SEVENTEEN

Cason

I TAKE ONE DEEP BREATH after another, trying to wrap my brain around Londyn's deception. What the hell is wrong with me? Am I the stupidest man on Earth? A garbled sound crawls out of my throat, because as I stare at the new domain name, owned by Randolph Harding, there can only be one answer to that. I am the world's biggest idiot.

The front door opens, and closes, and I shove my hands into my pockets and work to get my temper under control, but that's like putting toothpaste back in the tube. Impossible.

"Cason," she calls out, her voice shaky and a bit hesitant.

Does she really think I didn't recognize her on the street?

I step from my office and her eyes go wide when she sees me. There's no hiding my anger. We stand there for a long time, like we're in a goddamn stand-off, and my mind races with all the unanswered questions.

"Why?" I ask, not knowing where to start. "I don't understand. Did you know I was going to be at the gentleman's club that night?" That doesn't even seem possible to me, which makes all this that much harder to understand.

"Cason," she begins, her voice tired and weary. She shakes her head and her hood falls to her shoulders. Her hair is in a ponytail, her face makeup-free. The innocent look works on her, apparently. "It's not like that."

I laugh. "What is it like then, Londyn? What am I supposed to believe?"

Her face falls. "You think I gave my father insider information about your business." Her shoulders sag.

"He already bought the domain name. Soon he'll be selling women's apparel that caters to professional businesswomen who are either too busy to shop, or have limited funds but need to look professional. That sure sounds a lot like what we talked about."

"Yeah, I know but—"

"What I don't understand is why you didn't just go to him with your Soft Wear idea? Why bring it to me first?" I wave toward the laptop on my desk. A thought hits, and an almost manic laugh crawls out of my throat. "Oh, wait, I get it now. Your daddy's businesses are failing and you asked me so we could discuss designers and distributors." I look down the hall, and through the glass door, see her father's car drive by slowly.

"So that's what you think, Cason?" Her coat sags

on her shoulders as she exhales. "That's what you really think?"

"Yeah," I say, my heart splintering into a million tiny pieces. "That's what I think," I bark back, pain and anger mingling and fogging my ability to think with any sort of clarity. I'm being a total prick here, and I know it, but I'm so goddamn mad, I'm seeing red.

"You want me to leave?" she asks, her voice hitching.

I nod my head. "Unless there is something else you need from me. Any more advice, any other designers I could introduce you to?" She opens her mouth to speak, but I cut her off. "Although I can't imagine what else you could possibly take from me."

Her mouth closes, and tears fill her eyes. Her father's car drives by again. "You should go. Daddy's waiting." I take a step back, putting a measure of distance between us, physical and emotional. "I'll have your things sent to you."

She glances over her shoulder. "Cason, I—"

"Goodbye, Londyn."

She hugs her jacket to herself, and backs up toward the door, her footsteps wobbly and unsteady. She turns and opens the door. Her body vibrates as she takes a big breath.

"For what it's worth," she says quietly, talking to me over her shoulder. "It's not what you think. None of that matters though, because I made a mistake in the past, one I'm completely sorry for, but I was also going on misinformation, and that destroyed your trust in me. It's not something I'll ever get back, that's perfectly clear to me now."

"What are you talking about, Londyn?"

"My father told me you thought I was a silly girl, a joke. He actually had a recording of you saying that. I have no idea how he got it. I guess he must have had you followed." A cry lodges in her throat. "That would be just like him."

I grab a fistful of my hair. Will that man never stop screwing with me? What the hell did I ever do to him, anyway? "I never said that."

"I know. He wanted you out of my life because you were from the wrong side of the tracks. He didn't think you were good enough, didn't have the right pedigree. He manipulated me, and in the end, it destroyed us both."

I back up, grip the doorframe to my office, my pulse jumping in my throat, incredulous. "That's why you kept asking me if I thought you were silly?"

"Yes."

I shake my head, as I wrap my brain around all this. "You were pretty quick to believe the worst of me then."

"Sadly yes, and that was on me and not you. It came from a place of fear and insecurity." She swallows. "You said yourself I needed to believe in myself." She turns, and watery blue eyes meet mine. "But I'll leave. I'll let you throw me out of your life."

"What is that supposed to mean?" I shout back.

"You have insecurities that stem from your child-hood too, Cason. You're so afraid of getting hurt, you push others away before they can push you away." A long pause and then, "That's why you're so quick to believe the worst of me. Just for the record, my father is completely wrong about you. You're a good man."

I stand there staring, her words banging around inside my rattled brain.

"One more thing Cason. We don't have a future, I accept that, but you need to take some time, a lot of time, in fact, and work on you. There are people out there that want to love you, and I really hope you can see that, and not let fear drive your actions and push away the next woman who wants to be a part of your life. I want you happy."

She disappears through the door, closing it quietly behind her. I walk up to it, my heart crashing in my ears as she takes the steps to the walkway. Her father climbs from the car, a shit-eating grin on his face—like he was right about something—and circles it to greet her, but she shakes her head and walks past him, heading toward the downtown core. I have no idea what she's doing, and I shouldn't care. I shouldn't care one damn iota, but how can I not? I'm in love with her yet all this time, she was using me for information.

Does that really make sense, Cason?

But by leaving she was admitting her guilt, right? She didn't stay and fight to convince me I was wrong. I pace back to my living room, and look out over the water. My boat bobs in the sea and if it wasn't so damn cold out, I'd sail away and forget the real world existed for a little while. But it does exist and I can't hide from the harsh realities. Jesus, Londyn and I shared an incredible time together. We had so much, fit so perfectly. Just like we did back in college. Until her father ruined my life.

He didn't just ruin you, dude.

I shove my phone into my pocket, and needing fresh air I head out the door. I walk aimlessly, pausing by the gazebo where the Christmas movie was filmed. My heart aches a little more as I consider Londyn's kindness, her joy in helping the students with their costumes.

I take a breath but find it harder and harder to breathe. Eventually I find myself inside a bar, and I sit at the table and nurse a brandy, then another. A group of laughing women enter, and one of the girls makes eye contact with me. I practically snarl at her, even though she doesn't deserve my anger. Before Londyn, I would have approached any one of those girls, but now, well, now I'm screwed. How can I be with anyone when my heart belongs to Londyn?

I scoff and finish my drink. Maybe I should go take one of them back to my place, maybe that's the only way to get Londyn out of my system once and for all. My phone rings and my damn heart leaps, hoping it's Londyn, and shaking my head because of it. I am such a goddamn fool.

I check the screen and a growl crawls out of my

throat when I see it's Roman calling. I think about ignoring it. If I don't take the call, he'll worry about me, the way he always does this time of year. We go way back to college and not only is he Hard Wear's head web developer, he's one of my closest friends, and he deserves better from me.

"Hey, Roman, what's up?"

A pause and then, "You okay, buddy?"

"Perfectly fine. How was your holiday?"

Instead of answering, he says, "You sound like you've got something on your mind."

"Just work stuff. New spring designs," I say, wishing he couldn't read me so well. "Listen, I was going to call you about Peyton."

"Is she okay?" he asks, real concern in his voice. I smile at that. At least my buddy has my back and worries about my kid sister as much as I do.

"Yeah, I need a favor."

"Anything for you, you know that."

"She needs a pretend husband, as insane as that sounds." The line goes quiet. Did he hang up on me? "Roman?"

"Uh, what are you talking about?"

"It's for the teaching job in Malta."

"Pretty sure I'm not your guy."

Actually, he's the perfect choice. Not only is he off women after his fiancée left him, he'd never mess with my kid sister and he'll keep a close eye on her. As Hard Wear's head web designer, he can work anywhere for a few weeks.

I'm about to explain when another call comes in.
I check the display to see that it's Peyton. Shit, she
should have been in the air by now.

"I'll call you later and explain. Peyton is calling
and I have to take it."

"Yeah, okay, buddy," he says, his voice filled with
uncertainty.

I take Peyton's call. "Hey, was your flight delayed? Do you need me to come get you?"

"Where are you?" she barks at me.

I sit up a little straighter. "What the hell, Peyton?"

"I'm at the villa and you're not here. Where are
you?"

"I'm having a drink. I'll come back right now. Is
everything okay?"

"Everything is far from okay," she says, and I'm
already halfway out the door.

"I'll be right there." I hang up and practically run
through the downtown core. I'm out of breath by
the time I open my villa door and find Peyton glaring at me.

"Are you insane?" she asks.

"Yeah, probably, why?" I ask and follow her into
the living room.

"I ran into Londyn at the airport. She was a mess."
She pokes a finger in my direction. "And you, my
brother, are an idiot."

"An idiot and insane. This is getting better and
better."

She points to the sofa, and I sit.

"Do you really think she set this all up, Cason? Do you really think she knew you were going to be at the gentleman's club and went through all this trouble to get information from you?"

"Well, I know how it sounds—"

"Here's how it sounds. She hurt you once and you were so damn certain she was going to do it again, you just jumped to that conclusion."

"Her father, the website—"

I scrub my face, and try to put the pieces together but they simply don't fit.

"Cason," Peyton says, her voice softer as she sits beside me. "Mistakes were made in the past, and that's where they need to stay. You two love each other." I open my mouth, but how can I protest. I do love her. "You have this tendency to push people out before they can push you out."

I shake my head. "Londyn said something similar, and she told me I needed to work on myself."

She gives a humorless laugh. "Don't we all."

"You say she loves me, but she walked away."

"Did you ever stop to think why?"

"Because her father…" She shakes her head and my words fall off. My heart sinks to my stomach as I think about my exchange with Londyn. Her father tricked her once, who's to say he hasn't tried to do it a second time. No way in hell did I say those things about her back in college, and when I defended myself, she agreed—she believed in me.

You didn't believe in her, dude.

I exhale, loudly as my rattled brain settles, and the truth seeps in. "She left because I didn't trust her." Hell, I wouldn't even listen to her. "She left because she saw no future if I couldn't let go of the past."

"That's right, big brother."

I swallow, the world crashing in around me. "I was cruel."

"You struck out from a place of fear. She knows that."

"I'm sure she must hate me." My throat tightens. "I screwed up and ruined everything."

"Yeah, you did. Now what are you going to do about that?"

"I should call her."

"You need to do better than that, Cason."

CHAPTER EIGHTEEN

Londyn

IT'S BEEN ONE MONTH since I've been back from Cannes, and Cason has yet to send me my belongings. Not that I care. Everything in that suitcase will simply remind me of him, and my heart is already in pieces as it is. I've been working, however. On my own designs, and while my mother calls every day begging me to make amends with my father, that forgiveness will be a long time coming. I still can't quite wrap my brain around everything that happened, or why my father wants me to fall into the role of the perfect little daughter. Image and stature are important to him, apparently, and that all comes before my happiness—before his wife's. I see now that my mother might have all the jewels and shiny things, but deep down I'm not sure she's really happy.

What I truly can't wrap my brain around though, is that the second half of Cason's payment landed in my bank account shortly after I returned home. Why would he pay me? He still thinks my father's businesses are in jeopardy, and putting those funds into my hands only helps a man who has done nothing but try to destroy Cason. I guess that just goes to show Cason is a man who is true to his word, and is full of integrity and kindness, despite what the system did to him and how it destroyed his trust in others.

I don't want his money. I reached out to Peyton about it, and she's going to talk to her brother. Sure, I could use it to set up my own business, but I'd rather do it all on my own. I can start small and build. Speaking of Peyton, she called earlier and wants to come over to talk to me. Perhaps she's going to arrange a transfer of the funds back to Cason. I'm looking forward to seeing her, although the sight is going to be painful, after the happy memories we created over the holidays.

I set my notepad on the sofa beside me, and walk around my condo. I pace restlessly as I've been doing since I returned to New York, and I peer out my window, waiting for her car to pull up in front of my building. I drop the curtain and glance at my yoga pants and T-shirt. Good Lord, I should change before she gets here. My clothes have ice cream stains on them.

A car door slams. Shoot, too late.

I run my hand over my mess of hair and walk to the door as she knocks. Her eyes open wide when she sees me.

"I don't even have to ask," she says and pulls me in

for a hug. "But you have ten minutes to get changed and comb your hair. We're going out."

I back up, and shake my head. "What are you talking about?" That's when I notice she's wearing heels and a dress, covered by a wool coat. Her diamond earrings twinkle in the light, so does her necklace. "Do you have a date?"

"Yeah, with you. Now get ready."

"I'm not going anywhere, Peyton. I have things to do."

"Like what?" She reaches out and runs her fingers over the stains on my shirt. "Finish the tub of rocky road?"

"It's not rocky road, it's salted caramel."

She laughs. "I don't care what it is, you're done moping. Yes, my brother was an idiot, and—" She blinks. "Wait, you do still love him, don't you?"

My shoulders tense and I hug myself. "Of course I do, Peyton."

"Even after all the stupid things he said to you?"

"I know where they were coming from."

"Still doesn't make it any better. But I guess what I'm asking is, if he wanted to try to work things out, you'd be open to that?"

I snort, unladylike I know, but I can't help myself. "That's not going to happen," I say.

"Well, we're still going out. You have nine minutes to get changed."

"Peyton, I—" Before I can finish my protest, she's turning me around and pushing me down the hall.

"I'll drag you out in these clothes, but once you see where we're going you'll kill me for not making you change."

"Where are we going?"

"It's a surprise."

"I don't like surprises," I say. The last surprise I faced was at the auction. Look how that turned out.

"You're going to have to trust me on this." She taps her wrist. "Clock is ticking."

"Wow, you're as pushy as your brother."

She grins at me. "Eight minutes."

"Fine." I rush around my room, and tug a cocktail dress from my closet. I slide into it and run a comb through my hair. Since it refuses to cooperate, I pin it up.

"I like it up," Peyton says from the doorway and my heart skips a beat. Cason liked it up, too.

Ugh, stop thinking about him, Londyn.

I put on a pair of earrings, and leave my face makeup-free, except for a swipe of the red lipstick Jennie gave me that night at Movida's. Great, now I'm thinking how much Cason liked it the night I put it on.

"How do I look?"

"He's going to lose his mind," she says, her voice so low I have to strain to hear it.

"What?"

"Nothing." She shakes her head. "Did you make that dress?"

"Yeah," I say and glance at myself in the full-length mirror. "Do you like it?"

"It's fantastic. I want one."

"When I get my business up and running, I'll see what I can do."

"And that lipstick, it's a great color."

"My friend gave me this. Hang on." I dig through my purse. "I picked up another tube and it would go so great with your amber hair. It's yours."

"Are you sure?"

"Yeah, you'll love it." I snort, remembering the first time I put it on and how Cason reacted. "Be careful with it, though. The color is like an aphrodisiac."

She chuckles like she doesn't believe it. "Well thanks."

I step into the hall and pull a pair of heels from the coat closet.

"You're going to kick ass in the fashion world," she says as I slide into a winter coat. The weather is a heck of a lot colder than it was in Cannes.

We head outside to her car. I stare at the people walking along the sidewalks as she drives and soon enough she pulls up to Skylight Square.

"What the…"

"It's Fashion Week," she says. "And we're going."

"I…don't have tickets."

"I guess it's a good thing I do."

I climb from the car, hardly able to believe it. "But you're not really interested in fashion, are you?" I ask.

"I like a nice dress as much as the next person," she says with a grin. "Tonight is for you, Londyn."

"I can't believe we're doing this."

Twenty minutes later we're sitting in the front row. The front row! Surrounded by other designers.

"Isn't this exciting?" Peyton asks me.

"I'm still in shock."

"You just wait," she says with a grin. "I bet you're glad I made you change, now."

I laugh. "I would have killed you."

"I know."

The first model comes onto the stage, and my pulse leaps, but as she strolls the catwalk my heart falls into my stomach. I glance at Peyton who is staring at me, a huge smile on her face. What the hell is this? Cason's way of showing me what it's like to have your ideas ripped off? I turn back to the model, taking in *my* design on her body. Another model walks onstage, and once again she's in something I sketched while I was in Cannes. My stomach coils, and if I wasn't in the front row, I'd storm out of here. But I am not about to draw any attention to myself. Tears prick my eyes and I try to hide them.

"Hey, what's wrong?" Peyton asks.

I shake my head as one more model parades up and down, and the crowd claps. Well, at least they like my designs. With my throat tight, I wait for the designer to come out, to claim his glory, but when Cason walks onstage with Luis Laurent, I nearly sink to the floor.

Peyton grabs my arm and gives it a squeeze, but I barely register the touch as Cason takes the microphone.

"Let's give it up for the designer of these beautiful garments," Cason says, and my gaze slides to Luis. But he's staring at me. In fact, both men are looking my way. Cason holds his hand out, and my entire body tightens. What is going on?

"Can we please bring Londyn Harding to the stage," he says.

Peyton stands and hauls me to my feet. She guides me onto the stage and my knees wobble.

"Cason," I whisper. "What is going on?"

Luis takes the microphone. "This lovely and talented woman is responsible for these new spring fashions. She designed them, while my team created the final versions as a surprise to her. Can we give it up for Londyn?" Everyone starts clapping and Cason puts his hand around me to hold me upright. "I would like to invite her onto my team," Luis says, and I begin to shake. Luis winks at me. "I'll give you some time to think about that."

He hands the microphone back to Cason. Cason clears his throat and his eyes are on me when he speaks into the microphone and says, "I am so happy to share your beautiful designs with the world." He glances at the crowd. "You're going to be seeing a lot from this talented woman. But right now, I'm taking her backstage, because I don't feel like sharing her with anyone right now." Laughter erupts around us as he grins at me. "I want her all to myself tonight."

Tears fall down my face. I can't believe Cason did this for me. The crowd claps, and he takes my hand and leads me to the back where the models are rushing about. Without a word, he ushers me into a private room, and closes the door.

"You're a superstar," he says. "You're going to have a ton of orders."

"I can't believe you did this. How? When?"

"I wanted to tell you how much I believe in you, but after what I said, I wasn't sure words were enough."

"This…this is unbelievable. I never expected… I can't even…"

"Londyn, I would have come to you earlier, but I took your advice."

"My advice?"

"Yeah, you told me I needed to work on myself, so I did. I did a lot of thinking." He steps up to me, and his eyes are dark, full of warmth as he takes my hands in his. "Want to know what I concluded?"

"Yes?" I say, my voice as shaky as my hands. He dips his head, his lips close to mine, and everything inside me fills with the love I have for him. My throat tightens, and my heart squeezes as I stare up at him.

"I think I'm an ogre, and an oaf. You and Peyton were right," he says in a teasing voice.

"Cason…"

His face falls, and he goes completely sober as

he pulls me in and I rest my face on his chest, his heart pounding hard against my cheek. "Seriously, Londyn, I need to you listen to me. I have to tell you what I think. What I've been thinking all along."

"Okay," I say, my knees so wobbly that if he wasn't holding me, I'm sure I'd collapse.

"You are kind, generous and caring. You have untapped talent beyond belief and it's time the world knows who you are. I believe in you, and everything you do."

"You do?"

"Of course I do. Contrary to what you think, I have never hated you, and deep down, *a part of me* wanted our time in Cannes to be about revenge, but I'm just not that guy. I'd never want to do anything to hurt you, Londyn. I was an ass for the things I said, and for not giving you a chance to explain, and I hope you can forgive me."

"You never hated me?"

"No, in fact, I never stopped loving you. I struck out without listening to you, even though you believed in me. I'm sorry. I'm so sorry, Londyn. I made a mistake."

"I made mistakes, too."

"We both did. But how about we leave them in the past, and start fresh."

A bone-deep want seeps into my soul. I step back, and his eyes go wide. He swallows, and runs his hand over his face like he always does when he's worried about something.

I sniff. "You had your say, now it's time I had mine." He takes a deep breath, like he's preparing himself for the worst. "You remember I said by the end of our two weeks I'd come up with the perfect description of you, and you were a little worried about that?" He nods, his dark eyes brimming with unease.

"I've given it a ton of thought. You're right, you are an ogre and an oaf."

He nods, and looks at the ground, his eyes dark and full of sadness. "I understand if you can't forgive me."

"But you're also the kindest, most trustworthy guy I know. Don't think for a minute that I didn't know it was you who donated to the film class." A wide grin splits his mouth, and he looks up and whistles innocently. I step back into him and put my arms around his neck. "But you know what I think the perfect description is?"

His big hands wrap around me and drag me close. "No, what?"

"Cason Harrison, my fiancé."

"Is that what you think?" he asks, his eyes full of warmth and desire.

I poke him in the chest. "It's what I know."

"It's what I know, too," he says, grinning. He arches a brow. "Do you forgive me, Londyn? Or perhaps I should say, do you forgive me, fiancée?"

"Always," I say and go up on my toes. His lips find mine, and the world shimmers around me, my heart so full of love and hope, I'm sure I'm going to burst.

"There's one matter we need to discuss," he says.

"Oh?"

"You see, you left before you fulfilled your contract, and I believe I have a few more days with you."

I grin, liking where his mind is going. "You don't think I fulfilled my end of the contract?" I ask, even though we both know I did, but I'll play along, see where he's taking this.

"That's right, and I plan on taking what's mine."

"What are you saying, Cason?"

"I think we should fly back to Cannes, where I can tie you up, and do dirty delicious things to your body."

"Is that what you think?" I ask.

He scoops me up and I yelp with joy. "It's what I know."

* * * * *

FAST DEAL

FAYE AVALON

MILLS & BOON

For Mum, who's always been partial
to a 'naughty' story.

CHAPTER ONE

A COUPLE MORE MINUTES and he'd put a stop to it.

While the woman dancing on one of the low-level tables was nowhere near indecent, the suggestive way she was moving her hips to the music signalled things could be heading that way.

Connor Fitzpatrick sat back in his chair at the rear of the bar, nursing a whisky. His lower back complained, likely due to all the late nights he'd been pulling. He should be making time for the gym rather than running herd on a group of women who, from their laughter, had undoubtedly been upping his bar profits considerably.

While that was always good, it wasn't as if either of his London clubs needed much in the way of a boost. They were going great guns. He looked around the packed club with its soft ambient lighting, deep, black leather sofas and stylish features in chrome and glass. This club had been his first and had quickly gained favour amongst the young and fashionable. That was why he had been well placed to act when providence had smiled on him and dropped the property he'd been patiently waiting to buy—and then destroy—right in his lap.

About bloody time. Now he could get closure, payback, revenge. Whatever the hell anyone chose to call it.

The deal he'd made with Damian McBride had taken some ducking and diving, but Connor had no scruples about putting on the emotional screws. Offering over the market value hadn't hurt, either, which was why Connor was only a signature away from owning the now defunct Cabacal Club, the place that symbolised the lowest point of his life.

He had no idea what he'd do with it. Maybe just gut the place, or let it fall to rack and ruin. He didn't give a fuck.

It was no skin off his balls. And he should know, since they'd already been sliced and bruised enough for one lifetime. For the past five years he'd placed his focus squarely on building his business, taking pleasure in the rapid success his clubs had brought him. Now the acquisition of the property at the heart of his near-downfall would provide the last soothing layer of balm to heal old wounds right over.

He sipped his whisky, letting it drive down the bile of memories as his gaze drifted back to the woman still making full use of the table. While he liked his patrons to enjoy themselves, this one's impromptu dance wasn't exactly the kind he encouraged. No denying she had curves, displayed as they were in tight white jeans and a sleeveless grey top that had a zipper down the front, opened to reveal some tantalising cleavage.

Still moving, the woman pushed her hands underneath her long mane of dark-blonde hair, lifting it away from her neck and letting it cascade back down over her shoulders. The way she shimmied, her body undulating in perfect time to the music, had his already alert cock throbbing against the fly of his suit pants. Shit, this was all he needed. A frigging hard-on courtesy of Ms Footloose up there.

She held her arms out to the side, gyrating in a way that reminded him of a belly dancer he'd once encountered during a pub crawl with his mates. He had very happy memories of that night, especially the one where he'd peeled away all seven layers of flimsy gauze—in private, of course—before he and said belly dancer had fucked the living hell out of each other.

He took a healthy slug of his drink as he continued to watch the current show, imagining sliding down the zipper of her top to reveal breasts perfect for his hands and mouth. Since he could see the faintest outline of nipple, he'd bet she wasn't wearing a bra. He imagined feasting on her breasts, ruthlessly licking her nipples, then slowly stripping her out of those jeans. He wondered what kind of underwear she favoured. Those skimpy, lacy deals, perhaps? Or maybe she wore none at all.

He swallowed, his fingers curling tightly around the glass as his gaze zoomed in on her ass, looking for a distinct panty line. Shit, he had a full-blown throbbing erection now. And if he did then he'd bet nearly every other guy in the place did too.

Since he prided himself on running classy establishments, he knew the time had come to call a halt. With considerable reluctance, and hoping to hell his erection wasn't visible to all and sundry, he tossed back the remainder of his drink, placed the glass on the table and stood. Instantly, one of his security men was at his side.

The man glanced over at the group of women. 'You want me to deal with this, boss?'

Connor shook his head. It didn't matter how many times he told Nigel not to call him 'boss', the man was old school, an ex-copper, and seemed to prefer formalities. 'No.' Connor let out a long exhale. 'I'm heading home anyway, so I'll sort it on my way out. Keep an eye on them, though, and if they attempt a replay or start to get rowdy call them a cab.'

Nigel tapped two fingers to his temple. 'Consider it done.'

Connor walked across to the table, hoping that the raunchy dance hadn't offended his other customers. From his brief glance around the club, most seemed to be taking the unexpected entertainment in a genial manner.

As he neared the table, the woman reached down and took off one shoe. It was one of those lethal, spiky heels that looked as if it should come with a health warning. Not that he didn't enjoy seeing them at the end of a woman's leg—sexy as hell, especially when they wore nothing else.

Encouraged by her friends, the woman started twirling around, wobbling precariously on the one remaining heel. She bent, obviously intent on removing the other shoe, but toppled and stumbled back against him.

As Connor reached out to catch her, something lanced across his neck. He inhaled sharply, his fingers reflexively digging into her waist as she fell to her knees, still holding the recalcitrant shoe.

'Oh, shit. I'm so sorry.'

Caught in the startled green of her eyes, his hands tightened around her waist, holding her steady.

'You're bleeding. I've hurt you,' she said.

He tore his gaze away from hers long enough to turn his head, the spike of her shoe dangerously close to his head. 'It's fine. Just get that thing away from me before you poke my bloody eye out.'

Using his shoulders as leverage, she swivelled around, then sat on the edge of the table and put her shoe back on. All the while she peered at his neck. 'I'm really sorry.'

Connor touched his hand to the spot she was staring at, aware of the slight sting there. He wasn't sure if that sensation was because of the wound itself, or the intensity of her study, but when he drew his fingers away they were streaked with blood.

She reached up. 'You're bleeding on your shirt collar.'

Connor stepped away from where she was about to touch his neck. 'I've bled on worse things. Don't worry about it.'

From the small bag she had strapped across her body, she pulled out a wad of tissue. 'Here, press this hard to the wound. It will staunch the bleeding.'

He found himself doing as she said. It was those hypnotic green eyes. Or more likely the concern in them.

That unsettled him. Pulled up too many memories. He'd rather she poked his eye out with that insane heel than make him remember things he'd sworn to forget.

'Thanks,' Connor said. He turned from her, intending to head to his office at the back of the club, and almost bumped into Nigel.

'Have you got a first-aid kit somewhere?' she demanded of the burly bouncer, before turning back to Connor. 'We should make sure the wound is clean and dress it properly. There's no telling what germs are on the heel of my shoe—you might be infected by something nasty.'

'I'm sure I'll survive.'

'There's a kit in the office,' Nigel said, tilting his head towards the door, and Connor could have sworn the man was battling a grin. 'It'll be fully stocked with everything you need.'

Connor narrowed his eyes, fully intending to remind Nigel of his duty of care towards his employer, especially the part about protecting him from pushy females. 'Great. Then I'll thank you both for your unwarranted concern and be on my way.'

He was almost at his office door, and trying not to think about those eyes, those curves, all that bloody hair, when he felt her behind him.

Still pressing the wad to his neck, he looked over his shoulder and raised his eyebrows. 'I'm a big boy. I can take it from here.'

She shook her head, sending those luxurious locks brushing against her shoulders and—fuck—across her breasts. 'You really should let me have a look. I'm a qualified first-aider.' She glanced towards the door, then back at him. Her eyes went wide. 'Are you the manager, or something?'

'Or something,' he said, acknowledging that her cagey look was likely due to concern that she'd be charged with bodily harm. 'Look, it's okay. No harm done. I'm not about to press charges.'

Still, she hesitated, looking from him to the door and back again before moving right past him and into his office.

Connor closed the door, watching as she took a cursory look around before heading over to the three-tiered filing cabinet in the corner. 'Is this where you keep the first-aid kit?'

Damned if he knew. 'Probably.' He walked over, unlocked the cabinet and, as he knew the first two drawers were jam-packed with business files, slid open the bottom one. His efficient assistant had placed a green box at the back of the drawer, clearly marked with the universal symbol for first-aid supplies.

Before he could reach for it, the woman bent down and grabbed it from the drawer. 'Sit,' she instructed, crossing to the desk and sliding out his black leather chair. 'Let me take a closer look.'

Connor frowned. He should tell her to get the hell out of his office, remind her that he could deal with his own bloody cut, and if he wanted to sit in his damned chair he would—he didn't need a pushy siren giving him instructions. Instead, he found himself walking to the chair and sitting like a well-trained canine. His only excuse was that the sooner he let her do her nursing stint, the sooner she would be gone. At least, that was what he told himself.

She reached out to remove the bloodied wad at the same moment he did. Their fingers brushed, hands touching. Okay, nothing wrong with a little spark of chemistry, a zing of sexual awareness. Some very definite fire in the blood, and below the waist.

The subtle snatch of her breath as they touched, the way her heated gaze held his a moment too long before dropping to his mouth, confirmed she wasn't immune to that zing. One glance at her grey top confirmed his theory. Those nipples he'd imagined licking to peak were already reflecting the very outcome he'd visualised.

Maybe he was being too hasty in his desire to be rid of her. For the past several weeks, he'd been on a rollercoaster, his attention tightly focused on a driving need to buy the Cabacal and lay to rest old ghosts. He couldn't blame his body for starting to retaliate against having its physical needs denied for too long.

From her table-dance earlier, she was definitely a party girl, probably up for some fun, and the way she was sending his hormones on this happy journey signalled she was exactly the kind of woman to break his no-sex streak. Fun-loving, easy-going, obviously in touch with her own sexuality. Add this definite mutual attraction to the mix and it boded well for a little private party of their own.

She tossed the tissue into the waste bin, then she placed her hands on her knees and bent to peer at the wound with an intensity reserved for someone inspecting a new kind of species.

When she reached for the first-aid box she'd placed on the desk, Connor couldn't resist a quick glance down her top.

Nice, he thought, as his extremely interested cock responded with appropriate pleasure. He averted his gaze as she turned back. Instinct had him folding his hands in his lap in a bid to hide the evidence, but he was too late. Her eyes dropped to his hands before she returned her attention to his neck. 'You don't have to hide that,' she teased, dabbing the cut with a cotton ball. 'Was my dance responsible? Or just the fact I'm wearing a low-cut top?'

He liked her directness. Liked that she didn't seem at all interested in playing games, or pretending there wasn't a massive flood of pheromones renting the air between them. Appearances could be deceptive, of course, but it was refreshing to find a woman who seemed straightforward and down-to-earth.

Her directness warranted some of his own. 'It started with the dance, then you bent over the filing cabinet and then you bent over me. What's a man to do?'

She smiled, still dabbing. 'Can't blame you, I suppose. Men are such basic creatures.'

'Come on.' He winced as she touched a sore spot. 'You're not telling me your intention wasn't to get the men out there fired up?'

Not a hint of insult showed on her face, feigned or otherwise, nor in her actions. He liked that too. 'Why should it always be a woman's intention to turn on a man? Can't she simply enjoy moving her body for her own pleasure?'

'Fair enough, but why choose a crowded club to do it?' He waited until she looked at him. 'Or do you always like an audience when you give yourself pleasure?'

Tiny spears of colour bloomed in her cheeks, and she caught her bottom lip between her teeth. He enjoyed watching that spectacular mouth, maybe even more than the fact he'd managed to set her back a step.

His enjoyment was short-lived when she reached out to the box again. 'If you're trying to shock me, you'll have to do much better than that.' She undid the cap of a bottle with blue liquid and poured some onto a fresh cotton ball.

He grinned. 'You didn't actually answer my question.'

With a sexy pout that had his erection throbbing beneath his hands, she held the now doused cotton ball aloft and considered. 'Do I like an audience when I give myself pleasure? Hmm. Well, to be honest I usually do that in private. For my eyes only.'

She jerked down the collar of his open-necked shirt, smiled sweetly at him then stabbed him with the fire of hell. He shot back in his seat and grimaced. 'Whatever kind of bloody healing balm is that?'

All innocence and patience, she continued to administer to his neck, earning from him several more sharp intakes of breath as she worked. 'Men are such babies. And here I was thinking you were a grown man.'

'I'm man enough, sweetheart, with all the parts to prove it.' Suddenly irritated, both by the sting from that bloody liquid and the image of her pleasuring herself without him being there to see it, he reached up and curled his fingers around her wrist. 'I reckon I'm cleaned up well enough by now.'

She glanced down at his hand before bringing her gaze back to his. 'Are you allergic to plasters?'

'No.' Even if he were, he'd suffer through it if it meant getting this torture over with. Not just suffering at the hands of her less than gentle nursing techniques, or the growing temptation of sampling her very appealing attributes. It was also the way it made him wonder when a woman had shown this much concern for his welfare, if ever.

The sting of that liquid had not only cleaned the cut but had shaken him back to reality. Yeah, okay, he wanted her. He *really* wanted her. But the timing sucked. His priority was getting home, grabbing some long overdue sleep, checking final figures and documentation, then preparing himself for the six a.m. conference call with Damian McBride.

Normally, Connor would take his chances. What was one more sleepless night? Especially if he had the opportunity to share a bed with a hot woman. But he couldn't afford to take any chances with tomorrow's meeting. It was too important to him. He'd waited too long. He had every intention of making Damian draw up that contract pronto so they could both sign on the dotted line.

Which meant he had to call a halt to this extremely pleasant interlude and get his ass back home. He sucked in a breath. 'Won't your friends be wondering where you are?'

'They know where I am. They would have seen me come back here with you. If I'm not out in a reasonable amount of time, they'll call the cops.'

He realised he still had hold of her wrist, noticed how his hand fitted easily around the circumference of all that soft flesh. With considerable reluctance, he released her. Shit, but he really wanted to seduce his dancing queen, find out if all that bared skin was as silky as it looked. Let his hands slide easily over those sexy dips and curves as he kissed her full lips and drove them both insane.

'Well, stick the plaster on, and maybe you should go back and join them. I'd just as soon not have the cops banging on my door, if it's all the same to you.'

She laughed, took off the protective wrapping of the plaster then bent down to place it on his neck. He deliberately kept his gaze averted as she moved closer to smooth the plaster down at the edges, but her scent washed over him. Floral and earthy at the same time. Feminine and sultry. He wanted to draw her close, breathe her in.

Luckily, she straightened. 'There. Good as new.'

He was tempted to tease her, ask if she thought he'd be left with a scar. But, as he figured he had enough of those already, he declined. Some things weren't easy to joke about.

Since he didn't intend delving any deeper into that aspect of his past right then, he pushed such thoughts away and kept his focus trained on her.

He made a long, slow perusal of her as she stood there staring at his neck. Her tank top had ridden up, revealing a creamy strip of flesh around her midriff, causing saliva to pool in his mouth. And, maybe it was his imagination but the atmosphere was hot and enticingly tempting.

In the grand scheme of things, who said a man needed eight solid hours sleep anyway? He'd existed on far less than that during his thirty years on the planet and, while tomorrow's stakes had never been this high for him, there wasn't much that could go wrong. The negotiations had been undertaken, the sums agreed.

In which case…

Connor eyed her up and down, making sure she couldn't mistake his intention. No point wasting valuable time with unnecessary rituals and peripherals, like pretending they both weren't interested in each other.

'Since you've taken such good care of me, why don't I buy you a drink?'

'A minute ago, you were trying to get rid of me.'

Yeah. And he would wonder for ever what particular brain malfunction had brought about that insane notion. There was being cautious and there was being a complete dickhead. What man with his head on straight denied himself a quick roll in the hay with a hot and willing woman?

'I was just making sure we were thinking along the same lines.'

'Which are?'

'You. Me. A bottle of whatever is your pleasure.' She bit her bottom lip again and he could see cogs turning, wheels spinning. Determined to get her agreement, he tapped a finger to the plaster and pursed his lips in a pitiful manner. 'You can't surely be considering abandoning me so soon? I might start bleeding again.'

She laughed, a deep rumble of sound that shot fresh heat through his blood and promised extremely good times ahead. He leaned forward and reached out to take her hand, noticing how her fingers stiffened momentarily beneath his before relaxing. Not wanting to push things too hard too fast, he let go of her. 'Why don't you go and tell your friends you won't be needing the cops?'

She raised her eyebrows, amusement evident in her eyes. 'That might be a little premature.' She replaced the lid of the first-aid box. 'But say I agreed to one drink, I've got a feeling you wouldn't be satisfied with that. Am I right?'

He knew instinctively that he needed to change tactics, maybe back off a little. Despite that she seemed to be matching him in the verbal banter stakes, it was hard to deny her tentative manner as she'd asked him what his intentions were. He hoped to hell he wasn't making her uncomfortable.

Not that she'd appreciate any kind of subterfuge either.

Straight-shooter, he reminded himself. She didn't play games. 'Look, let me tell you where I stand. I think we've got this mutual thing going. I'd like to buy you a drink and see where it leads. If it leads us beyond that drink, then I'll be an extremely happy man.'

Her breasts hiked as she sucked in a breath. While he hadn't shocked her, he'd pushed her off-balance. He kind of liked that. There was a certain satisfaction

in unbalancing a confident woman. From nowhere
came the unsettling thought that right then he was
almost as desperate to get her affirmative response
as he was that contract from Damian McBride. What
the hell was that about? Perhaps he really had been
without female company for too long.

She didn't respond but kept eyeing him as if she
was trying to figure him out. He chanced an easy
smile. When she screwed up that delicious mouth, he
held his breath, willing her not to back out now. Not
when he had images of her doing incredible things
with that mouth.

Slowly, she picked up the box and took it back to
the cabinet where she bent and slid it into the lower
drawer. His throat went dry at the sight of her perfect ass in those tight-fitting white jeans.

She closed the drawer and stood. Her back went
ramrod straight as she looked at the captioned photograph on the top of the filing cabinet. The one taken
when he'd received an industry award last year.

He walked over to stand next to her, making sure
not to crowd her.

'Look, I think you're a woman who likes to call
it straight and, since we both know there's a strong
physical thing going on here, why waste time pretending otherwise?'

She continued to look at the photograph, then took
another deep breath and turned to look up at him,
making his pulse kick like a frigging donkey.

After a brief hesitation, she placed her palm

against his chest, and he swore her guarded eyes went a darker green. 'I do like straight talking, but I also like to think around things.'

'Then start thinking.' He winked, smiled. 'Make it fast.'

Another hesitation, then she laughed. Shit. He really liked that laugh, the way she paused before she got the joke and then the laugh bubbled from deep in her throat.

'Trust me, as much as I'm tempted, it's not a good idea. For a variety of reasons.'

'Name one.'

She blinked, as if she hadn't expected the question. 'Well, we don't know each other. Like you said, the response is physical.'

What the fuck was wrong with that? 'Physical responses can be the best ones,' he said with a waggle of his eyebrows. 'Less chance things get complicated.'

She laughed again, her eyes meeting his for long moments. It made him wonder if she was enjoying their flirtatious banter as much as he was but was determined to hold back, to fight against their obvious attraction. 'You may be right about that.' Her smile was a little wistful as she reached up to tap the plaster. 'Make sure to keep that on for a while.'

What the hell did that mean? Was she giving him the old heave-ho? He wasn't prepared to let her walk away that easily.

Maybe he really had come on too strong. She

said one of the reasons this was a bad idea was because they didn't know each other. Well, that he
could remedy.

'So, about that drink.'

She was at the door, her back to him and with her
fingers wrapped around the handle. For what seemed
like an age during which Connor held his breath, she
stood there, no doubt taking her time to deliberate.

Then she turned to look over her shoulder at him.
'I'll meet you at the bar.'

CHAPTER TWO

LOLA MCBRIDE TUGGED DOWN the edge of her top so that it covered her midriff and perched on a stool at the bar. Her friends were over on the small dance floor, having fun, but Lola needed a few minutes. Away from Connor Fitzpatrick's hormone-inducing presence, she was able to think again, to breathe again.

She still hadn't recovered from seeing that photograph of him on top of the filing cabinet, and the caption declaring Connor Fitzpatrick an entrepreneur to watch. Finding out *he* was the owner of the club and not just the manager had taken the wind right out of her sails. She'd imagined someone older, embittered, hardened, somehow. And while the man she'd just spoken to wasn't one you'd want to mess with—the hint of steel in his grey eyes alluded to that—he'd been kind of playful, flirty and...sexy.

She hadn't factored in the possibility that Connor Fitzpatrick would be insanely gorgeous and that they'd share an intense and instant sexual attraction.

What the devil had she been thinking, flirting with him right back, egging him on?

That was most definitely not part of her plan.

She'd expected to come here, suss out the joint and in the process have a little post-graduation fun with her friends. It never hurt to check things out, nor did it hurt to size up the man who would play a vital part in her achieving her goal.

But meeting him tonight and being attracted to him hadn't remotely figured in her plans. How was it that one glimpse of him had heated her blood and shot lurid little messages to every one of her nerve endings?

Lola tapped her fingers on the bar. Think… She had to think.

Damian would be in Singapore for another couple of weeks, plenty of time for her to get Connor's agreement to her plan before her brother got wind of it. If Damian found out, he would stymie it in the same way he'd stymied all her attempts to get the Cabacal property back. Her brother hadn't even done her the courtesy of looking at her business plan. He had just flat-out told her it wasn't a viable proposition, that the competition was fierce and that it would likely fold sooner rather than later. He'd told her to put her first-class business degree to better use than some airy-fairy notion of running a fitness studio.

The fact Damian had actually used 'airy fairy' in relation to her long-held dream had incensed Lola more than anything—perhaps even more than hav-

ing to fulfil the requirements of her trust fund. She'd
achieved the business degree and post-graduate qual-
ification demanded by her late father, yet she still
wasn't able to run her own show until her twenty-
fifth birthday.

Despite pleading with Damian to hold off putting
the property on the market for six months, until she
would be in a position to buy it for her studio, he'd
gone right ahead and entered into negotiations with
Connor Fitzpatrick.

Connor was owed, Damian had said. It was poetic
justice that the property should be his. Lola knew
that Connor had worked for her late uncle as manager of the Cabacal, and that he had been a victim
of her uncle's treachery as much as her mother had
been. All that aside, she didn't think Connor had as
much right to the property as she did. Built by Lola's
maternal great-grandfather for his beloved wife, the
Cabacal had been handed down the female line of
the family, right until her mother had been cheated
out of it by her only brother, Lola's uncle.

Now Lola had made it her mission to get the property back where it belonged.

While she appreciated the tenacity that Connor
had shown in outbidding two other serious buyers, it
didn't make things easy for her. So, denied using the
front door to achieve her goals, she had no option but
to go around the back. That meant ensuring that, if
Connor bought the property, she could convince him
to sell it to her as soon as she had the money from

her trust fund. She'd need to show him that her need to own the property was greater than his.

It was a long shot, of course, but she could hopefully sweeten the pot with an excellent financial incentive. Whatever it took, she was going to get her late mother's inheritance back, and in doing so would right a cruel wrong, rebalance the books and put the universe back on its axis.

She'd come close to jeopardising her plans by falling into lust with Connor, but how in heaven was a girl supposed to resist those eyes, or the way his dark hair brushed against his very kissable neck? Not to mention the impressive width of his shoulders, or the breadth of a quite spectacular chest.

Tempted to break her non-drinker status, she eyed the cocktail one of the bartenders was currently making and wondered if she should order one.

Despite her spontaneous dance routine—thanks to an equally spontaneous game of truth or dare—she hated the nightclub scene. It was in total contrast to what she loved. Keeping fit, active, healthy. Eating the right foods, nurturing her body, making sure she treated it so that it would serve her well.

During her enforced academic studies she'd moonlighted as a fitness instructor, taking part-time courses in health and wellbeing and massage therapy, eventually qualifying as a yoga instructor.

It had been her mother's dream. Now it was hers.

Deep in thought, Lola sensed a ripple of something around her and became aware of Connor a moment before he slid onto the stool next to hers. Her whole body responded sensually as his scent and his aura washed over her. 'What's your poison?'

As if by magic, a bartender morphed before their very eyes and was waiting expectantly. 'Virgin mojito, please.' When Connor raised his eyebrows, she shrugged. 'I'm not a fan of alcohol.'

As the bartender went off to fill the order for their drinks, Connor swivelled his stool towards her. 'You said there were a variety of reasons this was a bad idea,' he said, leaning his forearm on the bar. 'The first was that we don't know each other. What's the second?'

Distracted by the brush of his thigh against hers as he swivelled towards her, Lola swallowed. She didn't want to feel his muscular strength against her legs, notice the way his shirt collar flirted with his amazing neck or glimpse the light sprinkling of dark hair escaping the V of his opened shirt.

'I don't do one-night stands.'

She blurted it out, as much for her own benefit as his. If she kept that particular mantra at the front of her mind, she might just make it through this conversation without making a grab for that shirt opening and hauling him against her for a blistering kiss.

He raised his eyebrows. 'Sometimes it pays to broaden your horizons.'

Not right then, it didn't, Lola thought with a degree of desperation, trying hard to keep hold of her withering resolve. Thankfully, their drinks arrived, and Lola took a healthy swig of hers. Her body was doing the most incredible things. Her breasts felt so tender they actually tingled, and her nipples were hard buds scraping against the fabric of her top. As for between her legs…well, talk about achy and throbbing.

She glanced to where Connor's fingers leisurely stroked his glass, unable to keep from imagining just what kind of damage those fingers could inflict on her. If just the thought of that could turn her on, what would the reality do?

Okay, men had turned her on before, and a couple had turned into lovers. Neither one of them had made her body feel as if it was being twisted inside out.

'Why don't we backtrack here?' Connor said after taking a swig of his beer. 'What's your name?'

Lola couldn't think of any reason why she couldn't tell him. If by the slimmest possibility Damian had mentioned her to Connor, he would have referred to her as Louise, and not by her nickname.

Even so, she kept a careful watch for any hint of recognition. 'It's Lola.'

He gave a slow nod. 'Sexy. Like you.'

Remembering that she wasn't supposed to know his name, she raised her eyebrows. 'And you?'

'Connor,' he said, and held out his hand. 'Good to meet you, Lola.'

She slipped her hand into his and felt a definite punch of reaction from her breasts to her core.

Still playing along with the pretense that she had

no idea who he was, Lola sipped her drink again. 'So, this is your place? You're the owner?'

'Yeah,' he said matter-of-factly, but there was caution in his eyes. 'Is that a problem?'

Lola shrugged. 'Of course not. You must be quite the entrepreneur, though. The location alone makes this place a prime piece of real estate.'

His expression morphed from caution to amusement. 'What are you? An estate agent?'

With a smile, she shook her head. 'Just been doing some research. I'm planning to start my own business.'

He took another drink of beer. 'What kind of business?'

It was on her lips to tell him, but this question put her on shakier ground. Damian might have let it slip that his sister wanted the Cabacal property with the view to opening a health studio, but she couldn't imagine that was really a possibility, seeing as her brother barely acknowledged her dream. Still, it didn't hurt to be circumspect. She didn't want Connor putting two and two together, at least not until she'd had the chance to figure out his plans.

He leaned forward, obviously sensing her hesitation. 'Come on, it's only fair. Tit for tat. You know I own this place.'

She huffed. 'That didn't take much working out. You might not have *owner* emblazoned on the door of your office, but I would have guessed from the way your security chap sprang to attention when I scratched you, or the way the bartender popped up from nowhere as soon as you appeared, even when I'd already been waiting a full five minutes to be served.'

His eyebrows drew together. 'You'd been waiting that long?'

Realising how that sounded, she waved her hand in dismissal. 'A figure of speech. I was just making a point.'

'Even so...' He turned towards the bartender. 'He'll have to go.'

'No.' Lola reached out and grabbed Connor's wrist. 'He's lovely, and he's rushed off his feet, just like the rest of your bar staff.'

She drew back with a frown when Connor turned towards her with a grin. Releasing her hand from his wrist, she gave him a haughty look. 'Funny.'

He kept his gaze on hers. 'And it was hardly a scratch.'

'What was?'

With a mock-pitiful expression, he stroked his thumb across the plaster on his neck.

Lola laughed. She really liked his quick humour. 'Oh, for pity's sake.'

He leaned forward, serious again. 'Speaking of pity, are you going to put me out of my misery, Lola?'

Her stomach clenched along with her inner thighs. 'Don't do one-nighters, remember?'

'That was when we didn't know each other.'

She willed her hands not to tremble as she reached

for her drink and sipped the soothing liquid. 'You think knowing each other's names takes care of that?'

'We've shared a whole lot more.' He slid his hand across to where she held her glass and lightly stroked his fingers over hers. 'I know you're a qualified first-aider. That you care about my bartender keeping his job. That you're probably the only woman I've ever met who can do an erotic dance on a nightclub table without the aid of alcohol.' His eyes narrowed slightly, the grey darkening as he looked at her. 'And I know that you're sexy as fuck.'

She kept her focus on his hand, that slow, sensual slide of his fingers over hers. Hell, but she really wanted to know how it would feel to have those fingers toying with other parts of her body. Like her nipples, her breasts, her sex...

She drew her hand away from his intoxicating touch. 'None of which qualifies as an in-depth getting-to-know-you session.'

He winked. 'It's a great start.'

This really wasn't a good idea. It could badly affect her plans. What if they had sex and it all went wrong? Even if it didn't, how would he react when he knew who she was and what she wanted? It was already getting messy. If she told him now, he'd feel manipulated. How much worse would it be if they had sex and then she told him?

She knew of his history with her uncle—knew he'd been cleared of the embezzlement charges brought against him five years ago. Even though she had long since severed all ties with that side of the family, no doubt Connor would react unfavourably to her when he learned of the connection. She'd planned to reveal her identity alongside an explanation of what had happened to her mother, hoping that Connor would see some parallel with his own situation and be sympathetic to her plans to get the Cabacal back.

But things had taken an unexpected turn with this insanely inappropriate attraction between them.

She looked down, already regretting that she couldn't let this go any further. 'If things were different, I'd be on the same page as you.'

'I think we're already on the same page...about a lot of things.'

The way he said it put her on alert. Did he already know who she was? Had Damian spoken to him about her, warned him she might try something like this? Since she'd been deliberately cagey about her plans, she couldn't see that was likely.

Her stomach slid uncomfortably as she met his eyes. 'What things?'

He grinned. 'Aside from the extremely pleasant sexual attraction we have going? Looks like we're both actively looking to acquire property.'

This was the perfect place to just blurt everything out and hope that he'd understand. Except something stopped her. If she found out a little more about his reasons for acquiring the property, and what he intended to use it for, she might have a better under-

standing of how to set about convincing him that
her reasons were more justified. Knowledge was
power, right?

Watching him closely, she raised her glass to her
lips. 'Are you expanding your business?'

His casual shrug was in opposition to the dark
flash in his eyes. 'Haven't decided yet.'

'Then why are you acquiring property?'

There was a definite change in his demeanour
now. No trace of the easy charm, or the sexy glint
in his eye. 'Fate dropped an opportunity in my lap.
A property became available that I've wanted for a
while.'

'For another nightclub?'

'Like I said, haven't decided.' He twisted his
glass, round and round, seemingly mesmerised by
the movement…and maybe old, painful memories.
Then he gave another casual shrug, as if to toss those
old memories aside. 'There's no rush to do anything
with it. It's been empty for a few years.'

An optimistic band of hope settled around Lola's
heart. If he had no direct plans for the building and
would allow it to remain empty for the foreseeable future, then surely it wouldn't be too much of a wrench
for him to sell it on to her when the time came?

'We've gone off-course,' he said, his mood changing back to its easy, flirty style. 'Why would I want
to talk bricks and mortar when I'm in the company
of a beautiful woman?'

'Are you saying that women can't talk bricks and mortar?' she challenged. 'That we can't talk business?'

He held up his hands. 'Nope. Not saying that. Some of the hardest negotiators I've dealt with are women.'

She sensed he meant that and wasn't just tossing her a line. 'I'm pleased to hear it.'

He lowered his hands, grinning. 'All I'm saying is that I'd like to negotiate something else entirely right now.'

She laughed and tucked hair behind her ear. 'You're just too predictable.'

'I can live happily in that knowledge, especially if it gets my hands on you.'

The feeling of wanting his hands on her, of wanting hers on him, was almost overwhelming. She knew that Connor would be a fabulous lover.

No doubt his innate confidence would extend to the sack, making what they shared powerful and explosive. She was drawn to that confidence, to his easy wit, his ability to tease without seeming to belittle.

She chose that moment to glance over Connor's shoulder and caught the crazy butt-wiggles and thumbs-up signs her friends were giving her from across the bar. When she looked back at Connor's ruggedly handsome face, and the dark seduction in his eyes, she felt like doing some butt-wiggling herself. Except she couldn't. He was way out of bounds.

Of her friends, only her flatmate Emily knew her

plans, knew the history behind them. Lola looked over at Emily now, saw the concern in her friend's smile and gave a subtle shake of her head. She looked back at Connor. 'I'll just be a minute.'

As she swivelled on the stool, he leaned forward. 'Don't break my heart and dump me before you've even given me a chance.'

She laughed at his puppy-dog expression and stood. 'I just need to…' She pointed towards the cloakrooms. 'I'll be back. Even if it's only to tell you that we're no longer on the same page.'

He slapped a hand to his chest, and Lola laughed again, heading to the ladies' room as Emily did the same.

Emily didn't waste any time as they walked through the door together. 'I've been talking to Nigel and he told me that's Connor Fitzpatrick. Did you know? Have you told him who you are?'

'Yeah, that's him, and no, I didn't tell him. Couldn't find the words. I did have a hairy moment when I thought he might already know, but since he hasn't told me to piss off I'm pretty certain he doesn't.'

'He didn't look much like he was planning to tell you to piss off.' Emily nudged Lola's elbow. 'More like he was planning to rip your panties off and have you right there on his bar.'

'Bloody hell. Don't put that image in my head. I'm trying to contain myself as it is.'

'If he were anyone else, I'd say go for it. I mean,

hot dude, nightclub owner, single, probably got all his own teeth.' Emily slicked on fresh lip gloss and looked at Lola in the mirror. 'You know I'm worried.'

'There's no need. All I'm doing is trying to buy a property. If my stupid brother wasn't such a prick, he'd let me buy it straight from the estate and then I could go ahead with my plans and have guilt-free sex with Connor Fitzpatrick. It would be a win-win.'

'You know what I think. That you should just walk away from everything and start fresh.' Emily sighed and shrugged. 'But then you wouldn't get the property or the sex.'

'I can't do that, Em. I need the Cabacal back.'

Emily tucked her lip gloss in her bag and turned so that her back was to the counter. 'We never factored in you fancying the guy. This makes it ultra-complicated. You really should just walk away and think of another way to get what you want.'

'I know.' Somewhere between leaving Connor and entering the cloakroom, Lola had grasped just how crazy an idea this was. Not just having sex with Connor but asking him to let her have the property. 'I'm going to head home and rethink all of this. Find another way.'

'Good. Look, the others are going to party for a while longer, by the looks of things, so why don't I come home too and we can hash things out?'

'No. You stay. Enjoy yourself. I'll get a taxi back.'

Lola usually appreciated her friend's input when she was working around a problem. But tonight she

wanted some alone time to think of another way to
make her plans come to fruition after her interaction
with sexy Connor Fitzpatrick. After that, some sol-
itary self-pleasuring while watching late-night-TV
porn was on the cards.

Lola checked her watch. 'First thing tomorrow,
I'm going to call Damian, put on the emotional
screws if I have to. I'm going to make him read my
business plan, look at my projections and convince
him that I'm deadly serious about doing this. He can't
refuse me. I won't let him. If I need to, I'll get lawyers involved, prove that our mother was cheated out
of that property. If nothing else, it will delay the sale
for a while. Maybe even for six months.'

Lola felt distinctively nauseous at the prospect of
going head to head with her stubborn brother again,
but her determination didn't waver. It was a hellishly
long shot, but Lola was prepared to take it.

She said her goodbyes to Emily and, since she
didn't want to see Connor again, headed straight for
the exit.

Hopefully, she wouldn't have to wait too long for
a taxi. She had new plans to formulate…and a date
with a silver bullet vibrator.

CHAPTER THREE

THE DOORMAN SET ABOUT hailing her a taxi, although at this time of night Lola knew she might have to wait a while. She shivered as the cool air brushed over her bare arms, but the chill did nothing to diminish the heat still burning inside her, and the smoulder of desire for the man with gun-metal-grey eyes and deep, gravelly voice.

Lola shivered again, but this time it had nothing to do with forgetting to collect her jacket before she'd left the club. It had everything to do with her fevered thoughts about one incredibly sexy club owner.

She shot off a quick text to Emily asking her to grab her jacket, and almost dropped her phone when the voice came from behind.

'So, you decided to dump me after all.'

His voice rippled along her spine, setting all her nerve endings alight. She turned, meeting his equally powerful gaze. 'Yeah, well. I decided we'd slipped off the same page after all.'

Bloody hell. How was she supposed to resist him when he moved up this close to her, when she had to look up several inches even while wearing these treacherous heels?

In the relative safety of the ladies' room, with her bestie giving her support, deciding to leave him behind had seemed easier—the right decision. Now, with him here while she gazed into those gorgeous eyes, she was so damn sunk.

'That's a pity,' he said, sliding his hands into his trouser pockets. 'And just when I'd decided to go all out to seduce you with my winning ways.'

Okay, he was teasing her, but she really wished he was being serious. She wanted him to pull out all the stops. Not that he'd have to try too hard. She was already ninety-nine percent seduced, and it was only a pesky one percent that kept her from throwing caution to the wind.

'Can't have that,' she said, trying to bite back a smile. He didn't need any more encouragement. 'I wouldn't want to be responsible for robbing women of one more bad boy trying to make good.'

'It's true, then? Women really do like bad boys?'

'Of course. But then you already know that. Hence the dirty sparkle in your eye.'

He grinned. 'That dirty sparkle is all for you, sweetheart.'

If Lola had thought her blood was burning hot, it damn near raced through her in a fiery inferno now. 'I'm not really one for bad boys.'

'I'd have thought women who dance on tables don't want any other kind.'

With immense effort, Lola turned her attention back to the road, hoping the doorman would succeed in getting a taxi pronto and save her from herself. 'Don't believe all you see. My friends were all feeling punch-drunk at having been released from the shackles of university life, and they reminded me of a promise I made three years ago when I said that as soon as I graduated I'd be so happy that I'd dance on a table. What you saw was a woman letting her hair down after having it pulled up tight for too long.'

Bloody hell. Why had she told him that? What was it about him that made her spill so easily?

He tugged gently on the ends of her hair. 'Looks like it's well and truly down to me.'

'Yeah, well, looks can be deceiving.'

'Not with you. It's one of the reasons I'm attracted. You tell it like it is. No bullshitting.'

Guilt rippled along her spine and her heart gave one solid, culpable thump. 'I can bullshit with the best of them when I need to.'

'Nope. It's not your style, and believe me, I can tell.'

The feeling intensified. 'Maybe you don't know women as well as you think.'

A guarded look came into his eyes, then it was gone as he moved closer. 'I reckon I know you. You're a woman who knows what she wants. And, from experience, I know women who set their mind on something tend to get it.'

Lola was too busy basking in the compliment to concern herself with the damning truth of what he'd said.

She had waited the best part of her life to have someone—anyone—imply that she was strong-willed enough to make her own decisions, to choose what was best for her. She supposed that was what happened when you were raised by a headstrong father and an even more headstrong older brother.

Yet here was Connor, actually giving her the one thing she'd wanted for ever. An acknowledgement that she was not only capable of knowing what she wanted but was resolute enough to carry through with her plans.

It warmed her right through, heightened her confidence and solidified her determination to call Damian tomorrow morning and get him to sell the Cabacal direct to her. If Connor could see how competent and determined she was, surely she could convince Damian. She felt a little bad she'd be going behind Connor's back, but he didn't seem too interested in doing anything specific with the place.

Besides, all was fair in love and property acquisition, right?

There was another bonus, too. By persuading Damian to let her purchase the property, it meant Connor Fitzpatrick wouldn't be an obstacle. Which meant her reasons for keeping him at arm's length were null and void. Was there a reason to deny them both the pleasure of enjoying each other any longer?

Just like that, she felt her earlier resolve not to indulge in a one-night stand crumble. If she was ever
going to break that rule, then this was certainly the
time to do so. She couldn't imagine a man more
likely to give her a good time than Connor.

She eyed him—that glorious neck, the wide, muscular chest and those powerful thighs. She thought of
how Connor's thighs had brushed against her knees
while they had chatted at the bar, imagined how
amazing it would be to feel his legs tangled with
hers when they were both naked.

She took a deep breath as a taxi pulled up to the
kerb and leaned down to give the driver instructions
before turning back to Connor. 'There's a hotel near
my place with a pretty decent lounge and excellent
bar service. We could share a nightcap.'

The lights from the club entrance caught the glint
in his eyes. 'My place has the same. I've also got a
great view.'

She returned his smile. 'I'd really love to see it.'

Connor gave the driver fresh instructions then slid
into the taxi beside Lola. He was tempted to throw
whatever money he had in his wallet at the poor man
and order him to put his foot down on the pedal. On
arrival, he'd simply haul Lola from the car, toss her
over his shoulder and head up to the penthouse.

But something niggled.

What had changed her mind? She'd been happy
to dump him, to leave his club without telling him

why. She'd even given him a categorical no when he'd propositioned her.

Even as he cursed himself, he knew he wouldn't rest unless he understood the reasons for her change of heart. He was not usually one to look a freaking gift horse in the mouth, but past experience had made him wary. He had to know, had to make sure she wasn't playing him.

He'd been played before, and look how that had ended. At first Caroline had seemed like the perfect woman: beautiful, accomplished, loving, attentive. The daughter of his mentor, the man who had given him his first big opportunity in the world of business. Little had Connor known, when he'd accepted the manager position at their family's flagship casino, that he'd basically set himself up for the ultimate fall. He'd remained blissfully unaware of Caroline's ulterior motives, her desire to manipulate and use him. It wasn't until the police had come calling that Connor had realised he'd been set up, not just by his mentor, but by the woman he'd thought he loved.

Since then he'd been wary of history repeating itself, which was why he rarely got involved with women beyond easy, brief, sex-only deals. So, despite the fact that his body thrummed with the need to get his hands on Lola, he made himself sit back as the cab driver negotiated the busy late-night traffic. 'One question.'

Surprise lit her face. 'Okay.'

'What's with the about turn? No one-night stands, remember?'

Lola hiked up one shoulder. 'Can't a girl change her mind?'

'In my experience, if a woman changes her mind it usually ends up biting the man in the ass.'

She laughed, but there was an edge to it. 'Like I said before, I like to think my way around things. That's what I've been doing, and now what I want has changed.'

He had a feeling they weren't just talking about sex, but since they'd arrived at his place he shelved the conversation for now. From the throbbing in his pants, he had more urgent things with which to concern himself.

This was only a one-nighter, but it didn't mean he wouldn't keep his wits about him.

As soon as the taxi drew to a halt, Connor stepped out and went around to hold the door for Lola. He paid the driver, vaguely registering the man's thanks for the generous tip. He turned to Lola. Although he resisted hauling her over his shoulder, he couldn't stop from reaching for her hand. Her fingers curled tightly around his, and he pulled her to his side. Her generous lips slid into a smile and she looked up at him with eyes filled with temptation.

He managed to pull his gaze from hers long enough to jab the code into the security panel of the foyer door, then he hurried her through the marble-floored entrance hall and towards the bank of lifts.

While they waited, she pulled gently at the edges of his plaster with her free hand. 'That's dried up already. You must heal fast.'

He needed a moment to get his thoughts straight, as he was totally focused on the arrival of the damn lift and getting her up to his place pronto. 'It'll take more than a four-inch heel to put me down.'

She made a low, smoky sound in her throat that did interesting things to his rapidly escalating libido. 'How about six-inch ones?'

The vision of her wearing even higher heels made his abs clench. 'On you? That would not only put me down, it'd knock me clean out.'

'Have you got a shoe fetish?'

'Don't give a rat's ass about shoes, only the legs they accentuate.' Deliberately, he kept his gaze locked on hers. 'Especially yours.'

'A leg man, then.'

Still he kept his eyes on hers. 'Legs, breasts, ass and pretty much everything between. I'm not particular.'

Again, that laugh. He was tempted to ditch waiting for the lift and negotiate the twenty floors up to his apartment on foot.

'I don't believe that for a moment,' she said with a tilt of her head. 'I have a feeling you're very particular.'

He reached out and touched the ends of her hair that were so damned close to her breasts and those hard nipples poking through her top, which he *really* wanted to touch. 'What about you? Chest? Pecs? Butt?'

'My favoured attribute depends on the man.'

He stabbed at the lift button again, his chest tightening with the need to get his hands on her. 'How so?'

'Well, I like some men for their bodies. Others for their intellect. Others still for their ability to make me laugh.'

After a quick mental tot, he grinned. 'Never had any complaints about my body,' he said waggling his eyebrows. 'And, while I can't split the atom, I can hold my own in most conversations. As for making you laugh? I've heard that dirty laugh of yours enough times to know I score high in that regard.'

She gave him another sample of said dirty laugh. 'Okay, three strikes and you're not out.' She eyed him wryly. 'Yet.'

'Is there another set of manly attributes on your list?'

'Can't think of any straight off. Of course, there's sex. The whole "satisfying a woman in bed" thing.'

Connor swallowed. Yeah. He really liked the way she shot straight. 'That would make it four strikes, and still I'm not out.'

She huffed. 'You've got a healthy enough ego, I'll give you that.'

'No point indulging in false modesty. From what I've been told, I seem to have an uncanny ability to make a woman happy between the sheets.'

She took in a breath and let it out on a less than steady sigh. 'Ah, theory. Or maybe just hearsay. Me?

I like evidential proof. I've always been a practical girl.'

He glanced down at her cleavage. Hard not to when her breasts were moving up and down as her breathing rate increased. 'I'll bet.'

His own breathing was unsteady and, had his cock not been restrained by his trousers, it would have joined in the fun. As it was, it pressed painfully against his zipper.

He resisted a muttered expletive as he stabbed the lift button yet again, his legs almost sagging with relief when the doors pinged open.

He took Lola into the small space and, unable to resist any longer, pushed her against the far wall, then placed his hands either side of her head. He brought his mouth a whisper from hers.

'It's time to put theory aside, Lola.' He brushed her lips lightly, making sure to press his hips against hers to let her feel the force of his desire. 'And hearsay.'

'Fine by me.' She wrapped her arms around his waist, moving her hips in a subtle motion and almost making him lose it. 'Like I said, I've always favoured the practical.'

CHAPTER FOUR

LOLA HAD HEARD the expression that you could reel from someone's kiss, but she'd never given much store to it. Yet as Connor took her mouth she…reeled. Her knees all but buckled and fire zipped in her veins. She wasn't sure if the way her stomach somersaulted was because of the kiss or because the lift had arrived at Connor's floor.

'Hmm. I really like the practical,' she said, disengaging herself from Connor's arms and stepping back from him to get a few moments to steady herself. 'Much better than the theory.'

'Me too,' he said as, taking hold of her hand, he led her from the lift and out into the small hallway. There was only one door that she could see, and they headed towards that.

Connor slid the key card into the slot and let Lola enter first. He was right about the view. Across the wide living space, floor-to-ceiling windows dominated and the lights of central London flickered around them.

'Wow.' She walked across to get a better look.

'This is amazing.' Instinct had her looking across to the east and towards the area that housed the Cabacal property. Discomfort flared that she was kind of deceiving Connor by not coming clean about who she was. He seemed a decent enough guy. But as this was just a one-off deal, and she would likely never see him again, there didn't seem any real harm.

Connor came up behind her and wrapped his arms around her waist so that they both looked out at the view. He hadn't switched on any lights in the apartment, so what there was came from the reflection of the flickering London skyline beyond.

She loved the feel of his arms around her, the scent of him and the sheer animal magnetism that was uniquely his. One hand came up to cup her breast.

'You don't waste any time,' she said in a droll tone as his other hand cupped her other breast. 'I thought you might be the savouring kind.'

'I am,' he said, nuzzling her neck and making her tremble. 'This is me savouring.'

He squeezed her breasts lightly and rocked his erection against the curve of her ass.

'You feel damn good, Lola.'

The husky, muffled tone shot reaction from her breasts to her core. She moved her hips, not wanting him to have all the fun, and her reward was a needy groan. 'You feel damn good too, Connor.'

He kept one hand on her breast and slowly slid the other down to cup her between her legs. Lola moved against him as he gently touched her, encouraging him to increase the pressure. Thankfully, he took the hint.

'I was planning to take this slow,' he said in a low, sexy drawl. 'But the feel of your ass against my hard-on is kind of making that impossible.'

Reaching up and back, Lola locked her hands around the back of his neck, the movement pushing her breasts forward so that the hand cupping her breast squeezed lightly. 'Sometimes slow is overrated.'

He pressed harder against her, encouraging her to open her legs a little.

'I've got you for one whole night, which means we can do fast, slow and everything in between.'

She recalled what he'd said back in the bar about the benefits of broadening horizons, and if she was broadening hers then she was damn well going to enjoy every moment of it. 'We're still talking theory,' she teased. 'You might still be out on that fourth strike.'

He spun her around, stealing her breath. 'Not going to happen,' he warned as he hiked her up into his arms. She squealed, wrapping her legs around his waist and clinging to his shoulders as he took her through to his bedroom located directly off the living space, quickening his pace as he went.

Another huge room, Lola thought as he set her down on the bed. Another room with amazing views from floor-to-ceiling windows. 'Are the walls in every room of your apartment made of glass?'

'Just two,' he said, yanking the edge of her top

from her waistband. 'Are you planning on talking interior design right now?'

Lola laughed. She really did like his dry wit. It was sexy and a big turn-on.

'I'm just making pleasant conversation.'

Slowly, he drew the zipper of her top down, and she raised her arms as he pulled the top over her head. He took a moment to gaze at her bared breasts, then cupped them, his hands moving in drugging circles, thumbs flicking her nipples and hardening them into tighter buds. She arched, loving the way he touched her.

'You like your breasts touched?'

'Uh, huh.' She hadn't given it much thought before, but now her whole attention was focused on Connor's adept thumbs and skilled fingers manipulating her tender flesh.

He leaned forward, guiding her back until she was lying across the bed. He licked one nipple with the lightest touch but it sent shockwaves right through her body. His tongue felt hot, determined, and she hadn't thought she could feel any better about having her nipple licked until he increased the pressure.

Even as Lola closed her eyes, enjoying his attention, he took the bud into his mouth and sucked. She arched again, higher off the bed this time, resisting the urge to just lie back and let him do what he wanted.

But she had some wants of her own, and that meant getting her hands on Connor. As he continued to kiss her breasts, she pulled his shirt from his trousers and tried to shove it off his shoulders. Connor didn't seem in any hurry to get naked, grabbing her wrists and coaxing her arms back over her head.

He knelt, working his knees between her legs and holding her arms steady, then continued the sexy manipulation of her breasts.

Lola wondered if she'd ever been shot to peak quite so fast before, because she could feel the merciless throb between her legs and knew that it would only take one touch and she'd probably explode.

But Connor didn't release her hands. Instead, he curled his fingers more tightly around hers and anchored her to the mattress.

He moved down, kissing her ribcage, the skin across her waist. Bracketing both her wrists with one hand, he used his free hand to reach between them and unhook the clasp of her jeans. He moved her zipper down a mere inch, touching his mouth to the exposed skin. The only sound came from their deepened breathing. His tongue circled her navel, making the muscles between her legs clench hard.

He caught the zipper fastening between his teeth and slowly pulled it all the way down, then used his free hand to push her jeans open.

It was deliciously erotic and Lola moaned low in her throat.

Connor looked up at her, his grey eyes dark and hooded.

With her wrists still bracketed by his hand, Lola

swallowed and gave a half-hearted tug. 'Do I get to yank your kit off any time soon?'

He grinned, that deliciously sexy hike of his mouth doing amazing things to her equilibrium. 'All night, remember? First I'm having you. My way.'

'What does that mean?'

He trailed a finger down the line of the unfastened zipper towards the top edge of her panties just visible beneath her jeans. She shivered.

'It means I'm going to touch you, taste you, do what the hell I like. After that, maybe I'll let you do the same to me.'

Lola liked the sound of that, but she wasn't going to let him think he was calling all the shots. 'Who says you get to go first? Isn't there some leeway for negotiation?'

'We already negotiated.'

'We did? I must have missed that part.'

He kept his gaze on hers and pushed his hand down the opened fastening of her jeans. Lola sucked in her stomach to ease his way lower, wishing she hadn't worn such tight-fitting jeans. As it was, his fingers were barely inside the lacy edge of her panties.

'My place, my rules.'

'So, if I'd invited you to my place, I'd be the one with the negotiating power?'

He hesitated. 'That's how it works.'

'In whose world?'

'Mine.'

He released her hands but she kept them over her

head, wondering what he planned to do next. Her whole body was on fire, trembling, skin shivering and burning all at once. He lifted her hips and pulled the jeans from her legs so slowly that it made her feel exposed in a way she'd never felt before.

Having tossed her jeans away, he hooked his fingers into the sides of her panties. She thought he was going to tug them off too, but instead he leaned down and pressed his mouth to her lace-covered mound.

It was somehow more erotic having him kiss her with this flimsy barrier between them than if he'd just ripped the panties away and kissed her bare. Her whole body trembled as he hooked his hands beneath her knees and raised her legs so he could get more access to the place he wanted. His mouth was hot, his tongue determined as it flirted with the edge of her panties.

Bringing her hands down from above her head, she tried once more to get the shirt from his shoulders, needing to feel his skin beneath her hands and drive her fingers deep into his firm, hot flesh. But he didn't budge, just kept kissing her with a kind of determined focus.

'Connor?'

Her breathy plea echoed around the space, but Connor ignored it. She hiked herself up onto her elbows, her gaze falling to where Connor worked her so expertly. If the man could make her feel like this with her panties still on, what the hell would he be able to do when she was naked?

She didn't have to wait long to find out. Before she could track what he was doing, he tugged at the lace, dragged it down her legs and tossed it away to join her jeans on the floor.

He spread her, holding her open and looking his fill. She shivered as his head descended, and the first touch of his mouth to her raging heat shook her right through to her core.

She flopped back against the mattress in sensual surrender, her fingers curling into the sheet for purchase. It was like being devoured, like being ravaged, tossed in an erotic sea of pure sensation. All she could do was go with it, let the storm take her wherever it might. She closed her eyes, her muscles jerking with each press of Connor's tongue against her slit.

There was no time to prepare herself, no time to brace against the fury of the spasms that rocked her world. It was amazing, incredible, overwhelming, and as she came down she was already mourning the fact that this was temporary, one night only, no strings. No anything.

Lola flung an arm across her forehead, gasping for breath. 'Bloody hell.'

He inched up, bracing himself on his hands to lean over her. 'Yeah.'

'You're good at that.'

'I'm good at a whole lot more.'

'Condom?'

He grinned. 'Not yet. I haven't finished.'

Since she had her legs open with him lying between them, his impressive bulge pushing hard against her heat, she looked up at him from beneath her arm. 'When do I get my turn?'

'I thought you just did.'

'Funny. You won't even let me take your shirt off.'

'Plenty of time for that.'

She tried again to slip it from his shoulders, but he caught her hand. 'I told you I wasn't finished.' He grinned. 'Unless you want to miss out on my special technique.'

Lola gave him a suspicious look. She wanted to challenge him on his bossy attitude, his determination to get his own way. Getting involved with a man who liked to control to the extent Connor did should have sent out all kinds of warning signals, but her body was sending out its own signals right then. Her skin tingled and her muscles clenched in anticipation. She had to admit that she was intrigued and, as this was only a one-night deal and their paths were unlikely to cross again, she wasn't about to get too hung up on his need to call the shots. 'What special technique?'

He grinned, leaned down and kissed her breasts, taking his time to explore each nipple in turn. Then he moved down her body, kissing her lightly at the waist, exploring her abdomen and around her navel before touching light kisses down her thighs to her knees.

Lola moved in sensual pleasure, driving her fingers into his hair until he started to move up her body again and settled beside her. Their gazes met and Lola loved the deep, smoky look he gave her.

His hand moved down her body, his palm cupping her pussy.

Lola swallowed. She wanted to turn her face away from his intense look, but she couldn't seem to. Slowly, he teased her apart with his forefinger, stroking lightly across her wetness. She held her breath, expecting that he would push in deeper but, when he continued that drugging, barely there movement, she had to suck in a deep breath as her lungs squeezed.

He leaned down and brought his mouth to hers, kissing her in a way that mirrored what he was doing between her legs. Lola felt light-headed and realised she was holding her breath again.

He kissed across her mouth, her jaw, down her throat, but still the pressure of his finger remained light.

She arched her hips a little, coaxing him. He kissed her, this time pressing his tongue between her lips and delving into her mouth in a deep and sensuous exploration of her softness.

Lola moaned, moving her hips again. She was going to start bloody complaining if he didn't take the hint and just…

The breath caught in her lungs as he pushed inside her, swapping his forefinger for his middle finger and sliding in deep. As she closed her eyes, he started a slow push-and-release motion that soon had Lola gasping for air.

She heard herself cry out when he arched his finger, applying a gentle pressure against her clit. This time she really did feel the room spin, and she opened her eyes to see him watching her with those hooded eyes.

'You're right,' she managed between breathy gasps. 'That's certainly special.'

'We're not there yet,' he said in a deep and gravelly tone.

Before she could respond, he flicked his wrist, making his finger spin inside her, backward and forward as he varied the penetration, the pressure.

'Oh, my God…' Lola felt as if her whole body was being twisted as he continued to work her, and she wondered if she could take much more of this intense pleasure. She was riding high again, hurling up towards that precipitous edge, to be flung into the stratosphere with nothing to cling to.

She grabbed for his wrist, wanting the connection, wanting something to keep her from spinning into orbit. It was too late. Because she flew, she spun and all she could do was let go.

Slowly she came down, easing out her body like a sensual cat.

Were one-night stands supposed to rock your world? Were they supposed to make you…feel? Because she *did* feel, all kinds of things—warm, sensual, shaky, unsettled. It hadn't escaped her that he'd put her needs first, that he'd focused on her pleasure. It made her want much more than this single encounter.

Which was crazy, stupid, dangerous…

She pulled herself back from the perilous edge. 'Well, I can officially vouch for the specialness of your technique. Happy now?'

He withdrew his hand. 'Shouldn't that be my line?'

'You don't play fair.'

'You got that right.'

He looked serious, making her wonder at his meaning. All indications were that Connor loved to play, loved to tease, but the way he'd said it, the look in his eyes, alerted her to some deep, hidden meaning behind his words.

'I didn't have you down as a point-scorer.'

He trailed his fingers lightly across her abdomen, then shrugged. 'No point-scoring involved, just hot and dirty sex. Isn't that what you want?'

It was exactly what she wanted, and she really couldn't fathom why she had all these feelings spinning around inside her. Maybe that was what happened when you agreed to have sex with someone you didn't know that well. And when that someone turned out to be so very adept at making a woman's body sing. 'Absolutely. Hot and dirty sex. And now maybe it's time to show you one or two of my own special techniques. It's my turn to get what I want. To have my fun with you, right?'

He narrowed his eyes, as if he was trying to work out her meaning, then he turned and lay on his back. 'Go for it, sweetheart. Do your worst.'

CHAPTER FIVE

CONNOR HAD KNOWN she'd be a fire cracker in bed, that she wouldn't be shy about stating what she wanted, so why did her words put him on full alert? *It's my turn to get what I want. To have my fun with you, right?*

Maybe because he preferred to be the one calling the shots. It was safer that way. But Lola had so easily shifted the dynamic he liked to set up from the start—the one that gave him all the control.

When Lola straddled him, whatever else he'd been about to think flew out of the window.

She stripped away his shirt and undid the button of his fly. He was burning, his body one hot mass of need. Maybe that was what came of being without physical release for too long now.

Connor pushed away the nudge that warned it had less to do with that and more to do with enjoying this particular woman. Lola. Yeah, she was a fire cracker, all right. She'd said she liked to think things around in her mind, work out the pros and cons before making a decision. It seemed when this woman had done the weighing up she went straight for what she wanted.

And, right then, that appeared to be him.

The determination in her eyes set his blood on fire, sending a lightning bolt of raw desire through his system as she yanked down his zipper.

Her hand slid inside his trousers, her fingers playing just above the head of his cock. His abdominal muscles jerked, and a throbbing need to be inside her vied with his decision to let her take her fun. It was only fair. Yet, at the same time, he knew he needed to keep his instincts sharp because something about Lola could make him take his eye off the ball. And that was never going to happen again.

Was he getting to be such a suspicious bastard that he was seeing spooks where none existed? This thing between them was scratching an itch, right? It was just sex. Going nowhere.

Just sex. Going nowhere.

That became a mantra as she ran her free hand lightly over his chest, his pecs, across his shoulder, making every single muscle tremble beneath her touch. Light. Smooth. Devastating.

'You have great definition,' she said, making him lose the ability to breathe as her fingers inched closer to the tip of his erection. 'Gym?'

He shook his head, unable to tear his gaze away from the lusty look in her eyes. 'No time.'

She plucked at his nipple while her other hand

played dangerously close to where he wanted it. 'What do you do to keep fit?'

He grinned, although his chest was tight with anticipation of what she would do next. 'Fuck.'

Her hands stilled; her eyes went wide. 'Really? You must do that an awful lot to get this kind of result.'

He was about to defend himself against the subtext that he was some kind of man-whore when she grinned.

'I suppose you think you're quite the comedienne,' he said, waiting with what he considered stoic patience for her to start working his body again. His muscles had no such fortitude, and his cock jerked as his abs clenched.

She kept her gaze on his and, with a very feline smile, placed her palm flat on his chest so she could lean slightly forward, then pushed her other hand down into his boxers and wrapped her fingers around his cock.

Connor swallowed at the feel of her solid grip, marvelling at the strength in her small hand. She rotated her hips and, though her pussy wasn't touching him, his dick reacted as if it were.

He reached out, wrapped his hands around her hips and tried to bring her against him. She shook her head and tutted. 'Not yet. We have all night, remember?'

He narrowed his eyes at the way she batted his words back at him. When she started moving her hand over his erection, slow and easy, he called on some more of that stoic patience.

His breath caught, his chest tightened and he almost shouted his relief when she sat back and tugged at his waistband. 'Let's have these off, shall we?' she said, as she yanked both his trousers and boxers from his hips with surprising strength of purpose.

He raised his hips, already toeing off his shoes, and then sat up to help dispose of his remaining clothes. She straddled him again and placed both palms on his chest before looking down to where his dick stood at attention. 'Impressive,' she said. 'Makes me want to play.'

Before he could get a coherent thought into his frazzled brain, she inched down his body, her breasts jiggling and making him want to take them in his mouth again, to savour all that ripe and silky flesh.

Then he didn't even try for any kind of thought as she bent down, her hands on his thighs, and she licked across his head.

His throat went tight along with his body, and he arched his back, encouraging her to take more of him. She continued the slow slide of her tongue across his tip, her fingers pressing into his thighs as if to anchor him where she wanted him.

Briefly, Connor closed his eyes, his hands tight fists against his sides. She took him a mere inch into her mouth, her tongue wrapping around him, before withdrawing and again giving her attention just to the tip.

He was about to protest…make that plea…when she ran her tongue lightly down the length of him, at the same time sliding her hands higher up his inner thighs until she could cup his sac.

His breath came in desperate gasps now, his rib-cage locked as his muscles tightened almost painfully in his chest.

His fisted hands pushed hard against the mattress as she took him fully into her mouth, her soft lips curling around him, the light graze of her teeth a delicious friction as she moved up and down his length. Her hair trailed across his thighs and slid over his lower abdomen as she worked him slowly, then harder.

When his balls grew tight, he reached out for her, sliding his fingers into her hair and raking her scalp, encouraging her to release him. He wasn't going to last, and he didn't want to lose it with her mouth wrapped around him.

While he wasn't a stranger to a woman going down on him, or letting her take things to their natural conclusion, for some reason he didn't want that tonight. It made him feel too raw…

He didn't have time to question that, given he was seconds away from shooting his load. Instead, he sat up and grabbed for her arms, pulling her away from him.

She looked a little surprised, her green eyes wide, her soft lips full and pink from being wrapped around his cock.

'Need to be inside you,' he growled, reversing their positions until she lay on her back. 'Can't wait.'

He closed his eyes as his erection throbbed, trying to get his act together long enough to grab a condom from the bedside drawer. It didn't help that he was lying between her legs, her slick heat against his length and her breasts pressing against his chest.

He opened his eyes and reached out, fumbling for the drawer. Seconds later he had the condom rolled on, and he looked down at her.

A smoky green layer of pure lust filled her eyes as he eased her legs wider, then slid his hands beneath her backside to tilt her hips upward.

He pressed forward and, her eyes still on his, she arched her neck. Her lips parted and, barely inside her, he leaned down and kissed her, pressing his tongue inside her mouth. She gave a low sound in her throat as he released her mouth.

He slid deeper, her warmth and wetness aiding his way, her muscles drawing him in and clamping tight around him. Vaguely, it registered in that moment that he was powerless against the magnetism that seemed to burn between them.

But it was only sex.

To prove that he drove himself to the hilt, stealing the breath from them both, thrusting inside her as his mind switched off and his body took control.

A burning sensation hit the base of his spine, barrelling around to his pelvis, down the length of his cock. He wanted to hold off, make this last, but he was too far gone.

He managed to get a hand between them, pressing a finger to Lola's clit. Her frantic moan ripped away the last of his restraint and sent him over the edge.

He came. Pumping into the condom. Encouraged by Lola's needy rendering of his name and the clenching of her muscles as she gripped him tight.

He looked down at her as they both fought for air. Her face was flushed, her eyes heavy-lidded, and she looked so bloody beautiful it stole what little air he'd managed to grab into his tight lungs.

What the fuck just happened?

He moved back from her as if she were possessed by some strange power that could contaminate him. 'Okay?' he asked lamely.

She nodded, looking a little dazed. 'Yes. You?'

'Me?' He sucked in air, willed his breathing to settle and eased further away. 'I'm always okay. I make sure of it.'

Lola battled to regain a little balance. If she was going to break her rule about one-night stands, she couldn't have done it in a more spectacular fashion.

Maybe there was something to be said for casual hook-ups after all, especially if the sex could be as amazing as they'd just shared. She hadn't expected it to be quite so intense, so…breath-taking.

There'd been a connection between them, something she couldn't quite label as anything else, but maybe that was all part of the brief and temporary nature of a one-nighter. It was her first—how would she know?

What she did know was that it had been far more than she'd anticipated, even though she'd anticipated a whole lot of fabulous with Connor.

As he was already heading to the bathroom, Lola stretched, managed a deep breath and would have let it out on a contented sigh if something hadn't niggled.

Connor had seemed to be enjoying her oral skills until he'd unexpectedly called a halt by pushing her away at a vital moment.

Okay, she didn't have a mountain of experience when it came to sex, but she liked it well enough, and thought she could find her way around a man's body.

Emily had once declared that some men didn't like a woman to go all the way when it came to blow jobs because it made them feel vulnerable. Was that what had happened? Had Connor been annoyed that she'd tried to force him to lose control?

Since he was the epitome of strapping, confident male, she couldn't quite make the fit, but he'd certainly yanked her away from him fast enough.

Maybe an ex had hurt him in the past. Had a woman made him feel vulnerable? She thought back to when she'd suggested he might not know women as well as he thought he did. Remembered that guarded look he'd given her, and the cryptic comment about women who set their mind on something tending to get it.

Maybe that was at the heart of his need to control. To keep a tight handle on proceedings.

My place. My rules.

If Connor was deep into the control thing there was no way she wanted any more of that. She'd already had a lifetime of it. Men who liked ordering her around, who pressed their own agendas on her life, all the time citing that they were acting in her best interests.

Men like her father and her brother.

Okay, they loved her and wanted the best for her, but come on… When were they going to step out of the prehistoric age? Her father had been the kind who thought it was his absolute right to manage the lives of his wife and daughter, to provide for them, protect them. The problem was, his idea of protection and provision had been beyond autocratic. Like something out of Victorian times. According to him, he'd known what was best for the women in his life and that was that. End of story.

Unfortunately, her brother had inherited that same attitude. Damian had always been a chip off the old block, but in the three years since her father had passed away her brother had upped his game and taken on the mantle of family despot.

Once, although she'd fought against their unreasonable decisions, she'd had little choice but to go along with them. That was no longer the case. Now she was running her own show, and there was absolutely no room for more dictators in her life.

So why in heaven's name was she attracted to the same type of man? Why was she already wanting more than one night with Connor? More of that amazing, world-rocking sex?

And why was she ruining an intensely enjoyable evening by over-thinking?

All she needed to know right then was that he made her body hum. He lit her up in all the right places, and several she didn't even know she had. Being with Connor had given her an excellent yardstick by which to measure future sexual experiences.

Connor chose that moment to come back into the bedroom. Lola's mouth went dry as she feasted on his tall, muscular physique, and the easy way he strolled towards the bed with a predatory look made her want to reach out and yank him back pronto.

While she wasn't into control or dominance by men in general, she hadn't realised how much of a turn-on Connor's assertiveness could be. At least where sex was concerned.

'You've got a look in your eye,' he said as he settled on his side next to her. 'Makes me want to do things.'

Lola fluttered her lashes. 'That's why we're here, isn't it?'

He bent his elbow, supporting his head with his hand. 'Want anything? Drink? Something to eat?'

She shimmied against him. 'What I want you can't get from the kitchen.'

He brought his free hand to her stomach, flattening his palm over her navel and making her muscles clench. 'In that case…'

Lola placed her hand over his, determined to enjoy what was left of their hot night and see it as entrée into her new life. From the old to the new. From tyranny to liberation.

Tomorrow, she would go head to head with her brother over the Cabacal, convince him that she meant business. She'd show him how serious she was about her future plans, how determined she was to make a go of it, and she'd get him to change his mind. Whatever it took.

Then this night with Connor would be relegated to the ranks of one naughty, exhilarating, extremely hot encounter with her very own bad boy.

CHAPTER SIX

'WHY ARE YOU so determined to be difficult?'

Lola had spent the past twenty minutes video-calling her brother and pleading her case but Damian hadn't budged. She'd outlined her business plan, given him detailed figures and targets, walked through the accounts she'd kept for the last year while she'd been teaching yoga part-time—but he hadn't been swayed.

Frustrated beyond measure, Lola had then threatened to instigate proceedings to contest her late uncle's legal ownership of the property, citing how it had essentially been stolen from their mother. Damian had quickly poured cold water on that, reminding her that it had been contested at the time and that, since her mother had been considered of sound mind when she'd signed over the property, it had been deemed a lawful, if not moral, transaction.

Their father had been angry, although not particularly sympathetic. He'd blamed his wife for not having taken proper care of her assets and allowing the property to fall into her brother's hands. He hadn't been in the least bothered that the property meant far more to her mother than its financial value. That she'd intended it to provide a studio for health and wellbeing, a place where people could escape the increasing frenzy of city life.

Not only had her mother suffered the heartbreak of being duped by her only brother, whom she'd trusted and adored, she'd also lost what was to have been Lola's inheritance. Witnessing her mother's distress, Lola had vowed to one day make her mother's dream come true and open a fitness studio in the Cabacal property. Sadly, she'd lost her mother soon after making the vow, but her determination to fulfil her promise had never wavered.

'This property has done nothing but cause problems for this family,' Damian said. 'It caused a huge rift between us and Uncle Guy's family that I can't ever see healing, especially now Caroline has been released and has decided to move to Dubai.'

Lola couldn't find any compassion for her. She'd never liked her cousin and thought her spoiled and mean-spirited. Caroline had always protested her innocence in the embezzlement charges, but Lola didn't believe that claim for a second, and neither had the judge who had sentenced her to four years in prison.

'I don't want the rift healed,' Lola said. 'I'll never forgive Uncle Guy for what he did to Mum, and I'll never understand how you could accept the role of executor of his will.'

'Because there's nobody else,' Damian said, running a hand through his short, dark hair. 'Do you think it's been easy handling his affairs? He's left a mountain of debt, and the only real asset available for me to work with is the Cabacal.'

Lola could see the turmoil in his green eyes, and she knew that for the past six months since their uncle had died, he'd worked hard to negotiate the estate, and if her brother was finding it problematic then it really was complicated. Damian might be controlling and a bloody pain in her backside but he was one of the most astute businessmen she knew.

'Which is why my offer to purchase the property makes sense. You can have my trust fund, which basically makes me a cash buyer. There aren't too many of those around. Any other buyer and you'll have to wait for loans and mortgages to come through before you get an injection of cash.'

'I promised Dad that I'd take care of you,' he said in a tone that indicated he was fast losing his patience. 'That means not letting you waste your trust fund on some venture that'll see you broke before you even blink.'

'How can you say that? Along with my business degrees, I'm a specialist in therapeutic yoga and relaxation techniques. That puts me in a solid position to make my plans work.'

'New health clubs come and go so fast, it's hard to keep track,' he said, his eyes narrowing. 'The demand for gym classes might be high, but there are far too many establishments offering them already.'

Lola wanted to scream. Gym classes. *Gym classes.* Her brother really hadn't been listening to a word she'd said. She wanted so much more for her clients than a good workout. She wanted a place they could unwind from the stresses of life. A soft place to fall when life became overwhelming.

Lola held fast to her own patience. 'When are you back in London?' she asked, undaunted by Damian's persistent refusal to be reasonable. 'Promise me you won't do anything concrete until I can go through all my projections with you face to face. You'll see how thorough they are, and how serious I am about this.'

'Fitzpatrick is offering over the asking price, and the estate needs every penny it can get.'

'It shouldn't even form part of Uncle Guy's estate. It wasn't his to own. You can't feel good about this.'

'What I feel isn't the issue,' Damian said with a sigh, leaning back in that way of his that signalled he was done with the current topic of conversation. 'Mum signed away the property without telling Dad or even seeking legal advice. Nobody does that.'

'And nobody expects their brother, their own flesh and blood, to steal from them either.'

'Look, Louise. The sale of the Cabacal's a done deal. Connor Fitzpatrick wants the property and he's in a position to buy it. I spoke with him crack of dawn this morning and we agreed final details. Apart from his signature on the contract, and the transfer of his funds into the estate, it's in the bag.'

'You spoke to him this morning?'

When had that happened? She and Connor had been active pretty much all through the night and they'd shared breakfast. The only time they'd been apart was when she'd taken a shower.

Her heart took a major dive. Not just because her plans to obtain the Cabacal first-hand were fading into oblivion, but now she'd slept with Connor. If her only option was reverting to Plan A, and getting him to sell to her when she was in a position to buy, she'd have to tell him who she was. Now he'd think she'd used him and would likely tell her to go take a hike, or something much worse!

Her chest tightened as her breath hitched beneath her ribcage. She didn't want him to think her a liar, a manipulator, a cheat, but he would, and that made her feel hollow inside.

She called on her yoga background, reminding herself that the ancient practice taught calmness even in the midst of challenging situations. She took a deep breath and let it out slowly through her mouth as she mentally counted to six.

She couldn't believe that Damian had gone ahead with the sale to Connor, and it hurt so much to think that he wouldn't even consider her plans for the property. But since it was fruitless arguing with Damian any longer, she ended the call.

With a huge sigh of frustration, she sat back and

thought about what Damian had told her about Connor. He'd said Connor was owed the property, and despite feeling she was owed too, this intrigued her. What exactly had gone on between Connor and her uncle that Connor would offer above market value to purchase the Cabacal? Why would he want any reminders of his past there? Why would he want anything more to do with it?

If she'd been falsely accused of embezzlement, she would want to erase the whole sorry episode from her mind.

But then it wasn't really her business. Her business was to work out her next steps.

She sipped her coffee, considering. She could go ahead with her original plan, and ask Connor to sell the Cabacal to her, or she could start looking at other properties.

No. The latter wasn't an option. If she gave up on the Cabacal it would be like letting her mother down.

Her mother had been a gentle soul, less interested in profit and loss than she was in helping people and making them happy. Having her soft heart used against her by a money-grabbing brother, who'd known his sister wouldn't question whether he had anything other than good intentions, had been unconscionable.

Furious, Lola shoved the coffee away. The fight wasn't over yet. There was no way she was backing off. One way or another, she was getting her mother's property back.

Which meant there was only one thing for it.

Plan A was back on the table.

Connor would think she'd had sex with him in an attempt to seduce him into selling to her. He'd never believe she'd slept with him because she wanted to, because she was attracted to him, because she liked him.

She had to make him understand why she needed the Cabacal so much, and convince him that she'd only given in to the attraction between them once she'd believed she could convince Damian to sell her the property outright. The fact her plan had gone belly-up had now left her in a precarious position.

Speaking of precarious positions… Her mind skipped back to last night. The sex had been hot, no arguing with that, but being with Connor had been… fun. Despite the blip when she'd glimpsed that edgy side to him—something locked down, unfathomable, untouchable, controlling—she'd really loved his quick wit, his playful manner. He was exciting, adventurous. He'd made sex fun as well as wickedly erotic.

She hadn't experienced that before.

Her first time had been with a fellow undergrad who had been studying applied mathematics and had done everything, including sex, with precision and measured skill. It hadn't been the most exciting way to lose her virginity, but at least he was thorough.

Her second lover had been a guy she'd met while doing her MBA. He'd been studying for a doctorate and she'd had a feeling he'd enjoyed their conversations more than the sex, although when he had applied himself the sex generally had been satisfactory.

At least, that was what she'd thought until last night.

From now on, considering her plans, she'd have to keep any future interaction with Connor on a hands-off basis.

Regardless of anything else, she had to come clean.

She went into her tiny bedroom and started dressing for her midday yoga class, knowing that afterwards she'd have to contact Connor. She wasn't certain what concerned her the most. Facing his hostility when she told him the truth, or hurting him by doing so.

Whatever it was, she'd just have to deal with it.

Connor left his brother Logan's law office satisfied that the paperwork Damian McBride had emailed over to him was in order. Even though he liked Damian, and knew that the man was not a great fan of his late uncle or his business methods, Connor wasn't taking any chances, which was why he'd asked his brother to take a look at the contract.

While Logan specialised in family law, he'd worked for major players in the world of politics and commerce and for A-list celebs. Connor was satisfied that, if his brother gave the okay, all was solid and above board.

He thought about celebrating his win by heading across London to view his soon-to-be acquisition. He could stand and stare at the place, imagine it being bulldozed. At first Connor had thought about renovating; the place hadn't been empty long enough that it couldn't be rescued. But the thought of tearing it down was just too satisfying to dismiss.

Maybe he'd ask to operate the wrecking ball, take the first swing to demolish concrete and stone. How satisfying would that be? Perhaps, as the first brick crumbled, as the first wall fell, he would gain that elusive sense of liberation from his past. Feel his anger and frustration fade as the building leveled.

He'd rebuild, of course. No sense buying prime real estate in the capital and doing nothing with it. Apartments, perhaps. Something far removed from what it had been five years ago—an outwardly high-end casino which, he'd painfully discovered, had been used for nefarious purposes.

His hands fisted, chest tightening. He wanted that damn place. He wanted every last piece of what it had been and what it represented obliterated from the face of the earth.

Images came unbidden, filling his head with old and painful memories. Caroline standing beside the baccarat table, her green eyes lit with the knowledge that she'd successfully primed him to take the fall for her father's and her duplicity. The realisation that she'd professed to love him only to stab him in the back. The cops arriving to read him his rights…

Deliberately, he uncurled his fingers and took a deep breath. No point looking back. Everything was set to move forward to his satisfaction. Which made today a fucking good day.

He considered walking to the nearest of his clubs. His back was acting up this morning and a walk usually eased it. He could use the time to finalise details of Logan's stag party, make sure everything would be on point for his brother's last shot at freedom. Why the hell he wanted to tie himself down, Connor had no idea. Okay, Connor liked April well enough, and his future sister-in-law seemed like a good person. Most importantly, she made his brother happy.

Logan was a hero in Connor's book. His oldest brother had done everything in his power to keep their family together when their parents had taken off, leaving five children to fend for themselves. That, and the fact that Logan had saved him from the lash of his father's belt too many times to remember.

His brother was the only person Connor trusted.

He hailed a cab, sat back, and closed his eyes. The sun played across his lids, helping his muscles relax. He fought the pull of sleep as the cab trundled through the busy traffic, his drugged thoughts rolling back to the previous night and the reason for his current fatigue.

Lola.

Shit, but that woman was something else. Hot. Adventurous. Inexhaustible.

And fuck was she flexible, he thought with a grin. Bending her body with effortless ease and making him lose his damn mind as she took him to paradise…

Paradise? When had he ever used words like that? It was sex. That was all it was. Good, dirty, passionate, energetic sex.

His cock strained against his zipper and he shifted. He'd known he wouldn't be disappointed. When she'd left that morning, she'd made absolutely no demands to see him again. No hints that, although they'd agreed only to one night, maybe there could be more. No suggestions that they could hook up again some time if they were both at a loose end.

None of that. They'd shared breakfast. She'd kissed him, tossed him a smile and left his apartment. She was a female version of him. For some reason, that pissed him off.

He'd fought against her wanting to direct proceedings, yet he really shouldn't have concerned himself. She'd shown a determination to satisfy them both. The problem he'd had was more to do with her inherent softness, and he was suspicious of that. Who could blame him? He'd promised himself he'd never again be taken in by face value attributes. Yet Lola seemed genuine, which in itself rang warning bells and cautioned him to keep his instincts sharpened.

While she shot from the hip, she had conflicting layers: strength, gentleness, wildness, caution. All part of the fascination that made her so damn sexy, but which confused the hell out of him. Not that he should concern himself with that, either. They'd both understood it was temporary and no-strings sex.

Yeah…so why was he leaning forward and tapping the glass to direct the driver to her place? Ex-

cept he didn't know exactly where *her place* was,
apart from what he'd overheard her tell the driver last
night which was basically just the street and general
location. What the hell was he going to do? Knock
on every door until he found out where she lived?

Part of him warned he was pushing things, crossing a line by trying to track her down. The thing was,
he wanted to see her again. *Really* wanted to see her
again. Now that he had her in his head, he couldn't
resist the opportunity for another meet. He wanted
more of those conflicting layers, another chance to
get a handle on who she really was.

More fool him.

Fifteen minutes later, the taxi pulled up outside
one of several tall terraced houses in a long row of
similar residences. Connor paid the fare and got out.

As the taxi sped away, he stood on the pavement
and surveyed the nearest building, wishing he'd
thought to grab her mobile number so he wouldn't
be standing like an idiot on a busy London street in
the middle of the goddamn day, wondering what the
devil his next step was.

But asking for her number would have suggested
he wanted more. Would have given her the impres-
sion he was interested in seeing her again.

*Yeah, and standing outside her place isn't doing
that at all, is it, Einstein?*

Connor pushed back his jacket and slid his hands
into his trouser pockets, looking up at the property
like some kind of demented estate agent, hoping it
housed Lola's place.

With no real plan, he strolled up the half-dozen stone steps and glanced at the panel by the side of the door. He scanned the list of names but didn't see Lola's.

So, what did he do? Press every bell and ask for her? How the heck would that sound, some stranger pressing bells and requesting a woman in the middle of the day? Not suspicious at all.

Ten minutes later, he was sure that someone had probably already called the police. He'd tried to use his best appeasing tone and had been surprised at the trusting nature of several occupants he'd already tried. Other occupants seemed less unsuspecting.

One woman had demanded his name, his mobile number and the exact nature of his business before telling him to get lost when he'd said he was looking for a woman called Lola.

By the time he hit pay dirt, he was sure that he'd be hauled away in a wailing cop car any moment and would spend the night in the nearest nick. As he pressed what he decided would probably be the last button before he called it quits, memories hit him. A cold cell, echoing walls, drunken shouts of innocence from his neighbours.

He remembered the icy slab he'd slept on, the numerous questions, the looks of suspicion aimed at him from police officers, until Connor had finally caved and asked for his lawyer.

It had seemed like hours before Connor even knew what he'd been charged with—longer still until

Logan had arrived and demanded to know what the hell was going on.

He'd listened with a kind of disembodied disbelief as they'd outlined the charges and had realised he'd been framed, used as a scapegoat.

But that hadn't been the worst of it…

'Hello?'

He jerked back, almost toppling off the top step as the husky, familiar tone slapped him dead centre in his chest.

'Hey, Lola.'

There was a long silence, during which Connor wondered if he'd imagined hearing her voice, but then she spoke. 'Connor? What are you doing here?'

'I was passing. Thought maybe I could buy you lunch.'

Another silence, during which Connor started to question the wisdom of what he was doing. What the hell was happening to him that he found himself this attracted to a woman that he'd act so out of character? Okay, so it wasn't the first time he'd actually pursued a woman he liked, but this?

Was this bordering on stalker-ish?

Maybe his wanting to find out more about her had something to do with those layers. Her intriguing blend of assertiveness, strength, hesitancy, and doubt. It was an explosive mix in a woman, and it fascinated the hell out of him.

'How did you know where I lived?'

He jolted as her question drew him from his reverie. 'Heard you tell the taxi driver last night,' he said, more than a tad embarrassed at the admission.

Yet more silence. 'Give me five minutes.'

Turning, he sat on the stone step, both anticipating seeing her again and wondering what in God's name he was doing. He should have left it. Should have enjoyed their one night of great sex. Moved on.

She arrived faster than he'd anticipated, considering that a woman's five minutes could often stretch to infinity.

The door opened and he stood, turning to face her. She wore a white tee with a red diagonal flash across her breasts that announced *Forever Fit* in script lettering, and a snazzy pair of leggings that looked as if she'd poured herself into them. Her hair, all that glorious hair, was pulled back and up into a kind of messy bun.

She had a battered holdall flung over her shoulders.

Connor raised his eyebrows. While she looked sexy as hell, she was hardly dressed for lunch at Lavini's where he'd planned to take her.

'Sorry, but I can't do lunch,' she said, reading his thoughts. 'I've got a class.'

He should have been relieved. Should have shrugged, said 'Another time,' and walked away, but instead he slipped his hands into his pockets and stayed where he was. 'Quick coffee?'

She glanced at the big white watch on her wrist. 'Yeah, that would work. But mine would need to be decaf.'

'Where's your class?' he asked, taking the holdall from her before heading down the stone steps onto the pavement. 'We'll find a coffee shop nearby.'

She pointed along the road to a building that looked like a community centre. 'Just across the road.'

'Right.' He let her lead the way, wondering what the hell she had in the bag that made it feel like a dead body.

'What kind of class?' he asked as they crossed the busy road.

'Lunch time yoga.' She eyed him, an amused look in her sexy green eyes. 'Want to join us?'

He raised his eyebrows. 'Do I look like I want to join you?'

She eyed his suit, then laughed with that throaty sound that shot straight to his balls. 'Funny, but it's always the people who could use it most that are the most derogatory. Almost like they're scared to actually relax.'

'I relax,' he felt compelled to point out. 'I just prefer not putting myself into complicated positions and cutting off my air supply when I do so.'

She shook her head, the bun on top wobbling precariously. 'Another misconception. Some of the most effective poses are incredibly simple. Yoga teaches controlled breathing and only some of the practices involve holding your breath.'

'If you say so.'

This time she tutted, her expression making him wonder if he'd hit a nerve of some kind. As they'd arrived at the double entrance doors, and Lola was keying in security numbers on the pad beside them, he thought it best not to follow up his insights into the ancient practice.

Several people milled around in the entrance hall, and a couple of them waved to Lola. She went through more double doors and into a small coffee bar. Most of the tables were taken, so she headed to a bench counter that looked out onto a small garden area.

She sat on one of the high stools. 'This okay?'

Connor gladly put the bag down between them, then sat next to her. 'Yeah, great.'

Amused, she looked at him as he settled in. 'You have to go and order at the counter.'

He narrowed his eyes, but couldn't stop the smile. 'What happened to equality?'

'You invited me, remember? That means you go get the coffee. I'll have a small decaf Americano.'

Yeah. He really liked her directness. No side. No games. Maybe that was part of the attraction? What you saw was what you got. And he'd been watching closely.

He turned, almost falling off the stool. She gave a throaty laugh which, combined with the sight of her in all that close-fitting workout gear, went straight to his cock.

He wasn't sure how he was supposed to make it to the counter without disgracing himself but, as everyone seemed happily engaged in their own conversations, he walked off to place their order, hoping to hell nobody checked out the vicinity of his groin.

CHAPTER SEVEN

OF ANY SCENARIO Lola could have imagined, the very last one was having Connor turn up on her door step.

Her first thought was that he'd discovered who she was, but that didn't seem to be the case.

She had gone over half a dozen potential starts to the conversation she knew they needed to have about the Cabacal, but one look at him standing there looking drop-dead gorgeous in his business suit, his blue shirt opened at the collar, and she'd forgotten every single one.

She turned and watched appreciatively as he ordered their drinks, knowing that the impressive breadth of his shoulders had nothing to do with the impeccable tailoring of his jacket and everything to do with his muscular perfection. She glanced at his neck, wondering if beneath his collar he sported evidence of the fact that she'd taken big, greedy bites of it.

Her gaze slid down to his backside and she swallowed, recalling how firm he had been as she'd clenched her hands over his taut flesh, encouraging him to drive deeper inside her.

She blew out a breath and turned away. God, it was getting hot in here.

Seconds later, he was back. He slid onto the stool, grimacing a little as he settled there. 'What time's your class?'

She checked her watch. 'Forty-five minutes yet. I usually like to get here an hour before, but since I had a busy night, and a late start this morning, I'm a little out of sync.'

He grinned and looked at her as if he was remembering every dirty thing they'd done together. 'You like to warm up before class?'

Even if she did, she wouldn't need it today. Her body was impossibly hot already. 'I like to set up before class starts.'

He raised his eyebrows. 'You're the instructor?'

'Is that so unbelievable?'

He shook his head, his gaze travelling down her body and then back again. 'No, but I thought you'd just finished uni. Which was the reason you were dancing on my table last night.'

'I have just finished uni. Bachelors and then an MBA.'

'Where does yoga come in?'

'I did a part-time teacher training course. Practical and theoretical. It was almost like taking another degree.' She blew out a breath. 'It's a very profound and intricate subject that involves learning about anatomy, physiology and the philosophical side, too. I love it.'

Connor smiled, leaning forward to clasp his hands on the table. 'I can see that from the way your eyes light up.' His gaze held hers with such intensity that Lola felt the punch of it right down in her solar plexus. 'Are you planning to make a business out of it?'

'Uh-huh. I'm going to run my own studio.'

Habit had her bracing herself for what she feared might follow. Would Connor be like her father, like Damian, and try and convince her of the error of her ways?

'Your own studio,' Connor said, smiling at the waitress who brought their coffee. 'What are you planning to offer your clients?'

'Remedial yoga, relaxation therapy, Pilates, and therapeutic massage.'

Connor took a small sip of his coffee, pursing his lips as he nodded. 'What size studio do you have in mind? Are you planning to start off just by yourself, or will you take on other tutors immediately?'

Since there was no hint of censure in his questions, Lola leaned forward. 'I want to offer a variety of courses and therapies right from the start. There are a few well-qualified teachers on the circuit who are interested in taking on more work. But I intend to be really hands-on and not stick myself behind a desk doing admin.'

He nodded again. 'Yeah, I get that. It takes some organisation but it's doable.'

Lola caught her bottom lip between her teeth, her face pleasantly warm from the realisation that Connor seemed genuinely interested. It was so refreshing not to have to defend or explain her choices.

'That's what I'm thinking. I've done really detailed planning, based on my research of health clubs from a variety of UK cities, projected out for the next few years. That should give me a really good head start, and some leeway for changing things up if necessary.'

'That's why you're looking at property? Potential locations for your studio?'

She found it hard to look at him, knowing that now was the perfect time to come clean. To admit her plans for the Cabacal. 'Yes.'

'Found anything suitable yet?'

She raised her head, met his eyes. 'I have. A perfect property. Perfect location.'

'That's great.'

Her stomach gave a ridiculous lurch, leaving nausea in its wake. 'It would be, but there are complications.'

'What kind?'

She kept her eyes on his, trying to find the right words to minimise the damage of her confession. 'Somebody else is interested.'

'Then make sure the agents know that you're even more interested,' Connor said. 'Make them an offer they can't refuse.'

She thought of Damian. How she'd tried to convince him to sell direct to her. 'You make it sound easy.'

'If it's what you really want, go for it. Don't give

up until you've exhausted all possibilities. Until there's nowhere left to go.'

'Is that what you would do?'

A determined look came into his eyes. 'Every time.'

Lola knew they were both talking about the same thing, and again she wondered why he wanted the Cabacal property so badly. If it held bad memories for him, wouldn't he want to walk away, have nothing more to do with it? Or maybe it was more a case of laying old ghosts to rest. In which case, if she remained patient it wasn't unreasonable to think that he'd be willing to sell it to her.

Connor shrugged. 'You just need a plan of action. I'd imagine a woman who studies for a business degree, an MBA, and trains as a yoga teacher at the same time isn't exactly lacking in the smarts department.'

It was a strange and pleasurable sensation that filled her chest, for a moment pushing away the uneasy feeling that had settled there at the thought of coming clean about who she was. She really liked his faith in her abilities, that he considered her smart. It was refreshing to have a man who thought her capable of going for her dreams.

Yet layered beneath the pleasure of that was the nudge of guilt. He'd supported her as she'd laid out her plans to him, encouraged her to go for what she wanted, all the time unaware that those plans and wants were in direct opposition to his own.

On top of that, he'd told her that he liked her di-

rect approach, yet here she was continuing the deceit.
Her only defence was that she was really starting to
like him, and she didn't want her time with him to
come to an abrupt halt when she told him the truth.

He looked at her for several unsettling moments,
then flashed a devilish grin. 'So, yoga,' he said, looking at her over the rim of his cup. 'That explains why
you're so freaking flexible.'

Lola's body reacted to the sexy implication, an
arrow of heat firing through her veins. She clenched
her fists in her lap, annoyed that she'd let the perfect
opportunity to tell him who she was slip past. She'd
chickened out.

Wrong time. Wrong place. A coffee bar in the
community centre, a short time before she was supposed to instruct a class in the art of relaxation, was
not exactly the best place to confess all.

Admitting her identity to Connor would open
a whole can of worms that would need explaining. While she hadn't outright lied to him, Connor wouldn't see it like that. It would be a double
whammy for him. Not just because she'd been eco-
nomical with the truth about who she was and what
she wanted, but also because of her family connection to the man who had brought false embezzlement
charges against him.

That connection was tenuous, especially considering Lola had distanced herself from that side of
the family after what had been done to her mother,
and over the years she had cut herself off completely

from them with absolutely zero interest in their lives or what happened to them. Still, as Connor rightfully harboured a lot of ill-feeling towards her uncle, she knew her blood relationship would matter a great deal. Some people thought the apple didn't fall far from the tree.

She saw a couple of her students enter the building. 'I have to go,' she said, swigging down the last of her drink. 'People are arriving.'

Should she suggest another coffee meet-up? They needed to talk some more. Talk, not have sex.

Connor reached for her hand. 'I had a great time last night.'

Blood raced through her veins and sexy memories flooded her mind. 'So did I.' She reached down for her bag. 'But it was a one-nighter, remember?'

As disappointing as it was, she couldn't have sex with him again. It was one thing giving in to her hormones when she'd thought she wouldn't see him again but, now that they were essentially in direct conflict over the Cabacal, another hook-up was out of the question.

He squeezed his fingers around hers as she tried to pull away. 'It wasn't good enough to repeat?'

Sneaky bastard. She wanted to say something pithy, something that would wipe that cocky grin off his face. 'I surely don't need to stroke your ego by admitting that it was fantastic, do I?'

'Fantastic is always worth another go-round.'

Her core muscles clenched and she felt the pull in

her blood. 'I'm betting you can't afford the distraction any more than I can.'

'As distractions go, great sex always wins out.'

'Not always.'

'Why don't you let me take you to dinner tonight? Let me prove it.'

Hell, no. She wouldn't survive another evening with Connor and his particular brand of seduction. Dinner could so easily lead to so much more, and before she knew it they'd be in bed again. She was finding it hard enough to resist that smile of his as it was, the one that hiked up one corner of his mouth and made him look rakishly sexy. The gleam in his steely grey eyes that gave off a very definite bad-boy vibe. Not to mention the pure male energy that came off the man and surrounded her, swamped her, made her want to fall into his arms, despite her better intentions.

Absolutely not. No way. End of story.

She had to stay immune to him. She couldn't allow him to spin his magic over her again.

'What do you say, Lola? Want to be distracted again?'

No. No. No.

She took a deep breath. 'Okay.'

Lola turned away from the mirror and smoothed down the front of the simple dark-blue shift. She'd chosen the dress for its modest neckline and knee-length skirt, hoping it gave off a specific 'dinner with a friend' vibe.

In the time it took to shower and spritz herself with an innocuous floral body spray, she had to remind herself that having sex with Connor again was most definitely not on the cards. She had to keep him at arm's length—absolutely no flirting.

What she planned to do was use their time together to get to know him better. Find out what made him tick. She might be able to discover more about his reasons for wanting the property so badly, and what plans he had for it. If they were based entirely on drawing a line under his past experiences, to put those old ghosts to rest, then she might have a better chance of getting him to sell it to her.

In the grand scheme of things, since they'd already slept together, keeping the truth from him just a little longer surely didn't matter that much. While she wasn't entirely comfortable doing that, she had to believe that the means justified the ends.

Getting the Cabacal back meant everything to her. It was more than righting a wrong; it was her real link with her past, with her mother.

So many of her childhood memories were tied up in that building. Parties her grandparents threw there, where she and her friends dressed up in pretty dresses and imagined they were film stars.

Being allowed to watch from the little balcony at the back of the club with her mother while famous singers performed for the cream of London society.

Watching her adored grandparents, smiling at
each other and so in love as they danced together
on the club's crowded dancefloor.

As her throat tightened, she reached out for the
fitted denim jacket she kept on a hook by the front
door, took a fortifying breath and made her way out.
She'd chosen basic black pumps tonight—far more
practical, since she didn't possess a car and usually
took the tube or walked.

Emily was working a shift, which spared Lola
having to explain that she was seeing Connor. She
knew her friend still worried about Lola's Plan A,
and would have given Lola an earful if she'd known
what was going on.

The nearest tube station was around the block
from the West End restaurant Connor had chosen,
and her chest hitched when she saw him waiting on
the pavement by the entrance. The jolt to her system wasn't entirely unexpected. The man certainly
made an imposing sight. Well over six feet of nicely
honed muscle, confidence oozing from the set of
those impressive shoulders and an aura of strength
emanating from his masculine frame as he stood
surveying his surroundings with his hands in the
pockets of his trousers.

As he was looking the other way, Lola stopped
and took a moment to compose herself, to remind
herself that she had a very definite plan for the evening, and that plan did not involve ending up in bed
with him again.

Despite her self-talk, her mouth fairly watered as she watched him, as she took in the sight of all that male energy and leashed power. The muscles between her legs clenched in sympathy with her plight, and heat burned through her veins. It was as if her body already mourned the loss of all that excitement, adventure and erotic pleasure.

She started walking towards him and, as if he'd sensed her, he turned and met her gaze. Her stomach went into freefall.

'Hey.'

He leaned down and kissed her lightly, his scent washing over her and making her insides do crazy, stupid things. Bearing in mind that her intention was to keep things light, she failed miserably as she met his kiss and deepened it a little.

He grinned. 'How was your class?'

'Good. How was your afternoon?'

He nodded. 'Busy. Productive.'

Meaning that he'd been looking over the final contract for the Cabacal property before signing on the dotted line? A sinking feeling played in her stomach.

'Hope you're hungry.'

She was, and not just for food. Oh, hell. Why was she letting her desire for Connor overpower what she had to do?

Focus. She had to keep focused. 'I'm famished. Didn't have time to grab much of anything today.'

'Let's remedy that.'

Their table was on the mezzanine level in a secluded booth that nevertheless gave a bird's eye of the diners on the lower level.

'I've heard about this place,' Lola said. 'I thought they were booked out for months. How did you manage to get a table?' She raised her eyebrows. 'Or maybe you have a standing reservation?'

He smiled at her over his menu. 'Yeah, it's a necessity. Have to make sure I accommodate my revolving door of hot lovers.'

She really liked his ability to make her laugh. 'In which case you must have some recommendations as far as the menu is concerned.'

He kept his gaze on hers for long moments, during which her pulse kicked up. He had the sexiest eyes, all that steely grey that turned to smoke when he was aroused. Like now. 'Depends what menu we're talking about.'

'The one with food on it.' She shook her head, then went back to perusing the offerings. 'You've got a one-track mind.'

'And yours went straight there. Explain that.'

She kept her attention on the menu but lowered her voice. 'We're not having sex again tonight, Connor.'

He likely wouldn't want it anyway if he knew what secrets she harboured.

'In that case, I'd better give the oysters a miss.'

Lola made the mistake of glancing up and smack into the depths of that sexy grin. The man was too delicious to resist. Was there anything quite so irresistible as an intelligent and devastatingly gorgeous male with the hint of bad boy about him?

'I have no idea how anyone can eat them anyway.'

'I should have known,' Connor said with a shake of his head as he placed his menu down. 'You're going to tell me you're a vegetarian.'

'No, I'm not, actually. Not that there's anything wrong with that.'

He pursed his lips, holding up his hands. 'No argument from me.'

'I'm actually pescatarian.'

'Ouch.' He mock-frowned. 'Sounds painful.'

'It means I eat fish.'

'Okay.'

'Nothing with batter around it, though.'

'Whatever you eat, you look good on it.'

She put down her menu. 'Thanks. But still not having sex.'

Connor was laughing as the waiter arrived. Lola ordered the steamed haddock and seasonal vegetables, asking for a plain white sauce. Connor chose steak. Rare.

When they were alone again, he raised his wine glass and nodded to her sparkling water with its slices of lemon and lime. 'You're sure you wouldn't like something other than water. A mocktail, maybe?'

Lola picked up her glass. 'This is fine. I'm not especially fond of the taste of much else, to be honest.'

'Don't drink. Don't eat battered fish. If I didn't know otherwise, I'd think you didn't have any vices.'

Lola tried not to return his grin as he raised his glass to his lips, but there was just something too deliciously naughty about him that made that near impossible.

'Any more news on the property front?' Connor asked. 'About those complications, I mean.'

Lola frowned at the question. 'Not really. It's a bit of a stalemate at the moment.'

'What agents are you using? Maybe I can help.'

Why did he have to say that? Why did he have to be ultra nice and offer his help? It only piled on the feeling of being the biggest cheat. And what did she say to that anyway?

Actually, Connor. You can help. You can sell me back the property I've been deceiving you about from the get go.

She had visions of him tossing her over the balcony of the mezzanine, and she wouldn't blame him. She'd endure just about anything if it meant getting the Cabacal back, even Connor's wrath if she had to.

Since her throat was tightening up, she took a sip of the tart water. 'That someone I told you about has beaten me to it. Offered a really competitive price.'

'Do you still want the place?'

She made herself meet his gaze. 'Yes.'

'Then keep at it. Like I said, anything's possible if you want it bad enough.'

'The person buying it really wants it too. In fact, I think he might even have already signed the contract.'

Part of her wondered if he'd say how coincidental

that was because he'd also signed a contract today. But he didn't.

'Call the agent. Find out. You need to know for sure. If the buyer's stalling, you can get in fast with a counter-offer.'

She thought of Damian. Even if Connor hadn't signed yet, even if for some reason things had stalled, her pig-headed brother wouldn't budge. He wouldn't let her counter-offer because he wanted to ensure she didn't get to follow through on her plans, just as her father had tried to thwart her mother's dream.

'City people won't have time for such foolhardy nonsense,' her father had said one night, when Lola had been listening at the top of the stairs as their argument had become more heated. 'They're too busy making sound investments, keeping abreast of financial dealings, to worry about bending and stretching and chanting some mantra after a long day. If they want to let off steam they'll take a run along the Thames, or find the nearest bar that sells a decent malt.'

Her mother's protests had fallen on deaf ears, just as Lola's had with Damian. The two men had been cut from the same cloth.

But Connor hadn't been. He'd been supportive and had even offered to help her.

Before guilt could run its scratchy claws down her spine again, Lola asked, 'Would you ever stall on buying a property you wanted?'

'Can't see the point. You want it, or you don't.'

So the chances were that there wasn't a hold-up with Connor signing the contract. Which meant the transaction had likely already gone through.

She took a steadying breath. 'What if you bought a property then decided it wasn't actually what you wanted? That the reason you'd bought it was no longer valid?'

She watched him closely as he pursed his lips, considering. 'Hard to say what I'd do. Never been in that position before. But as long as it turned a profit, I'd find a way to make it work.'

As long as it turned a profit. Surely Connor was driven by more than financial gain in his acquisition of the Cabacal? There had to be more of an emotional reason for him, based on his history with her uncle. It couldn't primarily be because the property would make him money.

'Anyway, where is it?'

Lola had to refocus. 'Where's what?'

'This property you want so badly.'

'It's way across town.' She knew he'd probe and was thankful when the waiter chose that moment to bring their food. It gave her some thinking time. 'But there are a couple of other properties I've seen that show promise.'

Why the hell had she said that? If she let Connor believe that, it would weaken her position when she came to negotiate with him. But right then she had to get his attention away from the real property she wanted. Because she wasn't ready to tell him. While she hated lying to him, she still needed to know more about him and his reasons for wanting the Cabacal.

Should she allude to her own reasons for wanting it? Not directly, of course. She couldn't come right out and say she wanted it yet. But if she could allude to the reasons, demonstrate how important it was to her, he might be more accepting of her behaviour when she eventually told him.

God. She hated the thought of things ending between them. She liked the way he took her seriously, how he encouraged her to go for what she wanted. She really liked his company, liked being with him. He gave her more confidence to go for what she wanted, which was kind of perverse, considering the situation.

'I'd never recommend you compromise,' Connor said, slicing his steak. 'That's an easy out.'

Lola speared a green bean. 'Don't you ever compromise?'

Chewing, he shook his head. Then he swallowed. 'Not if I can help it. Compromised once and it bit me in the ass, big time.'

Did this have something to do with her uncle? Trying for nonchalance, Lola cut into her fish. 'That can't have been good.'

'It wasn't, but it taught me a valuable lesson.'

'Which was?'

'Trust your instincts. Don't get screwed.'

That hit her right in the centre of her chest. Was that what he'd think she was doing? Screwing him?

And not in a good way. What were his instincts telling him right now?

'Those other properties you looked at,' he said, giving no indication anything was currently amiss in the instinct department. 'Have you seen them at night?'

'No.'

'It's a nice evening,' he said. 'Let's take an excursion after we've eaten and you can show them to me.'

Her heart jolted at the quick-fire suggestion. 'Tonight? In the dark?'

'Yeah. It's worth checking out the areas at night since I assume you'll be offering classes until late?'

'Yes, that's likely to be my busiest period.'

'So you'll get a feel for each place that'll differ greatly from the one you'll get during the day.'

Despite the moment of panic at Connor's suggestion to see the properties, it was hard not to enjoy his obvious interest in her plans. The fact he'd actually give them some thought, and wanted to help her with the practicalities was incredibly addictive.

Just like him.

But then he was a businessman. That interest was innate.

'Makes sense,' Lola said, thankful she'd taken the opportunity at least to research other properties as back-up options. She hadn't wanted to imagine the worst-case scenario—that she would never get the Cabacal back—but if despite her best efforts her plans for acquiring the property collapsed she had every intention that the health centre would still go ahead.

'Great.' Connor picked up the menu. 'The chocolate torte here is the best you'll ever taste.'

'Then make it two. I never share dessert.'

CHAPTER EIGHT

THEY DROVE THROUGH the streets of London towards the address Lola had given for the first property.

Parking being what it was in London, they had to leave Connor's convertible and walk a few streets to the first property. It was in a relatively quiet back street, with not particularly good lighting.

'See, this was my point,' Connor said as he slipped his hands in his pockets and looked up at the terraced building with its fairly dilapidated windows and doors. 'You wouldn't want to think about somewhere like this for your studio.'

As Connor looked around, Lola tried to think of relevant points to illustrate why this was a place she'd seriously been considering. 'It's close to a tube station, though. That's an important consideration.'

'Yeah. Really important. But it's too quiet. Not enough footfall. You'd need good security lighting, state-of-the-art security generally. Maybe even someone manning the entrance. That would hike your start-up costs.'

Looking around, Lola agreed. She hadn't factored

in major overhauls to the outside of the properties, aside from general sprucing up, and Connor was right: there were too many dark areas once the surrounding small shops were closed up at the end of the day. Security would have to be a priority if she ever considered this place.

She thought about the Cabacal and its surrounding area. It was in a really busy, well-lit area with trendy bars where people milled about at all hours of the day and night. Security there wouldn't be much of an issue beyond the basic requirements of lighting, good locks and a building alarm. She certainly wouldn't need to hire a night guard.

The next property was an easy fifteen-minute walk. Connor reached for her hand, his fingers tightening around hers, drawing her close. His scent wafted on the evening air, doing delicious things to her insides and making her move even closer to him as they walked. She needed to focus.

'What sort of things would you look for when property hunting?' Lola asked, as casually as she could. 'I suppose it depends on what use you intend, of course, but would you always have an idea of that at the point of purchase?'

She glanced over as he considered her question. With a bit of luck, he'd give something away regarding his plans for the Cabacal, and she'd have more information on which to build her case to convince him to sell to her.

He pursed his lips. 'Can't say I always know, although I'd have a general idea seeing as night clubs are my business.'

'Then any other property you acquire would always become a night club?'

'Not always.'

Before she could probe deeper, they turned a corner and the next property came into view.

Lola tucked away her frustration that she hadn't been able to glean more.

'This has more going for it, location-wise,' Connor said as he perused what was this time a two-storey concrete block, freshly painted and with new windows and doors. 'Although it's not as close to a tube station. Plus, there's noise from that bar across the road, which might cause you some problems if you're trying to create a relaxing atmosphere.' He glanced at his watch. 'It's still relatively early, so things are likely to get livelier, especially at weekends.'

Lola looked towards the bar, her rueful smile indicative of the fact she might never have given that much thought. 'Good point. There's so much to consider.'

Again, she thought of the Cabacal. The trendy bars nearby were unlikely to get especially raucous since they attracted a different crowd, mostly after-work professionals who were stopping by to discuss business with a colleague, or taking the opportunity to enjoy a quick drink before heading home. Close to public transport, relatively quiet, yet busy enough that she wouldn't have to worry about extra security measures. Even if the Cabacal hadn't meant so much to her, she would be hard-pressed to find a property more suited to her plans.

'You've got your priorities straight,' Connor said, cutting into her thoughts. 'Location and access. Once they're in place, you can build on everything else. Where to next?'

As they walked to the final property, Lola had to admit that having Connor's take on the properties was insightful and incredibly useful, and his willingness to help her by giving valuable advice only seemed to increase the gnawing sense of guilt about lying to him.

She had no intention of purchasing any of these properties. She wanted the Cabacal. Yet she couldn't shake off the feeling of connection that was growing with Connor. He seemed genuinely interested in helping her. He was able to make suggestions and give insights, but in no way did he ever undermine her. He never dismissed her ideas out of hand, but somehow managed to make her question them herself to get things clear in her own mind.

She was starting to like him more and more as the evening went on.

The last of the properties was in an even quieter area than the first one. It was smaller than the others, but there was no denying it had a certain charm.

'I thought this one might work because there's

a tube nearby and it has good bus links,' Lola said. 'But I think it's probably too quiet. Too small.'

Connor came to stand beside her after he'd taken a cursory look at the front of the building. 'Yeah, it's quiet, but you could use the back entrance at night. Busier there and plenty of people around. And, while it might be small, there could be the possibility of extending into the next building at some stage.'

'Hmm. And I do want to expand the business in the future.'

Lola studied the building, thinking that at some time down the line this type of building might be an option, but right then there was only one place she wanted.

'Does it give you a good feeling,' Connor asked. 'Those instincts, remember?'

She looked up at him and met his gaze. *He* certainly gave her a good feeling. And all her instincts told her to grab him and kiss the life out of him. He was so incredibly gorgeous, standing there in the muted light of a quiet street, his hair ruffled by the breeze, his dark eyes filled with that sexy gleam. All big and masculine in a tailored jacket that fit him to perfection, his tie rakishly loosened so he could unfasten the top button of his shirt.

Her mouth positively watered just looking at him.

It wasn't just the way he looked, although that had the power to steal her breath clean away. It was much more than that. With every moment she spent with him she felt the attraction grow. He didn't dismiss her dreams but seemed intent on helping her achieve them. He encouraged, supported, offered her his own insights. It was such an alien concept to her, having that encouragement, that support. How could she even try to resist him?

She wanted him. *Really* wanted him.

As if reading her thoughts, he stepped forward. 'You've got a dirty mind.' He grinned and slid his arms around her waist. 'Here I am, trying my hardest to keep my mind on business, and you're looking at me as if you want to do very wicked and erotic things to me.'

His chest grazed her breasts as he pulled her closer and her nipples hardened to tight peaks.

'No harm in looking.' She hesitated for just a second, then slid her arms around his neck. 'I really like you, Connor. Just remember that.'

He grinned. 'Okay.'

Then his mouth took hers in a desperate, heated kiss.

He circled her closer to the building, kissing her mouth, her jaw, her throat, and soon she was a quivering mess of need.

'Why don't we take a closer look at the entrance?' Connor suggested as he placed open-mouthed kisses on her neck.

They moved into the stone-floored entryway and Connor angled her back against the door. She searched around frantically, looking for security cameras. 'This is insane, Connor.'

'Yeah.' He pressed her to the door. 'Let's be insane together.'

'I hope we're not being caught on camera,' she
managed as his erection prodded her and she opened
her legs a little. 'I don't want to be on *Crimewatch*.'

'I already checked,' he said between those heated
kisses, his hands moving to clamp around her hips.
'No cameras.'

He levered up her dress, pressing his knee between her legs and coaxing her to widen them even
more. 'We can't do this, Connor. Not here. What if
someone walks by?'

'We'll wish them a pleasant evening and tell them
to sod off.'

He grinned, quick and sexy.

Even as she spun between pure lust and the deca-
dence of having sex in a public place, Lola couldn't
find it in her to stop Connor from reaching for her
panties.

He stepped back so he could shimmy them down
her legs, and all the while Lola kept searching around
for hidden cameras. She gave a quick laugh as she
stepped out of her panties, and Connor shoved them
in his trouser pocket.

'Oh, hell. I can't believe I'm doing this.'

Connor grabbed his wallet from his jacket pocket and
took out a condom. He unzipped his fly, the rasping
sound in the quiet of the London back street doing

nothing except to spur him on. He couldn't wait any longer. He needed her now.

When he'd covered himself, he pushed her back deep into the door-well, satisfied that they were as sheltered as possible and offering up a silent plea that they'd not be disturbed. Lola grabbed for his shoulders and raised one leg to wrap it around his waist.

'Thanks be to the yoga gods for a flexible woman.'

Lola laughed and tightened her leg against him as she dug her hands into his shoulders.

'You haven't even scratched the surface of my flexibility.'

He grinned, squeezing her backside as his cock pressed against her heat. When her foot slid down his spine, pressing on that sensitive area of his back, he reached around and positioned her foot to ease the discomfort. Although, when she hiked up her hips and all her wetness curved around his erection, he didn't think he was capable of feeling anything other than his blood rushing through him in a frenzied blast of lust.

'Shit, Lola.'

Her response was to bring her hand down between them and curl her fingers around his cock. She closed her eyes and dropped her head back against the door, her hips curving upward, encouraging him to slide inside her.

He wanted to torment her, make her beg for him to take her. He wasn't sure how he did it, but he managed to string things out, even as his cock throbbed and that lust in his blood gathered strength. Leaning down, he kissed her neck, letting his teeth graze against her delicate throat.

Still her hips bucked and she gave an urgent, 'Connor…'

'What?' His voice sounded low, grazed, as if his throat was raw. 'Tell me what you want.'

'You know,' she complained, her fingers squeezing his thickness, her foot pressing into his back, her hips grinding as she tried to get him inside her. 'I'm not going to spell it out.'

She didn't have to, not when her wet heat was like a siren call to his dick. There was only enough torment he could take, only enough resistance he could manage.

He tapped her hand away, replacing it with his own as he positioned himself and pushed hard, deep and was inside her as she gasped and clung to him.

He pumped hard, each shove pushing her harder against the door, which answered with a shaky, clanging sound that indicated an unsustainable lock.

Each time he shoved into her she caught her breath, the sound travelling to her throat in a needy groan.

'Connor… Oh, God. Connor…'

She held him tight, her muscles gripping his cock, her fingers digging into his shoulders.

He drove into her like a freaking train, but in his defence she was making him bloody crazy with her tight, hot body and those needy gasps and moans.

Each time he pushed deep, the door gave way a bit, and in the small slice of his brain that still functioned with some coherence he had the thought that maybe the door wouldn't hold out much longer against the determined battering they were subjecting it to.

He placed his hands on her hips, squeezing tightly both to go even deeper inside her and to hold her safe in his arms in case the door gave way.

He came hard, over and over, as he felt her answering response.

He dropped his forehead to hers, their gasping breaths echoing around the silent back street.

'Do you think someone heard us?' Lola asked as she caught her bottom lip between her teeth. 'I think I was making a lot of noise.'

'Yeah,' Connor said as he withdrew from her. 'You were sounding off loud enough to wake the dead.'

She slapped at his shoulder. 'You weren't exactly quiet.'

She looked so thoroughly fucked, her hair all mussed, her lips full from his kisses, not to mention her dress up around her waist. He zipped himself, then leaned down and lightly kissed her. 'Let's go back to my place and really put on a show.'

She hesitated for a moment in the process of pulling down her skirt, and he knew those cogs and wheels were turning and trying to come up with an excuse. 'I should get home. I've got some lesson plans to write up and other admin to do.'

FAYE AVALON

115

He noticed she didn't meet his eyes and wondered if she was thinking the same thing he was thinking. That one-night stands were supposed to last one night, but neither of them seemed able to stick to that. They both wanted more.

He didn't want to dwell on what 'more' was. Didn't want to think around why he couldn't seem to get enough of her.

All he knew was that this was starting to turn into more than sex. He couldn't remember the last time he'd enjoyed being with a woman this much. Lola was easy to be around and maybe that was part of the attraction. She knew what she wanted. She was focused, intelligent, and fun. No side.

He'd enjoyed looking at those properties with her, getting a handle on what she was looking for and what she wanted for her business.

She had plans, dreams, and he sensed an innate determination to achieve those plans and dreams. That energy bounced off her like a living thing. It was addictive.

She was addictive.

Fuck.

Reality check. 'Look, I know this has been pretty intense,' he said as nonchalantly as he could manage while he battled with the idea that he wanted more with Lola than blow-the-doors-off sex. 'But in my experience this kind of chemistry burns out faster when acted upon and not denied.'

She reached into her bag and pulled out a tissue

for him to use to dispose of the condom. After he'd taken care of that with a visit to a refuse bin a few yards away, he came back to find her straightening her clothes.

There was a tightness in his chest and his breathing felt uneven. Unusual for him to feel stress after a great bout of sex, but something about Lola unsettled him. He wondered if it was because she might be about to say no. To walk away.

He wasn't ready for that. He hadn't been lying when he'd suggested letting this thing between them burn out naturally, except he was no longer sure it was that simple. Regardless, the last thing he wanted was to have her stick in his system and not be able to do a thing about it.

His mind flashed back a few years to the moment he'd realised Caroline had been manipulating him. Shit. That had hurt like nothing else. Maybe if he hadn't been so damned obsessed with her, hadn't allowed himself to fall too fast and too hard, he might have seen the signs, might not have gone against his instincts to slow down, take his time getting to know her better. Instead, he'd plunged straight into the deep end of the pool, only to come up gasping for air and finding himself in the role of scapegoat.

He'd been a damned fool, and his only defence was that he hadn't been thinking straight. When a man didn't think straight because of a woman, there was usually hell to pay. He'd learned his lesson, and that lesson included keeping things temporary, light, easy. Fuck a woman and get her out of his system before she had chance to take up residence there.

He knew he needed to do that with Lola, but it wasn't a real problem. This time he was giving the deep end of the pool a wide berth, and there was no chance of falling in. His eyes were open, and he wasn't about to be taken for a fool. Never again.

'How about I help you with that admin work you mentioned?' he said. 'Then you can stay the night and I'll make you breakfast.'

She looked up at him, her direct green gaze indicating she was trying to resist him but failing miserably. He really liked that she wasn't clingy and needy but was instead independent and focused on her own plans. Her determination to make her dreams a reality was refreshing, more so because she didn't seem the type to step on anyone to do it. He should know, since he'd been privy to enough treachery and deceit to last him a lifetime.

'You're a difficult man to say no to, Connor.'

'Then don't say it.' He slid his hands in his pockets. 'Look, this is fun, right? And that's what we both want. No strings, no commitment?'

She nodded.

'It doesn't have to mean anything for either of us beyond good sex. We're not making it into anything else. It won't go on for ever.'

Why did he keep saying this? Was he trying to convince her, or himself?

Caution filled her gaze, only adding to his own

sense of confusion and panic. What the hell was wrong with him? If she said no, he would let her go. No hard feelings. Nothing lost. He'd forget her, and the sex, soon enough. He'd make bloody sure of that.

'You're right,' she said with a nod. 'It doesn't have to mean anything else. It doesn't have to affect anything else. It's just sex, and it certainly won't go on for ever.'

Having her shoot his own words back at him pissed him off, and made him want to press her right back against the door and show her just how long it could go on.

It was bad enough that he wanted another night with Lola, but he feared he was already planning the night after that. And the next. He was at risk of stepping onto dangerous ground. What had happened to quick, easy sex-only arrangements? The kind that ensured he didn't have to look beyond what was on the surface. He didn't have to bother working out a woman's motivations or wonder what the hell she might be plotting or planning. He didn't need to figure out what her end-game was, and how it might bring him to his fucking knees.

Once bitten was more than enough for any man, and he'd vowed that he'd never let himself be vulnerable again. That he'd never totally trust. And, family excepted, he never had.

He stepped away from Lola so fast that he stumbled on the kerb.

He winced as his back muscles protested, and

Lola's hand reached out at the very moment he righted himself.

'Connor. Are you okay?'

He grimaced, his hand shooting to his lower back as pain ripped through him. 'Yeah, fine.'

'You're not fine. I've seen you flinch a few times now. What's wrong with your back?'

'Nothing. Just kicks up from time to time.'

She came around behind him and put her hand on his lower back. 'Where does it hurt?'

She pressed and prodded, making Connor think that if his back hadn't hurt before it certainly would after she'd finished with him.

'Your muscles feel really tight. I can help with that.' She came back in front of him. 'Let's stop by my place on the way to yours and I'll grab a few things.'

Tired of this particular conversation, Connor drew her closer, placing his arms around her. 'The only thing you need to bring is you. I'm planning to keep you naked and very contented for the whole night.'

'And what if your back seizes up?' she asked, cocking her head to the side. 'You're not going to be much use to me then, are you? Think about it. I'll be naked and there'll be nothing you can do about it.'

Connor drew in a breath. 'When you put it like that…'

CHAPTER NINE

EMILY WAS STILL OUT when Lola rushed up to their flat. She grabbed a few supplies then scribbled a note telling her friend that she wouldn't be home again that night.

Lola knew she needed to put Emily's mind at rest about what was going on. They'd spoken on the phone earlier that day when Lola had admitted that her conversation with Damian hadn't gone well. She knew Emily was worried about her spending time with Connor while this secret lay between them. So was she.

It doesn't have to mean anything for either of us beyond good sex. We're not making it into anything else.

Would he feel that way when he knew the truth? Would he shrug off what they'd shared as something that didn't matter? That didn't have to influence a business transaction between them?

She feared he wouldn't be able to do that. Hadn't he also said that he found it hard to trust?

Nausea settled in her stomach at the knowledge that she would be responsible for adding another cruel layer to his trust issues. The very last thing she wanted to do was hurt him and the longer this went on between them without her admitting who she was, the worse it would be for Connor.

And for her. Because she was getting herself in too deep. She was starting to really care about him, and about the consequences for him if she continued this charade. There was also the possibility that the longer she delayed telling him the truth, the more likely he was to refuse selling the Cabacal to her.

Despite everything, she couldn't seem to not want him. Couldn't deny herself the opportunity to spend another night with him.

Soon, everything would change between them, so couldn't she just have this one last time?

She wanted it. So much. And she was going to take it. She slipped a change of underwear in her bag, along with some toiletries from the bathroom, then headed back out to where Connor was waiting for her. She knew that she should have invited him up, but she didn't want him seeing anything that might make him suspicious. It was safer to let him wait in his car. Thankfully, he hadn't pushed.

The fact he had showed no interest in seeing where she lived confirmed that he saw this as a temporary thing between them. That it would burn itself out. There was no need for him to concern himself with the inside of her flat, or anything else in her life that didn't relate to their time between the sheets.

The thought sat heavily in her chest.

Perhaps this was a good thing. If he wasn't invested in anything they shared other than excellent sex, then her eventual revelation wouldn't hit him as hard. She might not add to his trust issues as deeply as she'd feared.

That was a cop-out, but it went some way towards alleviating her guilt. But only some way, because the spectre of her deceit was always lying there just beneath the surface.

Yet she didn't want that spectre to ruin what time she did have with Connor.

On arriving at his apartment, Connor busied himself getting drinks while Lola went into his bedroom and unpacked her bag.

When he came in with their drinks, he stopped dead. 'What's all this?'

She looked to where he stared at the bottles of essential oils she'd unpacked on his side table, the scented candle and oil burner, and the huge towels she'd fetched from the bathroom, one of which she'd placed across the centre of the bed. 'I'm giving you a massage.'

He frowned. 'Why?'

'Because your back muscles need one.'

A pained look passed over his face. 'My back muscles are fine.'

'They will be when I'm finished with them. This is one of the things I'm trained to do, remember? Therapeutic massage.' She bit back a grin. 'Honestly, anyone would think you're about to undergo a form of torture.'

'They'd be right.'

Now she did laugh. 'Get your kit off, lover. Then come and lie face-down on this bed.'

He raised his eyebrows, then took a large swig of his drink before placing their glasses down on the other side of the bed. 'That was going to be my line.'

Lola pouted. 'Poor baby. Would it help if we were both naked? Would that make this whole torturous experience less objectionable to you?'

'Wouldn't hurt.'

They eyed each other across the bed and, saying nothing, Lola reached behind her to pull down the zip of her dress. She slid the material off one shoulder, then the other.

Connor watched transfixed as she let the dress fall to her waist, revealing her bra. He only moved when Lola raised her eyebrows expectantly, and he slowly began unbuttoning his shirt.

It was Lola's turn to be mesmerised. With his heated gaze still fixed on hers, he tugged the unbuttoned shirt from his trousers to reveal the amazing muscled perfection of his chest. Her mouth positively watered as she imagined sliding her oiled hands over all that hard, masculine strength.

He tossed the shirt to the floor, then grinned. 'You next.'

Enjoying the game, she reached around and pulled the zip further down her back so the dress slid over her hips and to the floor. Then it was her turn to wait. But Connor didn't move.

'Haven't you forgotten something?' he asked with an arch of his eyebrow.

She glanced down at herself, then realised what he meant. She looked up, met the wicked gleam in his eyes then unhooked her bra. Only when she tossed it away, revealing her breasts to his hungry gaze, did he unhook his belt and draw it from the waistband of his trousers.

His slow striptease was really turning her on, and she hoped by the time they were both naked that she'd still be coherent enough to administer his massage.

When he was down to his boxers, he stood waiting again. 'Take them off. Make it slow.'

The now-familiar burn in her lower belly intensified, joining the throb of anticipation between her legs. But she couldn't let herself be distracted; she needed to work on Connor's back first. Ease some of that tension she'd felt beneath her hands when she'd checked him out.

Nevertheless, she'd promised him that they could both be naked when she massaged him. So she hooked her fingers into the sides of her panties and slowly lowered them down her legs to the floor, where she stepped out of them.

From across the bed, she heard Connor's breath hitch, saw his nostrils flare and his erection jerk hard against his boxers. He yanked off his boxers, his cock standing proud and ready.

Lola took a moment to enjoy the sight of him,

the exceptional physique and potent appeal, then she nodded. 'On the bed.'

She thought he would protest, say something like *You first*, but he did as she said. She had to wonder if his instant compliance was more to do with the prospect of having his sexual needs satisfied rather than having his non-sexual physical needs fulfilled.

She coaxed him into a prone position, noting how he pillowed his head on his folded arms and then turned so he could watch her. She poured some of the massage carrier oil into the bowl she used for mixing, then added several drops of lavender essential oil and some cooling eucalyptus, before pouring the mixture into an empty glass bottle.

'Smells like crap.'

She glanced down at him as she swirled the contents in the bottle. 'Open your mind to possibilities. This is going to make you feel really good.'

'If your intention is to make me feel good, then I've got a better idea. One that involves you lying beneath me with my cock inside you.'

'You've such a way with words, Connor. Romance just oozes from you, doesn't it?'

He turned his head a little more, a questioning glint in his eyes, making her wish she could take back what she'd said. Because romance didn't come into this thing between them; it was purely physical. It didn't matter that she was starting to want more. That she was enjoying the way he treated her like a woman who knew her own mind, who had good

ideas, whose dream he validated and supported. It
didn't matter that she enjoyed his quick wit, his attentive manner.

Because he didn't feel the same, and once he knew
the truth she might not be able to convince him that
what she felt for him wasn't all a lie. So this, right
now, was all that mattered. Being with him, attempt-
ing to ease his discomfort, enjoying him.

Everything else could wait just a little longer.

She cleared her mind so she could tune in to Connor's needs. She picked up a small hand towel and
placed it beside Connor's shoulders, then grabbed the
bottle of mixed oils and got onto the bed.

He looked amazing. All that lean and honed muscle across his back, the wide shoulders, carved shoulder blades and well defined arms. She wanted to
touch every square inch of him.

'This is more like it,' he said as she straddled him
and her wet heat pressed against the crease of his
buttocks. 'Your hot little pussy pressed against me
is all the massage I need.'

'Try and switch off your thoughts,' Lola instructed, trying not to react to the feel of Connor's
toned body against her. 'Soon, you'll be feeling so
good that you could go all night.'

He gave a low hum, making her smile.

She rubbed her hands together, warming the oil
between her palms before placing them either side
of his lower spine.

His muscles tightened a fraction, then released as

she moved her hands in slow, circular movements. 'Put your attention on the area I'm touching and imagine your muscles relaxing.'

'Uh-huh.'

She smiled at his muted response, sliding her hands along his spine in a slow up-and-down then circular motion.

'How's that?' she asked softly when his breathing deepened, slowed.

'Not bad,' he said after a moment. 'You've got magical hands.'

'You're really tense around here.' She worked on the area beneath his waist. 'How did you hurt your back?'

His muscles tightened a fraction. 'Old history.'

'I'd really like to know. It might help me understand just how deep a massage I need to give you.'

It wouldn't necessarily help her to do that, but Lola really wanted to know more about him, and getting him to talk while he was in a relaxed state would likely be the best opportunity she would have for that to happen.

'Got into some scrapes while I was in foster care.'

Lola straightened. She hadn't expected him to say that, but now that he had she was intrigued.

'Father took off when we were kids. Mother left to go find him. The five of us kids were placed in care. Wasn't long before I acted up and they transferred me out, away from my siblings. Maybe I deserved it. I was a cocky little bastard.' He went silent for a moment, then drew in a long breath. 'You stopped stroking. I was enjoying it.'

'Sorry.' She began working his muscles again, taking extra care as myriad feelings vied for attention. Her heart squeezed at the image of a scared little boy acting up because he didn't know what was happening to him, to his family. Not only losing his parents, but being separated from his siblings.

Anger simmered deep inside her at a system that didn't recognise the effect of that kind of trauma on a child. 'You've got four brothers and sisters?'

'Yeah. Logan's the eldest. I'm next. Then there's Aiden and Ty, who are in the forces, and Colleen's the baby. She's at uni.'

She forced herself to keep her strokes light. 'How did you hurt your back?'

He raised his shoulders in a lazy shrug. 'Took a tumble down the stairs, courtesy of a bigger kid's boot.'

Her chest burned. 'Little shit.'

'Him, or me?' His low scoff should have eased the anger inside her, but it didn't.

'What happened after that?'

'Wasn't long before Logan got himself a job. Got us all back together again.'

Lola hadn't met Connor's eldest brother, but already she liked him without reservation.

She couldn't imagine that kind of childhood. Her father and brother were controlling, but she knew they loved her, protected her. And her mother and grandparents had adored her.

After a few moments, Connor stretched a little. 'Have to admit, that feels really good.'

'Tension and stress will tighten your back muscles and cause pain, especially since you have a weakness in that area. You really should take time to learn to relax.'

'Yeah.'

She continued to work on his back, warming and pouring more oil to aid her manipulation of his muscles. She could feel them loosening by degrees, his breathing really deep and his body relaxed.

She thought about what he'd told her, about the circumstances of his injury. Although anger still burned through her, she knew it wouldn't aid her massage ability, so she took some deep, cleansing breaths and willed her hands to relax.

She loved touching him, helping him, and it didn't hurt that she could feast on his spectacular body at the same time.

Unable to resist, she leaned down and pressed a light kiss to his neck, then across his shoulders and down his spine. The fragrance of the oils combined with Connor's own exquisite scent flooded her nostrils. She shifted back a little and kissed each of his ass cheeks. This guy was certainly built.

'Do I get to pour oil over you and kiss your ass next?'

It made her laugh. 'How does your back feel?'

'Good. Why don't we test it out?'

Deeply moved by what he'd told her, she wanted to help him even more. That, and the fact she was enjoying the feel of Connor's hot and pliable flesh beneath her hands. 'There's something else we could try that might help you relax deeper.'

'Now you're talking.'

'You might like this even more. It has dual benefits.'

'I'm all ears,' he said, turning to look at her with slumberous, sexy eyes. 'Well, not all ears. I'm pretty much a whole lot of cock at the moment too.'

To confirm his statement, he turned onto his back.

Lola laughed and shook her head. 'So I see.'

She straddled him again, making sure to keep away from his erection which threatened to press against her heated core. 'Have you heard of Tantric sex?'

'Yeah,' he said, his hands on her hips. 'It's the kinky stuff, right?'

'No. It's really slow sex. It can lead to incredibly powerful orgasms.'

That got his attention. He raised his eyebrows, his hands leaving her hips to cup her breasts, his thumbs stroking slowly across her hardening nipples. 'Tell me more.'

'It's been around for thousands of years. It involves prolonging arousal.'

'Go on. I'm riveted.'

She kept her face impassive because she needed him to understand the real nature and purpose of the practice. 'You have to stick with it, Connor. Have to step out of your comfort zone. You can't change your mind halfway through and go for the whole wham-bam thing instead. It involves a lot of slow, steady touching.'

'I can do slow,' he said, illustrating his point by languidly sliding his hand across her stomach. 'And I can do steady.'

'I'll need to teach you a full yogic breath. Controlling your breathing is a fundamental part of Tantric sex. Now, are we doing this or not?'

He shifted on the bed, as if getting comfortable. 'Go for it.'

'Okay.' Still straddling him, she got comfortable herself, thinking how bizarre it was teaching someone how to breathe deeply while you were both stark-naked and one of you had a massive erection. 'Close your eyes. Concentrate on your exhalation.'

Surprisingly, he picked up the technique really fast, and before long was taking good, deep breaths.

He opened his eyes. 'When do we get to the good stuff?'

'This is the good stuff. It's not just about getting off. Do you know what chakras are?'

He grinned. 'Kinda'

She talked him through each one, pleased that he paid attention, although his hands found her hips again, his fingers possessively digging into her.

Closing her eyes, she deepened her own breathing. When she opened them again it was to find him watching her. 'You're so fucking beautiful.'

It knocked her sideways for a moment. Not just because of what he'd said, but the way he'd said it.

As if he was seeing deep inside her, looking past the superficial to what lay deeper beneath the surface.

It unsettled her, pushed at the guilt that she'd tried to put away for one more night. When he tried to pull her down against him, she batted his hands away. 'You're losing focus.'

He gave a lazy grin. 'I like my focus.'

'I'm going to touch you really slowly,' she said, battling to concentrate. 'You're going to breathe through it, and you're going to concentrate on being in the present. If you feel like you're going to come, pull the energy up from the base of your spine to the top of your head.'

He raised his eyebrows, his grin widening. 'The top of my head?'

'Connor. Are you going to take this seriously?'

He sobered, but she knew it took everything he had. It was his first introduction to esoteric practices and it was natural for people to be circumspect when they didn't know what to expect.

She took in a deep breath, filling her lungs with the fragrant oils and the heady scent of Connor, then placed her hands on his chest and slowly circled her hands over his skin, teasing his nipples.

It didn't take long before he cupped her breasts, brushing his thumbs across her nipples and sending delicious thrills through the entire length of her body. She shifted against him, rubbing her heat against his impressive erection, but making sure to take it really slowly and sensually, reminding herself that this was about the journey, about exploring each other, about making it last.

Soon they were both breathing heavily, with no thought of control, or of stringing things out. Connor curled his fingers deeper into her hips and held her tight as he flipped them both until she was on her back and he was leaning over her.

'Your back…'

'Is feeling great,' he ground out as he slid his hand between her legs. 'Those magic hands of yours.'

He had magic of his own, Lola thought while she still could. In his hands, and just about everywhere else. He pushed his finger in deep, sliding in and out in a slow and drugging rhythm until Lola was trying to delay her own orgasm.

She didn't want this to end. Not just the slow and easy way they were together like this, but her time with Connor. Deep inside her she knew she was on borrowed time, and she couldn't deny the truth of that even as Connor brought her closer and closer to the edge.

Not wanting to let that truth take root, she focused on what she'd told him and slowed down her breathing as her inner muscles began to contract. She pulled the energy from between her legs, imagined drawing it up her spine to the top of her head and found herself gasping for both air and control.

Connor withdrew his hand and reached out for a condom. Vaguely, Lola knew he'd covered himself and she opened her legs as he moved between them.

With his hands braced either side of her shoulders, he looked at her, their gazes connecting and holding, and Lola felt something move through her that was at once powerful, amazing and discomfiting. She sensed that Connor was fighting to keep control. He was trying hard to do what she'd told him and take this really slowly.

'Think I've just about reached the end of my journey,' he said as he nudged her opening. 'So, unless you object, I'm heading straight for my destination.'

Lola wanted to tell him it was okay, that she'd reached the end of her journey too. She was primed to take him inside her, to feel the length of him fill her and take them where they both needed to go.

Journey's end.

Instead, he took it slowly, his gaze locked to hers as he pushed in an inch before he withdrew, then another inch, and again a withdrawal. It was exquisite: the friction, the heat, the sheer girth of him. Each time he pushed forward, she gripped him hard, holding tight as he withdrew and earning a deep groan.

Like her, she knew he hovered at the edge of orgasm and, loving his attempt to keep things slow for as long as possible, she wanted to return the favour.

Reaching between them, she called on her theoretical knowledge of the practice and pressed her fingers beneath his balls. She was rewarded with a sharp, 'Fuck'.

'Sorry…'

He held above her, gritting his teeth, his eyes

squeezed tight for a few moments. Then he opened them and shook his head. 'Don't apologise. That's taken the edge off.'

'Really?' She released her hands and brought them to his shoulders. 'It was supposed to.'

He pushed inside her, a little deeper this time, before withdrawing again. 'Are you close?'

As if he had to ask. Surely her gasps and moans were indicative of her nearness to orgasm? But she nodded. 'Yes.'

Still moving slowly, but making sure he didn't push too deep, he dropped a kiss to her mouth. 'Want me to stop for a while? Slow things down?'

When she shook her head, gripping his shoulders tighter, he brought a hand down to her knee and raised her leg higher. The movement allowed him to push deeper and this time he drove in all the way.

Lola gasped and clung to him. 'Oh, hell. That's...'

The angle at which he penetrated her allowed him to rub against her slick walls and hit the exact spot where she didn't think any amount of Tantric knowledge would stop her from coming. She was powerless. Completely and desperately defenceless against the spasms that flung her over some metaphoric wall where everything was shot with colour, light and pure sensation.

Nirvana, she thought as the orgasm went on and on. This had to be the closest to nirvana anyone could get on this earthly plane.

With each shove inside her, Connor grunted, then

he was coming too, and she could feel each frenzied release reverberate inside her.

Their gazes clashed again and held. Their breathing was unsteady, gasping.

Connor blew out a long breath through his mouth, then dropped his forehead to hers. 'That was…some journey.'

Lola managed a smile as she reached up and brushed the back of her fingers along his stubbly jaw, her hands not quite steady. In fact, nothing about her felt steady. Her world had been rocked, shaken. 'Destination was pretty good too.'

His gaze held hers and for an instant she glimpsed something raw and unexpected in his grey depths. Had he been as affected by what they'd just shared as she had been? Had he experienced a tumble into the unknown, a wrench away from the norm? Whatever it was disappeared beneath the flash of his grin. 'How long before we can take the return trip? That squeezing thing you did was pretty neat.'

'I didn't do it right,' Lola said, still trying to make sense of what she'd glimpsed in his eyes. 'You came too soon afterward. Maybe I didn't press hard enough or long enough. Done right, you're supposed to be able to go for hours before climaxing.'

Connor's eyebrows rose. 'Anywhere I can press to stop you from coming so fast?'

'It's not so vital for women. Multiple orgasms, remember?'

'Even so. This Tantric thing has something to recommend it. Maybe I'll make a study of it.'

For some reason, his statement made her feel ridiculously pleased. Probably because he actually seemed serious, although she did wonder if he was just being glib. Whatever, she loved the fact that he hadn't dismissed it as being out there or new age, and seemed willing to keep an open mind.

She wanted to tell him they could do lots more practising, but that spectre of guilt hung between them. After her revelations she doubted there'd be any kind of relationship between them, let alone one that involved experimental sex.

A hollow feeling settled in her stomach, but she wasn't about to let it ruin what had been an amazing experience, so once more she locked it down inside her and refused to dwell on what she couldn't have.

Connor eased away from her and rolled onto his back. He didn't look at her as he asked, 'Have you tried anything like this before?'

'No. Any knowledge is theoretical.' She rolled onto her side and hiked onto her elbow, looking down at him to gauge his reaction. 'Although I have considered learning more about it and maybe adding it to my repertoire. I could give lessons.'

His head whipped around and the look of horror on his face was priceless, until he realised she was ribbing him.

'Give me some time to recover and I'll help you with a lesson plan.'

CHAPTER TEN

LOLA WOKE IN the early hours with Connor's arm around her shoulder, her head on his chest. She hadn't planned to stay the night again, but that Tantric session seemed to have wiped them both out.

She angled her head to look up at him and saw he was in a deep and seemingly restful sleep. The urge to wake him was strong; she couldn't seem to get enough of being with him. But she left him to it. The quality of sleep after a massage was often the purest form of rest. Not to mention the benefits of a hefty session of good and wholesome sex.

Carefully, Lola got off the bed and, as Connor's shirt was the nearest item of clothing, she shrugged into it, loving how his smell wrapped around her.

She fastened a couple of shirt buttons at her waist, checked the candles and oils had burned right out, then made her way to his kitchen. Interesting. His counters were clear, the whole space pristine-clean. Perhaps not unusual for a man who probably didn't spend much time at home. Despite that he'd taken some time having coffee with her in the middle of

the day, she sensed he was a workaholic, and probably spent more time travelling back and forth between his two clubs than anything else.

Lola found a glass and poured herself water. She
turned and leaned back against the sink, her gaze
landing on the breakfast bar in front of the large
floor-to-ceiling window that looked out over the
capital as it came awake in the soft glow of early
morning.

On the black marble counter lay a scattering of
papers, and on top of the pile was a copy of what
looked like the agent details for the Cabacal property. Lola walked over and picked up the document,
scanning the photos and the descriptions beneath
them. She stroked lovingly across the photographs
of the old Art-Deco-style building, remembering vis-
its with her mother when she was a child. Back then
her grandparents had been alive and the building had
housed a small exclusive cabaret club.

But Lola's mother had always planned that when
it became hers she would turn it into a fitness and
wellbeing studio with the sole intention of helping
people live better, healthier lives. It had caught Lola's
imagination from the start, and she'd listened with
rapt attention as her mother had declared what the
various rooms would be used for: the colours, the
equipment, the classes she'd planned. Lola had been
inspired, and from then on it had become her dream
too. Until her devious uncle had changed everything.

Saddened by old memories, she placed the details

back down, noticing the wad of official-looking documents off to the side.

The contract, Lola thought. For the sale of the property.

She tilted her head, trying to get a good look at the papers without actually touching them, all the while instructing herself to turn around and walk away. Was Connor in the process of reading through the document before he signed it? Wouldn't that be done in a lawyer's office? Why did he have the paperwork at home? Left so haphazardly on the breakfast counter? Was this just a mock-up of the real thing that Damian had sent?

Lola took a breath, then put down the glass. It wouldn't hurt just to take a peek, would it? She wasn't sure why she was torturing herself, but morbid fascination drove her onward. Maybe there was something in the contract, some clause, that could provide her with ammunition to persuade Connor to sell the property to her when she was in a position to buy it. Her fingers crept dangerously close to the bottom edge of the paper, but she pulled them back.

She couldn't do it. It wasn't right. It was intrusive, invasive and downright dishonest.

Connor had been good enough to try and help her with the properties he thought she was interested in. He'd taken her to each one and pointed out pluses and minuses. Okay, they'd punctuated their viewings with some very enjoyable back-street sex, but that wasn't the point.

He'd been interested in helping her. Which meant that she had no business snooping. Besides, she knew what was in the contract, the terms of the agreement. Damian had told her, labouring the point: full and final sale. As if she needed reminding.

It was strange, really. Connor was obviously willing to pay an extremely competitive price for the place, yet he'd admitted to having no real plans for it, and had even considered allowing it to remain empty for the foreseeable future. He hadn't really seemed that interested in it.

What exactly was the pull of the place for him? Why did he feel compelled to own it?

She knew how strong that compulsion could be, and although the property held wonderful memories for her she imagined Connor would rather forget what had happened to him.

As she mused about reasons, her hands found the countertop. Before she could stop herself, she nudged back the edge of the papers and flicked through them. All legal jargon, with the usual sections and clauses. No mention of intended use anywhere that she could see, but that wasn't unusual. If Connor planned another nightclub, it wasn't so far removed from the casino that her uncle had used it for.

Her eyes almost popped out of her head when her gaze fell on the agreed purchase price. How much? It wasn't just over the market value advertised but was more than Lola's trust fund could cover. Her heart took a dive along with her stomach. How was she supposed to persuade Connor to sell to her at a much lower price than he had agreed to pay for it?

Disheartened, Lola let the pages fall back and straightened the contract on the counter. But beneath it was more papers. She didn't even think about not looking now. Surely there was nothing else that could surprise her? Slowly, she drew out the remaining documents.

Pages of blue letterhead held a series of price quotations for construction work. Yes! Now she might get an idea of what Connor planned to do with the place.

The top quote was for some restructuring at the club where she'd first met him, to add a small rear patio area with lighting and outside heating.

The quote underneath made her heart stop.

To carry out demolition work at premises in south west London currently known as the Cabacal Club.

Demolition? Was he having it torn down?

Lola stared at the quote, reading every word over and over, as if she might have misread them. As if that word 'demolition' was actually something else. But it wasn't. He was having the property demolished.

She couldn't seem to swallow, couldn't stay the nausea that swam in her stomach. For long moments she just stood there in the quiet of Connor's kitchen, staring at the words which now blurred as her eyes went damp.

She shoved the quotes back beneath the contract

and stepped away from the counter, as if doing so would make what she'd just seen disappear. She sniffed, squeezed her eyes shut as anger coated the nausea.

There was no way she would stand back and let this happen. No way she'd let him destroy that wonderful old building.

She snatched up the property details again, knowing what a travesty it would be to tear down all that old architecture, all that wonderful marble and inlaid panelling. She thought about how her great-grandfather had built the property as a testament to the love he felt for his wife. How it had stood for almost a century, through turmoil and change, only to be obliterated from the face of the earth because Connor wanted some kind of payback.

If he went ahead and tore it down, then her mother's dreams for the property would be gone for ever, because then there was no way Lola could make them happen.

She smoothed her hand over the details again, searching for some way to convince him to change his plans and preserve the old building. If he really didn't want it, then why couldn't he sell it on to her? She had to talk to Connor. Had to tell him about her mother, how she'd been cheated out of the property. Maybe she could make him see that, like him, her mother had been a casualty of her uncle's treachery. That if he allowed her to buy the Cabacal back he'd be helping her put things right.

She heard a sound behind her and turned to see

Connor lazing against the door frame, his eyes languid, like a man just roused from sleep, but with an intensity in his gaze that was hard to miss.

Her first instinct was to lash out at him, demand he tell her what the hell he was thinking, demolishing such a wonderful building, but she couldn't do that. He might, quite rightly, do some lashing out of his own. He still didn't know who she was, or what the building meant to her. And that was down to her own cowardice in not telling him before now.

As it stood, he had every right to do what he wanted with his new purchase. But she wasn't going to give up without a damn good fight.

Connor didn't like how he'd woken from a deep, relaxing sleep and his first thought had been Lola. What they'd shared had been intense and unsettling. Not just the slow sex stuff, but the way she'd gotten him to open up about his past. He rarely talked about that. The last time he'd been persuaded to reveal his past, it had been used against him.

He'd learned long ago that women had their own agendas. They could wheedle every little bit of information from you and then twist it and turn it to accommodate their own desires.

Sounds from the kitchen stopped his thoughts from spiralling downward. He needed a distraction, and that meant getting Lola back to bed for some early-morning activity. He found her deep in thought and poring over some papers. His papers.

The sharp nudge of suspicion squeezed his chest.

What the hell was she doing reading his personal documents?

'Found something interesting?'

Lola started, the papers fluttering to the floor. 'Sorry.'

She picked them up quickly, then stacked them on the counter, her eyes not meeting his. It hiked his suspicion several notches, until he realised that he'd left the property details for the Cabacal in full view, and it was probably perfectly natural she'd take a look, given she was searching for a property of her own.

Was he just being paranoid?

'You should drink some water,' she said, coming across and handing it to him. 'You need to rehydrate after a massage.'

'I know what else I need after a massage.' He took the water, noting how her hands trembled a little. Was she unnerved because he'd startled her? Caught her snooping? He felt that poke of suspicion again, until he reasoned that this was Lola, not Caroline. Lola had always been upfront and had never given him reason not to trust her.

Yeah. He was likely being paranoid.

He placed the glass down and slipped his arms around her.

'My shirt looks good on you.'

'It was the nearest thing I could find.'

Although she laid her hands on his biceps, her manner was reserved, her voice tight. She didn't meet his eyes. He frowned, placing his hand beneath her chin and coaxing her to look at him. 'Everything okay?'

She gave a wan smile. 'Of course. How are you feeling?'

'Good.' Actually, he felt more than good. He felt fucking amazing. Except he knew there was most definitely something wrong with her. Was she still concerned with his wellbeing?

He didn't need that, or want it. He could look after himself.

From nowhere came the memory of concerned eyes looking down at him. That look had warmed all his cold parts until he'd discovered the duplicity, the treachery that could lie beneath feigned concern and the need for a scapegoat. Caroline had been an expert at deceit, making him believe she cared for him when all the time she'd been making plans behind his back to destroy him.

Shit. He needed to get his attention away from the past. Lola had stirred up things with her questions last night, and it was fucking up the good times. Good times he wasn't quite ready to end.

That knowledge was troubling in itself, but at least he had his finger on the pulse. Had his wits about him. He knew what he was doing. And right now that meant coaxing her back to bed, enjoying some early-morning sex. And in doing so he'd put a smile back on both their faces.

He popped open the three buttons at her waist, then slipped the shirt from her shoulders.

'The effects of your magic hands are wearing off a little. I'm thinking you should give me a refresher.'

He tossed the shirt to the floor and, wanting to demonstrate just how good his back felt, he hiked her up into his arms.

She stiffened against him, but her hands landed on his shoulders. 'You should take care for a while. No sudden movements.'

'Told you,' he said as he strode back to the bedroom. 'It's fine.'

'Just take things slowly for a while so you can gauge how it really is.'

'Oh, I can do that.' He deliberately misinterpreted her meaning, turning to the bed and taking his time lowering her down. 'There. Slow.'

Lola sighed as he moved over her, but her demeanour felt stilted. 'You really need to pace yourself. When you're stressed, you don't take the time to think things through. That's when you can end up making snap decisions that are irreversible. It never hurts to consider things from all angles.'

He searched his memory banks for a conversation they'd had which would make sense of what she'd just said, but found nothing. 'No need for concern on that front. I'm a man who considers every single angle.' Wanting to ease whatever was bothering her, he waggled his eyebrows. 'Or hadn't you noticed.'

'Connor, I'm really sorry for snooping, but I couldn't help noticing the property details on your counter.'

'Yeah. I saw you reading them.'

She took a huge breath. 'Are you really thinking of having that building demolished?'

He felt the punch in his solar plexus. He didn't much care about her looking at the property details, but he certainly didn't like the fact she'd gone through his private correspondence. It didn't pay to let anyone think they had more of a part in your life than you were prepared to give them. And Connor wasn't prepared to give an inch. When he gave that inch, the shit tended to hit the fan. 'That's my business.'

'Like I said, I'm truly sorry, but it's such a wonderful building.'

Not for him, it wasn't. The sooner the place was razed to the ground, the sooner he could draw a solid line under the past and start a new chapter.

'It's called progress,' he said, rolling onto his back. He felt irritated, both by her prying and by the fact she'd made him think back too much in the space of a few short hours. He'd felt too comfortable sharing things with her last night, and there was no space for that in their relationship. Their time wasn't meant for conversation, it was meant for hot, dirty sex.

She hiked onto her side and looked down at him. 'Progress doesn't mean destroying what's good about the past.'

'Believe me, there's nothing much good about that.'

'That's surely not true? Even with what you told

me last night, there had to be some good things, some good memories.'

'Yeah.' He thought about the moment Logan had brought his siblings out of foster care so they could live as a family again. It had been the happiest moment of his life. 'Maybe one or two.'

'Have I told you about my mother?'

Dangerous territory, Connor thought. Hadn't he warned himself against this? Against shooting things between them to another level?

'My mother was a yoga instructor,' Lola said before he could distract her. 'At the time she started teaching, the premise was way out there. My father didn't understand. He used to call it hippy nonsense. When he knew I wanted to follow the same path as my mum, he was livid. He insisted I get a business degree, obviously hoping that during my time at university I'd come to my senses.'

Connor frowned. He didn't hold with the idea of a parent manipulating a child and controlling them. Not that his father had been Dad of the Year. His old man hadn't been bothered enough to stay in his kids' lives, let alone try and manipulate them.

'At first, I wanted to tell my father to get stuffed. That I didn't need the carrot of a trust fund to achieve my dreams. But then I realised having a business degree was a wise step to take, considering my plans, and I certainly wouldn't have been able to afford to run my own studio if I didn't have the trust fund. So, like it or not, I was kind of over a barrel.'

Connor thought that she eyed him with the same
look that a person watching an angry snake would
have. Cautious. Wary. He had a feeling she thought
he would judge her for doing her father's bidding.
For accepting the trust fund.

'We have to take our breaks where we can,' he
said with a shrug. 'No point looking gift horses in
the mouth. And we're all products of our childhoods,
like it or not. And sometimes not just our childhoods.'

'What do you mean?'

He gave another shrug, not wanting to indulge in
any more revelations about his past, but she looked so
unsure, he wrapped his arm around her and coaxed
her to lie back. When she settled against him, he
drew her close so that her hand settled on his chest.

'My own particular gift horse came at a time when
I was trying to prove something,' he said. 'Prove that
I was better than my old man. That I could stick to
something, make something of myself. Got myself
involved in a situation where I should have trusted
my instincts and walked away.'

'But you didn't?'

'No. I didn't have a trust fund dangled in front of
me, but the carrot was too juicy for me to walk away
from. I got the opportunity to work for a man who
ran a string of successful casinos throughout London. He took me under his wing, eventually offered
me manager at his flagship club.'

He couldn't be certain, but he thought he felt her

tense a little against him. Then she shifted, relaxed, and he wondered if he'd imagined it.

'For a while things were great, then something happened and everything changed.' Beneath the steady stroke of Lola's fingers, Connor's chest tightened as he thought again of Caroline, of how she'd slowly coerced him to do her bidding and how he'd slowly begun to tie the noose around his own neck.

He took a breath, working to find the words to give Lola the potted version, and avoid having to dig too deep into the nitty-gritty. 'The guy I worked for was involved in some dubious dealings and, when he slipped up, I was right in the firing line.'

'What happened?'

'I was arrested.'

She didn't react, not even a snatched breath of shock, a momentary gasp or incredulous flutter of eyelashes. All she did was keep stroking her fingers soothingly across his chest.

'I was falsely accused of embezzlement,' he found himself confessing. 'Took my eye off the ball and managed to get myself into a shit-load of trouble. My fault. Should have kept my finger on the pulse, trusted those instincts.' He shrugged. 'Still, lesson learned.'

'I can't believe you can say that so calmly,' Lola said as she looked up at him. 'You were arrested for something you didn't do.'

'It was a hard lesson learned. Taught me to rely on my instincts and never doubt them again. I chose to trust someone I shouldn't have trusted, even after I'd started having doubts.'

She quickly looked away, then rested her head against his chest. Maybe it was because she wasn't pushing for more information that he found his tongue loosening even more.

'That property I just bought was the one I used to manage. I poured everything I had into that place and it came to represent what I wanted in life. Success. Personal achievement and satisfaction. Wealth.'

He took a moment to catch his breath as it backed up in his lungs. 'I thought I had a tight handle on everything that went on in that casino, but my arrogance made me myopic. Looking back, I realise I didn't want to acknowledge what my instincts said. I wanted to go on believing everything was legit because, if it wasn't, what did that say about my judgement?' He sighed, as if to help disperse the tension lodged in his chest. 'But I couldn't ignore it forever. The dodgy dealings...the dirty money. Before I could confront the owner, tell him I knew what was happening, the police arrived to arrest me.'

Her fingers stopped gliding over his chest. 'That's terrible.'

He thought again of Caroline. Of what she'd done. He'd fallen in love with her, assuring himself that she felt the same. He'd been bloody besotted with her. That was the only reason he could think of for his temporary insanity. The truth was he'd trusted her. He hadn't for one moment considered she had an ulterior motive. That motive being setting him up as the fall guy when the shit had hit the proverbial fan.

It was only when he'd been arrested that he realised he'd been set up to take the fall.

It was a story as old as freaking time: man trusts a woman too readily and ends up getting his balls sliced.

'How long before the police released you?'

'Pretty fast. Luckily they found evidence to prove I'd been set up. After what happened, I just wanted to see the place gutted, obliterated.'

'I'm so sorry, Connor.'

Lola's heartfelt words and her gentle touch were so comforting that Connor pulled her over him. He wanted to see her face, look into her eyes, have her as close to him as he could get her.

Her softness, her understanding, was like a balm to him. Perhaps a woman like her could make him believe that things could be different. That he could let go of that defensive wall he'd built around himself. Maybe even learn to trust again.

As she straddled him, she placed her hands on his chest and leaned down. 'You really didn't deserve what happened to you.'

She slipped her hands to his shoulders, leaning further down and placing a kiss to his mouth. It was tender, the pressure firm and determined. Connor felt something shift inside him. It had been a long time since he'd felt so raw, so pulled apart. Longer still since he'd allowed himself to remember the finer de-

tails of what had happened that night five years ago.
He layered the painful memories beneath his desire
to draw the line under that part of his life, to take his
own brand of revenge on the family who had tried
to destroy him by becoming the owner of what was
the symbol of his downfall.

Lola's kiss seemed to soften all the rough edges,
soothe the turmoil those memories had unleashed.
She was making him wonder about a better way, if
maybe his desire to stick that final pin in the bubble
of bad memories was worth the angst. Would he do
better to let it go? Move on?

A thought came to him. Lola had wanted a studio
in central London, and the properties she'd shown
him were so different from the Cabacal he couldn't
imagine it would suit her needs. Yet, what better way
to draw that line under his past than see the property used for positive means? A place where people
could go to be de-stressed, rejuvenated, invigorated.

It seemed fitting somehow.

He would run it past her. She could always say no.

But right now wasn't the time for that particular
discussion. Not when she was kissing along his jaw,
down his throat. Tender yet determined kisses that
sent blood through his veins in a frenzy that belied
the softness of her touch.

He'd think on it some more. Maybe drop a few
hints along the way as to whether she'd be interested
in using the Cabacal for her studio. He didn't want
to make her feel uncomfortable. He should probably

first try and discover what level of trust fund they were talking about. Since she was looking at central London for a venue, he couldn't imagine she was sitting on anything other than a substantial sum.

Maybe he'd offer to rent it to her first, then she could take her time deciding if it was going to be the right fit.

He'd give it some more thought. Maybe sound her out first.

Until then…

He placed his hands around her hips, anchoring her as she straddled him. She straightened, all that amazing hair tumbling around her shoulders, brushing against her nipples.

She stroked the back of her hand across his cheek. 'I'm so sorry for what happened to you, Connor.'

'Hey, it's not your fault,' he said as her green eyes went misty. 'We've all got our story to tell.'

'Maybe.'

He hated that she looked so sad, so reflective. Things had gotten far too heavy. His confess-all moment had dampened the mood. This wasn't what either of them had signed up for.

He held tightly to her hips and reversed their positions, making her laugh. 'I'm starting to think you've got a problem with me being on top.'

'I don't have a problem with any position you're in,' he said, leaning down to take one very desirable nipple into his mouth. 'As long as that position involves you being naked.'

He glanced up, expecting to find her expression one of mock censure, but instead she had that pensive expression again.

He tapped his finger to the worried lines between her eyebrows. 'What's with the solemn look?'

'Just thinking.' She took a breath. 'Nothing is ever black and white, is it? You think you've got things sussed, that you really know what you want, and then it all comes crashing down and you end up having to rethink it all out again. Find a new way to achieve your plans.'

'Huh?' Connor wasn't entirely sure what she meant, but then it wasn't exactly his brain that was spinning its gears right then.

She shook her head. 'Ignore me. Just thinking out loud.'

With a smile, she reached for him. 'Why don't we find something to do until the sun really breaks through? Then you can make me breakfast.'

Connor could get on board with that. He breathed a sigh of relief, sensing they'd left the deep and meaningful discussion behind and were now back to the fun stuff. He knew his way around pre-breakfast activities of the between-the-sheets variety, and he could certainly negotiate that far better than the heavy talk that had left Lola looking so downcast.

He moved between her legs, intent on really putting that smile back on her face.

CHAPTER ELEVEN

LOLA HAD KNOWN most of what Connor had told her, and she'd kind of filled in the blanks herself about what she hadn't known. But having *him* tell her what had happened to him—hearing the anger, the hurt and, yes, the self-loathing in his tone—made it so much worse. Her uncle, a man he'd looked up to, who had basically mentored him, had allowed him to be charged when he was completely innocent.

As the tube she was travelling on entered a tunnel, she looked beyond the window and into the darkness. It kind of suited her mood.

If she'd hated her uncle before because of what he had done to her mother, she hated him even more now because of what he'd done to Connor. She knew it was bad to have feelings like that, and she knew she should try and turn her anger into something more constructive. She remembered that saying about how being angry at someone was like drinking poison and expecting the other person to die.

The problem was, she couldn't help it. Her uncle had been so manipulative and cruel. He'd cheated her

mother out of her dreams and he'd almost cheated
Connor out of his liberty. He'd made Connor question himself when all Connor had wanted was to do
a good job, be a good manager and make some of his
dreams come true. She didn't think she could ever
forgive her uncle for that.

She'd felt so close to Connor as he'd told her of
his past, as he'd opened up to her, yet the guilt was
never far away. He still didn't know who she really
was or what she wanted. After he'd been so honest
about his own past, she'd had the perfect opportunity
to come clean, but she couldn't do it. She couldn't
hurt him further by admitting that she had also deceived him. Instead she'd wanted to comfort him,
hold him, make love to him and provide a salve for
his wounds.

Admitting the truth became harder the more time
they spent together, yet no matter how bad she felt it
didn't seem to stop the wanting.

Somehow her own feelings had grown past the
purely physical and had developed into something
deeper and more profound. There was so much about
him that she respected and admired.

His single-mindedness, for instance. His ability
to forge through adversity and come out the other
end, determined to make the most of it. He'd had
what sounded like a rotten childhood, and then he'd
been badly betrayed and falsely accused by someone he'd thought he could trust. Yet he'd refused to
be beaten down by his experiences and instead had

used them, learned from them and made the most of his opportunities.

Maybe Damian was right. Connor was owed the Cabacal. For him, it was symbolic, and he deserved to have the satisfaction of owning the property that had been instrumental in bringing him down so low.

But that didn't mean she would stop fighting for the property. While she understood what it represented for him, there was no way she was going to stand by and allow him to raze the building to the ground.

'You're a chatty little thing this morning.'

Lola turned to see Emily's raised eyebrows as they travelled towards Clapham where Lola taught three yoga sessions on Mondays, finishing early afternoon. Emily attended the first of Lola's classes and then headed back for her shift at a local coffee shop.

'Sorry.' Lola shook her head. 'Just trying to work things out.'

'Things? As in, certain sexy nightclub owner?'

Lola sighed. 'Him and other stuff.'

Emily had tried to convince Lola that she should walk away from both the Cabacal and Connor. She thought Lola was in too deep and that whatever she did from then on would only cause her hurt and pain. She'd argued that if Lola walked away now she would never have to admit the truth of who she was or reveal her original plans.

For Lola, neither was an option. She couldn't walk

away from the Cabacal and she couldn't walk away from Connor.

What they'd had on that first night was meant to be fun, but somehow it had morphed into far more. At least for her. She'd started to imagine building a relationship with him even before he'd given her glimpses into his past. He didn't share things easily, but he'd shared them with her.

Slowly, she'd been falling for him.

'I'm a bloody idiot,' Lola murmured to herself, but the nudge to her ribs signalled that Emily had heard.

'No, you just fell hard for a hot guy who happened to see you as an intelligent woman capable of achieving her dreams. He's probably the first man in your life who's actually supported you rather than thrown obstacles in your way.'

The concern in Emily's eyes made Lola feel worse. She hadn't betrayed Connor's confidence by telling Emily what had happened to him, or his reasons for wanting the property. That really *was* his business. But she had told her friend that she was really starting to like him.

'I should have come clean to Connor right from the start. Maybe he would have understood.'

'And maybe he wouldn't.'

'True,' Lola said, her heart weighing heavily beneath the enormity of what she knew had to be done. 'But I have to tell him the truth.'

He deserved that. If afterward he didn't trust her enough to continue to be with her, or if she lost the

Cabacal in the process, he still deserved to know everything.

Her heart clawed at her throat, stealing her breath. There was no other way.

She had to tell Connor.

All her classes were full that day, but it didn't keep her from thinking about her impending confession and its potential consequences.

She intended to talk to Connor as soon as her work day was over. There was absolutely no point in delaying any longer.

Connor was a reasonable man, wasn't he? Surely he'd allow her to explain what she'd done and why she'd done it? He knew what it was like to be exploited, used. Surely he would see that her mother had been treated the same way, and how important it was for Lola to make things right.

She'd make him see, make him understand, and she wouldn't stop until she did.

It was hard to imagine not seeing him again, not having him in her life. But the possibility sat like a heavy brick on her chest, making her stomach feel hollow.

Without him, there would be a big yearning gap now. Because she'd let him sneak right under her skin and straight into her heart.

While she packed up her things after her class, her phone buzzed. Since they'd exchanged numbers before she'd left his place earlier, she wasn't entirely surprised that it was Connor.

'Finished for the day?' Her heart leapt at the sound of his deep voice, its rich tone edged with velvet. 'If you don't have any plans, maybe we could meet up. There's something I'd like to show you.'

She couldn't be distracted by the fact he wanted to see her, or that he'd remembered her classes ended early on a Monday. She had to keep focused. 'Connor. I need to talk to you.'

'Then why don't you grab a taxi and come on over?'

Before she could ask where he was, he rattled off an address which made her heart stop.

He was at the Cabacal.

Mixed feelings vied for attention: the pleasure of seeing the property again…the pleasure of seeing Connor again…but taking priority was the fact she'd be revealing her identity to him in the very place they both wanted. The place that stood between them.

If he didn't plan to demolish the building before, he certainly would after she'd told him she'd been lying to him.

Lola spent the taxi journey mentally rehearsing how to start the conversation she'd been dreading, her nerves escalating with each moment that passed. To make matters worse, what should have taken fifteen minutes took more than double that thanks to emergency road works. Unable to sit still any longer, Lola paid the driver, gathered her bags and walked the remaining half-mile to the property.

It was a good area, bordering the River Thames,

and, while busy, it was not so heavily populated with visitors as the rest of the city.

The weather was fine, so the sun sparkled on the surface of the water, reminding Lola of the times when she and her mother had come to visit and had chosen to sit on the stone steps leading down to the water's edge, where they'd talk about anything and everything.

It wasn't just memories of her mother that constricted her heart as she sat and looked out over the river now. It was the possibility she might lose Connor. What if she couldn't convince him that she had never meant to hurt him by keeping her identity a secret? What if he saw her silence as a sharp betrayal and was determined not to forgive her?

Her vision began to blur but since tears wouldn't solve anything, she inhaled deeply, gave herself a metaphorical dusting down then stood. She'd come here for a reason. She had to get on with it.

A short walk brought the Cabacal into view. She'd seen the outside several times while it had been unoccupied, but even neglect couldn't diminish the sheer beauty of the exterior. Like a sponge, Lola soaked up the architectural details. Art Deco in style, with a flat roof covering its geometrical shape, angular corners and large curved windows. Testament to an elegant time now long since past.

She wondered how the interior chrome, decorative glass motifs and beautiful limestone floor would look. Probably dulled and sullied—five years of ne-

glect would do that—but likely still as stunning beneath the surface. It bordered on criminal, allowing
a beautiful place like the Cabacal to rot this way.

It was even more criminal to have it demolished,
although she intended to fight that possibility with
everything she had. There had to be a way to make
Connor change his mind.

'Hey.'

Lola swung round, dropping her yoga bag in the
process, and her gaze met Connor's. Dressed in a
sharp business suit, he stood at the side entrance of
the property, smiling.

He strolled towards her, his sexy grin warming
the icy little pockets of discomfort that had settled
inside her. 'You look good,' he said, sliding his hands
around her waist and pulling her close up against
him. 'Smell good, too.'

How was it that he could set all her nerve endings
alight just by breathing? How could he make every
thought and worry disappear so that all she could
think about was being in his arms?

He leaned down and took her mouth in a deep,
passionate kiss, his hold on her tightening as the
kiss went on. She tried to resist, tried to break away
from him, but his pull on her was just too great. So
she sank into the kiss and just let herself be with
him while the inevitable confession nudged at her
conscience.

When his hold on her eased a fraction, he looked
down at her and smiled. 'How was your day?'

Her hands lay heavily on his shoulders, as if the weight of what she held inside her fused at that point. She hoped those broad shoulders would withstand the battering they would receive so that they could both find a way through the resultant storm.

'I really need to talk to you.'

'Same here.' His sexy wink turned her already feeble legs to mush. 'Want to see inside?' He picked up her yoga bag and grabbed her hand.

Thanks to her mental rehearsal in the taxi, she thought she'd had her moves all planned out, but he'd stripped all that away. 'Inside?'

'Yeah, as in through the front door. Then I get to kiss you the way I really want to kiss you, out of the glare of prying eyes.' He brought her closer again, his smile fading as he looked at her. She felt the punch of his intense gaze right down to her toes. 'I've really missed you.'

His hoarse tone had an awkward edge, as if he'd summoned the words and their meaning from a deep, dark cellar which he hadn't opened in a very long time.

Why was it so difficult for him to say them? Had he said them once before, and they'd been thrown back in his face? Perhaps by an ex who had hurt him and caused him pain?

But he'd said them to her, and they had the power to close up her throat, to bring tears to her eyes and to make her heart ache for something she hadn't even known she wanted.

But she did know what she wanted. She wanted him. More than anything else.

He brought his hands down to link with hers. 'Come on. I'll show you around.'

'Connor...' She tightened her fingers around his and pulled him back as he started to move. She couldn't go inside without having told him. It would only be delaying the inevitable. But then this might be the last chance she'd have of visiting the Cabacal, the last time she'd get to walk through the wonderful old place and relive precious memories.

It was too compelling to resist. So she loosened her hold on him and nodded. He took a bunch of keys from his pocket, selected two and used them to open the locks on the double doors.

He stood back and Lola stepped into the vestibule.

A gazillion memories tumbled over themselves as she took in the pink marble inlays and chrome fittings. She had a vision of her grandfather escorting her inside when she'd had lunch there as a special treat for her tenth birthday. She'd worn a pretty blue and cream floral dress, the detail of which was as vivid right now as it had been on that day.

As memories swamped her, she pushed them away. Because it was too much. She already felt raw and emotional, especially as Connor stood beside her and said nothing. She had the crazy notion that he knew—that he realised the place had a special meaning for her. But that was impossible. She hadn't had the guts to tell him yet.

His phone buzzed, breaking through her frenzied thoughts and the eerie silence of the empty space. She turned to see him checking the display. 'I need to take this,' he said. 'Look around. I'll be right back.'

As Connor went outside, Lola stepped through into the main hall. She froze. While the vestibule and entrance were unchanged from what she remembered when her grandmother had been alive, the main hall provided evidence of what her uncle and his greedy hands had done. Most of the stunning architectural features remained intact, thank God, but there was no trace of the beautiful, elegant interior her grandmother had created. In its place were the garish and showy remnants of the casino.

Taking a breath, she wandered further into the space. Since she'd never seen the appeal of gambling, Lola didn't know to what use the dusty, discarded tables had once been put. Poker? Black jack? The only game she recognised was roulette, with its distinctive wheel still in evidence.

At the far end of the main hall was a bar, its rich mahogany surface covered in layers of dust and grime, its shelves now empty, having once held glasses and alcoholic beverages showcased by the old etched mirrors running along the length of the back bar.

As she walked towards it, she glanced up to the mezzanine and spotted some old slot machines juxtaposed with a smaller bar which, she imagined with some cynicism, had allowed punters to refill their drinks with as little disturbance as possible to their game-playing.

Her footsteps echoed on the dusty limestone floor as she wandered past the bar and towards the wall that had once held clear windows looking out over the river. That would have been the first change she'd have made, Lola thought somewhat innocuously. Reinstating those wonderful views.

She turned back to look around the hall. It would have been an amazing space in which to run her studio. The main hall could easily have been partitioned into smaller units without losing the sense of light, of space. On fine days she could've thrown the windows open, maybe even had a deck built on the grassy ledge outside for outdoor classes when the weather allowed.

She wandered into one of the annexes off to the side, imagining it as a cloakroom with lockers for her clients. Then into another room that would have been perfect for storing class equipment.

Before long she would have removed all traces of the travesty her uncle had made of the space, but in the absence of being able to do that she was damn sure she was going to make certain that Connor didn't get to obliterate the property completely. She couldn't bear to think of all its lovely architectural features lying in a pit of rubble on the beautiful limestone floor.

She heard Connor, his voice getting louder as he neared the door to the main hall. 'Okay, I'll wait for you,' he said to the caller. 'It'll save me a trip to your office.'

Steeling herself for the conversation to come, Lola came back into the main hall as Connor tucked his phone back in his pocket.

'What do you think?' he asked, coming to stand beside her. 'It's a big space, but it'd be easy enough to have it made into smaller areas. The two pillars at the sides aren't load bearing, so they could be removed easily enough, which means that the smaller annexes could be knocked together.'

Lola found it hard to concentrate on the rest of what Connor said. She was too busy trying to make sense of what she'd already heard. Why on earth was he waxing lyrical about the potential of the place?

Her heart stuttered. 'You're not going to have it knocked down?'

His eyebrows rose. 'Well, no. Not if you think it would work for you.'

She swallowed, her throat so tight it was hard to breathe. 'Work for me?'

Had she slipped into some alternative reality? A parallel universe? What the hell was he talking about? She didn't even want to consider what she *thought* he was talking about.

'Like I said, those pillars aren't a problem, and if you want the hall sectioned off some good stud walling would be an easy enough fix.' With his hands in his pockets, he strolled around the room. 'How many people are you planning to have in each class?'

Lola's heart was flipping about like a mad thing, but she couldn't take his words at face value. She searched his face but there didn't seem to be any artifice in his expression or demeanour. No suspicion in his eyes telling her he'd found out who she really was and was messing with her. Connor didn't play those sorts of cruel games. If he'd known who she was, she would have seen it in his eyes, would already be facing his wrath.

'Ten students per class is the norm,' Lola said, her throat like sandpaper. 'Twelve, tops.'

Connor nodded thoughtfully. 'This space could easily accommodate those numbers.'

As she still wasn't entirely sure what was going on, whether or not he had some sort of agenda, Lola kept her gaze steady on his. 'I don't understand.'

He shrugged. 'I've got a property, you need one. None of the others you showed me seemed suitable. This one does. I'm willing to rent it out to you until such time as I'm ready to sell it and you're happy it'll work for you. Unless you already know it won't work.'

Lola bit her bottom lip. Everything she'd planned for had fallen into her lap. Just like that. So how come, instead of celebrating her luck, she had a hollow feeling settling in the pit of her stomach? He was willing to do this for her when she hadn't even had the decency to tell him who she was, and that this very scenario was the outcome she'd been planning all along.

'It would work perfectly,' she said as guilt clawed its ugly way around her heart.

She couldn't let this continue, couldn't let him make this huge gesture until she had come clean. He would no doubt retract his offer. And she wouldn't blame him.

Yet she had to make this right.

'Connor. I can't tell you how much I appreciate what you're offering me. But we really need to talk.'

'Hold that thought,' he said, already moving towards the entrance door as his mobile buzzed. 'I just need to take care of some business. Hand over some papers. If it's the cost of renovation that's worrying you, we can work that out.'

It was only delaying the inevitable, yet Lola was glad of the breathing space. The chance to formulate her words in a way that would cause Connor the least damage, the least hurt. She was about to throw his generosity back in his face, and she hated what that might do to him. He'd already been manipulated and betrayed by her uncle, and the fallout had taken him years to work through. How would she feel when she not only opened up all those old wounds, but inflicted even more new ones?

She wrapped her arms around herself, as if to stop her insides from spilling out. It felt as if she'd been flayed right through to the core of who she was because she couldn't bear the thought of hurting Connor this deeply.

She heard him speaking with someone outside, a

vague shiver of recognition trembling down her already icy spine.

The door swung open and Connor walked through, closely flanked by Damian.

As Lola met her brother's angry gaze, she knew any chance she had of making Connor understand had just disintegrated like dust on the limestone floor.

CHAPTER TWELVE

ANY FOOL WOULD have noticed the tension that snapped between Damian and Lola. Just as any fool would have noticed the colour leeching from her beautiful face.

Connor looked between them, his eyes narrowing. 'What the hell's going on?'

Damian kept his attention on Lola. 'That's what I'd like to know. Maybe you'd like to explain, Louise.'

Louise?

'What are you doing here, Damian?'

The man raised his eyebrows, showcasing the confusion in his eyes. 'The real question is, what are *you* doing here?'

'Somebody better start explaining,' Connor said, his chest squeezed so tight that his ribs started to ache. 'And soon.' They obviously had some kind of history, and clearly not good. Were they once lovers? That possibility made him want to pound his aching chest in a direct display of male possession so that Damian knew with absolute certainty that Lola was his now.

Lola seemed to have turned even paler. 'This is none of your business, Damian. You should leave.'

A hint of perception replaced confusion in Damian's now narrowed eyes. 'Have you gone behind my back? After everything I said?'

Gone behind his back doing what? What the fuck was going on?

'You didn't give me any choice.' On the surface, Lola sounded firm, but Connor heard the hitch in her voice. 'This wasn't what I wanted. It certainly wasn't what I planned.'

Damian turned to Connor. 'Have you agreed to anything?'

'About what?'

Damian took a deep inhalation. 'My sister can be very persuasive.'

His *sister*?

Connor looked between them again, his gaze settling on Lola even as his head buzzed. Lola was Damian McBride's sister? What the fuck?

Why hadn't she told him? She must have known he was doing business with Damian over the Cabacal, which meant…

Shit. It meant she'd been lying to him.

His head pounded and the straitjacket that was now around his ribcage tightened further. He needed to think. To work this out, make sense of it.

'Lola?'

Strands of hair fell free of the messy bun as she shook her head. Her eyes were over-bright, shining with the truth of what his fevered brain was slowly, painfully, figuring out. She'd lied to him. All the time they'd been together, she'd had her own agenda. And he'd slowly been falling for her, allowing the wall around his heart to crumble brick by brick, allowing himself to contemplate the possibility that he might be able to open himself up enough to trust a woman again.

Fucking idiot.

'Connor. I need to explain everything to you.'

He thought he'd known pain before. As a child abandoned by his parents, as a budding entrepreneur betrayed by the man he'd considered his trusted mentor, as a lover cruelly manipulated by the woman he'd thought himself in love with. All those things had cut him like a thousand blades, but nothing…not one of those things…had ripped him apart like the pain of knowing that Lola had willingly, blatantly deceived him.

His blood was a torrent of rage as it swept through his veins. 'Damn right you need to explain. Start with why you lied to me. Right from the start. You fucking lied to me.'

Her throat contracted, her eyes deep pools of agonised green, but no way would he let his guard down. For all he knew, it was another act. Another attempt to manipulate him, draw him in, make him soften. Right now, he wanted answers. He wanted the truth.

'I always intended to tell you who I am, but first I

wanted to get to know you, to understand your reasons for wanting the Cabacal.'

Damian stepped forward. 'I told you Connor was owed. That should have been good enough. Why didn't you let it go?'

Lola turned to her brother, the paleness of her complexion highlighted by the spears of heat that flashed across her cheekbones and echoed in her eyes. 'You wouldn't even listen to me. Wouldn't even give me the chance to buy this place back. It belongs to our family, to me. You should have given me the option.'

Connor didn't want to know the ins and outs of who she thought was the legal owner. All he cared about was getting answers. From Lola.

'What were you hoping to gain from your lies?' he demanded, ignoring the way she flinched.

'At first I hoped to get you to agree to sell it on to me when my trust fund becomes available in six months' time.'

She threw a look at Damian, who had paced over towards the window, before bringing her gaze back to Connor's. Connor's mind was still trying to process everything. He was battling the sense of betrayal. The lies. The deception.

The need for answers to so many questions.

'That first night, at my club, you knew who I was?'

'Yes.' Her voice sounded thready, as if she couldn't quite catch her breath.

'And what? You thought you'd get me nice and

mellow? Is that what the dance was for? Work me up, then present me with the dotted line on which to sign?'

His gut burned. He couldn't believe he'd been so gullible. Couldn't believe he'd been so easily duped again. Hadn't he been careful? Hadn't he shut himself off enough not to let a woman close again? History, it seemed, really did repeat itself.

'No. I didn't even know you were in the club when I did that dance. It was a bet, remember? It wasn't until after I'd stabbed you with my heel and saw the award photo in your office that I knew who you were.'

Damian had now moved across to the entrance door, obviously sensing there was more going on than a property war.

A red haze misted across Connor's vision, his anger renewing with each confirmation of Lola's continued subterfuge. 'Wait,' he called, striding across the space to snatch up the papers Damian had left on the old bar before continuing towards the door. 'You'll want these.'

Connor was more determined than ever to own the Cabacal. Damian was right. He was fucking owed. The place had been at the heart of not just one, but two of the most destructive and deceit-filled periods of his life.

'You're sure?' Damian glanced at his sister, then back at Connor.

'Never more so. I want immediate completion on this. No delays.'

Damian nodded, then with a concerned look at his sister took the documents and walked out of the door.

Connor shook his head, hoping to shake some clarity into the chaotic mess that was his thoughts. 'Shit, I virtually played into your hands. Offering to rent you the place. Bet you were close to congratulating yourself on pulling that one off.'

'That's not true at all. Before Damian arrived I was planning to tell you the truth. I never meant to keep it from you this long. I swear I'm being honest.'

His laugh was as hollow as his stomach. 'I don't remember you being too worried about telling the truth that first night at the club when you went all out with the seduction routine. How can I be sure that wiggling your butt at me and shoving your breasts in my face wasn't all part of the act?'

'I told you. When I did that dance, I didn't know who you were. And if we're talking seduction, from what I remember you pressed pretty hard.'

Connor narrowed his eyes. 'And from what *I* remember, you refused me. Then you changed your mind.'

'I was attracted to you but, considering what I planned, there was no way I was going to sleep with you. Then I decided that if I could make Damian change his mind and sell direct to me, there was no reason not to act on the attraction. It wasn't until the next morning, after we'd slept together, that I realised you had both already agreed on a deal and that you were on the verge of signing, or even that you'd already signed. That's when I knew that I had to keep you at arm's length, that I couldn't sleep with you again. Not when I had to go back to my original plan and try and persuade you to sell the property to me.'

With each word, her voice grew stronger. She didn't falter, didn't hesitate. Connor wanted to believe what she was telling him, but he couldn't quite make that leap.

'Yet we ended up having sex again anyway, and I don't remember having to push too hard. What? Did you think it would give you the edge? Sex and business? Quite an explosive combination if you could make it work.'

'I didn't plan it, it just happened. You were pretty hard to say no to. And I certainly didn't intend having sex to give me any kind of edge. I was attracted to you, and I really enjoyed spending time with you. There was no way I ever intended for you to get hurt.'

Connor shoved his hands in his pockets and curled his fingers into his palms. 'Do you know what the really crazy part of all this is? I'd convinced myself that you were a straight-shooter, that you didn't do pretence. I'd been made a fool of before by a woman who I thought was different. Now I realise it must run in the family, that easy slide into deception, the ability to work on a man until he doesn't know which fucking way is up.'

She had the grace to look perplexed. 'I'm not sure I know what you mean.'

'Is that right? You expect me to believe you didn't know about my history with your cousin?'

Her brow furrowed. He wanted to believe she really didn't understand. Once, he might have done. But now he knew differently, and he wasn't buying the act.

'Maybe you swapped stories, is that it? How do I know that she didn't even give you pointers? Tell you my weak spots.'

'Connor, I really—'

'She'd damn well know them better than anybody. Caroline prided herself on reading people.'

The look of shock that passed over her face, that set her back a step, was worthy of an award-winning actress. 'Caroline?' Her hand went to her throat, her face turning pale again. 'What's she got to do with anything?'

Connor knew he shouldn't fall for it, but there was a stupid part of him that wanted to give her the benefit of the doubt. 'She played me,' he said. 'Primed me good and hard, so that when she was ready I walked straight into the trap.'

Her eyes flicked sideways, back and forth, and Connor knew those cogs and wheels were turning. He hated that he knew that about her, detested that he'd allowed her to get under his skin so far that he knew her ways, her expressions, her mannerisms.

Her hand stayed at her throat, her fingers sliding across her collar bone. 'Are you saying it was Caroline who set you up? Who got you arrested? I thought it was my uncle.'

'They came as a pair. She was cunning, manipulative, but it was Daddy who pulled the strings. She was his willing little puppet.'

She looked him square in the eye and, although he fought it, his gut twisted. 'You were lovers?'

Connor kept his face passive. 'Yes.'

She took in a breath, then bit down on her lower lip. 'I always assumed it was my uncle who was responsible for implicating you. I didn't for a moment consider Caroline had a part in it.'

'They carted her off to jail soon after my release, for God's sake. You didn't think she might have had a role in incriminating me?'

'I wasn't in touch with that side of my family, so I didn't know all the details.'

She shook her head, sending more strands loose to float around her face. He had to curl his fingers into his palms to stop from reaching out and brushing them away. Stop himself wanting to tilt up her chin, look into her troubled eyes and tell her everything was going to be okay. Because it wasn't going to be okay. It never could be. Not for them.

Her gaze settled at his throat. 'I'm so sorry, Connor. You must really hate my family. You must really hate me.'

Damn it, but he wanted to. He wanted to tell her to get the hell out of his life. He didn't need reminding that he'd allowed himself to be taken in by yet another scheming woman intent on using him to further her own desires.

Yet she seemed surprised by the knowledge her cousin had been complicit in his downfall. Genuinely concerned about what had happened to him.

Shit. It was making his head explode.

'Let's just put it this way,' he said, deciding he was done with it all. 'It doesn't make a difference to me that you weren't in touch with that side of your family, and I don't give a damn that you say you didn't mean to deceive me, manipulate me. The fact is, you didn't have the guts to come clean and tell me who you were and what you wanted.

'How do you know I might not have been sympathetic? That I might not actually have agreed to what you wanted, had you given me the courtesy of being honest? As it stands, I want nothing left standing of this damn building and nothing more to do with your family, or with you.'

Lola felt the punch of Connor's words deep in her solar plexus. Her insides were being scraped by some kind of vicious knife that wouldn't let up. She couldn't defend herself against his diatribe, because every word he said was right. Except in her heart she hadn't meant to manipulate him. She might have deceived him, but she'd never imagined that it would open so many old wounds for him.

She couldn't believe it was her cousin who had betrayed him so badly. Not that Lola didn't deem Caroline capable of such treachery, but she hadn't even considered the possibility that Connor had been attracted to someone like her mean-spirited cousin.

Lola wondered if she would have been able to keep from confronting Caroline and telling her just how evil she was if Caroline had been easily accessible, and not off hiding overseas after her release from prison.

Although right then Lola had more urgent and important things that she had to try and salvage. The most vital of which was trying to make Connor understand that she had never meant to upset him so badly.

Oh, he was angry, and rightfully so. He had every reason to be. But beneath that anger she knew she had wounded him. He hid it well, but the bleakness in his stormy grey eyes was evident to her. It cut her to the very depths of her being.

'I'm sorry for what I did, Connor. When we met I was really attracted to you and I never for a moment meant to lead you on. I certainly never wanted to cause so much hurt. All I intended was to persuade you to sell the property to me. I didn't realise what it represented to you. I can understand why you want it demolished, but please will you at least take some time to consider if that's really the best thing to do?'

Lola took a breath, trying to find the right words of appeal. She didn't want to fight for the Cabacal so soon after he'd told her about Caroline and how badly her cousin had treated him, but she couldn't afford to remain quiet. She at least had to try to save the property that had meant so much to her mother.

'My uncle cheated my mother out of this property,' she said quickly, unsure how long Connor would let her speak before he marched her out of the building. He was at least going to know what had prompted her to act in the way she had. 'My great-grandfather built it and it's been passed down through the women of the family. My mother planned to run it as a health studio until she was tricked out of her inheritance. I wanted to get it back. Make her dream come true. I know it doesn't change anything, but I just wanted you to know how important it is to me and why I did what I did. You don't owe me a thing, Connor, but please don't destroy this wonderful place without really taking some time to consider.'

When he didn't respond, Lola knew that, while he'd listened to her, he hadn't really taken what she'd said to heart. Maybe she'd hurt him too badly to expect any kind of compassion.

She sucked in a thready breath. 'I don't want you to hate me.'

He raised his eyebrows, piercing her with a look. 'We don't always get what we want.'

His words were like a physical blow aimed straight at her heart, smashing it to pieces. Her blood flowed like ice in her veins; her legs were hollow.

She closed her eyes against the torrent of hurt, before opening them to look straight into Connor's merciless gaze. 'Is there any way I can make this right?'

He shrugged. 'No. I was lied to once by your family. Cheated, deceived, fucking sliced in two. Thankfully, this time I found out before any real harm was done.'

His eyes bored into hers, the steel in their grey depths cold and unforgiving. It broke the final fragile shards of her heart.

In that moment, she knew she had lost him. That there was no making it right, no coming back from the dark place she feared she'd driven him to.

Lola turned and gathered up her bags, then suffered the cold, hard look in his eyes as he glared down at her. 'I really am so very sorry, Connor. Please believe that.'

His nostrils flared as he drew in a breath. 'Bye, Lola.'

She hurried across the space, barely seeing anything as her eyes blurred dangerously. She didn't give much thought to the fact this was the last time she would be inside the Cabacal building, the last time she would get to glance around it as she left it for ever.

All she cared about, all she thought about, was that she had ruined every chance she might have had with Connor. She had destroyed whatever they might have built together.

Just as she knew he would now destroy the Cabacal. She'd seen it in his eyes, heard it in the words he'd spoken.

And she couldn't find it in her shattered heart to blame him.

CHAPTER THIRTEEN

THE VERY LAST THING Lola wanted to do was have lunch with Damian. Her brother had called numerous times since that day at the Cabacal, but she'd refused to answer or return his calls. She felt a little bad about it, but she'd needed time to herself. She'd needed the break. Time to lick her wounds. Three weeks since her confrontation with Connor, and they were still as raw. Still as painful.

It was impossible to count how many times she'd gone over everything in her head, driving herself insane with thoughts of 'what if she'd done this?', 'what if she'd told him that?'. But it always came down to one thing.

She'd screwed up.

How was it possible to miss someone so much? How could the pain of losing them hurt quite so deeply? She couldn't pinpoint the exact moment that she'd fallen for him. Couldn't isolate the precise instant that she'd slipped from liking him to falling so deeply in love. Because she did love him. With every ounce of her being.

What they'd shared wasn't supposed to be meaningful. Yet it had so quickly morphed into the most extraordinary relationship of her life. And she'd thrown it all away because she hadn't had the courage to tell him the truth.

Now here she was, with her heart broken, and there wasn't a bloody thing she could do about it.

Ruthlessly, she pushed thoughts of Connor aside as she rode the lift to Damian's office. She'd spent far too many hours pining and crying and missing Connor. What good would it do to continue down that route? He didn't want her. He hadn't contacted her.

It was over. She had to move on.

Somehow. Some way.

Yet she knew her brother would want to know the ins and outs of her relationship with Connor, and she braced herself for the barrage of questions no doubt coming her way. Not that she needed to explain anything to him. It was her business. He had no right delving into her personal life any more than she had his. She'd make sure he respected that.

What she did intend to tell him was that she had found a suitable property for her studio. After a second viewing yesterday, she was putting in an offer. He had to realise that she wasn't seeking his permission, but that she was forging ahead with her plans, in her own way, on her own terms.

Oh, she understood that Damian cared for her, that he wanted to look out for her, but there were limits. She'd half-expected to find him waiting outside the Cabacal three weeks ago, ready to confront her, but there had been no sign of him. He'd called that same evening, though, and had found Emily in fierce guardian mode, telling Damian to sod off and mind his own business.

Lola could only imagine her big brother seething through the phone. Damian and Emily had never hit it off, and Lola suspected that her friend had taken great delight in giving the *arrogant and entitled dickhead*—her words—a piece of her mind.

She exited the lift and headed through the classy reception of her brother's investment company and towards his office. Having been waved straight through by his EA, she found Damian looking out of the window, his back to the door as he spoke on the phone.

He turned, finished the call, then came around to draw Lola into his arms. His brotherly embrace threatened to undo her resolve to move on with her life and her breath hitched dangerously. He held on for several moments, then drew back and placed his hands on her shoulders. 'Are you okay?'

As her throat had tightened from the unexpected warmth and support in his gesture and tone, all she could do was nod.

'I thought we could have lunch here,' he said, glancing to the meeting table laid out with coffee and sandwiches. 'There's something I need to talk to you about.'

'That's fine. There's something I need to talk to

you about too.' Lola took the property details from her bag before walking over to place them on the table. She thought it best to tell him her plans before she let him say whatever was on his mind. That way he'd know her mind was made up. 'Do you mind if I go first?'

'Louise.' Damian placed his hand over hers. 'I understand you're still pissed at me, and maybe I can't altogether blame you for that.'

'None of it matters now. I'm just interested in moving on. Which is why I'm putting in an offer for this property.' She nodded towards the details. 'I've spoken with the bank and they're prepared to advance me the deposit in lieu of my trust fund being released.'

She considered moving her hand out from under his but didn't. He was her brother and, despite everything that had happened, she needed him. She loved him.

'You still believe that I was being vindictive by not letting you have the Cabacal.'

'I know you were acting on Dad's wishes, although I suspect you agreed with his reasoning. You don't think I have the intellect to make my own business choices.'

'That's not true.' He looked at her for a long moment, then nodded to the nearest chair. When she sat, he settled beside her and reached for the jug to pour them both coffee. 'Do you know the real reason

Dad insisted on a business degree before you could access your trust fund?'

'Yes. Because he thought I was incompetent, in the same way he thought Mum was. He knew that, like her, I wanted to set up a health studio at the Cabacal, but he didn't think I was capable of making it work. He thought I'd be tossing away my inheritance.'

Damian sipped his coffee then looked down thoughtfully into the dark liquid before he met Lola's gaze again. 'I've learned the hard way that you've got a hell of a backbone, Louise.'

She was so busy basking in the startling compliment that she almost missed his next words.

'Dad never wanted you to know, but I think you deserve the truth.'

'What truth?' Her insides flipped uncomfortably, probably because Damian's expression signalled it wouldn't be to her liking.

'The Cabacal wasn't the only part of her inheritance our mother lost.'

Lola frowned, her breath shuddering. 'I thought it was the whole part. The property.'

'Our grandmother left her very financially secure, but Mother always had a guilt complex about that. She became involved in charity work, sat on committees, was actively involved in fundraising events. Unfortunately, her need to help people wasn't matched by a good head for business. She was easy prey, a target for manipulation by some unscrupulous types. She gave every penny of that inheritance away, and probably would have done the same with the Cabacal, except she'd earmarked that for her studio. It was symbolic for her.'

He took a breath, his face turning ashen. 'By the time father found out and stepped in to try and salvage the situation it was too late. All she had left was the Cabacal.'

Lola wrapped her hands around her cup, needing something to clasp as she tried to make sense of what her brother said. She hadn't known anything about her mother's extra inheritance—had never heard mention of it.

'Dad felt that if mother had invested her wealth wisely and made better business decisions she could have helped even more people, but she just acted rashly and without much thought. Then when she lost the Cabacal—'

'She didn't lose the Cabacal, she was cheated out of it.'

'Dad didn't see it like that, at least not totally. He saw it as yet another instance when mother didn't keep tighter control of her assets. She trusted too easily.'

'Nobody expects their own brother to steal from them.'

'Uncle Guy wasn't exactly trustworthy at the best of times. How many dubious dealings was he involved in? How many start-ups did he have that didn't get off the ground? His own parents didn't trust him to run their affairs, yet our mother decided that he was working in her best interests?'

'We all know how manipulative he could be.'

'Exactly. So you can't blame Dad for becoming paranoid about protecting you. He wanted to ensure you had a good financial grounding so that you'd make sound business decisions. That's why he set up the condition that you get the degree before you get your trust fund.'

Lola frowned. 'Did he make the same conditions for you? Did getting your trust fund require that you meet certain stipulations?'

'Yes. But I had to prove myself in business. Reach certain targets.'

That stopped her in her tracks. 'Really?'

She had always suspected that she'd been singled out, but if it was true that Damian had had to jump through similar hoops then it changed things.

Or did it?

'Then you should have been more understanding of my position. Even after I'd got my degree, proved myself capable, you refused to listen to my business proposal. You should never have withheld the acquisition of the Cabacal from me. You should have talked to me, discussed it as I asked. You wouldn't look at my projections, my ideas, my financial data. You completely dismissed me.'

'I know, and I'm sorry for it. My only defence is that I was still trying to protect you. That property had already caused so much heartache for our family, I didn't want it back in our lives. I didn't want you hurt any more.'

Damian scraped his hand through his hair, then pushed his coffee away. 'I need something stronger.'

He walked to the small bar in the corner and held up the whiskey decanter.

Lola shook her head. 'I don't drink. You'd know that about me if you took the time to find out instead of thinking you have to save me from myself all the time.'

Damian returned to his chair, whiskey tumbler in hand. 'Fair comment.' He sipped his drink. 'I've been wrong to dismiss your plans out of hand, and from what I hear you've got it all down pat. The figures, projections, anticipated profit and loss for the first five-year trading period. Not to mention ideas for promotional activities to set your studio apart from others offering similar things.'

Surprised, Lola raised her eyebrows. 'Where did you hear that from?'

Damian frowned. 'Your friend the ball-breaker, for one. She gave me an earful when I called and asked her to give you the message about lunch today. Told me that if I took my head out of my backside long enough I might learn something. Then, as if I hadn't been reprimanded enough, I got an earful from Connor.'

Lola shot forward as her heart jumped into her throat. 'Connor?'

Damian took another sip and nodded. 'Met him

at the official handover of the keys. Apparently, he's refurbishing the place after all, turning it into another nightclub. I happened to say that it was a good move.' He paused, watching her. 'He asked about you. I told him you weren't taking my calls. That you were still pissed at me.'

Lola's brain had latched onto the fact he'd asked about her, and her insides were currently doing a crazy, hopeful dance.

'He said he couldn't blame you,' Damian went on, unaware that his sister was having difficulty breathing. 'That the least I could have done was listen to your proposal, seriously consider your plans for your business instead of dismissing them like they didn't matter. He said you had a good head on your shoulders, that you thought things out, knew your own mind. According to him your plans to open a studio are sound. He finished by saying I didn't know jack shit about you.'

Lola's hand went to her throat, which was currently threatening to seize up. 'He said all that?'

Damian shrugged. 'Maybe he was right. Somehow it slipped my notice that you're all grown up now. A formidable woman who knows what she wants and goes all out to get it.' He smiled, looking vulnerable, something she'd never associated with her strong, opinionated brother. 'I'd really like to get to know that woman.'

She felt a loosening around her heart and smiled back. 'I'd like that too.'

Damian was half out of his chair before she could finish the sentence and they came together in a hug.

'Forgive me?' Damian asked when they drew back.

'Of course. You're my big brother. I know you're looking out for me and I appreciate it. Just do it a little less often, maybe? And hear me out?'

'Agreed. But maybe I can stick my nose into your business just one more time before I leave the dark side?'

Lola raised her eyebrows, expecting that he'd have something to say about her putting in an offer on the property she'd seen. 'Go on.'

'Hopefully you now understand where Dad was coming from when he placed the stipulation on your trust fund, and now that I've explained my actions you've forgiven me. Don't you think that maybe Connor would understand your reasons if you explained them to him?'

She toyed with the cup. 'I tried. But I've really hurt him. I never meant to, but I have.'

She hated what she'd done. If she'd felt manipulated by her father and brother, how much worse did Connor feel? He'd been manipulated, lied to, betrayed. Twice, she thought as her heart twisted. By her cousin and by her. Did she really think that a few words of apology would make it right?

'What happened to my formidable sister? The one who knows what she wants and goes all out to get it? Are you telling me that sticking to your guns despite everything, and fighting for your own studio, means more to you than making things right with Connor?'

Her head shot back. 'No.'

Connor meant everything to her. Certainly more than any studio. More than anything she had ever wanted, and would likely ever want. Which made him worth fighting for. With everything she had. Whatever it took.

Before she could second-guess herself, she stood, leaned down to peck Damian on the cheek and grabbed her bag as she headed for the door. 'Sorry, can't stay for lunch.'

At the door she stopped and looked back. 'As older brothers go, you're okay.'

She bolted from his office, her breath tight. Had Connor really said those things to Damian about her? That had to mean he would be willing to listen, didn't it? That he'd be open to letting her explain how she felt.

Her brother was right. She had fought for her dream of owning her own studio. But that didn't come close to how much she wanted Connor. Not having him in her life was like a huge slice down the middle of every dream she'd ever had and she wanted nothing more than to stick those parts back together, with Connor at the very centre.

She had to make him see that. Had to make him understand that she'd never intended to hurt him, deceive him. He needed to realise that he could trust her. That she cared only for him.

During the tube journey she planned what she would say, dismissing each and every attempt at an explanation almost as soon as she'd considered it.

She visited both his clubs, but he wasn't at either of them. She struck pay dirt when she bumped into the security man who had been there the night she'd first met Connor. He told her that his boss was busy sussing out his new club premises over on the South Bank and wasn't expected back until that night.

With her heart in her mouth, she hailed a cab and headed straight for the Cabacal.

Connor walked through the property with his foreman. Renovations had started and by rights he should have been pleased with progress so far. News of his plans for his latest club had already garnered interest, and his investors were happy that he was sitting on a potential gold mine.

Yeah, he should be on Cloud Fucking Nine, but the truth was he found it hard to give a damn. Maybe his plans for the place were foolish, but they seemed right somehow. Fitting.

And maybe he was a stupid prick who needed a reality check.

He walked across the newly renovated limestone floor and tried to focus on what he was creating here. He'd always been lucky that he could visualise how something would turn out, and various consultants had agreed that his vision for the place was spot on.

So why the fuck was he thinking of Lola again?

Slowly, his anger towards her had dissolved, and in its place was this damned melancholy.

In retrospect, it might have been better to renovate this building along the lines of his other two clubs, but the idea had entered his head and stuck there. Then he'd mentioned it to Logan and to a handful of other people whose opinions he valued. Spurred by their enthusiasm, he'd rolled with the idea and now there was no going back.

Maybe he'd been naive thinking that he could keep Lola from his thoughts. Every time he stepped foot in the place all he could do was remember how she'd looked wandering around the space, probably imagining how it would feel to run her studio there, in the place that had been in her family for generations and which held her mother's cherished vision. Her expression had turned wistful as she'd run her hands over the soon-to-be-refurbished pillars with their pink marbled inlays.

It had been her dream to run the studio in this building and there was a part of him, way down deep beneath the anger and the hurt, that suffered a sting of remorse that he had been instrumental in denying her that dream.

As for his own dream? He didn't rightly know what that was.

To expand his empire? Open more clubs? Go international?

Maybe.

He looked out through the windows towards the river knowing that, while those things might once have comprised his dream, lately his vision had morphed into something else.

Something far more valuable and precious.

Because somewhere in all this jumbled mess, despite the deceit and the lies, his dream had become... *her*.

Shit. He was a fucking moron. Acting like a love-sick fool.

Love-sick?

That hit him with the force of a truck and he came to an abrupt halt. He pulled his wayward thoughts together, or tried to.

Love-sick?

It was just a word. One he'd plucked out of thin air. A word with which his treacherous heart thought to torture him. Taunt him. Make him suffer.

Which was fair enough. A man who had allowed himself to trust again, despite his experiences, his promises not to get involved, deserved nothing less. He'd let Lola sneak under his defences. He'd let her take up residence in his head, in his heart, and now here he was. Raw. Disheartened. Dispirited.

Bloody *love-sick*!

Fuck that.

He gave himself a mental shake. All this maudlin introspection was doing nothing for his mood, and today of all days he needed to keep from sliding further into his self-imposed pit of gloom. Tonight was

Logan's stag party, and his brother deserved better than Connor's dark attitude.

His foreman chose that moment to bring Connor the latest sketch for the renovation of the glass panels beside the rear exit doors, the ones that would reinstate the views of the River Thames beyond. The man was an artisan, and Connor felt lucky to have him at the helm of the refurbishment. Determined to focus on his newest acquisition, he gave his full attention to the sketch pad and his foreman's animated explanations.

Until the door to the building swung open…

CHAPTER FOURTEEN

EVERY SINGLE THOUGHT in his head disappeared when his gaze fell on Lola, and then a barrage of emotions shot through him, each one urging him to go to her, kiss the very life from her, tell her that they could work things out.

Except they couldn't. He knew that. He'd lain awake too many nights these past few weeks, considering things from all angles, but every avenue brought him back to just one.

She'd conned him. Thought to trick him. There was no way back from that.

He met her gaze, noticing the slightly bruised look beneath her eyes. Had she been having trouble sleeping, like him? A well of concern hit him out of the blue and made him want to gather her up and make all her problems go away. Not that he should care. He *didn't* care. All she was to him now was a part of his past that, while painful, had thankfully been brief.

She raised her chin as she walked towards him: upright, resolute, full of confidence. Only those tell-tale shadows hinted at a different story. His peripheral vision shimmered to a blurry haze, his full attention riveted on her and the way she pulled so many conflicting emotions from deep inside him.

With Caroline, there'd been only one emotion. Anger.

With Lola? Damn it, there were too many to count.

She stopped in front of him, her gaze yet to leave his. Terrified he might disgrace himself and pull her into his arms, he slid his fisted hands into his pockets.

'Shall I come back later, boss?'

Vaguely aware of his foreman's presence, Connor nodded, although he couldn't seem to tear his eyes from Lola. 'That'd be great, Sid. Thanks.'

His blood began a slow and steady burn. She was so close that her citrus and floral scent wrapped around him, layering over the smell of newly plastered walls and freshly cut wood.

She took a breath and looked off to the side, past the half-dozen builders working in different areas, until her attention landed on the beginnings of a curved raised floor in the corner. 'I heard you were renovating after all. It's starting to look amazing.' A noise from the opposite side of the room garnered her attention. 'You're having the two smaller rooms incorporated into the main space? It'll look great.'

There was no disapproval in her tone, no sadness evident in her expression. Instead, she looked animated, almost enthusiastic. He wasn't about to let his guard down. 'If you're here for one last try to get me to sell to you, then I'll tell you straight off. You're wasting your time. Because I'm not selling this place to you, or to anyone else.'

Connor wasn't entirely sure how he managed to get all that out, seeing as his damn chest was squeezed so tight. His voice sounded firm, gruff. But inside he was in bloody turmoil.

'That's not why I'm here. In fact, I'm putting in an offer on a place I've found close to where I live.'

'Good for you.'

He wanted to pull her into his arms. He wanted to draw her close, lose himself in her, but he kept his distance.

She looked straight at him, her eyes clear and earnest. 'How's your back?'

His jaw tightened as he clenched his teeth. Her question wasn't welcome, nor was the concern in her stunning eyes. He didn't need a reminder of how amazing his back had felt that night when she'd massaged away the tension in his muscles. When they'd shared parts of themselves, and he'd wondered if things could be different and if he could learn to open up to someone again.

'It's fine.'

Another noise came from the side, followed by heavy banging. 'Can we go somewhere quieter?' she asked, hiking the strap of her bag higher onto her shoulder. 'There are things I'd like to say to you.'

He looked around, barely resisting the urge to

wrap his fingers around her arm as he nodded towards the open terraced doors that led onto the embankment.

A measly slice of sunlight crept through the heavy clouds, only to disappear again as Connor closed the doors behind them. It was quieter out here, although the steady undertone of noise as people went about their business in the capital was a constant hum in the background.

Lola turned to face him. 'I'm going to get straight to the point. I came here for one reason, and I hope you'll listen to what I need to say.'

She spoke with her trademark directness, that openness he'd admired from the start, but which lately he'd tried to convince himself had all been an act.

'I want to apologise again,' she said, her fingers curling more tightly around the strap of her bag. 'What I did was deceitful. All I can say is I was blinded by my own aspirations, my need to right a wrong. I was tunnel-visioned, and because of that I didn't acknowledge that more than one person had been wronged, or that I was hurting the people I really cared about.'

His heart took a ridiculous leap until he told himself she was referring to her brother. That was who she cared about hurting, not him. Damn it. Hadn't he learned anything from all this? Did he still want to hear her say that she cared about *him*?

Shit. He really was his own worst enemy.

'I should have come clean to you right from the start. Just blurted out who I was and, if you'd still been prepared to listen, ask if you'd be willing to consider my proposition. Instead of doing any of that, I just kept on withholding the truth from you.'

She took a breath. 'God. I'm babbling. I've been thinking about what to say to you for ages, working it all out so I'd have the best chance of making you understand that I mean every word. But when I walked in and saw you everything went full out of my head and I'm just—'

'I'd take a breath if I were you. Preferably a full yoga one.'

She stared at him, her breath hitching, then gave a wan smile. 'Have you been practising that?'

'No.' He wasn't entirely sure why he was torturing himself this way, making reference to that night again. Remembering their closeness, her gentleness, as she'd tended to him. What he should be doing was blocking everything they'd shared out of his mind.

'That's a pity.' She raised her chin again, looking him square in the eye. 'I had every opportunity to tell you who I was and you deserved to know.'

She put her weight on one foot, then the other. 'I spoke with my brother today. He told me things about my mother that I didn't know, things that he and my father had kept from me. It hurt me. Not what he told me, but that they'd never considered I had a right to know.'

She swallowed. 'I told you that the Cabacal was

my mother's inheritance. Mum knew my father wasn't interested in her plans to run a fitness studio so she went to her brother, my uncle, for advice. He told her she'd need loans to get the business up and running and said she'd need to use the Cabacal as collateral. She didn't know he was the one loaning her the money, and when she defaulted he took the property. It seemed he'd planned it all along.'

Connor hung tight to her every word, surprising himself with the raptness of his attention. He didn't want to see the parallels between his own situation and Lola's mother's, but it was hard to deny.

Trusting someone and having them deceive you was the hardest blow.

Yet as he looked at Lola he knew that she'd never meant to deceive him. She'd been trying to find a way to honour her mother, to right an injustice. She'd never deliberately set out to hurt him.

Fuck. He wasn't sure which way was up right then.

He knew what it was to be consumed with a need for revenge, that unshakeable drive for retribution. It drove everything—a man's thoughts, words, actions. He'd always felt it was a righteous desire. But now he wondered if that was true.

On the surface, he and Lola weren't that different in their need to pursue what could be considered a noble quest. The righting of a wrong. A balancing of the books. The difference between them was that, unlike his, Lola's attempt to balance the scales wasn't driven by revenge. It was driven by love. For her mother.

'Anyway,' Lola said as he remained silent. 'I just wanted to tell you the reasons behind my actions in the hope that you can begin to understand and maybe in time come to forgive me.'

His continued silence wasn't helping Lola's nerves. It felt good, telling him everything, and she knew she'd done the right thing, especially since his fierce expression had slowly softened. She'd hoped he would at least begin to understand why she'd done what she had, but now she had her doubts. She couldn't begin to gauge his thoughts.

She searched for more to say that might help but her mind came up blank. Then he turned and walked to the railing that separated the embankment from the edge of the river.

He leaned his forearms on the railing. 'Right from the first moment, you've had me turned upside down and inside out. That was the whole problem. I thought I had a handle on women…thought I could read them, see through any pretence.'

He stared across the river, his eyes bleak and his jaw tight. Lola wanted to step up to him and rub at the tension she suspected had moved into his shoulders, slide her hands down his back and, despite his earlier assurances, ease any pain he might have there.

But she knew he wouldn't welcome it, and any pain he felt was likely less to do with physical discomfort and more to do with having his perception of himself and his ability to read people destroyed. By her.

Mirroring him, she leaned on the railing beside him. 'I'm as sorry about that as I am about everything else,' she said, looking down at her clasped hands.

'Don't beat yourself up about that. I'm not blameless in all of this. When I first saw you, my only intention was to get you into bed. I didn't much care about anything else. Not exactly honourable, was it?'

'You'd had a really bad experience.' She could only imagine the way her cousin had used him, leaving him doubting himself and his ability to make sound judgements. 'It's natural that you'd be circumspect after what my family put you through.'

'No excuse.' He turned to look at her. 'If you hadn't got under my skin, I'd have dumped you as soon as I'd got what I wanted from you. I was using you to get what I wanted, so in some ways that makes us similar.'

'You got under my skin too.' Lola took a chance. 'I really wanted you that night. I still do.'

His gaze travelled over her face and butterflies took flight in her stomach. 'You said you're putting in an offer on a suitable place for your studio?'

The question killed off all those butterflies and replaced them with a big, fat hole of disappointment. She'd told him she still wanted him and he'd changed the subject.

'Yes. It's a good location. Plenty of space for what I need.'

Silence stretched until he sucked in a breath. 'I'm having this place restored, and as much as possible, I'm planning to keep the original features.'

'Yes. I can see that.' Her stomach fluttered, and she wanted to fling her arms around him as emotion filled her chest, but his insouciant expression put paid to any such notion. 'That's really wonderful. It should be restored. Thank you.'

As happy as she felt about that, she would much rather he'd told her he'd forgiven her. All her pleasure at knowing her precious Cabacal would be saved disappeared beneath a knot of despondency.

'You don't want to know what plans I have for it?' he asked.

No. She didn't. Because she really didn't care. Not anymore. Whatever he used it for it would now always be a painful reminder of exactly what she'd lost. And that was far more precious than bricks and mortar.

She kept her fingers wrapped around the railing, but she turned to him. 'My myopic need to get this property back has caused me more misery than I ever imagined. By the time I came to my senses, it was too late, and I'd lost something far more important to me. So, whether you decide to demolish it, refurbish it or float it out along the river, I really don't care.'

He pursed his lips, but there was a glimmer that softened the steel in his grey eyes. 'And here I was thinking that I'd maybe invite you to the opening.' He shrugged. 'But if you don't care...'

'Don't be flip, Connor. You'll insult us both.'

He pushed away from the railing. 'I did some checking,' he said as he looked up at the property. 'In your grandmother's time, this was a cabaret club. Quite the place to be seen, apparently. Unique, quirky and booked up months in advance.'

'I remember it really well,' Lola said, her heart a little lighter as she remembered all the times she'd visited the club as a child. How she'd loved exploring all its nooks and crannies, imagining she was one of the glamorous singers up on the stage...

'That raised curve in the corner,' she said, her eyebrows drawing together. 'Is that going to be the new stage?'

He nodded, looking down at her. 'Your brother gave me some old photographs and we're working to restore the interior as close to the original as we can get it.'

Lola's breath caught as the full weight of what he was doing took hold. 'Why are you doing that? Won't it be a reminder for you? I thought you wanted nothing more to do with my family.'

He stepped closer and touched the ends of her fingers with his, making her heart do a strange stuttering thing. 'You don't count your uncle or your cousin as family, and that's good enough for me. What's in the past should stay there.'

She closed her eyes, hardly daring to believe what

he was saying. When she opened them, she saw a warmth in his expression that she'd never expected to see again.

'Connor?'

'What do you say we put everything that's happened behind us and move forward?'

'Move forward? You mean with the renovations?'

He tightened his grip on her hands. 'No, I don't mean the fucking renovations. I mean you and me. Us.'

The heat that radiated through her chest, around her heart, made her breathless, light-headed. 'Us?'

'Yeah.' His throat contracted as he swallowed. 'I'm sorry for not letting you explain. For lumping you in the same league as your cousin. You wanted to right a wrong, and you did it out of love.'

'I never meant to hurt you,' she said, her voice hitching on the last word. 'I would never do that, Connor. Can you forgive me?'

'If you can forgive me.'

When he let go of her hands and slid his arms around her waist, she all but fell against him. She breathed him in, melting into the muscular heat of his chest.

He kissed the top of her head. 'We're a couple of bloody fools, one way and another. We should rectify that.'

'Absolutely.' She held tight, her arms around him, her ear pressed to his chest so she could disappear into the beat of his heart. The words she wanted to say bubbled up from deep inside her, and since she'd already risked too much by withholding the truth from him, she looked up at him and took another chance. 'I love you, Connor.'

His eyes went stormy, but he didn't hesitate. 'I love you too.'

As Lola wallowed in the moment, Connor lowered his head and touched his mouth to hers. The kiss was light, but it sent a fiery need racing through her body, turning incendiary when Connor pulled her closer and turned the kiss from light to passionate and then bordering on indecent.

They only pulled apart when they heard cheering, and turned to see Connor's renovation team on the other side of the windows grinning and applauding.

Connor laughed but didn't let her go. 'Only fitting we should give them a good show, seeing that this place is soon going to be famous for entertainment again.'

'We obviously didn't do a good enough job, since they're already getting back to work.'

'Only because they know I'll dock their pay.'

Lola laughed, but Connor turned serious. 'We're not so far along that I can't change my plans.'

'Why would you do that?'

'If you still want this as a studio, I can—'

Lola touched her finger to his lips. 'That's not what I want. I've got plans of my own now, and I'm excited about them. Besides, my mother would love what you're doing here. She'd see it as a tribute to my grandmother.'

He nodded and drew her in for another heated kiss.

'You know when you asked me how my back was doing?'

She frowned, suspicious. Maybe because of his wicked, sexy grin. 'Yes.'

'Well, come to think of it, I am suffering a few twinges here and there.'

'Really? Maybe I should help you with that. I've got some new massage oils that might be exactly what you need.'

He waggled his eyebrows. 'It's not the oils I need.'

She laughed and leaned into him, looking up into his sinful gaze. 'Then tell me what you need and I'll make sure to have whatever it is permanently on tap. Just for you.'

He grinned. 'Yeah? Then maybe you could throw in some more of that Tantric stuff. I wouldn't complain, neither would my grateful cock.'

'I'll bet. Want to come back to my place? Emily is away for a couple of days.'

'Sounds perfect.' He winced. 'Shit. It's Logan's stag night.'

Lola stroked the back of her fingers down his cheek. 'Come by after. It'll give me time to prepare.'

The glint in his eyes sent little arrows of anticipation straight to her core. 'For what?'

'Let's just say it involves a special relaxation technique I was reading about. You'll probably be in need of that after an evening of strippers and booze.'

He shook his head, his mouth turning up in a hard-done-by grin. 'Strict instructions from Logan. No strippers.'

'Then maybe I'll make up for that and put on a special show for you later. Wouldn't want you missing out.'

'No chance of that.' He dropped his forehead against hers. 'You're everything I need, Lola.'

'And you're everything I need, Connor.'

In the shadow of the building that had threatened to pull them apart, Connor drew her in for another scorching kiss.

Eventually he drew away with that devilish grin on his face. 'So, tell me more about this special technique…'

EPILOGUE

'WILL YOU PLEASE put that away? You must know it all by heart now.' Lola laughed as she tried to take the small wad of notes from Connor as they waited by the entrance of the reception hall where his brother Logan stood with April, his new bride, greeting their guests.

'I can't remember a bloody word,' Connor said, opening up the notes for his best man's speech again. 'It was bad enough checking my pocket all the time just to make sure the ring was still there, now I've got this fresh hell to negotiate.'

'Just stop,' Lola said, trying not to laugh again as she fixed his tie for the umpteenth time that day. 'You'll be fine.' She looked up into his smoky eyes. 'Do your yoga breathing.'

He gave her a speculative look. At least she'd got his attention off his nerves.

For the last couple of weeks, they'd spent every possible moment together and it had been the happiest time of her life. She loved him so much.

'Not sure I should do that,' Connor said with a

wicked grin. 'Not if I don't want to disgrace myself in front of all these people.'

She finished straightening his tie, then tapped his arm in admonishment. 'It's not supposed to always lead to sex, Connor.' Although, every time she'd instructed him through a relaxing breath-control technique, it almost always had. 'It's supposed to help you calm down.'

He leaned down and kissed her, not concerned at all about the people milling around. When she pulled back, he grinned, but he kept his arms around her. 'That's all the calming down I need.'

'Good. I've never known you this nervous. It's just a speech. I'm sure you've given a few of those in your time.'

Connor kept his gaze on hers, his expression turning serious. 'It's not the speech that's got me all wound up.'

Lola raised her eyebrows. 'What else? Is everything okay?'

He swallowed. 'Yeah. Everything's great. Perfect. Maybe if it wasn't, I wouldn't be this nervous.' He tightened his hold on her. 'I've been looking on this speech as a kind of practice run. For when I'm in Logan's shoes.'

Lola's heart tripped. 'In his shoes?'

'Yeah.' He gave a quick smile. 'How about it, Lola?'

Lola just stared at him, trying to work out if he meant what she thought he meant, or if her crazy, loved-up heart was playing tricks on her. 'How about what?'

'You've got the smarts,' he said, frowning. 'Work it out.'

Oh, hell, she was actually going to cry. She placed her hand at her throat, hoping to stay the waterworks. 'Okay.'

'"Okay" as in *yes*?'

'Uh-huh.' It seemed she had completely lost the power of speech.

He grinned. 'I was thinking we could use the Cabacal for the reception. A private event right before opening night.'

Lola bit her lip, nodding her agreement. She could barely see Connor clearly now.

'I love you, Lola,' he said, pulling her so close against him that he cut off what little air she could get in her lungs. 'So fucking much.'

Looking into his eyes, she felt joy spread through her. Maybe it wasn't the most romantic of marriage proposals, but she'd take it. Just as she'd take everything the future held for them. As long as she had Connor, she had all the romance she would ever need.

And one of these days, maybe she'd teach him to take a full yoga breath that didn't end up with them lying naked between the sheets.

Or maybe not, she thought as she fell joyfully into his kiss.

* * * * *

COMING SOON!

We really hope you enjoyed reading this book.
If you're looking for more romance, be sure to
head to the shops when new books are
available on

Thursday 29th October

To see which titles are coming soon, please visit

millsandboon.co.uk/nextmonth

LET'S TALK
Romance

For exclusive extracts, competitions
and special offers, find us online:

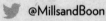 facebook.com/millsandboon

@MillsandBoon

@MillsandBoonUK

Get in touch on 01413 063232

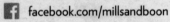

For all the latest titles coming soon, visit
millsandboon.co.uk/nextmonth